Out of the Dark

Gregg Hurwitz is the *Sunday Times* bestselling author of *Orphan X* and *The Nowhere Man*, the first Evan Smoak novels. He is also the author of *You're Next*, *The Survivor*, *Tell No Lies* and *Don't Look Back*. A graduate of Harvard and Oxford universities, he lives with his family in LA, where he also writes for the screen, TV and comics, including Wolverine and Batman.

Out of the Dark

GREGG HURWITZ

MICHAEL JOSEPH
an imprint of
PENGUIN BOOKS

MICHAEL JOSEPH

UK | USA | Canada | Ireland | Australia
India | New Zealand | South Africa

Michael Joseph is part of the Penguin Random House group of companies
whose addresses can be found at global.penguinrandomhouse.com.

Penguin
Random House
UK

First published in the United States by St Martin's Press, an imprint of Macmillan Publishers 2019
First published in Great Britain 2019
001

Copyright © Gregg Hurwitz, 2019

Set in 13.5/16 pt Garamond MT Std
Typeset by Jouve (UK), Milton Keynes
Printed and bound in Great Britain by Clays Ltd, Elcograf S.p.A.

A CIP catalogue record for this book is available from the British Library

HARDBACK ISBN: 978–0–718–18548–0
OM PAPERBACK ISBN: 978–0–718–18549–7

www.greenpenguin.co.uk

MIX
Paper from
responsible sources
FSC® C018179

Penguin Random House is committed to a
sustainable future for our business, our readers
and our planet. This book is made from Forest
Stewardship Council® certified paper.

To my intimidatingly astute copyeditor,
Maureen Sugden

Who for sixteen novels has raised my game
and saved me from countless embarrassments
with razor-sharp wit and feather-soft nuance

1997

Prologue: *Perennial Rain*

Evan is nineteen, fresh off the plane, trained up, mission-ready. And yet untested.

His first assignment as Orphan X.

He adjusts rapidly to this foreign place, a city with drizzly rain, imperious ministry buildings, and men who kiss on both cheeks.

His backstop is impeccable, endorsed by visas, a well-stamped pass-port, verifiable previous addresses, and phone numbers that ring to strategically placed responders. Jack, his handler and surrogate father, has built for him a suitably banal operational alias – enterprising young Ontarian, recently separated from his equally young wife, eager to shep-herd his family's home-siding business into territories unknown. He and Jack worked the identity, kneading it like dough, until Evan was aligned with it so thoroughly that he actually felt the sting of his domestic setback and the fire of ambition to expand into this brave new market. Evan has learned not to act but to live his cover. And he does his best to stash away the part of him that does not believe his alias until the point at which he will require it.

He moves frequently around this gray city to prevent degradation of cover. Now and then in the streets, he comes across others his age. They seem like creatures of a different species. They don backpacks and trickle in and out of hostels, drunkenly recounting school tales in foreign tongues. As always, he remains separate – from them and everyone else. The United States has no footprints in this country. There will be no rolling-car meetings, no physical contacts from an embassy. If he fails, he will expire in a cold prison, alone and forgotten, after decades of suffering. That is, if he's not fortunate enough to be executed.

One night he is meditating on a threadbare blanket in a hotel seemingly as old as the country itself when the mustard-yellow rotary phone on the nightstand gives off a piercing ring.

It is Jack. 'May I speak to Frederick?' he says.

'There is no one here by that name,' Evan says, and hangs up.

Immediately he fires up his laptop and pirates Internet from the travel agency across the avenue. Logging in to a specified e-mail account, he checks the Drafts folder.

Sure enough, there's an unsent message.

Two words: 'Package waiting.' *And an address near the outskirts of the city. Nothing more.*

He types beneath: 'Is it a weapon?'

Hits SAVE.

A moment later the draft updates: 'You're the weapon. Everything else is an implement.'

Even from across an ocean, Jack casts arcane pearls of wisdom – part koan, part war slogan, all pedagogy.

Evan logs off. Because they communicated within a saved message inside a single account, not a word has been transmitted over the Internet, where it could be detected or captured.

On his way out of the rented room, Evan freezes, hand wrapped around the wobbly doorknob. He has been tasked. Once he goes through that door, it is official. Seven years of training has brought him to this moment. His body is gripped by a comprehensive, bone-crushing fear. He doesn't want to die. Doesn't want to crack rocks and eat goulash in some labor camp for the rest of his days. Doesn't want his last moments to be the pressure of a Tokarev nine-mil at the base of his skull and the taste of copper. The perennial rain streaks the window, a tap-tap-tapping on his nerves. He's sweated through his shirt, and yet the tinny doorknob remains cool beneath his palm.

Like a prayer, he hears Jack's words in his ear as if he were right beside him: Envision someone else, someone better than you.

4

Stronger. Smarter. Tougher. Then do what *that* guy would do.

'Act like who you want to be,' Evan tells the stale air of the hotel.

He vows to leave his fear behind him in that room. Forever.

He opens the door and steps through.

The bus out of the city reeks of body odor and sweet tobacco. Sitting in the back, Evan applies a thin sheen of superglue to his fingertips to avoid leaving prints. He prefers this to gloves because it looks less conspicuous and allows him better tactile sensation.

Uneven asphalt erodes into a winding dirt road carved into a mountainside. Eastern Bloc municipal rigor dissolves into hamlets in shambles. Bedsheets flap in the wind. Buildings lean crookedly. Riding a wet gust, a muezzin's call to prayer. It is as though they have traversed not communities but continents.

The address belongs to a walk-up apartment overlooking a cart-congested road. Evan mounts the curved stucco staircase, padding across blue-and-white Turkish tile, and knocks on a giant arched door, its wood embellished with rusting metal straps. It creaks open grandly to reveal a round man in loose-fitting clothes of indeterminate style.

'Ah,' he says, wireless spectacles glinting. 'I trust your journey was safe?' A sweeping gesture of arm and draped sleeve accompanies his softly accented English. 'Come in.'

The ceiling is high, churchlike. A Makarov pistol rests in plain view on top of a television with rabbit-ear antennae. The man and Evan pass through clattering bead curtains into a cramped kitchen and sit before shallow teak bowls filled with figs, dried fruits, and nuts.

The man produces a small plastic bag with EYES ONLY Magic Markered on the label in Cyrillic. Inside the bag is a single bullet casing. Evan examines it through the plastic. A copper-washed steel cartridge from a 7.62 × 54mmR round.

It dawns on him that this shell holds a fingerprint, that it is to be left behind to direct blame elsewhere for what Evan will be instructed to do.

He thanks the man and moves to rise, but the man reaches across the table, wraps his brown fingers around Evan's wrist. 'What you hold in your hands is dangerous beyond what you can imagine. Be careful, my friend. It is an unsafe world.'

The next morning Evan takes to the city neighborhoods he has been scrupulously exploring for the past few weeks. He knows where to make inquiries, and these inquiries land him in the back of an abandoned textile factory, speaking to a trim little Estonian over an industrial weaving loom on which Sovietski rifles are laid out at fastidious intervals.

The preserved shell in Evan's pocket requires a round that fits a limited range of guns. He looks over the Warsaw Pact offerings, spots a surplused-out Mosin-Nagant with a PSO-1 scope. He points, and the Estonian, using a clean gun cloth, presents it to him. As he observes Evan examining the Russian sniper rifle, his smile borders on the lascivious.

The gun will give Evan a two-inch grouping at a hundred meters, which is all he needs, but he affects a negotiator's displeasure. 'Not a world-class rifle.'

The man folds his soft pink fingers. 'It is not as though you are going to the National Matches at Camp Perry.'

Evan notes the reference, tailored for him, a North American buyer. He lifts a wary eye from the scope, regards the little man in his ridiculous suit and pocket square.

The Estonian adjusts his tie, dips his baby-smooth chin toward the rifle. 'And besides,' he says, 'three million dead Germans can't be wrong.'

'Alvar?' A weak feminine voice turns Evan's head.

A beautiful young girl, maybe fifteen, stands in the office doorway, naked save for a ratty blanket drawn across her shoulders. Her eyes sunken and rimmed black. Bones pronounced beneath her skin. Behind her, Evan spots a filthy mattress on the floor and a metal cup and plate.

'I'm hungry,' she says.

Evan catches her meaning through his grasp of Russian, though he presumes she is speaking Ukrainian. He makes a note to add this linguistic arrow to his Indo-European quiver.

The Estonian seethes, an abrupt break in his middle-management demeanor. 'Back in your fucking bedroom. I told you never to come out when I am conducting business.'

She doesn't so much retreat as fade back into the office.

Evan hefts the rifle, as if he will be paying by the ounce. He flicks his head toward the closed door. 'Looks like she keeps you busy.'

Alvar grins, showing tobacco-stained teeth. 'You have no idea, my friend.'

To the side a pallet stacked with crates of frag grenades peeks out from beneath a draped curtain. The Estonian notices Evan noticing them.

'My friend, 1997 has proven good to me,' he says. 'It is the Wild West here now. Orders coming in faster than I can fill them. High quantity now. These are the kinds of movers who move nations.'

'For which side?' Evan asks.

The man laughs. 'There are no sides. Only money.'

At this prompt a wad of bills changes hands.

Seventy-two hours later, Evan finds himself in the sewer beneath a thoroughfare, stooped in the dripping humidity, Mosin-Nagant in hand. He stands on the concrete platform above a river of sludge, waiting. The eye-level drainage grate set into the curb grants him a good head-on vantage down the length of the boulevard. In the distance, squawks from mounted speakers and the roar of an erupting crowd. The parade drawing nearer.

Various coded dispatches from Jack have filled in some of the blanks. The target: a hawkish foreign minister gaining power by the day, vocal about nuclear development. Breathing the swamplike air, Evan waits. A cheer emanates from the street above him. He lifts the rifle, the tip inches from the mouth of the curb inlet, and clarifies his view, allowing the scope to become his world.

Children held aloft on shoulders laugh and clap. On the banked curve of visible street, sawhorses hold back the masses. Miniature flags flicker before faces like swarming insects.

The front of the processional, a phalanx of armored SUVs, turns into view several hundred meters away. The vehicles head up the stretch of asphalt toward Evan. His view is slightly offset from each windshield as it flashes in the muted midday sun.

Evan aligns himself with the rifle to reduce recoil and allow for quick repeatability if he has to cycle a second shot. He calculates the mechanical offset – the one-and-seven-eighths measurement between the crosshairs and bore axis. Then he adjusts the intersection point for ninety meters, the spot where the vehicle spacing is optimal for the angle he requires. His field of view will diminish the closer the car gets. If the target passes the mark, his shot will grow more difficult by the meter. It must be ninety meters – no more, no less.

He sets himself in position. Aside from the breath cooling his pursed lips, he is still.

At once, looming large in the scope, is the target. A tall, balding man with a dignified bearing, lean in a dark suit, surrounded by various generals in full regalia and his wife in a flowy aubergine dress. Waving to the crowd, they are clustered in an open boat of a vehicle that brings to mind the Popemobile.

One hundred ten meters.

One hundred.

There is a problem.

The foreign minister's wife turns to face the opposite side of the street, completely blocking Evan's view. Her head right in front of her husband's.

Ninety-five meters.

Panic. In a split second, Evan falls apart and regroups.

If he has to go through her, it's better to penetrate the eye socket so there's only one chance for the skull to deflect the round. Evan lays the crosshairs directly on her pupil.

Ninety-three.

He takes the slack out of the two-stage trigger, breathes breath number one.

He is looking directly into her eye, into her. Mascara on the curled lashes, joy crinkling the upper lid. She is not part of the mission. Should he disregard her as collateral damage? In the corridors of his mind, Evan listens for Jack but hears nothing aside from the hiss of passing tires and the frenzied stir of the crowd.

Second breath. Exhale. The final half breath before the shot.

If he waits any longer, a host of new problems will present themselves.

A one-millimeter movement of his finger pad gets it done.

Inconveniently, Jack's voice announces itself now, a whisper in his ear: The hard part isn't turning you into a killer. The hard part is keeping you human.

The vehicle coasts forward. It is on the X. The dark dot of her pupil, the minister's head pulling back, aligning perfectly behind her. Now.

And then they are past.

Evan discards the half breath. Sweat stings his eyes. His mind races, recalculating, adjusting intersection points, dialing back the magnification, faces zooming and shrinking as he fights to hold the mission together in the circle of the scope. As he's feared, his field of view diminishes, complications stacking on top of complications.

He breathes. Focuses.

Slack out of the trigger. Mag dialing back, back. There will be a moment, one moment, to get it done right and clean, and when it presents itself, he will be ready.

The generals shuffle around the wife, smiling beneath mustaches, the minister's face popping in and out of view, there and then gone. Seventy-five meters now, the preceding vehicle squeezing the angle tighter and tighter, diminishing it to a slice.

The universe is reduced to the tunnel of the scope. There is nothing else, not even breath. The wife turns, her sturdy bosom filling the vantage, the minister drifting again behind her. Evan waits for her arm to rise for another wave to the crowd, and at last it does, a sheet of cloth draped wing-like beneath her arm. The minister is invisible behind it, but Evan has tracked his movement, anticipates how far to lead him.

He exhales slow and steady, then pulls. The bullet punches through the gauzy cloth an inch and a half below the wife's straightened elbow.

Evan's hands move of their own volition, manipulating the bolt for a follow-up shot, the shell spinning free and clattering at his feet. But there will be no need for a second bullet. The foreign minister leans propped against two of the generals, his eyes vacant, one cheek dimpled by a hole the size of a thumb. His wife's mouth is stretched wide and trembling in a scream, but Evan can hear nothing over the eruption of the crowd.

He drops the weapon into the stream of passing waste below. After pocketing the kill brass, he takes out the plastic bag and shakes onto the dank ledge the copper-washed steel shell case with its invisible fingerprint, a fingerprint that he now knows belongs to a Chechen rebel of some reputation.

They will search the crowd, the surrounding buildings, the parked vehicles before they will think to look beneath the earth, but nonetheless Evan runs to his exit point and emerges through a manhole cover into a park five blocks north. He walks three blocks east, away from the quickening commotion, and boards a bus. A few klicks later, he exits, flips his reversible jacket inside out, and zigzags the city, the spreading news on the lips of passersby, wafting in snatches from café tables, blaring from car radios.

Once he's safely back in his rented room, he logs in to the e-mail account and creates a new saved message consisting of a single word: 'Neutralized.'

A moment later the draft updates: 'Close the operation.'

Evan stares at the words, feeling the glow of emotion beneath his face. He runs a hand over his short hair, and his palm comes away damp *with perspiration. He stands up, walks away from the laptop, walks back. Types:* 'Request phone contact.'

He hits REFRESH. *Hits it again. Nothing.*

Jack is thinking it over.

Seventeen anxious hours later, Evan finally receives a response, and two hours after that he is standing at the specified cross street, having reached Jack at a pay phone from a pay phone. He's caught Jack on the front edge of an East Coast morning, though he seems as alert as ever, his station-agent's mind shaping his responses into neat packets of words, articulate silences, loaded intonations.

'All he did is provide a cartridge case,' *Evan says.*

Jack says, 'That's all he did of which you're aware.'

'He seems loyal. An asset.'

'Don't believe everything you think.'

The breeze blows flecks of moisture into Evan's face, and he hunches into the collar of his jacket, turning this way and that, watching pedestrians, vehicles, the windows of the towering, stone-faced buildings all around.

'He's not a friend to us,' *Jack says.* 'He's a friend to everyone. A businessman. He doesn't just sell cartridge cases with fingerprints. He moves weaponry.'

'Weaponry?'

'Fissile material. Highest bidder. He is a complicating factor in our work there. That has to be enough for you.'

'What about the Sixth Commandment?' *Evan says, anger creeping into his voice.* ' "Question orders." '

'You've questioned them,' *Jack says.* 'Now execute them. Close the operation. Your friend and anyone else you might have used. This cannot – will not – come back on us.'

The steady hum of a dial tone follows.

Evan wanders the neighborhood until he comes upon a GAZ Volga, a four-door sedan as common on these streets as a Chrysler in Detroit. He hot-wires it and leaves the city, driving into a bruise-colored sunset. He parks several blocks from the apartment with the curved stucco stair-case and then closes the distance under cover of the rapidly falling night. Only once he's reached the blue-and-white Turkish tiles does he remove his pick set. The rusting lock on the arched wooden door gives itself up within seconds.

Evan steals silently across the dark front room with its vaulted ceil-ing. The Makarov pistol remains in its place, resting atop the antique television. It is loaded.

In the rear of the apartment, the kitchen is lit, and carrying through the beaded curtain is the static-filled sound of an animated radio announ-cer rattling on in a language with which Evan is unfamiliar. Tajik? Bukhori?

How little he knows of this life he is about to extinguish.

The hanging beads slice his view into vertical slats. The man sits at the small chipped table, facing away, spooning soup from a bowl. An old-fashioned radio rests on the counter beside a hot plate. A prosaic little portrait: Man Eating Dinner Alone.

Evan steps through the curtain, the clattering beads announcing his presence. The man turns and looks back through his wireless spectacles. There is a moment of recognition, and then the lines of his face contract in sorrow. There is no anger or fear — only sadness. He nods once and turns slowly back to his soup.

Evan shoots him through the back of the head.

As the man tilts forward, his chair slides back a few inches and his body remains resting there, chest to the table's edge, face in the soup.

Evan lifts him out of the soup, upright into the chair, and cleans his face as best he can. His left eye is gone, and part of his forehead. As Evan returns the dish towel to the counter, he comes upon a crude clay ashtray, shaped by a child's hand.

He vomits into the sink.

After, he finds a bottle of bleach in a cabinet and sloshes it into the drain.

As he exits onto the dark staircase, he becomes aware of a man easing up the stairs, drawn perhaps by the sound of the gunshot. The man's left fist gleams even in the shadow.

They freeze midway down the stairs.

The man is all dark silhouette to Evan, just as Evan is to him. The man's head dips, orienting on the pistol in Evan's hand. The man lowers his own gun, opens his other palm in a show of harmlessness, and shakes his head. Evan nods and brushes past him.

Ten minutes later, halfway back to the city, his knotted chest still prevents him from drawing full breaths.

His next stop is the abandoned textile factory. As he enters, darting through the warren of giant fabric rolls, the trim Estonian appears suddenly. He holds a no-shit Kalashnikov, its curved magazine protruding like a tusk. Evan has brought a pistol to an AK-47 fight. They are standing by the industrial weaving loom where they met before.

The Estonian cocks his head with benign curiosity, but his grip stays firm on the assault rifle, his small eyes hard like pebbles. Even at this hour, roused from sleep, he wears neatly pressed trousers and a tailored shirt, though one flap remains untucked. The door to the office behind him is closed, but a smudged glow illuminates the fogged glass of the window.

The men square off in an uneasy truce, not aiming their weapons but not putting them away either.

'I need your help,' Evan says. Slowly, cautiously, he raises the Makarov, then fiddles with the slide. 'It keeps jamming.'

The Estonian's smile appears, a neat arc sliced through soft pink cheeks. 'That is because you did not buy it from me.' He reaches for the gun. 'But seriously, this is a statistical near impossibility. Makarovs do not jam.'

Evan knows this, but it was the only excuse he could fabricate in the moment.

The Estonian shakes his hand impatiently. Beneath his other elbow, the muzzle of the AK nudges forward. 'Well?'

Evan is forced to relinquish the pistol.

The Estonian takes it, then sets down his own weapon on the loom. He drops the magazine, examines it, then grins at Evan's ignorance. 'The underside of the magazine feed lip has a burr from grinding on the clearance.'

With the toe of his loafer, he hooks a cardboard box and tugs it out from beneath the loom. Digging through the contents, he produces a new magazine, jams it home, and hands the pistol back to Evan.

'I'm sorry,' Evan says, and shoots the man through the chest.

The Estonian falls back, his palms slapping the concrete. He is trembling, his arms wobbling violently. A cough leaves a coat of fine spittle on his blue lips. His pupils track up in little jerks, find Evan. Never has Evan seen such terror in another person's face.

Evan crouches, takes his manicured hand. The nails are clean and cut short. The Estonian clutches Evan's fingers, grips his forearm with his other hand, pulls him closer. The partial embrace in another context would be affectionate. Perhaps it is even now. Evan lowers him gently to the floor, cradling his head so it doesn't strike the concrete. He holds the man's hand until it goes limp.

Then he rises, walks back to the humble office, and opens the door. The girl, bloody-lipped and ashen, lies balled up on the mattress. A heroin kit rests on a metal folding chair. She is naked, spotted with bruises, skin tented across bones. Her left shoulder looks dislocated. It is impossible that she would not have heard the gunshot.

On a metal desk across from the mattress, a cigar box brims with bills. Evan picks it up, sets it on the floor by her thin arm. 'You're free to go now,' he says.

She rolls her eyes languidly toward him. 'Where?' she says.

He leaves her there with the box full of cash.

That night he beds down at a different hotel, logging in to e-mail and leaving a draft for Jack. 'Operation closed.'

He checks departure times out of the second-largest airport of the neighboring country. Tomorrow will be a busy day.

And tomorrow, and tomorrow, and tomorrow.

Now

1. Face in the Crowd

A man melted into the throng of tourists gathered along the E Street walkway. He was neither tall nor short, muscle-bound nor skinny. Just an average guy, not too handsome.

A Washington Nationals baseball cap was pulled low over his eyes to thwart the security cameras. He'd shoved rolls of dental cotton above his molars to alter his facial structure and thwart the biometrics software that the Secret Service ran on every face in the crowd. He wore fitted clothing that showed the contours of his body, no out-of-season overcoat that might conceal gear or weaponry and draw unwanted focus.

He had flown to DC from the West Coast – as he had the time before and the time before that – under a passport in another name. He'd rented a car using a different identity and checked in to a hotel using a third.

He slurped the Big Gulp he'd picked up at 7-Eleven, another prop to augment the T-shirt from the National Air and Space Museum and the Clarks walking shoes he'd bought last week and tumbled in the dryer with dirty rags so they'd look broken in. The soda tasted like what it was, sugar soaked in corn syrup, and he wondered why people willingly put this type of fuel through their system.

He knew which visual triggers to avoid; he wasn't sweating and was careful to make no nervous movements – no protective hunching of the shoulders or jittering from foot to foot. He didn't carry a bag or a backpack and he kept his hands out of his pockets.

Evan Smoak knew the Secret Service protocols well.

He'd spent the past half year assembling intel piece by piece and tiling it into a larger mosaic. He was nearing the final stages of general reconnaissance. It was time to get down to mission planning.

He set his hands on the bars of the eight-foot-high gates. The trees of the South Lawn formed a funnel leading to the White House, which would have been a fine metaphor for Evan's own narrowed focus if he were the type to bother with metaphors.

Setting his Big Gulp on the pavement, he raised the camera dangling around his neck and pretended to fuss with it. In order to slip it between the bars of the fence, he had to remove the hood from the 18-200mm Nikkor lens. When he put his eye to the viewfinder, a zoomed-in image of the White House's south side loomed unobstructed.

Lost in a mob of tourists taking pictures, he let the lens pick across the grounds. The obstacles were impressive.

Strategically positioned steel bollards dotted the perimeter.

Subterranean beams waited to thrust up from the earth at the slightest provocation.

Ten feet back from the fence line, ground sensors and high-res surveillance cameras lay in wait, ready to capture any flicker of movement or tremble of the earth on the wrong side of the bars.

Uniformed Division officers stood at high-visibility posts at intervals across the terrain, backed by an emergency-response team equipped with FN P90 submachine guns. In keeping with Secret Service stereotypes, the agents wore Wiley X sunglasses, but the shades had a strategic advantage as well: A would-be assailant could never be sure precisely where they were looking. The high-visibility posts kept people in the crowd from seeing all the security measures they were supposed to miss.

At the southwest gate, a pair of Belgian Malinois commanded a concrete apron that was thermoelectrically cooled so it wouldn't burn their paws in the summer heat. They sniffed all incoming vehicles for explosives. They were also cross-trained to attack in the event a fence jumper made it over the spikes. If there were worse places to wind up than in the jaws of a seventy-five-pound Malinois, Evan wasn't sure where they were. The dogs were bona fide assaulters, way above their weight class; SEAL Team Six had gone so far as to parachute into the Abbottabad compound with a specimen of the breed.

Next Evan swiveled the camera to the White House itself. The semicircular portico of the south side, like the rest of the building's exterior, was outfitted with infrared detectors and audio sensors, all of them monitored 24/7 by on-site nerve centers as well as by the Joint Operations Center in the Secret Service headquarters a mile to the east.

Agents at the JOC additionally monitored radar screens that showed every plane entering the surrounding airspace. They maintained an around-the-clock interface with the Federal Aviation Administration and the control tower at Reagan National Airport. If a drone or a superhuman pilot managed to steer through the gauntlet of early warning mechanisms, an air defense system loaded with FIM-92 Stinger missiles was hard-mounted to the White House itself, standing by for dynamic air interception.

Evan tilted the zoom lens up to the roof above the Truman Balcony. A designated marksman with a Stoner SR-16 rifle held a permanent position providing overwatch for the south lawn, where enormous red coasters marked the landing zone for Marine One, the presidential helicopter. Countersnipers

patrolled the roof toting .300 Win Mags, good to fifteen hundred meters out, which created a protective dome stretching a mile in every direction.

It wouldn't merely be tough to reach the White House. It would be impossible.

Not that it got easier if some lucky soul managed to get to the building's threshold.

Between metal detectors, guard stations, and magnetometer wands, nothing entered the White House that hadn't been painstakingly screened. Not a single one of the million pieces of annual incoming mail. Not even the air itself. Electronic noses at all entrances detected the faintest signature of airborne pathogens, dangerous gases, or any other ill wind blowing no good. The Technical Security Division ran daily sweeps on every room, checking for weaponized viruses, bacteria, radioactivity, explosive residue, and contaminants of a more exotic stripe.

Even if by a miracle someone was able to actually penetrate the most secure building on earth, the White House was equipped with further contingencies yet. The interior hid not just countless panic buttons, alarms, and safe rooms but also multiple emergency escape routes, including a ten-foot-wide tunnel that burrowed beneath East Executive Avenue NW into the basement of the Treasury Department across the street.

Lowering the camera, Evan drew back from the reinforced steel bars and let out an undetectable sigh.

Killing the president was going to be a lot of work.

2. An Absence of Light

Orphan X.

That was Evan's designation, bestowed upon him at the age of twelve when he'd been yanked out of a foster home and brought up in a full-deniability program buried deep inside the Department of Defense. It wasn't just a black program; it was full dark. You could stare right at it and comprehend nothing but an absence of light.

About a decade ago, the inevitable ambiguities of the operations Evan was tasked with had reached a tipping point. So he'd fled the Orphan Program and blipped off the radar.

He'd kept the vast resources he had accrued as a black operator and the skills embedded in his muscle memory. But he'd also kept the bearings of his moral compass that had, despite the blood he'd spilled across six continents, stubbornly refused to be shattered.

Now he was the Nowhere Man, lending his services to the truly desperate, to people who had nowhere else to turn. He'd been content to leave the past in the past. Even within the intel community, the Program had remained largely unknown. Evan's code name, Orphan X, was dismissed as a figure of myth or an urban legend. Few people knew who Evan was or what he'd done.

Unfortunately, one of them happened to be the president of the United States.

Jonathan Bennett had been the undersecretary of defense for policy at the Department of Defense during Evan's incipient years in the Program. Through a trickle-down system designed to maximize plausible deniability, Bennett had given the mission orders. Evan had been the most effective operator on Bennett's watch, killing enough declared enemies of the state to fill a graveyard. Evan knew where the bodies were buried; he'd put them in the ground.

Years later, when Bennett had become president, he'd set about erasing any record of the constitutionally questionable program he'd overseen. Through sweat, blood, and hard work, Evan had discovered that Bennett was particularly obsessed with eradicating any trace of the 1997 mission.

Which put Evan at the top of the hit list.

He didn't know why the mission held a special place in Bennett's paranoiac heart or why that assassination in that distant gray city was relevant today. On that cold fatal morning, what mysteries had lingered outside the periphery of Evan's scope? In pulling the trigger, had he toppled a domino, sparking a chain reaction with momentous consequences? Or in the dankness of that sewer, had he waded into something intimate, putting himself in the crosshairs of a personal vendetta? He didn't have any answers.

Only that Bennett wanted him eliminated.

And that he, in turn, wanted to eliminate Bennett.

But Evan's motives weren't merely self-protective. Bennett was morally corrupt in the most profound sense, a rot seeping down through the chain of command. From the highest office, he had ordered the deaths of a number of Orphans, executing those who, under his tenure, had risked their lives for their country. And he'd had someone else killed as well, a man so steadfast and true that Evan had come to view him as a father.

That had been a miscalculation.

24

Which was why Evan was here now, pressed against the White House gates with a gaggle of tourists in the sticky June heat, waiting for a sign of the Man.

The woman to Evan's side rose onto tiptoes, funneling her children before her to provide them a better view. 'Look! I think that's him! I think he's coming!' She swatted her eldest on the arm. 'Close out that Pokémon nonsense and take some pictures for your Instagram.'

Evan lowered the camera and retrieved his Big Gulp as the phalanx of vehicles rolled into sight, tailing down the circular drive as they departed the West Wing. The motorcade was the so-called informal package, eight Secret Service G-rides and three indistinguishable presidential limos. The three limos forced potential assassins to play a shell game when choosing a target; they never knew for sure which one the president was riding in. The decoys pulled double-duty as backup vehicles in the event of an attack.

As the convoy neared the South Lawn, it halted abruptly.

Excitement flickered in Evan's chest, the lick of a cool flame. Was this the opportunity he'd been waiting on for 237 surveillance hours spread over the past six months?

He lifted the camera again in time to see an aide jog out from the edge of the Rose Garden, a soft-sided leather briefcase in hand. The trees cut visibility, the aide flickering in and out of view as he neared the motorcade. To keep the aide in sight, Evan threaded through the crowd along the gate.

The aide halted by the middle limousine, barely visible between the trees. The door popped open, just barely, and the aide slid the briefcase through the tiny gap.

The door closed once more.

The episode could have been witnessed by only a dozen people standing in the right vantage point along the gate.

It was indeed the break Evan had waited half a year for.

Bennett had shown his hand.

But because the president was in the middle limo now, that didn't mean he'd be in the middle limo next time. Or that the limos drove in the same order each time.

Evan's mind raced, grasping for variables.

The president might not have a favorite presidential limousine. But he'd almost certainly have a favorite *driver.*

Evan had to watch not the limos, but the drivers.

Or more precisely – since the drivers were hidden behind tinted windows in identical vehicles – Evan had to watch how the drivers *drove*, identifying any distinctive feature of how the middle wheelman commanded his vehicle.

He locked his primary attention on the central limo while also letting his vision widen to encompass the other two. The sun beat at the side of his neck. The crowd jostled with anticipation, the air smelling of Coppertone and deodorant. The Instagram kid whined that he was starving and sagged as though he'd misplaced his spine.

Evan maintained perfect focus.

As the convoy started up again, the end vehicles turned their wheels *before* the vehicles moved, rotating them in place on the asphalt while the limos were still at rest. But the middle driver turned the wheels only as he coasted forward, providing a smoother ride for the president.

A poker tell.

If Evan were one to smile, he would have now.

Instagram Mom tugged her kid upright. 'Stand *up*, Cameron. The president's coming this way.'

As the convoy banked around the curved drive, Evan put himself on the move, carving not too briskly through the onlookers, heading to where E Street intersected with East Executive Avenue.

President Bennett preferred this route, as it allowed him to avoid Pennsylvania Avenue, which ran across the front of the White House and provided a view of Lafayette Square, where an ever-growing mass of protesters gathered to call for his impeachment. They wielded signs and banners decrying a host of constitutional violations. Contravening the Arms Export Control Act. Funneling money and weapons illicitly to foreign fighters. Initiating widespread NSA surveillance of Americans. Monitoring domestic political factions that opposed him. Transgressing international conventions. Providing special access to defense contractors. Circumventing Congress. Usurping judicial powers.

But Bennett had masterfully erected a force field around his administration, fogging transparency sufficiently to hold his detractors at bay.

Evan was not interested in politics. Bennett's transgressions of office, while appalling, were not what had Evan here on the sun-baked concrete outside the White House. It was not about the vast and the conspiratorial. Not about whispered conversations in the corridors of power. Not about kingdom-altering back-channel deals or the Rube Goldberg machinations that disguised originator from outcome, cause from effect.

It was the faces of the dead.

And the fact that the president of the United States had personally ordered the murder of men and women who as children had been taken from foster homes and trained and indoctrinated to spend their existence serving their country. They had done the best they could with the life that had been imposed on them. And he'd snuffed them out for the sake of his own preservation.

Ending Jonathan Bennett was the ultimate Nowhere Man mission.

Finally the motorcade reached the intersection and halted. Again the drivers of the bookending limos turned the tires while stationary, grinding tread against asphalt. And again the wheels of the middle limo rotated only as the driver pulled out.

It had not been a fluke, then. But a habit.

The convoy banked onto E Street and headed for Evan.

He adjusted his baseball cap and slowed his breathing until he could sense the stillness between heartbeats, the sacred space he occupied the instant before he pulled the trigger of a sniper rifle, when even the faintest thrum of blood in his fingertip could put him off his mark.

In less than a minute, the presidential limo would pass directly in front of Evan, bringing him at last within several meters of the most inaccessible and heavily guarded man on the face of the planet.

3. Identified Threat

Excitement electrified the crowd cramming the sidewalk. People surged toward the curb, strained their necks, waved dumbly. A flurry of hands bearing smartphones rose in unison, most people twisting around to capture themselves in the photos. The motorcade barreled forward, the sight that launched a thousand selfies.

As reviled as President Bennett had proved to be, he was still good for a social-media status update.

Surrounded by civilians, Evan watched. The air was East Coast heavy, rippled by a humid breeze. The taste of soda lingered on his tongue, coating his teeth.

The vanguard of G-rides and the front decoy swept by, the presidential limousine coming into clear view. Dubbed 'Cadillac One' or 'The Beast,' it deserved both nicknames.

Set down on the chassis of a GMC truck, the limo was nearly eight tons, each door the same weight as a cabin door of a Boeing 747. Military-grade armor, an amalgam of ceramic and dual-hardness steel, was coated with aluminum titanium nitride. Slabs of ballistic glass a half foot thick composed the windows. A steel plate soldered beneath the vehicle guarded against the possibility of a frag grenade or an improvised explosive device. Even if a hail of bullets shredded the puncture-resistant, run-flat, Kevlar-reinforced tires, the limo could still drive away on the steel rims beneath. The limo was designed to take a direct hit from a bazooka.

Evan had a Dr Pepper Big Gulp.

If need be, Cadillac One could serve as a self-sustained, fully functional emergency bunker. Bottles of the president's blood were stored beneath the rear seats. At an instant's notice, a designated backup oxygen supply fed the air-conditioning vents. Firefighting gear stowed in the trunk was accessible through a hatch behind the armrest. The gas tank self-sealed, preventing combustion. Encrypted comms gear maintained continuous contact with federal and state law enforcement.

Evan had cotton wads in his cheeks.

Behind the wheel of Cadillac One was a master driver from the White House Transportation Agency. The driver would have received highly specialized army training in evasive maneuvers, route analysis, tactical steering, and vehicle dynamics.

Evan had comfortable dad shoes.

The presidential limo coasted up level with Evan, and for a split second he stared from the sea of faces at the tinted window behind which Bennett drifted in a cocoon of safety and comfort.

Close enough for Evan to spit on the pane.

The motorcade drove on.

He reminded his face to relax as he watched it go.

Jonathan Bennett did not sweat.

He never issued a nervous laugh, a tense smile, or gave an accommodating tilt of the head.

And his hands never quavered. Not when as a special agent for the DoD he'd found himself at gunpoint on multiple occasions. Not when as an undersecretary of that same department he'd pushed a button in a command center and watched a black-budget unmanned aerial vehicle unleash hell halfway around the globe. Not when he flipped the pages of his rebuttal notes during his first presidential debate or his sixth.

Body control was a learned skill, one he'd been taught in his early training at Glynco and which he used every day as the commander in chief. Without uttering a word, he could assuage the concerns of the American public and project power on the world stage. He sold himself to the populace not by appealing to their better angels but by manifesting subtle dominance displays that voters registered in their spinal cords.

The fact that he'd been largely successful at appeasing the population was testament to his sheer force of will. His detractors had gained a bit of traction, yes, but he knew precisely which levers he'd need to pull before the midterm elections to maintain control of both houses.

He settled into the butter-smooth leather of the presidential limo now and scanned the urban-development report he was due to weigh in on at this afternoon's cabinet meeting.

When his driver negotiated the presidential limo into a left turn more abruptly than usual, Bennett registered a slight uptick in his pulse.

He looked at his deputy chief of staff, his body man, and the Secret Service agent riding in the rear compartment with him, but none seemed to have registered the deviation.

He waited two seconds, and then the Secret Service agent stiffened, his hand rising to the clear spiral wire at his ear.

Bennett thought, *Orphan X.*

He checked in on his breathing, was gratified to note that it had not changed in the least.

The agent's hand lowered from the radio earpiece. Bennett waited for him to say, *Mr President. We're deviating course. There's been an identified threat.*

The agent said, 'Mr President. We're deviating course. There's been an identified threat.'

Bennett said, 'Has there, now.'

He pointedly caught the eye of his deputy chief of staff and then turned and watched the buildings slide by beyond the tinted glass.

Secret Service agents stacked the seventh-floor hall of the upscale residential building. Despite the lush carpet, they moved delicately on the balls of their feet as they eased up on Apartment 705.

The lead agent folded his fingers into his fist – *three, two, one* – and the breacher drove the battering ram into the door, ripping the dead bolt straight through the frame.

They exploded into the apartment, SIG Sauers drawn, two-man teams peeling off into the bedroom and kitchen.

'Clear!'

'Clear!'

They circled back up in the front room, stared at the sight left in clear view of the open window. A tired breeze fluffed the gossamer curtains and cooled the sweat on the men's faces.

No sounds of traffic rose from F Street below; the block had been barricaded once the sighting had been called in.

The lead agent looked around the apartment, taking stock. 'Well, fuck,' he said. 'Ain't this theatrical.'

The breacher glanced up from the windowsill. 'It's been wired,' he said. 'The window. Someone slid it up remotely.'

'How long's the place been rented?'

Another agent weighed in. 'Manager said six months.'

There was no furniture, no boxes, nothing on the shelves and counters.

Just a sniper rifle atop a tripod there in full view of the open window along President Bennett's route.

'Someone contact that new special agent in charge over at Protective Intelligence and Assessment,' the lead agent said. 'Templeton's kid.' He tore free the Velcro straps of his ballistic vest to let through a little breeze, his mouth setting in a firm line of displeasure. 'Someone's been planning for a long time.'

4. What's It Gonna Be?

Evan moved swiftly along E Street a few blocks from the commotion. The closure had backed up traffic through the surrounding streets, though the presidential convoy had already made its retreat, doubling back and darting away before the public was let in on the ostensible threat. Evan had wanted to leave a message for Bennett, yes, but he also wanted to note the driver's procedures for altering the route in the event of an emergency.

Commuters were laying on their horns, a symphony of displeasure. Cops jogged by at intervals, spreading through the area. This section of DC, a sniper round's distance from the White House, had as many CCTV cameras as a London street corner, so Evan kept his head lowered, his face hidden by the brim of the baseball cap.

The Secret Service's Forensic Services Division had cutting-edge software that would review all footage in the area. Not wanting his movements to be pieced together after the fact, Evan paused directly beneath a cluster of cameras on a street-light, stripped off his Windbreaker so it fell casually into the gutter behind him, and heeled it back through a storm drain. He let the Nikon camera swing low at his side before delivering it to the same fate.

He waited for the crowd to swell and wash him up the sidewalk. A trash bin waited ahead at the edge of a crosswalk in the blind spot beneath another streetlight. He gave a swift scan for cops, found none close enough to take note of him.

Quickening his pace, he removed his Nationals baseball hat, palmed the cotton rolls out of his mouth, and trashed them together. From his back pocket, he pulled out a worn Baltimore Orioles cap and tugged it on before stepping back into the sight lines of the CCTV cameras overhead.

In his peripheral vision, he noticed a face holding on him for a beat too long. He risked a glance across the heads of the pedestrians crossing the street with him and grabbed an instant of direct eye contact with a square-jawed woman in a sweatshirt.

She turned away hastily, raising a cell phone to her face.

A band of pale skin showed on her finger; she'd removed her wedding ring to avoid its snagging on a trigger guard. In an instant he read her build and bearing – a plainclothes officer scouting for suspicious behavior.

Like, say, a man switching baseball hats in the middle of an intersection.

Careless.

And lazy.

Evan berated himself with the Second Commandment: *How you do anything is how you do everything.*

He could see the woman's mouth moving against the phone. Up the block, two uniformed cops keyed to their radios.

He kept walking.

The woman followed him.

The cops split up, taking opposite sides of the street, fording the current of passersby, heading in his direction.

Three tails were manageable. No one needed to get hurt.

People spilled out of bars and restaurants. A guy was handing out flyers for the Spy Museum. A frazzled father had gotten the wheel of his baby stroller stuck in a sewer grate. Chaos was helpful.

Evan cut around the corner just as another pair of uni-formed officers spilled out of an alley ahead, blocking his best route to freedom. An older cop with a ready-for-retirement bulge at his belt line and a muscle-bound kid who couldn't have been a year out of the academy.

Twenty yards apart the officers and Evan stared at each other.

Evan nodded at them.

And then stepped off the sidewalk and into a bustling café.

The pair of officers would reverse and cover the rear as the other three flooded into the front.

Evan had ten seconds, maybe twelve.

Given his training, that was a lifetime.

Evan threaded through the packed tables, requisitioning a mammoth latte mug from the service counter. In the back of the café, a brief hall led to a gender-neutral bathroom and a rear door with an inset pane of frosted glass. To the side of the hall, a small table remained bare, having just been wiped down.

Heading for the open seat, he plucked an ice-water jug from a busboy's hands and sloshed it across the tile floor in front of the table. As he swung into the chair, he reached between the couple dining beside him and snatched their saltshaker.

The wife aimed a do-something stare at her husband, who managed a feeble, 'Dude, what the hell?'

Evan didn't answer. He was down to five seconds.

He unscrewed the top of the shaker and poured its con-tents into his fist. Then he tilted back in his chair so his shoulders touched the rear wall, tasted the matcha green tea latte, and waited.

On the surface of the latte, a swan was rendered in steamed milk, its tail smeared to peacock proportions by Evan's sip. Over at the service counter, an artichoke and sun-dried-tomato panini sizzled on the press, releasing delightful aromas. Evan watched the front door.

At the behest of a harried manager, a waitress approached, clutching a menu to her chest in withholding fashion. She looked down at the wet floor and then up at Evan, uncertain where to start. 'Sir, I'm sorry. You can't just sit here. We have to seat you.'

He reached into his pocket, pulled out a wad of hundred-dollar bills.

'We're not a nightclub. We're, like, a café. We don't take *bribes.*'

He kept his eyes on the front door. With his foot he pushed the table away from him another six inches, getting it into position. 'It's not a bribe,' he said.

'No?' She regarded the proffered bills. 'What's it for, then?'

'The damage,' he said.

The plainclothes officer and two cops shoved through the front door of the café, spotting Evan immediately.

Evan sensed the waitress's head swivel from him to the officers and back to him. There was a slight, mouth-ajar delay as she processed his meaning. Then the hundreds lifted from his hand and she scurried back to the manager.

The energy in the café shifted as the officers advanced through the tables. One of the men unsnapped the thumb strap on his holster, and a kid screamed, and then there was yelling and jostling as the place cleared out.

The cops crept forward, hands hovering over their holsters in case Sergio Leone decided to bust in with a crew and start filming.

Evan sipped the matcha tea once more. It wasn't half bad. He wondered at the kind of life that called for a steamed-milk waterfowl decorating one's hot beverage.

The officers stopped ten feet from his table and spread out. But not enough.

The café suddenly felt quite silent.

'Why are you chasing me?' Evan asked.

'Why are you running?' the plainclothes officer said.

'Because you're chasing me.'

'We had an incident a few blocks away,' she said.

'An incident.'

'That's right. And then I saw you switching your hat.'

The two uniformed cops unholstered their Glocks. They didn't aim at Evan, not yet, keeping the muzzles pointed at the floor. An ice cube crunched under one of their boots.

Evan looked at the three cops facing him down. 'So that's why you're all here? Because I changed hats?'

'Why would you do a thing like that?' the woman said.

'The Nationals need some heart-of-the-order bats,' he said. 'I decided the Orioles are a stronger bet for the postseason.'

'And you decided this in the middle of E and Eleventh?'

He liked her.

'I did,' he said. 'And while I know that civil liberties have been under assault by the current administration, I would think you could overlook an epiphany regarding the national pastime.'

The amusement went out of her eyes. 'Why don't we stop fucking around?' she said.

Evan took another sip of the tea. Hot, not scalding. 'I'd like that.'

'I'm gonna tell you what's gonna happen next,' she said.

'No,' Evan said. 'I'm gonna tell *you* what's gonna happen next.'

He was still tilted back in his chair, casual as could be, but beneath the table he pressed his foot to its base. The uniformed cops were holding their Glocks too stiffly, seams of white showing at their knuckles. The muzzles were now aimed halfway between the tips of their boots and Evan's table.

'You're gonna let me walk out of here,' Evan said.

One of the male cops laughed, and the female officer blinked twice. 'Or?' she said.

'I'm gonna throw salt in your eyes at the precise instant I kick this table over. While you're busy blinking, the table's gonna hit *you*' – Evan's gaze flicked to the cop in the middle – 'right in the solar plexus. That'll knock your gun to the side. Maybe you'll fire it into your partner's leg. Maybe not. Either way he's gonna be distracted, because I'm gonna throw this overpriced latte in his face. Around then, when you're all scrambling to react, you'll notice just how slippery those wet tiles are that you're standing on.'

He turned his focus to the cop on the right. 'I'm gonna come over the top of the table, swinging my chair, clipping your wrists, which'll knock away your Glock – if you've managed to hold on to it by that point. Then I'm in your midst. Which means – even if you could see, even if you still had your weapons – you wouldn't be able to fire at me without hitting one another.'

Back to the cop in the middle: 'You'll be doubled over on the floor at this point, because . . . well, we've already covered that. I'm gonna break your nose as cleanly as I can with a quick left jab to make sure you don't get your vision back anytime soon. Let me apologize in advance for that. I know you're just doing your job. Then, with my right foot, I'm gonna kick you into her' – his gaze slid to the plainclothes officer – 'while she's still clawing at the salt in her eyes.'

'But you're not gonna break *my* nose,' she said, 'because you're chivalrous.'

Evan gave a one-shoulder shrug of assent. Then continued, 'After you three are tangled up and useless, it'll take me four and a half strides to reach the end of the rear hall, where your backup's waiting. The mirrored side of the espresso maker there on the service counter's giving me a nice clear reflection of the back door with the frosted pane. Your boy with the extra Y chromosome is throwing a shadow from the hinge side. He's holding his service pistol too far from his body, so when I kick the door open, it's gonna knock it back into his teeth. He'll go down hard, because that's what muscleheads do. The veteran cop on the other side I'll take down gently with a chicken-wing arm control, but I won't break anything, because: respect. Before they can recover, I'm gonna bolt up the alley and disappear into the rear entrance of one of the shops that I scouted earlier, but I won't tell you which one, because I don't want to be predictable, and let's face it, at this point that would be gilding the lily.'

He lowered the giant mug to the top of his stomach, and all three cops inadvertently tensed. Their hands were too tight on the grips, and too tight meant tremors and imprecision. Evan was unarmed, and his body language was so unaggressive it verged on soothing, a dissonance they clearly found blindingly bewildering.

Evan scanned the three officers, frozen where they stood. 'So, guys. What's it gonna be?'

In answer, all three muzzles raised to aim at him.

'Okay, then.' Evan adjusted his grip around the mug, readied his loose fist around the salt, firmed his foot against the table base. 'Are we ready?'

5. A Not-Unfamiliar Coldness

The park bench by the artificial pond looked like a movie prop, set at an artful slant beneath a Rockwellian maple tree. In the pond a family of plump ducks paddled by, ignoring the embarrassment of bread crumbs on the shore.

The man sitting on the bench was clean-shaven, save for a patch of hoary stubble at the point of his jaw. His once-rugged face had crumbled under gravity, giving him jowls. His eyes were a touch milky, his still-brawny forearms liver-spotted.

Jogging at a pace just shy of a sprint, Naomi Templeton took note of the bench from a good distance out and decided to accelerate until she passed it. Racer-back tank top over a jog bra, black running tights, sports headphones blaring Alicia Keys – all designed to make her run faster, go harder, be better. *This girl is on fire.*

She crossed the finish line of the bench and leaned over, hands on knees, taking a few minutes to recover. Then she circled the bench, sat on the end opposite the old man, and flipped out her earbuds.

As she caught her breath, the old man looked over at her, gave a double take. 'You remind me of my daughter.'

She said, 'Is that so?'

'Yeah, she's sturdy like you. And don't go getting offended. I mean well built, not fat.'

'Noted.'

'Her brothers are fit, too. Athletes, both of them. Lacrosse. You shoulda seen their muscles when they came home from college. Put me to shame – me in my prime, I mean. I think she was always trying to keep up.'

Naomi leaned forward. A breeze blew across her bare shoulders, turning her drying sweat pleasingly cool. 'Girls'll do that.'

'Yeah, especially with her mother gone early.' His trembling fingers found the cross nestled in the gray chest hair visible below the notch of his throat. His shirt was buttoned wrong, misaligned. He shivered a little. 'She's a tough one, my daughter. Always tried to please me, I think.'

Naomi stared at the water. 'Girls'll do that, too.'

'She never learned that you can't ever please anyone by *trying* to please them.'

'That's a tough lesson to learn, I guess.'

For a moment they sat and watched the breeze ripple the pond's surface. It was faux idyllic here, which made it easy to disregard the countless TVs blaring too loud from countless windows in the industrial block of a building set behind the strip of artificial turf, the wheelchair platform lift waiting at the base of the stairs, the direct-care specialists – all lovely, all patient, all ethnic – heading back from their breaks along the gently sloped walkways. All you had to do was squint a little, breathe the fresh air, and you could pretend you were in the real world, that everything was okay.

The old man shivered again.

Naomi said, 'What do you say we get you inside, Dad?'

She stood at the nurses' station in the assisted-living facility, looking over the latest medical report. The facility's name, Sunrise Villa, always struck her as optimistic and perversely cruel. Assessing her father's lab work, she felt a not-unfamiliar coldness wash through her gut.

42

She sensed Amanaki's eyes lift from behind the counter. The nurse, with her empathic gaze and lilting Tongan accent, seemed preternaturally aware of subtle emotional shifts, a human tuning fork. 'Everything okay, honey?'

'Yeah, thanks. It's just . . . The labs . . . I have to call my brother.'

Amanaki's eyes took on a knowing gleam, and she busied herself again at the computer.

Naomi stepped away from the desk and dialed. Jason picked up on the third ring. 'What up, Nay-Nay?'

'I'm at Dad's place. They took him off Exelon –'

'Off what?'

'One of his meds. They took him off it for nausea and dizziness, but he's dizzy without it, too. They tried the patch form, but that doesn't work either.' She ran her fingers through her bluntly cut blond hair. 'His complex-motor stuff's getting worse, and I guess he threw his pills at a nurse this morning.'

'Did they hit her?'

'Jason.'

'Okay, I'm sorry. Look, that's what the nurses are there for.'

'To have pills thrown at them?'

'You know what I mean. We pay good money for the care. It's a nice place.'

'I know. I've actually seen it.' She realized she was making a fist around her hair at the back of her head. 'I'm just saying, you should probably get out here and see him. Soon, I mean. And Robbie. Hell, Robbie I can't even get on the phone.'

'But he sends a check. It's been fair all the way through.'

'This isn't about *fair*. We're not eight years old, Jason. I'm here every other day –'

'That's because you live in DC. And look, it's your choice, N.'

43

'No shit it's my choice. I'm talking about *your* choices. It would mean a lot to Dad if you got your ass on a plane once in a while. You know how he feels about you and Robbie. It's different.'

'It's not different.'

The lie was half-hearted; Jason barely bothered to disguise the nicety with a tone shift. She could hear voices in the background, someone shouting out a ticker update.

'Look,' Jason said, 'with Tammy and the kids, you know, four schedules, four directions. You don't appreciate how hard it is when you have a family.'

'Jason, I've met your family. I appreciate how hard it is.'

He laughed. 'You know what I mean. And come on, the old man wouldn't recognize me anyway. He's lucky to have you there.'

She resisted the urge to fill the silence.

Jason finally said, 'I'll send you more money next month so he can get . . . I don't know, more time with the staff or whatever.'

'I don't need more money. I need – *he* needs – someone else here who loves him. He still likes listening to music and looking at his and Mom's wedding album –'

The workplace noise grew louder in the background. 'I gotta hop, N. News just hit the tape, and I've gotta whack some bids. Talk later.'

The call severed with a click.

Naomi pocketed the phone, walked back to the nurses' station, and looked down at her father's file.

Amanaki clacked away at her keyboard. 'I been here a lotta years, and I can tell you, women are better at this.'

'At not being selfish dicks?'

Amanaki's smile felt, as always, like the clouds had parted

to let through a blast of soul-warming beauty. 'Yeah, I'd say we are. Men talk a lot. Women stay and take care of what needs to be taken care of.'

Naomi's phone vibrated in the zip pocket of her tights – Jason calling back? The flare of hopefulness she felt was accompanied quickly with a pang of self-recrimination. When it came to her brothers, she knew better than to allow naïve optimism to worm its way to the surface.

As she dug in her pocket, she realized that it wasn't her personal phone that was vibrating but her secure Boeing Black smartphone.

She thumbed the ANSWER icon. 'This is Templeton.'

'Special Agent in Charge Templeton?'

'The very one.'

'We need you here immediately.'

6. X Marks the Spot

Arms crossed, Naomi regarded the scene in Apartment 705 as agents from Forensic Services worked up the room all around her. She'd been recently promoted within Protective Intelligence and Assessment, and though she'd worked a file drawer's worth of cases since, the other agents still seemed to be adjusting to her. More precisely, they were still adjusting to the last name that came attached to her.

For three administrations her father had run the 'big show' – the Presidential Protective Detail. In that time he had pioneered enough security and safeguard innovations that his name had literally become synonymous with perfection within the Service. *Did you Templeton the rope line? We need Templeton coverage from the hotel advance team. The motorcade route has been Templetoned.*

It's not that anyone believed that Naomi hadn't earned her promotion. At thirty-one she was young but not too young, and there was no arguing her work ethic or performance. But most everyone came at her armed with a quiver full of assumptions. Was she a guru with a genetic gift for security matters? A haughty prima donna? If they shook her hand, would some of the old man's magic rub off?

Few circumstances were as emotionally confusing as growing up in the shadow of a not-known-to-the-public celebrity. Her father's fame – if it could be called that – was a spark that threw no light beyond a circle of cohorts. The problem was, she happened to share those cohorts now.

She was Hank Templeton's kid first, Naomi Templeton second. Despite the complexities that presented, she did not deceive herself into believing that this was not without its advantages.

After getting the call at the assisted-living facility, she'd changed hastily in the car and raced to the scene. Door-to-door through rush-hour traffic in twenty-three minutes, a reaction time even her father would have found acceptable.

She returned her focus to the bolt-action sniper rifle sitting atop its tripod at the front window.

A Russian piece of gear, a Mosin-Nagant with a PSO-1 scope.

Given its placement, there was no way the motorcade's advance team could have missed it. It was positioned to be seen.

The weapon was common enough, millions of them were scattered around the globe. Yet the choice of rifle struck her as odd.

Given the high-rent real estate of the apartment and the high-value target the assassin hoped to capture in the scope, the rifle was decidedly second-rate. Mosin-Nagants were like AK-47s. You couldn't throw a rock in a war-torn country without hitting one. They were cheap, durable, and easy to use. But they had their problems. Sticky bolts, worn-out ejectors, screws falling out of the stocks. This one looked beat-up and dusty.

She would have expected something professional and top-tier, maybe a Remington M700 with a Leupold Variable-Power Scout Scope.

One of the forensics men, a towering guy with a drippy nose, announced his presence behind her with a sniffle. 'Serial number's been scoured off, probably with a bench grinder.'

'How deep?' she asked.

'Deep enough that there's no way we can recover it with an etching reagent. But that's not what's noteworthy. The rifle? It's not usable. The barrel's warped, and there's no firing pin. It's totally sterile.'

Naomi lifted her eyes to the four blown-up surveillance photos that tiled the wall behind the rifle. Each featured a face in close-up, and each face had a letter Magic Markered across it.

A middle-aged man in what looked like a Venetian piazza: *J.*

What appeared to be a homeless man in a mall: *C.*

A handsome guy smoking a cigarette in a parking lot: *L.*

And the last, a photo of a man in his sixties, this one without a letter scrawled across the head. A square face, weathered and handsome, with a well-practiced squint.

The staging of the rifle and photos made clear: This wasn't an aborted assassination attempt. It was a message.

But to whom?

Naomi flicked a hand at the photographs with the weird markings. 'How 'bout those?'

'Those are sterile, too. We managed to digitally capture the faces beneath the markings and run them through facial recognition. Nothing. These people? They don't exist. Except for him.' The agent pointed at the man in the unmarked photo. 'Former station chief with the Agency, mostly through the seventies and early eighties. His personnel record gets hazy after that. His name's Jack Johns.'

'Where is he?' Naomi asked.

'Went missing about six months ago, just vanished off the map.' The agent scratched his neck. 'Maybe these are photos of past victims of the shooter.'

Naomi tried the theory on, found it ill-fitting. 'You pull any prints from the pictures?'

48

'No. They're clean.'

'Did you dust the backs?' she asked.

'Yes.'

'You pulled the photos off the wall and put them back up?'

'They're taped, so we lifted them to dust the backs.'

'You dust the tape itself?'

'We did. Along with everything else in the apartment.'

'There isn't anything else in this apartment.'

'Doorknobs, countertops, toilet flusher.' The agent retrieved a handkerchief from a back pocket and wiped his nose. 'There's not a single print here. The guy's a ghost.'

She gestured at the photos. 'What's with the letters?'

'I don't know,' the agent said. 'But there's one more.'

'One more what?'

'Letter.'

'Where?'

He waved Naomi over to the rifle. The bolt had been manipulated back, revealing the round in the chamber. A single letter had been etched into it.

X.

'We found it like that,' the agent said. 'X marks the spot.' He gave a nervous laugh that sounded like a giggle.

Naomi looked from the round to the photos on the wall and back to the round. 'It's not a mark,' she said. 'It's a signature.'

'Why do you think that?' the agent asked. 'Doesn't it make more sense that it's the name of the target? Ye olde "bullet with your name on it"?'

'*X* stands for the unknown. President Bennett isn't *X*. He's the best-known human on the planet.'

'After Kim Kardashian,' the agent said.

'After Kim Kardashian,' Naomi conceded. She studied the scrawled letters covering the faces in three of the four photos.

'So the would-be shooter is in on the same side as the men in these photographs. If my theory is right.'

The agent shrugged. 'I wouldn't bet against a Templeton.'

'Then you'd lose a good percentage of the time.' She met his gaze, which had grown nervous, shifty. 'I need your ideas. Not your deference.'

He nodded.

She moved on. 'I was told PD had a run-in with a suspicious party on E Street after the rifle was spotted.'

'Yes, ma'am. Five officers.'

'When can I interview them?'

'Right now, if you'd like. Micelli just brought them up, has them waiting in the hall.'

She nodded and stepped out of the apartment.

The cops were huddled up by the elevator – a female plainclothes officer and four men. They turned as Naomi approached. She drew up short, taking in their ragged appearance.

The big rookie's front teeth were chipped. One of the uniforms had a broken nose, bruises already coming up beneath his eyes. The other had swelling that stretched down one cheek and across his neck.

After introductions were made, Naomi said, 'What's with the red blotch?'

'Matcha green tea,' the officer said.

'What?'

'Nothing.'

The cop with the incipient black eyes stepped in. 'Look, he got the better of us, okay?'

'And it looks like you caught the worst of it.' Naomi tilted her head back, appraising the nose. 'Jesus. At least it's a clean break.'

At this the man scowled a little.

Naomi turned her attention to the veteran cop and the woman. 'Seems like you two got off okay.'

The woman shrugged. 'I did get knocked down pretty hard. When Kryzanski was kicked into me.'

Naomi said, 'Lucky you didn't crack your head.'

'I think the attacker . . .' The female cop cleared her throat.

'What's that?'

'I think he cradled my head on the way down.'

Naomi nodded and then nodded again, unsure what to make of that. 'Romantic,' she said. A closer look showed the female officer to have red-rimmed eyes. Naomi decided not to ask about that at the moment. Instead she said, 'How 'bout you tell me how this all kicked off.'

'The guy threatened us,' Kryzanski said.

'Well,' the woman said, 'he didn't really *threaten* us. More like he told us what was gonna happen.'

The cop with the slight facial burn added morosely, 'And then it did.'

Naomi chewed the inside of her cheek. 'What did he say precisely?'

They told her.

Naomi said, 'Huh.'

They all stared at one another for longer than was comfortable. Though the incident had occurred nearly two hours ago, the cops still looked glazed. Regarding them now, the word that popped into Naomi's head was 'shell-shocked.'

She lifted her hand to help form her next question but then dropped it. They stared some more. 'So he just went ahead and did all that? When you were *expecting* it?'

'Well, not *exactly* like that,' Kryzanski said. 'Before he . . . *went* . . . he said . . . He said the slide on my Glock was out of battery.'

'Was it?' Naomi asked.

'No.'

She grimaced. 'Did you check?'

He hesitated, then gave a faint nod.

'Then what?'

'I don't remember much after that.'

'Is it fair to assume that's when the flying-table sequence started?' Naomi asked.

The female officer said, 'I believe that's fair to say, yes.'

'What'd he look like?' Naomi asked. 'This guy?'

'Average height, average build,' the female cop said. 'Regular features. He had a baseball cap pulled low, so it was hard to tell.'

'But you three were right there within a few meters of him in a well-lit restaurant.'

'I don't know.' The cop shook her head. 'He looked like a guy. Like anyone.' She was staring at the floor, still shaking her head. 'He looked like anyone.'

One of the forensics agents stuck his head out of 705 and called in a shout-whisper up the hall, 'Agent Templeton?'

His tone sounded sufficiently alarmed that Naomi hustled back to the crime scene, vowing to get a full debrief from the cops later. The din of clamoring voices inside 705 rose as she neared. She came into the room to find a man in a suit plucking the photographs off the wall.

'Who the hell is he?' she said. 'Who are you?'

The man turned around, sliding the photos into a manila folder. It took a moment for Naomi to place the round boyish face here, out of context.

Douglas Wetzel, the deputy chief of staff.

With curly chestnut hair a touch longer than DC standard, a full but neatly trimmed beard, and a suit priced well beyond the range of his salary, he looked like a trust-fund hipster conforming reluctantly to professional expectations.

She knew better than to take the laid-back adornments at face value. Wetzel was President Bennett's hatchet man, a political pit bull through and through.

As Wetzel clasped the folder to his chest and started out, Naomi stepped to intercept him. He was around her age, early thirties, and thick – a big-boned guy with some extra padding. She remembered reading somewhere that in order to match Bennett's schedule he functioned on three hours of sleep, snatched at intervals throughout the day. His entire existence was designed to remain at the president's beck and call 24/7.

'I'm Special Agent in Charge –'

'Templeton,' Wetzel said. 'We're aware.'

'What's the president's deputy chief of staff doing at my crime scene?'

'Invoking executive privilege.'

'You're tampering with evidence in an active investigation –'

'I was told it had been processed.'

'– and last I checked, you weren't the commander-in-chief.'

'I'm acting on the president's authority. He needs this contained.'

'The president's safety comes first,' she said. 'Containment second.'

Wetzel moved to step around her, and she moved as well, keeping her body between him and the door. He glared at her, and she held his stare. A number of her agents sidled up behind her casually, pretending to aim their focus elsewhere.

Wetzel's glare snapped off, replaced with a smile that showed little amusement. 'It's okay,' he said, taking a step back. 'You're new. You don't understand how this works yet.'

As he pulled out his phone and dialed, Naomi cast a glance over at the sniper rifle and the left-behind tape on the wall. A tableau staged to send a message.

Wetzel's appearance made clear who X had intended the message for.

Wetzel muttered into the phone and then looked up at Naomi. 'He wants you in his office *now.*'

Naomi felt herself flush. 'Director Gonzalez?'

Wetzel extended the phone, and she took it, pressed it to her ear in time to hear an all-too-familiar voice say, 'No. The president.'

7. First Domino to Fall

Evan had taken the southwest corner penthouse suite at the Hay-Adams. The hotel was suitable for a number of reasons. The building itself, a venerable Italian Renaissance–style beauty, had pleasing architectural flourishes, from walnut wainscoting to Elizabethan ceiling treatments. The service was superb – old-fashioned and discreet. Its 145 rooms provided relative anonymity.

And it had a superb view of the White House.

Sitting at his picture window, snacking on Virginia poached oysters bedded with cauliflower mousse, caviar, and a touch of yuzu, Evan let his Steiner tactical binoculars scan across Lafayette Square once more and lensed in on the northwest gate, the first point of entry to the West Wing. He'd been down in the park yesterday in an appropriated Parks and Recreation uniform, moving among the stalwart protesters and strategically trimming branches to clear the sight lines.

Despite the advent of dusk, he maintained a perfect view of the guardhouse now, the range-finding binocs designed for low-light conditions. A cable ran from the binoculars to his laptop, feeding it a steady stream of data.

He paused to slurp another oyster and took a sip of mint tea.

It was a civilized way to conduct an assassination.

Down at the gate, a woman in a royal-blue pantsuit hit a buzzer and spoke to a uniformed agent through the bulletproof glass. She gestured with annoyance, waving a yellow pass, but was turned away.

As she stomp-hobbled away in blocky high heels, Evan regarded his laptop, which mapped the woman's facial features, identifying her as a congresswoman from Florida's sixth district.

Another oyster. More tea.

He could get used to this.

The overhead vent wafted a cool current across his shoulders. The air was perfumed with French-milled soap from the bathroom. He was shirtless, an Egyptian cotton towel still wrapped around his waist from the shower; he hadn't bothered to get dressed.

Today Evan had announced himself to President Bennett. The rifle was the make and model Evan had used for his first assassination in 1997, the mission that – for whatever reason – Bennett was trying to eliminate any trace of all these years later. The photos Evan had taped on the wall were a few of the Orphans murdered at Bennett's command. Those men were no longer invisible, unseen and unmourned, but displayed as proudly as the stars carved into the white Alabama marble of the Memorial Wall at Langley.

And Jack.

Jack's face had been taped up in Apartment 705 as well, watching as Evan made his preparations, setting up the rifle, etching the round, parting the curtains to allow that first domino to fall.

For the past forty-five minutes, Evan had been set up here on the one-armed chaise longue of his hotel suite, waiting to see who Bennett would summon to handle the investigation. So far all Evan had captured in the lenses was a parade of White House workers and the occasional politician. He was hoping for a sign of Eddie Gonzalez, the Secret Service director, and whichever deputy assistant director he'd bring with him to run point on the investigation. Evan had figured that President Bennett would want to oversee the matter in person but, given the delay, he was beginning to think that Bennett might handle it over the phone.

A Jeep Wrangler parked beyond the gate, and a woman emerged. Tough-pretty, athletic build, her blond hair artlessly cut. No makeup, no jewelry. She was dressed nicely – dark jeans, white button-up, black fitted blazer – but not too nicely, as an aide or politician would be.

Promising.

The Steiners were a great set of glass, crisp up to a mile, refined enough that Evan could see the pierce holes in the woman's ears. As she reached the guardhouse, he screen-captured her on the laptop and ran facial recognition.

Naomi Jean Templeton, special agent in charge, Protective Intelligence and Assessment.

Evan pulled up her record from the databases and scanned it.

She was a pay grade below the agents Evan had been anticipating, and newly promoted at that.

Bennett would think she was malleable, controllable.

There was nothing the president valued more than control.

Evan adjusted the focus and watched the agent in the guardhouse tapping on his computer, a hardline telephone shrugged to one ear.

Naomi Templeton waited, penned in, the outer fence closed behind her, the inner fence not yet open. The guard gestured, and she placed her credentials in the pass-through tray. He examined them and sent them back.

The inner fence rolled smoothly open, releasing her from the sally-port pen, and she started for the West Wing.

A marine sentry guarded the entrance, motionless as a carving, his spit-polished shoes throwing a gleam even at this distance, even in this light. As she neared, he pivoted with automated grace, held the door for her with a white glove. His spine was a steel rod.

Evan watched Naomi disappear inside.

At last he rose and let the towel fall away. He'd made the opening gambit. It was time to formulate the next move.

8. Presidential Shit Management

The air in the Oval Office tasted of velvet. Perhaps it was the purity afforded by the filters, or perhaps it was just the flavor of the rich furnishings, of history itself. Naomi never got used to it. She'd been here three previous times with her father, all when she was small enough that he'd carried her in.

This was the first time she was here under her own power.

As she entered, President Bennett waited on one of the couches, his legs crossed. His eyes moved, but the rest of him didn't, a haunted-house-portrait effect. They tracked her progress in.

'Mr President.'

The rest of him became animated. Slightly. 'Agent Templeton.'

Somewhere behind Naomi, she heard the assistant secretary withdraw, the panel door suctioning shut, locking them in with an emphasis that called to mind the securing of an airplane cabin. The air hummed with silence, a vacuum-sealed effect.

Bennett's wire-frame eyeglasses conveyed a certain loftiness while adding a protective layer between himself and the world, augmenting his inscrutability.

'Why don't you sit,' he said.

Not a question.

She looked at the scattering of chairs and couches, realized that choosing her spot was a test of sorts. She took the couch directly opposite him, an assertive selection. Then she made full eye contact, though it was uncomfortable. He'd left the curtains at his back precisely parted to throw a slice of light into her face if she picked that seat.

He said, 'I heard you're not acceding to my wishes.'

'With all due respect, Mr President –'

'Is that phrase ever followed with due respect, Templeton?'

She pursed her lips. Recalled what her father used to say: *Ultimately a Secret Service agent is a babysitter. He just happens to be babysitting the most powerful person in the world.*

A memory flash kicked her in the gut – her father standing right there backlit on the carpet, broad-shouldered and stolid, and her reaching up to hold his hand.

Two hours ago, when she'd left him at the hospital, he'd been asleep, a bony fist clutching the top of the blankets, the downward slash of his mouth gapped with exhaustion.

She gathered herself, squared her own shoulders now. 'Okay, Mr President. Shall we get straight to it, then?'

'I'd appreciate that. I'm told my time is valuable.'

She cleared her throat and smoothed down the fabric of her pant leg, immediately annoyed at this release of nervous energy, especially given Bennett's motionless perch on the couch. He radiated latent power and menace, a coiled snake.

'My job isn't to accede to your wishes,' she said. 'It's to keep you safe. If you interfere with my investigation, I can't do that. I'd rather have you displeased with me and alive than happy and dead.'

He studied her for a moment. Then he smiled faintly. After the stone-faced commencement of their conversation, it felt like a full-body hug. She realized that this was a practiced technique, that he was conditioning her to react favorably to minor displays of reinforcement. She was a rat, and he controlled the rewards she'd receive if she pawed the right levers.

'My shit,' President Bennett said.

Her throat had gone dry, but she resisted clearing it. 'Excuse me?'

'When I travel abroad, a special portable toilet is flown with me. My feces and urine are captured and flown back to be disposed of here.'

He was studying her closely, gauging her reaction to the unusual tack. This was also a test – with Bennett everything was a test – and her reaction would determine her fate.

She went for unflappable. 'And?'

'Do you know why that is?'

At last, familiar ground. Presidential shit-management tales were among her dad's favorite anecdotes.

'So foreign intelligence can't capture it in specimen canisters and have it analyzed to determine what medical conditions you might have,' she said, striking a tone that bordered on disinterested. 'We did it to Gorbachev in the late eighties. The Mossad did it to President Assad when he traveled to Jordan for King Hussein's funeral.'

The president leaned forward on the couch, the slight movement as impactful as if he'd leapt to his feet. 'My *waste* is a national-security issue. I was the undersecretary of defense for policy at the DoD for two administrations and the secretary for a third. I've sat behind the Resolute desk' – at this, a hand flicked to indicate the wooden behemoth pinning down the oval carpet – 'for five years now. Do you really think I need you to explain my own safety to me?'

Naomi said, 'Evidently.'

It was a big gamble, and during the ensuing silence she envisioned herself clearing out her desk at headquarters, working security for a jewelry shop in Falls Church.

He absorbed this without reaction. When it was clear that

no response was forthcoming, she said, 'Your job is to run the world. My job is to cover your blind spots in one specific arena. That's all I do and all I'm here for. Will you let me do that for you?'

His snake eyes glittered, flat and impenetrable. He was still sizing her up, determining whether she was an asset or something worth eating.

'You catch a lot of flak being a female agent?' he asked.

'My SIG P229 shoots the same regardless of my anatomy.'

'That sounds like a well-rehearsed line.'

'It's a tired question, Mr President,' she said, then added, 'with all due respect.'

A hint of a smile teased the corners of his mouth but faded before it could get up steam. 'Let's try this one, then. You catch a lot of flak for your last name?'

She hesitated, saw that he saw it. It was like opening a tiny window into her soul. She packed down her regret, slammed the window shut. But it was too late. 'Nothing I can't handle.'

'Okay. Then let me ask you the generic question you've been answering since you stepped off the graduation dais at FLETC. Would you take a bullet?' His index finger jabbed into his chest, left side, slightly off the midline. 'For me?'

'That's not my job,' she said. 'My job is to keep that bullet from ever being fired. If it comes down to me having to play target dummy, I've already failed' – she caught herself – 'Mr President.'

He must have been breathing, though she could discern no rise and fall of his chest, no flare of his nostrils, no parting of his lips. Just the stare.

The discomfort of waiting grew until it became physical, expanding in her torso. She went on offense. 'You mentioned that your time was valuable,' she said. 'I'm gonna take you at your word. Which means I'd like to discuss the investigation.'

No nod, which she took as an invitation to continue.

'Everything about what we uncovered in that apartment is concerning to me,' she said. 'Not just the extent of the planning but the presentation of specifics. I believe your would-be assassin was speaking to you. And I believe you received the message.'

Something shifted in Bennett's expression, a loosening of the mask, and she saw that her words had turned a key in him. His locked-down posture eased, finally allowing a bit of slack in his muscles. He gave a faint nod.

She was in.

'My job is to cover every contingency,' she began.

'You *can't* cover every contingency. Not against him.'

She paused. 'Do you know who the suspect is?'

'No one does. Not really.'

She wasn't sure what to make of that. 'There was a run-in with an unidentified individual in a café minutes after the threat was spotted. His face was blocked by a hat in all CCTV footage, but we're looking to see if any of the mikes picked up audio. If so, we can match his recorded voice with those from threat calls we have in the database.'

'I read the report,' Bennett said. 'It was him. He won't have spoken in range of the surveillance units. And he won't be in the databases.'

She regrouped. 'The letters he wrote over the faces in the photographs. We can analyze the handwriting and backtrace the ink. We've got just shy of ten thousand ink samples in the International Ink Library, and a lot of manufacturers are adding invisible tags to help us —'

'Handwriting analysis will give you nothing. And the ink won't be traceable.'

'Okay,' she said, a touch of frustration leaking into her voice. 'Then we can start with the records we already have. You know the formula. Does he have a prior history of mental illness? Has he had military training? Does he have the capability to execute a plan? Exactly how serious is the threat?'

'No. Extensive. Yes. Grave.'

They stared at each other.

The panel door swung inward, and the assistant secretary stuck her head into the room. Without moving, Bennett said, 'Not now,' and she withdrew.

Naomi pursed her lips. 'The team is reviewing the squeal sheets and pulling Class 3 threats from records going back –'

'Don't bother.'

'We have twenty-five hundred working investigations –'

'Drop all of them,' Bennett said.

He was staring through the windows in the direction of the Rose Garden, but his eyes were unfocused.

'Mr President?'

He swung his gaze back to her.

'What the hell is going on?'

He smiled now, an actual smile. 'It seems as though we're talking. But that's not what's really been happening.'

'No? Then what has been happening?'

'I'm deciding.' That stare, direct and unremitting.

She weathered it, gave him back the kind of loaded silence he was so skilled at deploying.

'You're now in charge,' he said.

'Of what?'

'Everything,' he said. 'At least everything that pertains to this case. Which means, from my perspective, everything.'

'I have a deputy assistant director who's running point,' Naomi said. 'Plus Director Gonzalez –'

'That's no longer relevant. You will have the full resources of the Service at your disposal. You will focus exclusively on this investigation.' He paused for two seconds, an effective emphasis. 'Be advised, what I am about to tell you is classified, not just at the highest level but at a level you aren't even aware of. Understand?'

The question hung there, a threat. She held his gaze. 'Yes. I understand.'

He rose, circled the couch, and rested his hands on the back, looking across at her. 'The man trying to kill me is a US-trained black operative who has gone rogue. Code name: Orphan X.'

Naomi suddenly became aware of the chilled air in the room, a tightening of the skin at her nape. 'I thought . . .' She cleared her throat. 'I thought that program was apocryphal. Conspiracy-theory stuff.'

Bennett said, 'No.'

'The photographs –'

'Former Orphans, also rogue. Now eliminated.'

'And what information do you have on . . . Orphan X?'

It felt odd, saying the name as if it were something real.

'About as much as I just gave you,' Bennett said. 'We are dealing with a specter.'

'Then until I can get a handle on this investigation, we have to dial back your public exposure.'

'That can't happen. These are critical months, ramping up for the midterms. Speeches and fund-raisers. I have a party to feed. Plus, I've been besieged by claims of obfuscation. So the "optics," as the pundits like to say, must show me in contact with the populace.'

'Okay. We can hold the events, but we're gonna have to shuffle your schedule around and make additional game-day adjustments to throw Orphan X off.'

Bennett gave a slight nod.

'If you insist on working the rope lines, you can only interact with smaller groups of prescreened people. We'll add another layer to checking media credentials so he can't infiltrate the press corps. Any events you do, no matter the size, every last attendee goes through magnetometers.'

Bennett's mouth downturned faintly, just shy of a grimace. 'That'll make fund-raisers trying.'

'A lot less trying than getting shot.'

'I'm running a keep-control-of-both-houses campaign.'

'And I'm running a keep-you-alive campaign.'

He came around the couch, offered his hand to indicate that the meeting was ending. 'You don't relent, do you?'

'No, Mr President.'

His grasp was cool, firm, and dry.

'One more thing,' she said.

He halted, his loafers silent on the monochromatic oval carpet. The Presidential Seal was rendered in bas-relief, the eagle and stars sculpted into the pile itself.

She said, 'If I'm going to protect you from a threat of this magnitude, I need you to share all relevant information with me.'

'You have my word that I'll keep you apprised of everything that pertains to this matter. In return I expect that anything that comes up in the course of your investigation is brought immediately to me.'

'Yes, Mr President.' She exited into the secretary's office.

Bennett enjoyed the empty room for a moment. A moment of solitude was generally all he got at a time.

Sure enough, another door opened and Doug Wetzel stepped through. 'What'd you decide?'

Bennett said, 'I trust her enough to let her run things from the Service side.'

'She skates by on her old man's name.'

'Don't make that mistake. She's highly competent.'

'I haven't had time to get full background on her yet,' Wetzel said. 'How do you know?'

'Because that's what I do.' Bennett paused to assess the displeasure emanating off his deputy chief of staff. 'We're not going to rely on her solely,' Bennett said. 'She can't play offense against a threat like this. Neither she nor the whole goddamned Secret Service has the skills or the capabilities. If we want to get Orphan X, we can't rely on official channels.'

Wetzel leaned against the desk, scratched at his beard. 'So what do we do, then?'

Bennett said, 'Release him.'

'Who?'

Bennett just looked at him. Watched his Adam's apple bob, a particularly evident swallow.

Wetzel's voice, hoarse with apprehension: 'Right away, Mr President.'

He withdrew.

Before summoning his next meeting, Bennett took a deep breath and exhaled. The more lines he crossed, he'd discovered, the more he found necessary to cross. But this one in particular merited a respectful pause.

Once you unleashed hell, it was goddamned hard getting it back on the leash again.

9. Eternally Trapped Souls

Judd Holt awoke in his cell as he had every morning for the past 1,779 days. Physically, he was located inside a prison, but the issue of his legal whereabouts was more convoluted.

On a quiet winter day in 2006, Indiana's Federal Correctional Complex at Terre Haute inaugurated a euphemistically named Communications Management Unit, which floated inside the larger prison. The unit's nickname, Little Guantanamo, was more apt.

Like its cousin in Marion, Illinois, the Indiana CMU was created without any formal review process required by law. Mind-fuckingly, the unit was located on US soil while somehow not existing on sovereign land – a clever Schrödinger's-cat contortion designed to suspend prisoners' inalienable rights once they entered the sealed, windowless box.

CMU detainees – mostly terrorists or suspected terrorists – were deprived due process. Once ensconced inside the complex, they had radical restrictions placed on their phone calls, visits, and written correspondence.

For Judd Holt, this was perfect.

He needed to stay hidden as much as President Jonathan Bennett preferred him to be hidden.

Of course, Holt could have done without the incarceration bit, but he'd fucked up, stepping into an FBI sting operation that was too high-profile to cover up. Almost five years ago in the East Ward of Trenton, New Jersey, he'd illegally acquired an FN M249 SAW.

If he was going to kill Orphan X, he knew he'd require a serious platform.

He'd also acquired a Predator backpack that could hold eight hundred linked rounds to feed the rifle. Then he procured that amount of firepower four times over, in case it took more than a minute-long sustained burst to put down Orphan X. He'd driven to an isolated patch of woods outside Langhorne, Pennsylvania, to test the weapon. When the task force closed in, he'd been wearing the bulging rucksack on his back, unleashing on a stand of yellow birch like Ol' Saint Nick with a rage-control issue.

He could've obliterated his pursuers with a twitch of his trigger finger, but as accustomed as he was to bloodletting, he didn't need deaths of federal agents on his conscience.

So he'd allowed himself to be taken.

They couldn't believe that he was planning to use so much firepower for anything but a public massacre. They didn't understand the man he was hunting.

Needless to say, they had no idea who he really was. He lived under a false identity buttressed by authentic government-issued papers that were backstopped at the highest level.

Gun laws came with sentencing guidelines as draconian as those for drug laws, so he'd been slapped with two sixty-month sentences, one for the hog and the ammo, one for transporting across state lines.

He didn't expect to survive his first night in jail. He figured he'd be neutralized as soon as the sun dropped. Those were the rules of the game. He'd been caught – in the act of executing a personal mission, no less – and being caught risked exposure for those above him. The people who really mattered.

But that night a proxy had arrived who'd given him a

choice. A deal could be cut to take him off the boards. Holt would be buried in a CMU, out of sight and out of mind, where he'd finish his sentence. He wasn't to make any noise or file any appeals. He'd get out once his time had been served or when he was required – whichever came first.

He never went to trial. He zippered his mouth and got on the bus and had lived inside this box ever since. It was so cramped that when he lay on the cardboard-thin mattress of his cot, his outstretched arms could touch the opposing walls.

Of the three thousand prisoners housed in the entire complex, Holt was the most lethal, despite the fact that he'd already breached his fifties. He was a 'balancer,' one of the few non-Muslims scattered throughout the population to inoculate the unit against lawsuits. He'd been told more times than he could count that he looked like he had Scottish blood, but he didn't know where his people hailed from any more than he knew where he did.

He was built like an anvil, a whisper over five-nine, broadened with veiny, bulging muscle. His short-cropped hair, dull brown tinged with copper, receded into a severe widow's peak, a monk's tonsure beginning to crown in the back. A beard crowded his face, bristle so dense it looked like wiry fur. Under armed guard he was allowed to shave in his cell twice a week, and he required a fresh razor each time.

He was given fifteen minutes of yard time in a pen every Sunday – when it wasn't raining, when there were no threats of riots, when no irregularities had occurred during the week. During that time he had kept to himself, as was his habit, but he'd observed the others closely and forged a few alliances, not for protection but because he never knew when savage men might come in handy.

Today was not Sunday, which meant that he had sixteen hours to fill inside this six-by-eight-foot cell before he could go to sleep again.

That was fine. His training had prepared him for this. Time was money, and he had plenty to spend in here, 1,779 days with nothing to do but hammer his body into shape, hone his mind, and stoke his personal obsession to a high blaze. The instant he walked free from these four walls, he'd be ready to resume his mission.

Murder Orphan X.

Holt lay on the cot now, eyes still closed, feeling the warmth of sleep depart his face. The air was cool and smelled strongly of industrial cleaner. He let his lids part.

Directly over his head, a grapefruit-size orb bulged from the low ceiling, sufficiently tinted to hide the surveillance lenses inside.

The air felt different. He sensed it before he even sat up.

When he did, his cell door was standing open.

He stayed perfectly still, focused on the door, waiting. Ten minutes passed, maybe twenty.

He rose and knuckled the door gently. The rarely used hinges creaked.

He stepped into the hall.

The gate at the end was rolled back.

He moved toward it, drifting past other cells. Through the tiny glass squares, pairs of eyes watched him glide by.

Silence prevailed.

He reached the gate.

The guard chair just beyond was empty, a folded-back *Sports Illustrated* left on the padded seat.

Holt stepped through.

Now he was in a wider corridor that led to a solid steel door and a guard station. He kept on.

The guard on duty was watching the morning news.

Holt approached slowly and stood in full view of the tempered glass. The guard didn't remove his eyes from the small TV screen. His hand dipped beneath the counter, a buzz electrified the air, and the steel door clicked open.

Holt grasped the cool handle and pulled it wide. He stepped through into the gen-pop unit, two stories high. The range floor was spotless, broken only by floating staircases to the second-level catwalks. The animals were all in their precast-concrete houses, still behind locked doors, a face darkening every tiny glass window.

Holt ambled across the empty plain of concrete, sensing myriad heads swiveling to note his progress. Breath huffed across the tempered panes, fogging them sporadically.

So enormous was the hall of warehoused humans that it took Holt a full ninety seconds to traverse its length. Total silence accompanied him at every step. Given the height of the ceiling and the number of lives housed under it, the quiet felt thunderous, weighty, religious – as if he were moving through some netherworld, passing beneath the gaze of eternally trapped souls.

He reached the controlled entry point at the far side. He stopped and faced the security camera above.

The locking mechanism disengaged. He opened the door.

He was in the reception center now, where he'd been screened and processed nearly five years ago. An obese guard sat at the counter, working her gum like a cud. In the pass-through tray, a neatly folded stack of clothes waited.

It took Holt a moment to recognize them as his own.

As he approached, the guard swiveled on her chair, turning her back with evident disgust.

He stripped off the gray prison jumpsuit and stepped clear of it, leaving it puddled on the tile floor. For security reasons he'd been issued no undergarments, so he stood naked now, the air cold against his flesh.

He crossed to the counter, retrieved the clothes he'd last seen 1,779 days ago, and dressed. Olive drab vintage fatigue pants, worn T-shirt, steel-toed boots. A hundred bucks in gate money rested in the tray next to the wallet holding his authentic if illegitimate driver's license. He folded the five crisp twenties into his pocket and headed out.

A guard stood by the concrete façade of the entrance, twelve-gauge shotgun in hand.

The men stared at each other, and for a moment Holt wondered if he'd misread the situation, that he'd been led to his execution.

But the guard spit in the dirt and turned away.

Holt started across the dusty yard. In the tower the sniper kept up his watch, his wraparound shades winking back the sunlight. Holt watched the sunglasses scan right past him as if he didn't exist.

Which, he supposed, he didn't.

He came to the front gates, two layers deep, topped with coils of concertina.

They parted like the Red Sea.

He walked through one and then the other.

The instant he stepped free, a bizarre chime sounded, accompanied by a vibration against his thigh.

He reached down to one of his cargo pockets and lifted free an old-fashioned flip cell phone. He had never seen it before.

He snapped it open.

A voice he didn't know said, 'There's a Nissan Maxima across the parking lot to your right. No, *farther* right.' He adjusted his gaze. The voice continued, 'The keys are in the ignition. The destination is in the GPS.'

The call severed with a click.

Orphan A closed the phone and ambled to the waiting car.

10. Last Chance and Final Offer

The ride up the center of the marble obelisk took a full sixty seconds. The transparent elevator allowed for a mine-shaft effect, burrowing past carved blocks donated by various states and nations.

It was early on a Tuesday, so the number of tourists was thin. Evan stood in the back of the lift. He wore a roomy button-up shirt, nylon cargo pants, and a floppy sunhat. The Steiner binoculars, a favorite of bird-watchers and sightseers, dangled around his neck. He wore a fucking fanny pack, which he'd stuffed with sunscreen and maps so the security guards at the base would have something to paw through.

The doors parted on the Washington Monument's observation deck five hundred feet above the ground, and he shuffled out after the others into the narrow hall encircling the elevator shaft. Observation windows, two per cardinal direction, gave postcard views of the iconic scenery.

Across the National Mall, the morning sun bronzed the dome of the Capitol Building. Evan circled to the north window, which provided a crystal-clear vantage onto the White House, the Ellipse, and, just beyond, the streamer of 16th Street rising up, up, and away.

He posted up with his binoculars and waited. The president was scheduled to meet the Israeli prime minister at the National Gallery of Art for the ribbon-cutting of an exhibit featuring Nazi-looted art. Evan was tempted to attend, but at this stage of his operational planning he had to keep his distance. After yesterday's events the Secret Service would be deploying even more electronic surveillance to feed in real time to the Joint Operations Center on the ninth floor of HQ, where facial-recognition software would be applied.

Given that, strolling in wearing Groucho Marx glasses seemed ill-advised.

Evan faded back to let a few other tourists take a turn with their faces to the window. But even from the rear, he kept his binoculars raised.

Sure enough, at ten past the hour he saw movement across the White House's South Lawn. A number of motorcycle units peeled out first, fanning wide and posting themselves at intersections, a heightened security measure. Evan watched them position themselves, the observation deck giving him an ideal perspective to take in the grid of the city.

Finally the motorcade pulled into view, the three limos in a row crawling like beetles.

This time the convoy took a new route, cupping the edge of the White House lawn before cutting west to 17th Street NW.

A roundabout way to get to the Smithsonian. The Service was varying routine now, striving for unpredictability.

That was good.

Orphan X's message had been received loud and clear.

Evan adjusted the focus of his tactical binoculars, watching the tires of the three limousines, waiting for the telltale smooth rotation.

There it was.

President Bennett was in the rear limo.

The people in front of Evan rambled off, and he pressed forward, alone for the moment. As he leaned against the frame with an elbow and zoomed in on Cadillac One, he heard a distinctive ringtone sound from one of his pockets.

With its hardened rubber case and Gorilla glass, the Roam-Zone was a durable piece of gear. It was also impossible to trace. Each incoming or outgoing call was broken into digital packets and shot through the Internet, pinging through a network of encrypted virtual private network tunnels around the world before establishing the connection. Evan kept a filter on as well to screen out background noise that might provide clues to his location.

The phone number – 1-855-2-NOWHERE – was established for the pro bono clients he helped as the Nowhere Man, people in desperate need, grasping for a last lifeline before they went under for good.

Evan always answered the phone the same way: *Do you need my help?*

But as he eyed the caller ID screen now, he felt his pulse quicken in the side of his neck.

It was blank.

A few others – a *very* few – also had this phone number.

He thumbed the icon to answer, held the RoamZone to his face, said nothing.

A voice came through. 'Orphan X.'

Evan said, 'Mr President.'

'I received the message you left for me in Apartment 705. Given that you announced your intentions rather than simply trying to take a shot, I assumed you wanted to establish contact with me.'

Evan said, 'Affirmative.'

'You want to negotiate.'

Evan said, 'Affirmative.'

He tracked the convoy as it cut across Constitution Avenue NW, passing horizontally before him.

The measurement stadia of the binoculars marked off the

precise distance, .5-mil hash marks graduating to .1-mil hash marks toward the edges. Evan didn't need to measure now. But later, when he had to account for windage, minutes of angle, and the exterior trajectory of the projectile, it would become necessary.

'I can give you an unconditional presidential pardon,' Bennett said. 'For this current . . . situation. And for everything you've done before. I know you're highly trained. If you have a continuing interest in making use of that training, I could offer you a position not unlike the one you used to occupy. Except at the head of the table this time. Or you could walk away with full immunity and start a real life. An ordinary life.'

Evan thought of Mia Hall, the single mother who lived downstairs from him back in Los Angeles. The scent of jasmine on her skin and how the light caught in her curly hair. The loving disarray of the condo she shared with her nine-year-old son.

As he imagined everything that Bennett was ostensibly offering, a smirk touched his lips. *Isn't it pretty to think so?*

Bennett let the silence speak for a moment, and then he said, 'But permit me to be clear: This is your last chance and final offer.'

'Oh,' Evan said. 'You misunderstood me. I established contact to give *you* a final offer.'

A cough of a laugh, transmitted from blocks away and routed through four continents, reached Evan on a slight delay.

'Yeah?' Bennett said. 'What's that?'

'Step away now, resign the office, and I won't kill you.'

This time there was no laugh.

'You're joking, right?' Bennett said. 'Do you have *any idea* of the power I've got at my disposal?'

78

'I do,' Evan said. 'You've used it to kill so many of us already. And you're going after the rest. To make it as though we never existed.'

Bennett had been clear: He wanted them all dead. Former operators like Evan who had left the Program – who'd retired or fled or simply been used up and spit out. Who were overcome with PTSD and regret, pain and longing. They had known nothing but the inside of a foster home and the Program, but they'd gotten free somehow and fought their way back to a normal life. They were now wives or fathers or lost souls putting themselves together in a homeless shelter, a fragment at a time. As soon as Bennett finished with Evan, he'd resume hunting them.

The convoy detoured once again, heading north on 14th Street before zigzagging back toward the Mall – serpentine progress to keep out of the executioner's scope.

'Let's say this fanciful theory of yours is correct,' Bennett said. 'How about what *you've* done? Your life's work? Is that so different?'

It wasn't. And it was. Either way it was not a conversation Evan was interested in having with Bennett.

'The ends justify the means,' Bennett said. 'That's how you were trained, why you exist as what you are. If you're *really* good at it, do you know where you wind up?' The slightest crackle signaled his lips parting in a smile. 'The Oval Office.'

A family came up to claim a spot at the window, and Evan withdrew to the rear wall. Still he tracked the president's limo, threading its way to its destination.

'When it happens,' Evan said, 'it'll be over before you have any idea it's started. This is your last chance. If I hang up this phone, you will die.'

Bennett's laugh sounded like the jangle of silver.

Evan's hand tightened around the Steiner binoculars. Cadillac One hooked around 4th, coasted up Madison Drive to the National Gallery. Agents lined the steps from the limo to the museum entrance.

Evan said, 'I've killed generals. I've killed foreign ministers. I've killed captains of industry.'

The voice came back, calm as ever. 'But you've never killed the president of the United States.'

For a split second, Evan saw the man himself bob into view, just the back of his head and the top of a bespoke suit jacket framing his shoulders. One arm was raised, a phone pressed to his ear.

Evan said, 'Not yet,' and severed the connection.

11. Active Nightlife

On the dashboard of Evan's rental car, pressed up against the windshield, was a blocky electronic unit that resembled a police scanner. He was parked across the street from a brick building that wouldn't have been out of place at an Ivy League school. Adams Morgan, a diverse neighborhood in Northwest DC, was known for its active nightlife. People streamed out of bars and restaurants, providing plenty of movement to get lost in.

Evan had been sitting here unnoticed for the past hour and forty-seven minutes.

Waiting.

The unit on his dashboard was a cellular tower device interceptor, better known as a Stingray. If a targeted mobile device came within its transmission range, it would force the device to affiliate with it rather than with the nearest legitimate cell tower.

Law-enforcement cell phones featured increasingly effective encryption. But they had an Achilles' heel in the authentication process.

Authentication works in two directions – to and from the cell phone.

One of those directions was rock solid, the network going to extreme lengths to confirm the validity of a phone before allowing it to connect.

But the other direction was essentially unprotected. A phone did virtually nothing to determine that the network it was joining was in fact the network it claimed to be.

The Stingray on the dashboard was, like Evan, presenting itself as something it was not.

He'd lived under false cover for so many years that he wondered if he'd even know what it felt like to be real anymore.

Peals of laughter snapped Evan out of his thoughts. A cluster of college-age kids strolled past, cheeks flushed with alcohol – *You know you* so *want to hook up with him!*

They swept right past his car.

The guys sported man-buns of different sizes. The women wore strikingly similar designer jackets, cigarettes stubbed up between manicured fingers, their lip gloss uplit by the screens of their iPhones.

Watching them go, Evan had the experience he often did when looking at normal people: that of gazing through aquarium glass. They flitted by in happy schools, apart but somehow in concert, their movements choreographed to music that existed at some dog-whistle pitch he couldn't hear.

He'd been raised outside the mainstream, his childhood hours spent not at movies or the shopping mall but on rifle ranges and in dojos. He didn't understand the unspoken rules of intimacy, but he knew precisely at which angle to thrust a finger strike to dislodge someone's eyeball.

Ahead, one of the girls pressed a guy up against a brick wall and kissed him, one foot lifted behind her as the moment demanded. They broke apart a bit breathlessly and ran laughing to catch up to the others and the promise of the night ahead.

For an instant Evan wondered if he'd be willing to trade his knowledge of a well-directed finger strike for the ability to go out into the night – just once – with the sole purpose of enjoying it.

Across the street Naomi Templeton appeared.

Her Jeep Cherokee cruised up to the curb, and she hopped out, head lowered, already thumbing at her Boeing Black smartphone.

Evan raised the small Yagi directional antenna from his lap and aimed it at her.

The Stingray lights blinked on and off, a low-key Christmas display, waiting for Naomi's cell phone to affiliate itself with Evan's impostor network.

It did.

Now that the small box on the dashboard was the end point of Naomi's connection, it no longer mattered what kind of encryption was used, because Evan had all the keys.

He pulled his laptop over from the passenger seat, straining the cord connecting it to the Stingray, and alternated his attention between Naomi and the screen.

She headed for her apartment, phone pressed to her cheek.

He thumbed up the volume on his laptop and heard her saying, '– still catching up to this. Look, Director, he said Doug Wetzel would be my main interface, and as much as I'm flattered by the president's faith in me, I don't trust that guy.'

Director Gonzalez's voice came through Evan's speakers next. 'You don't have a choice, Templeton. This is what's happening now. If the president wants you dealing with his deputy chief of staff, that's who you'll deal with.'

'So I'm running point on the investigation.'

'You're not just running point. You're running the whole fucking thing.'

The call severed with a click, and Evan watched Naomi shoulder through the building's front door a bit harder than seemed necessary.

He scrolled down his laptop screen, scanning over her text messages. He could see inside her phone, and he could see inside everything the phone saw inside – data packets going back and forth, applications, her desktop calendar.

The big question would be whether he could use her phone to breach the Secret Service databases, which resided on a private secure network unhooked from the Internet at large.

To answer that, he'd have to get back home.

For now, his work in DC was done. He'd given Bennett a final chance. The bridge had been torched, the last thread severed. Bennett wouldn't call back.

The next time the RoamZone rang, it wouldn't be someone hunting for Orphan X. It would be someone who needed the Nowhere Man. Evan wondered what that mission would be and – given the danger of what he was about to embark on – how the hell he'd manage it.

Maybe fate would look upon the daunting task before him – the murder of the most powerful and protected man alive – and take that into consideration before directing some innocent to reach out to him in time of direst need.

He could always hope.

12. High-Functioning

Trevon Gaines walked from the bus stop to Mama's place. It was three blocks up and two over – but really two and three-fifths blocks over if you counted by house. Westchester was a nice neighborhood, and you got to look at planes flying overhead from LAX even though right now you could mostly only see their blinky lights 'cuz it was dusk. Tonight was a family dinner, and all his aunts and uncles and brothers and sisters would be there except Kiara 'cuz she was in Guatemala and Leo 'cuz he was at home with a broke jaw and Gran'mama 'cuz she was in the home and Daddy 'cuz he was in heaven.

Trevon had a bottle of Two-Buck Chuck from Trader Joe's, 'cuz you always showed up with something – that was a rule – but it was confusing because it wasn't chuck, it was 'Shiraz' which was almost like that girl's name from PE back in high school, the one who wore the tight shirt and he'd watch run around the track but not stare because staring made people nervous.

The bottle was also confusing because it didn't cost two bucks, it cost $1.99, which was one-sixth of what Trevon made an hour as the night watchman at the warehouse. Actually, it wasn't one-sixth, it was 16.5833333 et cetera percent, because the penny made it not perfect. He didn't like not perfect, but Mama always told him that not perfect was just fine, because things and people were made all different ways and they were all just as beautiful and you still loved them just as much.

It was a lot to spend for the Shiraz, because he wouldn't drink any of it, but Mama never let him show up without bringing something no matter how small even though she was rich and had a nice house and gave him money every month to help him stand on his own two feet 'cuz he was a twenty-seven-year-old man now and how was he ever gonna meet someone if he didn't stand on his own two feet. If you thought about it, he was just spending Mama's money to ride the bus to Trader Joe's and buy something to bring back to her, which didn't make sense, because why couldn't she just go to Trader Joe's and buy it herself, but that was a rule about how people did things, and rules were important to follow even if they didn't make sense.

He shoved his thick glasses up his nose and headed up the walkway and saw that the front door had been left open, and that was weird because Mama wasn't raised in a barn.

It was a heavy wood door, and the hinges creaked when he pushed on it. It was quiet inside, and it was cold. The tiles on the floor were red Spanish tiles, and there were forty-eight of them in the front hall, and they were too small to walk on and not step on cracks, but that was one of his rules and not a real rule so he didn't have to follow it, and sometimes it was even better not to.

He went down the hall to where it hit the big kitchen and living room and family room and the glass sliding doors that stacked back onto each other and opened wide to the yard.

He stopped.

He stood there for a minute blinking.

His first thought was of sangria, splashed on the walls, spilling off the accent table, staining the tile. He accidentally drank it once as a kid 'cuz it looked like juice, and he'd chewed the orange slices and then got all dizzy-headed. This looked like someone had dropped a pitcher. Or pitcher*s*.

Then he looked at what he was trying not to look at like he used to try not to look at Shyrece's chest when she ran laps in PE.

There were bodies, and they were sprawled on the couch and the floor and slouched against the walls, and they were the bodies of his aunts and uncles and brothers and sisters.

He heard his mouth make a noise that sounded like a groan, and then he was saying, 'Oh my gosh. Oh my gosh.'

He closed his eyes, and he hummed a little.

Then he opened them and looked at the twenty-seven drops of blood on the third tile from the back wall and the thirteen plastic spoons sticking out of the cup on the counter and the eighteen slats of the heating vent.

He blew a shaky breath and walked out through the slid-back glass doors into the backyard. His cousin Aisha was lying on a lawn chair and Uncle Joe-Joe was floating in the pool and Auntie Tisha was on the lawn with her dress all tangled and –

Mama was in her usual spot by the BBQ, except she was propped up in her chair now with her head nodded back so you could see all the rolls of her chin.

Trevon stared at her and felt hot beneath his face. And then he blinked hard, because we don't cry and we don't feel sorry for ourself, and he said, 'That's okay, Mama. Don't be scared. You're in heaven.'

It was getting harder to see everything, because dusk does that at the end, goes away fast. But Trevon heard footsteps crunching the gravel by the side of the house, and he turned around and the footsteps were getting closer, and he could feel his heart jerking in his chest.

Two shapes came out of the dark and turned into two

men. One had the kind of outlined muscles you don't find in nature but you see sometimes on TV. He had a tattoo of a half skull on each forearm, and Trevon could tell that if he held his arms together, they would make a full skull.

The other man reminded Trevon of how Uncle Joe-Joe always described that Johnson boy who lived around the block – raw and lean and all hungry-looking like.

They approached. They were wearing white gloves like the surgeons do on TV, and the gloves were stained red like they'd just performed surgery.

'Please,' Trevon said. 'Don't.'

The raw one smiled, and his pointy tooth glinted in the glow from the BBQ. 'Don't what?'

Trevon pointed at Mama and Auntie Tisha and Uncle Joe-Joe in the pool even though you couldn't see him in the dark anymore.

'Oh. *That.*' The silver tooth gleamed again. 'Nah, we got something better in store for you.'

'Damn,' the muscley one said. 'Those are some Coke-bottle motherfuckers.'

It took a sec, but then Trevon figured out he was talking about Trevon's eyeglasses, 'cuz that's what Clyde Johnson called them.

The muscley one said, 'You're Trevon Gaines, right?'

Trevon said, 'Uh-huh.'

'Night watchman at SoCal First Bonded Warehouse?'

Trevon said, 'I was Employee of the Month in February and April.'

The men looked at each other.

'This should be easy,' the muscley one said. He walked over to the trash can by the BBQ, lifted out the liner, and dumped the trash on the lawn. 'He's a fucking retard.'

'No,' Trevon said. 'I'm high-functioning.'

'Either way,' the raw one said, flicking open a folding knife, 'you're coming with us.'

The muscley one put the trash bag over Trevon's head, and everything went dark, and he got panicky and sucked in, but the bag filled the whole inside of his mouth.

Then a hand palmed the back of his head and something punched through the trash liner into his mouth and nicked the side of his cheek, and then he could breathe through the slit in the bag, but only barely if he sucked in and blew out really hard.

The Scaredy Bugs were running crazy inside his body, but he breathed as hard as he could to get air and told the Scaredy Bugs they weren't in charge, that he was the boss of them, and when the men shoved him to walk toward the gate, he didn't complain, because we don't cry and we don't feel sorry for ourself.

13. Good Little Lamb

From Terre Haute, Indiana, to the outskirts of DC was a straight shot on 1-70, ten hours and change without traffic.

But traffic had gotten worse in the past 1,779 days, and by the time Judd Holt steered the shitty Nissan Maxima into the motel parking lot, it was full dark.

He'd no sooner parked than the flip phone buzzed in his pocket. He thumbed open the clamshell and read the message: RM 7.

Okay, then.

Public housing loomed all around. A crackhead jittered across the crosswalk, head back, lips parted, ruinous yellow teeth grinning at the moon. Dealers were out, sitting on the hoods of cars, floating by in lowriders, working on their scowls.

Knox Hill wasn't the worst neighborhood Orphan A had operated in. Next to Jalalabad, it felt like Palm Beach.

He got out of the Maxima, ambled over to the row of bushes hemming in the parking lot, and took a long and satisfying leak.

He didn't like to head into trouble with a full bladder.

He walked over to Room 7 and knocked.

There was no point bothering with surveillance or a cautious approach. They wouldn't have had him drive all this way just to put him down.

The door opened. The guy inside was not what Holt expected.

White boy, soft from good meals and good living, some

college-athlete muscles in there attempting to hold on. He wore a gray plaid suit like it was 1955 and sported one of those beards that was trying too hard to be noticed.

Holt said, 'Who the fuck are you?'

The guy bristled. Stepped back.

Only once the door was closed behind them did he say, 'I'm our mutual friend's deputy chief of staff. The fact that I'm here personally should show you the importance of what we're about to discuss.'

Holt sat on the bed, bounced a bit to test the mattress. 'The fact that I walked out of a federal penitentiary showed me the importance of what we're about to discuss,' he said. 'So I don't need no foreplay.'

'The Orphan Program is no longer what it was,' the man said, sitting on the other bed and facing Holt so their knees almost touched. 'It's virtually shut down, and there are . . . compliance issues with our former operators.'

'Meaning they know shit that could be trouble for the Man.'

'Because of your shared history, there's a level of trust between you and the president.' The man licked his lips. 'You're the only Orphan he ever interacted with directly.'

Holt pulled his shoulders back and down, stretching them. He'd gotten used to it in the box, all the small, compact movements to keep his muscles from languishing.

He thought back to when Bennett was a star on the rise at the DoD. As the inaugural Orphan, Holt had been tasked with reading him in on the Program. He'd also helped Bennett in the operational planning of the first missions he'd overseen.

'He wasn't like the other DoD suits with their shiny little Glocks,' Holt said. 'Naw, he was steel. Could've just as easily been on our side of the fence. Yeah, we saw eye to eye.'

'That's why we want to entrust you with this essential job.'

'Doing what?'

'Eliminating Orphans.'

'Which ones?'

'All of them.' The guy reached for a briefcase on the ugly-ass comforter next to him and popped the brass catches like he was in a spy movie. He removed a few files. 'As you can imagine, information has been scarce. But we've managed to locate a few.'

Holt lifted a hand, palm up, and flicked his fingers inward. 'Give 'em here.'

He took the files and flipped through them.

The first contained a phone bill with a few matching numbers circled and nothing else.

The second showed a woman in her late thirties, now a single mother of two in Albuquerque. Holt stared at her face, the PTA makeover. As a former Orphan, she'd be harder to catch off guard than her appearance dictated, but she had kids, so there'd be strings to pull, levers to tug, plenty of incentive for her to go to slaughter like a good little lamb.

The third held a surveillance-screen grab from Grand Central Station. The Orphan looked unwell, a bulge at the waistline, gaunt cheeks, eyes wide and paranoid. He'd be rusty. Holt studied the wrecked face and thought about where he'd place the bullet.

He thumbed through the remaining files, most of them sparse. Each Orphan's personal background information and operational history had been redacted; all that remained was intel that pertained to tracking them down.

'As you can see, we've been hard at work these past months.' The guy clearly feared a good old-fashioned silence. He loosened his tie and undid his top button. Then he fished up a lanyard and showed off the flash drive dangling from it like a pendant. 'We have it cached digitally as well, but I was told you were more old-school.' The drive vanished into his collar once again, and he tidied himself back up. 'These files – like the Program – are deep black, totally off the books.'

Holt scratched at the stubble curling from his jawline and stared at the man. Aggressively. To his credit, the guy held Holt's gaze, but Holt could smell the fear coming off him, leaking through the pores.

Holt said, 'What's your name, son?'

'Doug. Wetzel.'

'Wetzel. Let me tell you something. This is all well and good.' Holt dropped the stack of files back into the kid's lap. 'And I will get to them. I can promise you that. But it's gotta wait. There's something I need to take care of first. When I'm done, I'll come back and we can run the table with these fuckups.'

'What's so pressing that you'd turn down a presidential order?'

'I think you know the answer to that. You didn't move heaven and earth to get me released to handle this non-urgent bullshit. So refine your sales pitch instead of trying to walk me into a honey trap.'

Wetzel folded his hands. His fingers looked like little sausages. 'Our interests are aligned.'

'No shit. I want Orphan X. He's got the most dirt on Bennett.' Holt stood up. 'This meet? Didn't need to happen. All you had to do is unlock that cell door and leave me the fuck alone.'

'Sit down,' Wetzel said. At Holt's stare he quickly held up a hand. 'Please,' he added. 'There's more.'

Holt said, 'Speak.'

Wetzel told him about the assassination threat and the sniper rifle they'd found with the photographs of dead Orphans.

Holt sat back down, the springs complaining under his weight. 'What about the Secret Service?'

'The Secret Service can't hunt.' The knot of Wetzel's tie was still pulled to the right side from his show-and-tell with the flash drive, but the rest of his getup was unrumpled, butter smooth. 'We'll get you anything you want. Guns, rifles, explosives.'

'I'll let you know. For now I'm gonna go – What'd you call me? "Old-school." But I do need one thing.'

'What's that?'

'Cannon fodder. Going up against X, I'll need numbers.'

'This is totally covert. I don't know how we can provide you –'

'At my prison,' Holt said, 'there were two brothers, went by Sound and Fury. They'll do just fine.'

'You want us to release these men?'

'You said you'll get me anything I want. Well. I want.'

'What are they in for?'

'Torture, rape, homicide.'

Wetzel said, 'Oh.'

They stared at each other some more.

Wetzel finally said, 'You expect me to free convicted rapists and murderers from prison?'

Holt said, 'Yes.'

Wetzel smoothed his beard. 'I don't know that that's –'

'You want to get a job done, you need the right tools,' Holt said. 'Wade and Ricky Collins are the right tools.'

Wetzel sipped in a breath. 'I'll see what I can do.'

'You said you're the deputy chief of staff. Act like it.' Holt dug in his pocket, removed the flip phone, and snapped it in half. He handed Wetzel the pieces. 'I bought me a new phone on the way here.' He told Wetzel the number. 'Got it?'

Wetzel nodded. 'I'll be in touch to coordinate our efforts, and we'll give you a contact number at the DoD. We have people there we trust more than the Service. We'd like you set up away from the president but always nearby. You can shadow his movements, run your own reconnaissance ahead of our advance teams, surveil from a slight remove.'

'Like X is.'

'Just so. You're the only one who can see this situation through his eyes.' Wetzel grinned. 'It takes an Orphan to catch an Orphan.'

Holt wondered how long he'd rehearsed that line.

'I ain't gonna *catch* him,' Holt said. 'I'm gonna *end* the motherfucker.'

Wetzel nodded, his chin tight against the tie. 'If you're caught, you're on your own. This is a full cutout operation.'

Holt considered punching Wetzel in the throat for being obvious. Instead he just stared until Wetzel cracked, fiddled with his briefcase, and rose.

'You're welcome to stay,' Wetzel said. 'This room is paid up for the next month. There's forty thousand dollars in the nightstand drawer next to the Gideon Bible. It can be replenished as needed.' Producing a disposable phone, he thumbed in the number that Holt had told him, let it ring once, and then hung up. 'That's the contact number you'll use should you need me.'

He started for the door and then paused. 'There is one more thing.' He set the briefcase down on the cracked wooden table, opened it, and removed a last file. 'Your arrest, your records, your trail in and out of the penitentiary have all been scrubbed clean. No one will remember anything or care to.

Except. The prosecutor, as you might recall, is a shark. Takes cases personally. Perfect record. Dots every i, crosses every t. And, we're told, keep tabs on every last conviction.' Wetzel rested the file on the table, tented his fingers on it for a moment as if blessing what lay within. 'Provide photographic evidence when it's done.'

'To be clear,' Holt said. 'We're talking about a federal prosecutor.'

Wetzel lifted his hand from the file and exited quietly.

Holt stood for a time in the motel room, breathing in the scent of mold and Lysol. Then he pulled open the nightstand drawer and scooped up the cash.

On his way out, he took the file from the cracked wooden table.

14. Expensive Fish

Pitch-black.

The Scaredy Bugs were running like crazy beneath Trevon's skin, and his mouth tasted salty from the blood, but he was trying hard not to notice. The little knife slit in the trash bag over his head was just enough to let the air trickle through if he worked really, really hard. His glasses were crooked, and he could tell they were foggy from his breath even though he couldn't see almost anything.

He wondered why they were doing this to him, but then he remembered that Mama always told him that bullies were just jealous of people who were special 'cuz they didn't feel special themselves.

Mama.

He bit his lip to keep it from trembling, but only for a sec, 'cuz he needed his mouth open to try'n get air.

They'd been in a car for a while – actually a truck or SUV, 'cuz he'd had to step up to get in the back. So far they'd turned left, left, right, left, right, left, left – and then he'd lost track 'cuz he thought of Mama.

Mama.

There was a slurping sound from the front seat.

Raw One's voice said, 'What's that shit?'

And then Muscley One said, 'Protein drink, fifty-four grams. Check out these sick gains.'

The seat belt made creaking sounds.

Raw One said, 'Be sure'n take lots of gym selfies before your kidneys fall out.'

The trash liner was wet against Trevon's face. 'Um,' he said. 'Excuse me? Could you please take this off?'

They both laughed, and Muscley One said, 'Sure, we'll get right on that.'

'Thank you,' Trevon said.

They laughed again, and he waited for them to help.

He kept waiting.

When they tore the garbage bag off his head, he gasped and gasped. As soon as he caught his breath, he said, 'Thank you.'

They were standing in a gravel lot in the middle of nowhere. There was a tall fence surrounding them, and on top of the fence there was barbed wire, except not the type that looks like little stars but the big swoopy kind with razor blades.

Muscley One shoved him hard in the kidney, and he said, 'Ouch,' but he moved where they wanted him to, toward a big cinder-block building that looked like a warehouse. It was dark, and there were no lights except for one over the only door he could see.

At the door Raw One tapped a code into a panel, and they stood there. Trevon looked at Muscley One's half-skull tattoos, and Muscley One said, 'The fuck you looking at?'

'Your tattoos. They're scary.'

'Not as scary as what you're about to see.'

Trevon said, 'Oh, no.'

The door buzzed open, and they stepped inside.

They were in a front room, and there were seven other guys like Raw One and Muscley One, and they all had guns strapped to their hips like it was nothing, and they were leaning against the walls and tables and looking all sullen-like. The walls were covered with eleven thick metal plates like it was some kinda shelter to protect them from a alien invasion.

Raw One said, 'How's his mood?' and Rat-Face One said, 'How the fuck you think his mood is?'

Fat One flicked his chins at Trevon and said, 'That the poor fool?'

Before anyone could answer, a voice came over a loud-speaker and said, 'Bring him in here.'

Raw One and Muscley One pushed Trevon toward a closed back door that was all thick and metal. Next to it was a big mirror that took up half the wall.

The voice came back on and said, 'Did you frisk him?'

'Believe me,' Raw One said, 'it's not a concern.'

And the voice said, 'It's *always* a concern.'

Then Raw One and Muscley One touched Trevon all over like they weren't supposed to, and he thought about Stranger Danger and that he'd have to tell Mama later.

Mama.

Instead he could tell Gran'mama or Leo, because they were family and family will take care of you. He wished Kiara was here instead of running around helping folks in Guatemala 'cuz she was the oldest and the sweetest and his favorite, and she always understood him better than anyone.

The big metal door buzzed, and then Raw One and Muscley One pushed him through. It was a nice office here in the middle of the warehouse with a desk and a blotter and tables with scales on them like they weighed lots of stuff in here, and there was a man sitting behind the desk with his boots up on the blotter.

He had a big face.

Muscley One and Raw One shoved Trevon down into a

leather chair facing the desk. Behind the desk were doors that opened onto other corridors with other doors, like the building kept going forever.

Trevon was sweating a lot, and he wiped at his forehead and straightened his glasses. He looked behind him and could see right through the mirror into the front room like magic, and then he realized it was like a interrogation room on a cop show. The other men were relaxed and joking, with big hand gestures and big smiles, and Trevon watched how happy they looked and couldn't imagine ever feeling like that again.

Big Face let his boots thunk to the floor, and he leaned forward over the blotter. 'Do you know what you did wrong?'

Trevon didn't, and he wanted so bad to cry but he didn't, because we don't cry and we don't feel sorry for ourself.

Instead he said, 'No, sir.'

'I'm an importer. In a particularly cutthroat business.' Big Face's voice was calm, but it was fake calm, like when Uncle Joe-Joe got real mad. It sounded weird, stuffed-up-like but also deep. 'Do you know how long I've been doing business successfully?'

Trevon shook his head.

'Forty-four years. How do you think I've gotten by this long?'

'I don't know.'

'Do you think it's by letting myself be taken advantage of?'

'No, sir.'

'Last Friday you were working the night shift at SoCal First Bonded Warehouse when my container arrived from Suriname.'

'Yes, sir. Intermodular container, series one, number BL322-401. It weighed in at 29,456 kilograms. External dimensions:

nineteen feet and ten point five inches by eight feet by eight feet and six inches. Internal dimensions –'

The voice was quiet, but it cut him off like a blade: 'Do you know what it held?'

'Frozen fish.'

'Sure,' Big Face said. 'Eighteen million dollars of frozen fish. My profits of forty-four years put on the line for this deal.'

Trevon said, 'That's expensive fish.'

Big Face breathed a few times. A vein squiggled in his throat, and his face was red. He looked like he might explode, but then he breathed himself back to calm. 'Yes,' he said. 'And this container – *my* container holding *my* profits of forty-four years – was supposed to go in the front and right out the back before the customs officials got there for the CBP examination. That was my understanding with Chava.'

'Chava got food poisoning.'

'But he told you what you were to do.'

'Uh-huh.'

'I had another container, a replacement container, right there, ready to be scrutinized. You just had to smile and look the other way.' Big Face picked up a letter opener and put the pointy tip into his finger and twisted it. 'But you didn't, did you?'

Trevon's throat was dry. He couldn't find his voice, so he shook his head.

'Instead you called customs and went home for the night. And now here we are. Me with my problems. And you with yours.' Big Face's teeth clenched. 'Do you think my . . . trading partners will cover my losses? Do you think they'll say, "Oh, there was a mix-up? That's okay. We'll cover your losses. We'll send you another shipment."'

'Oh!' Trevon said. 'One time I bought berries at Trader

Joe's, and when I got home the ones on the bottom were all moldy-like, and so I took 'em back . . .'

Big Face's eyes got wide, and Trevon figured he didn't like his story so he stopped telling it 'cuz that was something Mama had taught him about reading social cues.

Mama.

Big Face said, 'You didn't listen to Chava.'

Trevon wiped at his forehead again. 'Where's Chava now?'

'Chava? Chava is dead.'

Trevon felt his throat closing up, trying to make him cry, but he wouldn't. 'He is? Oh, no. Musta been really bad food poisoning.'

Muscley One and Raw One laughed behind him, but then Big Face looked up at them and they went silent.

'In direct violation of Chava's orders – of *my* orders – you called customs,' Big Face said. 'Why would you do such a thing?'

''Cuz that's what the rules say. And it's the right thing to do.'

'Are you happy with where that got you?'

'I don't . . . I don't know. What are you gonna do to me?'

'To *you*? Oh, I'm not gonna touch a hair on *your* head.' Big Face leaned forward, and his chair made a creaking noise. 'Instead I'm gonna tell you a story. When some piece of shit commits an act of terror in Israel, do you know what the Israeli army does?'

'No, sir.'

'They demolish the houses of the raghead's family. Every last family member. Every last house. Because, you see, merely punishing the offender doesn't work as a deterrent. It doesn't help ensure that this will *never happen again*.' Big Face took a few more breaths. 'What the Israeli army does is a fine policy. But my trading partners? They make what's going on in the

Middle East look like a playground. They could well imagine that with my coffers low and my merchandise flow interrupted I am weak. They are uniquely attuned to smelling weakness. So I require a show of strength. One that reminds them that I am not weak but that I am to be *feared*. Which requires measures much more severe than those used by the Israelis.'

Trevon felt pins and needles all over his body.

'Jesus Christ.' Big Face looked up at his friends. 'I'm dealing with someone who is *literally* too stupid to appreciate how fucked he is.' He stood. 'I'll try'n break it down for you clearly, Trevon. Everything that happened to your family? Everything that is *going* to happen? It's all your fault.'

Trevon tried to talk, but his throat was all dried up. He swallowed and tried again. 'What else is gonna happen?'

'I'm going to eliminate your people from the face of the earth. I will kill every relative and loved one you have. Wipe away any trace that you exist outside of the terrible thoughts bouncing around inside your damaged, useless skull.'

Trevon thought of his cousin Aisha on the lawn chair and Auntie Tisha on the lawn and Mama in her chair.

Mama.

Big Face interrupted his thoughts. 'Your grandmother? In the nursing home?'

Trevon's voice sounded like a croak. 'Gran'mama?'

'My associates mixed weed killer into her morning yogurt. She'll die, certainly. But it will take *hours.*'

Trevon shook his head back and forth hard, trying to make the pictures in it go away.

'Your brother Leo? Home right now with his jaw wired shut? My friends here replaced his meds with emetics. Can you imagine what it's like to vomit again and again when it has nowhere to go?' Big Face twisted that letter opener into the pad of his finger, bringing up a tiny bead of blood. 'It took him nearly twenty minutes to suffocate.'

Trevon waited, forgetting to breathe, his chest burning and burning.

Somewhere inside his brain, he realized that Big Face hadn't mentioned Kiara, which was good 'cuz Kiara was his favorite and she was in Guatemala helping folks and she barely never even checked e-mails no more.

She was safe. Kiara was safe.

But Gran'mama. And Leo. And Mama.

Mama.

Big Face was talking some more. 'Your lineage has been exterminated. And not just backwards but into the future. Forever. If you ever date, if you ever marry, if you ever have kids, we will be there. We will take everything and everyone from you as you took forty-four years of hard work from me.'

Big Face nodded, and Muscley One and Raw One came forward and grabbed Trevon's wrists to control his hands. He screamed and tried to fight, but they were way, way too strong.

They shoved Raw One's folding knife into Trevon's hand and made him grab the sticky handle before taking it away. Then they did the same thing with a machete and a gun and a pill bottle. They put all the stuff into a plastic bag.

Big Face nodded at the bag. 'Do you understand what this means?'

Trevon shook his head.

'These murder weapons have your fingerprints on them. If you go to the cops, if you talk to *anyone*, we will make sure these weapons are found. You will be known as the psycho retard who murdered his entire family. And I can promise you, you will not fare well in prison among real murderers. And rapists.' He licked the dot of blood from his fingertip. 'Do you understand now?'

It took some effort for Trevon to make his head move up and down.

'Maybe one day you'll decide that you can tell a police officer. Share your burden with a co-worker. Maybe you'll think you can run away, leave the city, go to Mexico. If you think I won't find out, think again. You don't do what I do over four decades without building connections everywhere. *I will know.*'

Big Face walked around his desk now in front of Trevon and crossed his arms and looked down at him. He smelled of fancy cologne.

'You exist now for one purpose and one purpose only. To be an advertisement to my trading partners, to my workers, to the world in which I move that no one is *ever* to take steps to harm my interests. You will wake each morning and breathe and suffer as a living testimony to my power.'

Trevon leaned over and vomited on his shoes.

Big Face said, 'Get this imbecile the fuck out of my office.'

Muscley One and Raw One lifted Trevon by the arms. His legs didn't work, so they carry-dragged him back out through the front room, into the gravel lot, and over to the truck.

Muscley One reached into the backseat and threw a little towel at Trevon's face. 'You're cleaning your ass up before you get in my new truck.'

Trevon wiped at his mouth and his shirt. Then he held the little towel tight in his hands as they put the trash liner back over his head and pushed him in. The air smelled like the blue tree he'd seen dangling from the rearview mirror.

As they drove off, the Scaredy Bugs went crazy inside

Trevon, running around so fast he wished he could unzip his skin and crawl out. He tried to hum to himself, but it didn't help any. His hands were shaking and his arms were shaking and his legs were shaking. He twisted the little towel between his fists and rocked himself, but that didn't help any.

The Scaredy Bugs had won.

15. Outside the Purview

After a roundabout trip home – an early-morning flight from DC into San Francisco, a commuter plane to Long Beach Airport, a vehicle switch at a long-term-parking lot, and another at one of his many safe houses – Evan drove his Ford pickup through the Wilshire Corridor. The harsh midday sun glinted off the glass of the condo high-rises thrusting up on either side of the boulevard.

Evan turned in to the porte cochere of his own building, the pompously named Castle Heights Residential Tower.

Mia Hall sat on the bench by the front doors with her nine-year-old son, Peter. They were eating ice cream, though more of Peter's seemed to be dripping over his fist than remained on the cone. He smiled a chocolaty clown smile and gave a wave that would have been visible several blocks away.

Evan slowed as he passed, the valet jumping at the chance to – for once – park Evan's truck. Evan put a traffic-cop 'stop' hand up at the valet, who sank dejectedly back into his chair, and then looked through the passenger window. It couldn't roll down. The Kevlar armor that Evan had hung inside the door panels prevented the glass from retracting. That was one of a variety of hidden security measures with which he'd outfitted the F-150. At a glance it looked like a regular pickup.

Just as Evan looked like a regular guy.

Peter leapt up from the bench at the sight of him. 'Evan Smoak!'

Evan opened his door and stepped up onto the runner so he was looking at Mia and Peter over the roof of the truck.

Mia was eating mint chip and doing an elegant job of it. Her wavy chestnut hair had been cut shorter, which accented her cheekbones and her wide-set eyes.

Not that he paid attention to things like that.

'I'll park and come back around?' he said, realizing too late that he'd pulled the sentence up at the end like a question.

'Sure,' Mia said. 'But don't expect me to share my ice cream.'

Evan slid back into his seat. He tipped the valet a twenty, because it wasn't the kid's fault that Evan wouldn't let him touch the war machine, and then he zipped down into the subterranean parking lot.

He came up the stairs, through the lobby, and out to the front of the building. Peter ran at him. 'Catch me!'

The kid, sticky fingers and all, was airborne.

Evan barely had time to get his arms up before Peter koala-clamped onto him. Evan patted his back twice awkwardly and set him down. It took Evan a great effort not to scrutinize the chocolate finger marks left on his shirt.

'Where were you?' Peter asked in his raspy voice.

At the White House, plotting to execute the president.

'A boring work thing,' Evan said.

Mia paused from attending to her cone, her lips slightly pursed. Her gaze, which she'd cultivated as a Grade III district attorney, conveyed equal measures of incisiveness and skepticism. 'No luggage, huh?'

He couldn't tell if there was a suspicious edge in her voice or if he was reading into it.

Mia did not know what precisely Evan did professionally, but she knew that he was not an importer of industrial cleaning supplies as he claimed to be. Over the years she'd gleaned that his actual work fell outside the purview of what she or her office would find acceptable.

Or legal.

Evan mustered a smile, though he felt it sitting flatly on his face. 'I travel light.'

'As one does. For boring work things.'

Peter was tugging at Evan's chocolate-stained shirt. 'Guess what happened to Ryan?'

'What happened to him?' Evan asked.

'No, not *Boy* Ryan. *Girl* Ryan.'

'What happened to Girl Ryan?'

'In Ms Bracegirdle's class –'

'Wait,' Evan said. 'Stop right there. You do *not* have a teacher named Ms Bracegirdle.'

'I swear to God I'm not lying,' Peter said.

'It's true,' Mia said, rising from the bench at last, leaving her satchel briefcase behind. 'It seems Roscomare Elementary went with a Dickensian motif this hiring season. I'm thinking if Peter fails out, he can become a chimney sweep.'

'So Girl Ryan?' Peter continued, undeterred by the sidebar. 'Girl Ryan's dad went on a trip, and, like, he always brings home presents, because, you know, that's what dads do.'

Peter's own father had died six years ago, and though the boy's delivery was just-the-facts-ma'am impassive, Evan thought he might have detected a note of longing in his voice. Out of the corner of his eye, Evan saw a shift in Mia's face, emotion flickering to the surface.

Peter steamrolled ahead. 'And her dad got her ...' He paused for dramatic effect, hands fanned like a magician before the prestige, charcoal eyes wide, his blond hair lank save for the perennial cowlick in the back that hinted at improper combing. 'A Eiffel Tower kit. You build it with wood microbeams –'

'Microbeams,' Evan said.

'I know, right? And you cut 'em yourself and glue 'em, and then when you're done, the whole thing lights up, and she brought it into class. But during nutrition break, Jesse M. played with it and it *caught fire.*'

'So what'd Ms Peerybingle do?'

'*Bracegirdle,*' Peter said. 'She got really mad and turned all red. Which looks even funnier since she has orange hair that sticks out and sorta a mustache. She looks like the Lorax.'

'Who's the Lorax?'

'You know, the guy who saved the trees and flew away. And so Ms Bracegirdle stomped out the Eiffel Tower, but she wears these hippie skirts, and, you know.'

'First-degree burns,' Mia said. 'Class canceled.'

'So that's why you're eating ice cream?' Evan asked. 'Celebrating the injury of Ms Flintwitch?'

'We are celebrating a half day off school,' Mia said as Peter ran into the lobby to throw out his ice-cream wrapper. '*And.* The successful conclusion of a particularly important case of mine.'

'Which was?'

'Stalking, criminal threats, forcible rape, three counts of injuring a spouse, dissuading a witness – who happens to be the defendant's four-year-old daughter – from reporting a crime. Seven felony counts. It was tough for a rat's nest of reasons I won't bore you with. But. I went seven for seven. That's what happens when I get mad. And then? I eat mint chip ice cream.'

Mia popped the end of the cone into her mouth and came closer. She wore what he'd grown to recognize as her court outfit – shadow-striped slacks and jacket with a sleek silhouette, fitted blouse, no jewelry. Freckles were scattered across her nose in an undisciplined fashion, which he found unbearably charming. Her wavy hair was unbound and by all conventional standards should have been considered a mess but instead looked amazing.

'This was one of the ones that keeps you up nights,' she said. 'I mean, the domestic-abuse photos alone.' She paused. 'I interviewed the four-year-old. Dirty clothes, tangled hair, and she had this untreated rash covering one whole side of her torso. When the social worker asked her what her name was . . .' She shook her head, her eyes misting. 'This beautiful little girl said it was "Idiot."' She looked away, squinted the incipient tears into submission, took in an uneven breath. 'Worst thing I ever saw.'

Evan gave her a moment. Then he said, 'I'm glad it was you who caught the case. And that you're good at what you do.'

'You don't understand,' she said. 'There's always the next one. And the next one. Guys like that piece of shit, they think they're above the law. You know what I mean?' She caught herself, smirked darkly. *'Don't* answer that.'

She held out her arms, and he hugged her, and she leaned into him. He could feel her stomach against his, and it was the best thing he'd felt in a month and change.

There had been a time when their chemistry had quickened to the point that it seemed they might be on the verge of an actual relationship, whatever that was, but the conflict between her profession and what she knew of his made it impossible. There were whole swaths of his life about which she could make no inquiries, and if she had, he could offer no answers. If she learned anything about it, she'd be obligated to prosecute him. And she also thought correctly that if they were together, the dark underworld in which Evan operated – even the tiny bit she knew of it – could pose a threat to Peter. On that front Evan also agreed.

So they were stuck in the same residential tower, nine floors apart, making a continuous effort to fight off an attraction.

He could feel her breath on the side of his neck as he took in the delightful smell of her. He noted a different fragrance – not lemongrass but lavender.

'You changed your lotion,' he said.

She pulled back and looked at him.

Embarrassment swept through him, a hot tide.

To cover, he gave an uncharacteristic one-shoulder shrug. 'I notice everything.'

She kept a straight face, but amusement filled her eyes. 'Oh, do you? Like what?'

Like the birthmark by your left temple. Like that you chew your left cheek when you're concentrating. Like that your eye color changes depending on the color of your shirt.

He stepped back from her.

'Like the seven security cameras on this side of the building,' he said. 'Like your briefcase is unsnapped, showing the file tab inside, Oscar Esposito, case number PA 338724. Like the make and model of the past dozen cars that have driven past.'

At the last, she raised her eyebrows.

'Reflection off the door,' he said.

She nodded, still amused. 'So lemongrass to lavender might as well be a blinking neon sign. I'm surprised you could focus with your senses being assailed like that.'

The front door opened now, and Peter flew back out. 'Mom, *Mom* – can I use the mail key?'

Evan took advantage of the distraction to slip away before Mia could continue her cross-examination.

16. A Bucket of Warm Spit

The President's Dining Room was a quaint piece of shit. It had once been a bedroom where Theodore Roosevelt's daughter Alice had lived; she'd even had her appendix hacked out beneath this pale yellow ceiling. After first daughter Helen Taft, the Coolidge boys, and a host of other presidential offspring had done whatever the hell kids do in bedrooms, it had been converted into a family room where Truman had lounged humorlessly behind his wire-rims, restrained and self-important. Then Jackie had overhauled the joint as Kennedys did, plastering the walls with antique wallpaper depicting battle scenes from the American Revolution. Johnson and Nixon, man's men and assholes to the marrow, had left it untouched, but a passel of Fords, Carters, Reagans, Bushes, and Clintons had fought it out ever since until the room had lowest-common-denominatored its way into its present state, where bland cream wall coverings and frilly valances prevailed.

Jonathan Bennett had no kids, thank God, and no wife. He didn't give a two-minute fuck about design, leaving such matters in the hands of his underlings.

In the few seconds per twenty-four hours he had alone, he wanted to use the dining room to dine. And that meant eating select meals procured from prescreened suppliers, transported to the White House by the Secret Service itself, unpacked and prepared by chefs and food handlers with security clearances.

The proverbial 'they' said that Bennett was the most

paranoid president since Nixon. Perhaps that was because he had accrued the most enemies since Tricky Dick flashed his preternaturally long fingers in the V salute and banged drunkenly around the Oval Office.

And besides, as the tired aphorism went, they can't call you paranoid if you're right. Given Bennett's decades at the Department of Defense, he knew this better than the politician saps who'd occupied the West Wing before him.

He knew what was out there.

He'd played in those sandboxes.

Hell, he'd put the action figures *into* those sandboxes. He'd used them to play his *own* games.

He smeared foie gras onto crostini now and washed it down with a two-thousand-dollar Domaine de la Romanée-Conti Richebourg Grand Cru.

Orphan X was out there somewhere, living rough, holed up like the international war criminal he'd been designated as since he'd left the Program. That was all well and good. Bennett sat in his fortress at the nucleus of power in the known universe, enjoying the finest pleasures life could offer.

He heard high heels tapping and smelled the Hermès perfume before she stepped into view.

He took another bite, enjoying his last moment of solitude.

'Jonathan,' she said.

He closed his eyes, let the full-bodied burgundy burn a delightful trail down his throat. Then he turned to face his vice president.

Victoria Donahue-Carr was by most accounts a formidable woman, highly capable and – at fifty-four – in the political sweet spot as far as age was concerned. Old enough to be considered an adult with enough experience under her sensible pantsuit belt to lead the free world should the need arise. And young enough to preempt any charges of being too long in the tooth to run once Bennett had served out his second term.

She leaned against the chair opposite his but didn't sit, her jacket bunching beneath her crossed arms. She'd sworn off horizontal stripes after their first term due to midsection spread. Once shapely, she'd turned into an obstinate block of a woman, which Bennett supposed was a fine metaphor for the deterioration of their relationship.

He read her face, her body posture, picking up a host of nonverbal tells that signaled discomfort.

'You're here to discuss the congressional subpoena that's rumored to make an appearance next week,' he told her.

'I am.'

'I have executive immunity. They can't *compel* me to appear at an investigative hearing.'

'Let's think this through, Jonathan. Yes, you can claim executive privilege. But the investigation is centered on activities that predate your time in office. They have nothing to do with the presidency itself. Which means you'll be hard-pressed to claim immunity.'

Donahue-Carr was a former constitutional lawyer and never tired of reminding him about it.

He swirled his wine, checked its legs.

'The constitutional demands of due process of the law are going to outweigh executive privilege here,' she continued. 'This isn't some penny-ante case, Jonathan. It's a multi*billion*-dollar investigation. And leaving questions unanswered – questions about relationships with defense contractors – we can't afford that.'

'Careful, Vicky, you sound like you believe what you're reading on the *Huffington Post*.'

'Wilson, Truman, Ford, TR – all of them testified before Congress,' she said. 'Even fucking Lincoln.'

She was growing exasperated. Exasperated was good. It made people ineffective and careless. He noted that she was gripping the back of the chair. Still, he did not invite her to sit.

'Voluntarily,' he said calmly. 'They appeared voluntarily.' He took another sip. 'I can ignore a subpoena.'

'Can,' she said. 'But shouldn't. There's talk of impeachment.'

'Impeachment.' He allowed himself a rare chuckle. 'It didn't matter for Andrew Johnson. Didn't matter for Clinton. And it won't matter for me. Impeachment of the president of the United States has a perfect record: oh for two.'

'The sample size is hardly reassuring.'

He set down his fork and his knife, streaked with organ meat. 'When I first took office, they were serving on the Reagans' china pattern. Bold red border rimmed with a gold band. I found it too . . . obvious. So I went with the Wilson service here.' He picked up his plate and tilted it so the food slid off and plopped onto the tablecloth. He displayed the smudged face of the china. 'The first one to be manufactured in the United States.'

Donahue-Carr took in the sight.

'You know what both plates have in common?' he asked.

'The Presidential Seal,' she said.

'That's right,' he said. 'In case I forget who I am.' He set down the plate, thumbed the outer band of matte gold encrusted with stars and stripes. 'The thing is? I don't forget. Not for a single moment since I put my hand on that Bible. Ask a dozen people what the president's job is and you'll get a dozen answers. But above all else, the job of the president is to demonstrate order. To maintain security. To project power. That keeps citizens from the realm of chaos. It keeps them from having to *contemplate* the realm of chaos. It keeps them happy and industrious, minding the laws of the land and paying their taxes and letting the grown-ups do what needs to be done. Having the president hauled before Congress undermines those American necessities.'

'I'm not sure you're aware of just how bad public sentiment is, Jonathan. You're balanced on a seesaw right now. One step the wrong way and the whole thing tilts. There's only so much we can sustain.'

'We?' He looked up at her. 'Because I'm feeling like *I'm* the one doing all the sustaining these days, Vicky. So when you say there's only so much *we* can sustain, do you mean our ticket? Or our party?'

'I mean the *country*.'

As soon as the words escaped, he saw the regret writ large on her face. The wrinkles around her eyes had rearranged themselves, her lips taut and bloodless.

So there it was. He'd pushed her buttons and forced an outburst, and the truth was laid bare. She'd shown that her loyalty, already worn down from the attrition of the past years, had grown dangerously thin.

Helpful data.

He couldn't stretch the fabric of his influence so tightly that it gave way. And judging from the expression on his vice president's face, it was reaching that point. If she turned on him, the whole house of cards would collapse.

'I'll take your counsel under advisement, Vicky,' he said.

'Thank you, Mr President.'

She started out.

'John Nance Garner said the vice presidency isn't worth a bucket of warm spit,' Bennett said. 'It's likely apocryphal, but hell, you catch the drift. I don't think that's a fair character-ization of the office. Do you?'

Donahue-Carr cleared her throat. 'No, I don't.'

'After all,' Bennett said, 'you've done your job for me. You delivered Pennsylvania twice. And we squeezed just enough mileage out of that one-eighth of you that's Venezuelan to get over the hump with the Hispanics. Didn't we?'

The rims of her nostrils reddened, but she held her com-posure admirably. 'We did.'

'The unions have your respect. That proved helpful. And your track record gave me cover against concerns that I was in bed with Wall Street. You're pretty but not threatening. That helped bring men to the polls while not putting women off. I owe you for that as well.'

When he slid his chair out, it made a scuffing sound on the square-patterned rug. He stood, set his napkin beside his plate. 'What do all those benefits you offer have in common?'

Her breathing had quickened, the rise of her chest visible. 'I don't know.'

'They're all in the past. I've won both of my elections already. You'd do well to remain useful to me in the future.'

Her nod was more like a tremor. 'I understand, Mr President.'

She exited, her footfall quicker than before.

17. Stray Dogs

Evan dined a few blocks from Castle Heights at a restaurant specializing in 'New American' cuisine, a designation he found simultaneously meaningless and redundant. Sitting at the patio's edge, he ordered a whole branzino roasted in a parchment wrap with a side of steamed kale. Though the bar offerings were extensive, none of the vodkas rose to his palate, so he opted for Pellegrino, which he drank garnished with a wedge of lime.

It was a consummate Angeleno night – warm edging into cool, neither too dry nor too humid, a soothing breeze. Looking into his glass, he pictured Jonathan Bennett's face swirling behind the bubbles and wondered what the president was doing at this very moment across the breadth of the continent. Readying battle plans of his own? Gathering intel on the other wayward Orphans so they could be put down like stray dogs?

Sipping from his glass, Evan registered the sting of betrayal as something physical, a knife between the ribs. He was reviled by the country he'd served, unwanted and deemed not worthy of living, hunted on the authority of orders issued at the highest level.

They had made him who he was and then found their creation to be unacceptable.

His pleasures now were simple. Using his skills to help those not merely in need but also worthy. And sipping sparkling water alfresco on a glorious California night.

He engaged in a quiet sitting meditation, timing his inhalation, doubling the count for his exhalation. And again.

The Fourth Commandment: *Never make it personal.*

This would be a mission like any other.

Except infinitely harder.

He checked the RoamZone, confirming that the display showed no missed calls, which brought a wave of relief.

He settled back in his chair, scanning the restaurant. Eating by himself gave him the freedom to study everything around him even more closely. One of the regulars, an older woman, sat alone in her usual booth. Stiff tweed suit, face done up, cell phone on the table. She drank a single glass of white wine with dinner every time. She always overtipped. The phone never rang.

She broke his heart ten different ways.

He glanced away so as not to be caught staring and noticed a homeless man stumble up the sidewalk with the aid of a crutch. Just beyond the patio, the man sat, slumped against a parking meter. He was missing a leg below the knee. His battered cardboard sign read HOMELESS VETEREN WITH PTSD IM NOT ASHAMED ANYMORE BUT NEED HELP.

His head was lowered, his good leg kicked wide, the cardboard sign propped against his belly. His clothes were filthy, his face covered with grime.

The Veterans Affairs Medical Center abutted these streets, and affluent Westwood received plenty of spillover from the facility.

The man rustled the sign in his lap. Passersby lived up to their designation, neither slowing nor looking up from their phones. When the veteran scratched his cheek, his finger carved a white streak through the grime.

The waiter circled by and topped off Evan's sparkling

water. He followed Evan's gaze. 'Would you like me to have him removed, sir?'

Evan said, 'No.'

The server gave one of those ridiculous half bows inherent to waiters and barons and started to withdraw. Evan grasped his forearm. 'I'd like another branzino, please.'

The waiter's pupils jiggled a touch nervously. 'Very well, sir.'

Fifteen minutes later the dishes arrived. The waiter hesitated.

Evan gestured at the place setting across from him. 'The extra one goes there.'

The waiter stiffened, his posture verging on displeased. He dispensed the dishes as directed and retreated inside.

Evan stared across the sidewalk at the veteran, and, feeling the heat of his gaze, the man looked up. He rumbled to his feet, picked at his beard, his eyes on the steaming meal sitting before the empty chair.

'What's that?' he said.

Evan said, 'Yours.'

The man stood a moment longer, the cardboard sign crumpled between his loose fists. Then he hobbled onto the patio and sat opposite Evan.

He ate hungrily but not impolitely. The other diners either took no notice or competently pretended not to. Evan and the man dined in perfect silence, focused on their meals.

Sometime later they finished.

Evan held up his credit card, one of many in one of his many different names, and the waiter materialized to retrieve it.

As Evan signed the check, the man gulped down his water and wiped his mouth on the napkin. 'Good fish,' he said.

Evan looked across the table until at last the man looked up.

'Thank you for your service,' Evan said.

The vet nodded. With some effort he rose, leaning heavily on his crutch.

As Evan headed out, the man resumed his position against the parking meter, holding up his unread sign as patrons streamed past.

18. Coldly Modern

Evan's penthouse condo, a seven-thousand-square-foot sprawl, was open design and coldly modern – slab counters, streamlined appliances and fixtures, workout pods sprouting like mushrooms from the poured-concrete floors. It was also a fortress protected by rigorous alarms and surveillance systems, bullet-resistant polycarbonate thermoplastic resin windows, and armored sunshades. A freestanding fireplace dotted the center of the great room, and a spiral staircase rose to a reading room that he rarely made use of.

A black suede couch and an area rug, miniaturized by the vast space, fulfilled the homey quotient.

Still disgruntled by the restaurant's standard booze offerings, Evan breezed into the kitchen and tugged open the freezer drawer of the Sub-Zero. Lined neatly inside was a selection of exceptional vodkas. He plucked out his bottle of choice for the evening.

Fog Point was made with water harvested from San Francisco fog. To capture the Bay Area mist, mesh fog catchers designed to emulate water-capturing plants were positioned high on the hilltops around Outer Sunset and Sutro Tower. A full day's harvest amounted to a mere few cups of the precious liquid.

Evan filled a cocktail shaker with purified ice, poured in a jigger, and shook it until his hands adhered to the metal. From the freezer's middle shelf, he removed a stainless-steel martini glass, frosted from the chill, and poured in the mist's newest iteration.

He sipped.

Hint of citrus. Maybe honeysuckle.

Lovely.

He circled the kitchen island to the so-called living wall, a vertical rise of germinating herbs and vegetables, and snapped off a sprig of basil, which he let float among the ice crystals.

Then he washed and dried the shaker and jigger and put them away. A few drops of water remained on the counter, so he wiped them and then wiped the rest of the counter for good measure, and then he wiped it again to get rid of the wipe marks.

He told himself, '*Stop.*'

Padding across the great room, drink in hand, he passed between racks of kettlebells, his shoulder brushing a heavy bag.

A single hall led to the master bedroom, where his Maglev bed literally floated above the floor, repelled from it by unreasonably powerful neodymium rare-earth magnets. A cable anchored to each corner moored the bed to keep it from flying up and smashing against the ceiling.

In the en suite bathroom, a nudge of his knuckle sent the wide glass shower door rolling aside on its barn-door track, and then he stepped inside and gripped the hot-water lever.

An embedded digital sensor read the print of his curled palm and allowed him to twist the lever through the point of resistance. A hidden door, disguised seamlessly in the wall tiles of the shower, swung inward, and he entered the concealed four hundred square feet he mentally referred to as the Vault.

Part command center, part armory, the Vault was where Evan did the majority of his operational planning. The underbelly of the public stairs to the roof crowded the space in the rear, where weapon lockers stood aligned. In the center of the room, an L-shaped sheet-metal desk supported a proliferation of computer hardware.

Right now there were no monitors in sight.

With a finger, he clicked the mouse and three of the four walls – a horseshoe wrapping the desk – shimmered to life. Over the past few weeks, he'd tiled those walls with OLED screens, made of glass embedded with mesh so fine it was undetectable to the bare eye. When not engaged, the screens shut off, transforming into invisible panes.

With everything up and running now, the Vault came alive with color and movement. One screen rotated through pirated feeds of Castle Heights' surveillance cameras, showing angles of hallways, the lobby, and surrounding streets.

The other mounted screens hosted a profusion of evidence pertaining to Evan's 1997 mission. Operational details, archived newspapers from the era and region, maps detailing every location he'd visited as a nineteen-year-old formulating his first hit. There were compiled records on the targeted foreign minister, his wife, the generals who had occupied the vehicle with him that day. The round man who'd supplied the steel shell casing with the fingerprint, the Estonian arms dealer, the heroin addict tucked in the shabby office of the abandoned textile factory who had overdosed in early 1998 – each had a painstakingly assembled dossier as well.

Evan had resurrected every last thread of evidence as he conducted his own postmortem, but nothing he turned up showed the assassination to be anything but a standard kill.

Not one piece of intelligence had produced a worthwhile lead.

A flowchart of Jonathan Bennett's career through 1997 dominated the right wall – every known post, every documented trip and meeting, every on-the-record colleague and contact.

All dead ends.

Evan still had no idea why his first mission was so important to Bennett and why it was so threatening that Evan had to be neutralized for the role he'd played in it.

What – all these years later – was he still not seeing?

If the right wall was an attempt to diagnose the past, the left wall diagrammed the future. It was a living tableau, aggregating data that would aid in the assassination of the president.

Evan immediately noticed a number of changes on the left wall since his latest excursion to DC.

The White House's Web site had taken the president's public schedule offline. *No information available at this time.*

Evan looked down at the pinecone-shaped aloe vera plant nestled in a glass bowl filled with cobalt glass pebbles. 'Okay, lady,' he told her. 'It's all up to you and me now.'

Aside from the living wall, Vera II was the only other living organism of note in the penthouse. He watered her by slipping an ice cube between her serrated spikes once a week, which was all the caretaking she required and all the caretaking he was capable of.

He returned his focus to the screens. Mentions of the president's movements from other credible Web sites showed his agenda in sudden motion, fund-raising events sliding around, speeches put on hold, ceremonial events delayed until further notice. Bennett wasn't holing up, but the Secret Service was smart enough to obscure his comings and goings so as to give little advance notice of his itinerary to Orphan X.

The president had no unavoidable, predetermined

appearances scheduled in the upcoming months, such as an address to the UN or a G8 summit. The State of the Union, another palatable opportunity, wasn't until January.

A media feed showed the usual screaming headlines – an arms deal with Syrian rebels gone to shit, Bennett resisting pressure to testify before Congress, gerrymandering resolutions sneaking their way onto ballots before the midterms.

Evan sank into his chair and took another sip of the Fog Point. Definitely a trace of honeysuckle.

He refocused on the task before him.

The Stingray he'd used to such fine effect last night now rested on the sheet-metal desk, downloading data and encryption keys into an out-of-the-package Boeing Black smartphone he planned to use as a mirror for the one belonging to Special Agent in Charge Naomi Templeton.

He'd already transferred the data onto his hard drive and spread it around the OLED screens facing the desk. A GPS dot showed a nice, strong signal from her apartment.

He remotely activated the microphone on her smartphone, picking up the noise in the room.

A doorbell.

A barking dog.

And then Naomi's voice. 'Hush, Fenway. Hush.'

There was some rustling, perhaps as she moved away. Then her words came again, less clearly. 'Hey, thanks for stopping by. I wanted to see, you know . . . any chemistry.' Sounds of movement, and then she said, 'He likes you.'

The next exchange was obscured. When Evan could again hear Naomi's voice, she was saying, '– so it's forty bucks to walk him, fifty-five to drive him over to visit my dad during the day, and a hundred for a hike and a grooming, yeah?'

A low-pitched man's voice murmured something Evan

couldn't make out. He switched his focus to Naomi's calendar, notes, and e-mails, also up on display. An algorithmic software program scrolled through her information, grabbing data indicative of future movements.

Lots of meetings at headquarters, interagency consultations, countless visits to her father's facility. No social plans. No documentation of specific movements with or regarding the president.

Any information concerning Bennett was wisely kept off a phone that could be misplaced or stolen.

'Okay,' Naomi's voice cut in again. 'So he needs a walk every day? I don't know all this stuff yet. He's my dad's dog, and I'm . . . I'm sorta still catching up to all this.' More masculine mumbling, and then Naomi said, sharply, 'No, I don't want to *get rid of* the dog. My dad likes seeing him. Christ, Fenway's the *only* thing that makes him happy.'

On the screens Evan brought forward another window. Before he'd left for dinner, he'd deployed Hashkiller's 131-billion-password dictionary on every last piece of encryption on Naomi's phone, hoping to grind through a portal and bust onto the Secret Service's private secure network.

On the activated microphone, he heard a door close, and then Naomi said, 'Maybe I *should* give you away, you mongrel.' A scrabbling of paws answered her. 'How am I supposed to take care of you in the middle of all this?' More footsteps, more scrabbling paws. 'Dad would know exactly how to help me, but he's not really Dad anymore, you know?'

Evan heard the puff of a deflating cushion – Naomi had plopped onto a couch? – and then another, louder plop as the dog presumably landed beside her.

Naomi sighed. 'Looks like it's up to you and me, Fenway.'

Evan glanced at Vera II and pictured Naomi a dozen

states away conferring with her own loyal adviser, plotting to catch Evan just as he was plotting to evade her.

On the mounted screen, Hashkiller continued to make superb progress on Naomi's applications and log-ins, but Evan watched with rising pessimism as gateway after gateway led nowhere he wanted to be. Despite all his machinations, he'd hit a hard roadblock and had to figure out how to get around it to the useful data, the data hiding safely on the Secret Service's secured network. Those databases would hold a treasure trove of information on everything from Bennett's contingency motorcade routes to which company supplied chemicals to the White House dry cleaner.

Unfortunately, the network – and all the computers on it – looked to be air-gapped, unhooked from the Internet and any external devices.

Evan's middling hacker skills couldn't get him in.

He knew only one person good enough for the job.

Perhaps it was time to pay her a visit.

He'd just started researching tickets to Milan Malpensa Airport when his line rang. Not the RoamZone. His home line.

He'd forgotten what it sounded like.

He jogged out of the Vault and all the way to the kitchen, picking up on the fifth ring.

It was Mia.

She was screaming.

19. Bad Men

Trevon didn't know how long he'd been walking. The whole day was like Swiss cheese with big holes in it.

He remembered Muscley One and Raw One throwing him out of the truck.

He remembered his shoulder hitting the ground hard and the sound of the truck driving away.

He remembered when he clawed the garbage bag off his head it was that bluish light of early morning and he was in an alley behind a dumpster and his eyeglasses were bent at the arm really bad.

He remembered stumbling out of the alley holding his shoulder and thinking, *Ow, ow.*

He remembered there wasn't a street but a big empty parking lot that glittered with broken glass, and the only person in sight was a hobo with a long scraggly beard who smiled a toothless smile at him and said, 'Right on, man. I been there.'

He remembered thinking to find a street sign, because he knew every street in all of Los Angeles and could list them in order and that made him special.

He remembered finding a street sign, and now the arm part had snapped off his eyeglasses at the hinge and so he had to hold them in place so they didn't get tilty when he read the sign.

He remembered realizing that he was near downtown and that if he walked long enough, he could find a bus stop.

He remembered finding a bus stop and waiting forever

and finally getting on a bus and making a connection and then another to get home.

He remembered trying to keep the Scaredy Bugs down, but then on the third bus they filled him up, starting with his feet and then his legs and then his stomach and then – *Oh God, oh God.*

And now he was walking again because the bus driver had throwed him off the bus, but it was so far to walk still since he had to cross South Central Avenue and Griffith Avenue and Stanford Avenue and South San Pedro Street and Trinity Street and –

All of a sudden it was dark and cold and he was sitting beneath a freeway underpass and some guys were huddled around a fire in a trash can warming their hands and he wanted to warm his hands so bad, too, but they looked like Bad Influences and Mama told him to steer clear of Bad Influences, because who you surround yourself with makes up part of who you are, and so he kept walking even though his feet were so sore.

Mama.

He had the little towel he'd used to wipe off his pukey mouth still crammed in his pocket, and he thought he should probably throw it out, but it was like Blankie when he was a kid and it was all he had in the world now and what if he puked and needed it again?

A guy was selling flowers by the on-ramp and Trevon walked by and the guy said, 'Fuck you, *ése*. I got this corner,' and Trevon said, 'Excuse me, sir. I'm sorry,' and had to take the long way to get across the 110, holding his shoulder even though it didn't help stop the pain any.

He could see the moon overhead like a eye staring down at him, and he felt as alone as anyone had ever been in the world, because they were all dead, Uncle Joe-Joe and Gran'mama and Leo and everyone except Kiara, 'cuz she was gone in Guatemala helping folks and out of touch and he had no one to call in the whole entire universe.

He stopped at the side of the road, and cars were whizzing by, and he stared up at the Moon Eye and the Moon Eye stared back at him and the Scaredy Bugs went crazy in his chest and he thought his heart was gonna stop and he couldn't breathe and he knew he was gonna die and he thought maybe that was okay 'cuz it would be better than living now.

The sidewalk zoomed up and hit his cheek, and then he curled up on his side and drew his knees up to his chest with no one but Moon Eye even noticing him and the Scaredy Bugs danced in front of his eyes and he was trying to find air to breathe, and then he heard a screech of brake pads and footsteps coming up, and then a hand rested on his shoulder and a voice said, '*Hola*. Hello? Hello, my friend? My friend, are you okay?'

And Trevon said, 'Uh-uh.'

'Did someone hurt you?'

'I don't know.'

'Do you need to go to the hospital?'

Trevon could hear the cars whizzing by still and felt the cold of the nighttime pavement against his cheek, and he fought the Scaredy Bugs as hard as he could, because we don't cry and we don't feel sorry for ourself, and the man kept his hand on his shoulder, and that helped because it was another person touching him but not in a Stranger Danger way, and right now that meant he wasn't so alone.

Trevon sat up.

'That's right, *amigo*. Just take a deep breath. And then another.'

'Yes, sir.'

Now he could see the man's face, crinkled and kind, and the dark hair with some white mixed in like Uncle Joe-Joe's.

Trevon said, 'What's your name? 'Cuz I'm not allowed to talk to strangers, but if I know your name then you're not a stranger.'

The man made a smile, but it wasn't a happy smile, just the shape of one. 'Benito Orellana.' The smile shape faded. 'What happened to you?'

'I can't tell you.'

Joven, what happened to you?'

'Leave me alone.'

Joven –'

'Go away!'

Mr Orellana drew back, and then Trevon felt guilty 'cuz it wasn't respectful to raise your voice at nobody, and so he said, 'I'm sorry.'

Mr Orellana said, 'That's okay.'

Trevon cleared his throat. 'They said I can't tell *anyone.*'

Mr Orellana sat down on the pavement next to Trevon. He stayed like that for a full minute and then another. His car was double-parked at the curb, and another car honked as it passed, all rude-like.

At a hundred and thirty-seven seconds, Mr Orellana said, 'You know my name, so that means we're not strangers, right?'

'Right.'

'We're sort of friends, even.'

Trevon gave a reluctant nod. His shoulder hurt and his cheek hurt and his heart hurt.

'I was in big trouble once,' Mr Orellana said. 'With my son. And I needed a friend. A friend I could trust.'

'They said I can't talk to anyone.'

'Who did?'

'Bad Men.' Trevon bit his lip 'cuz it was wobbling and he wasn't gonna cry or feel sorry for himself 'cuz that would be disrespecting Mama's memory.

Mama.

Trevon said, 'They hurt my family, and I can't tell anyone or they'll make it my fault.'

Mr Orellana made a noise in his chest like the Bad Men had done it to him instead of to Trevon.

'See?' Trevon said. 'You can't help me. No one can help me. Ever again.'

Mr Orellana got up and dusted off his pants. He crouched over Trevon and rested both hands on his shuddering shoulders.

He said, 'Can you remember a phone number?'

20. Yes, Please

Evan flew down nine flights of stairs and spilled onto the twelfth-floor hall. At the end, the door to Mia's condo stood open. He ran up the corridor and into 12B.

Mia stood facing the couch, shifting her weight from foot to foot as if she wanted to break into a sprint. Peter was whimpering. Evan couldn't see him over the back of the couch except for the swirl of blond hair sticking up above the cushions.

Heeling the door closed, Evan went to Mia's side. 'How'd it happen?'

She said, 'He dove off the counter playing Batman and hit the coffee table.'

Peter looked tiny on the couch. He was wearing only tighty-whities and a torn bedsheet knotted around his throat. The low-rent cape had been swept aside to reveal the dislocated shoulder. His right arm hung lower, pulled down out of the socket. In place of the deltoid was a divot deep enough to be shadowed. Peter glanced down at the scoop of hollowed skin, crunched up his features, and turned away again. His face looked hot, humid with smeared tears.

Evan said, 'Batman doesn't fly.'

Peter stopped sniffling. 'He can glide,' he whimpered.

'Gliding's trickier than it looks,' Evan said.

'Evidently,' Mia said. 'Now I need to move him to the car, but he won't get up and I can't carry him —'

Peter broke in. 'It hurts too much to move.'

'– and I've gotta get him to the hospital.'

'No hospital!'

'Okay.' Evan held up his hands. 'He doesn't have to go to the hospital. I'll do it.'

'You know how to fix a dislocated shoulder?' Mia asked. 'Wait – of course you do. Why would I even . . .' She shook her head in exasperation. 'Okay. How do you do it?'

'There are about two dozen ways,' Evan said. 'I prefer the one that's the least painful. How 'bout you, Bruce Wayne?'

Peter nodded.

'Okay, I'm gonna sit down next to you on the couch. But I'm not gonna touch you at all yet. Okay?'

Another nod.

Evan eased onto the cushion on Peter's right side. 'What would you say the pain's at on a scale of one to ten?'

Peter blinked through his tears. 'What's one? Like a paper cut?'

'Yes.'

'And what's ten? Like someone rips your face off and then sets it on fire?'

'Sure,' Evan said. 'But maybe they set it on fire first, because once your face is ripped off, you don't really care if it's lit on fire after that.'

Peter considered. 'I meant they light where your face *used to be* on fire. Like the underface.'

Since her own face was buried in her hands, Mia's voice came out muffled. 'Boys? Maybe we can get to it?'

'Like a six,' Peter said.

'Okay,' Evan said. 'Here's what's gonna happen. I'm gonna rub your back right here, okay? This won't hurt much. I'm just loosening up the muscles, because they're spasming and pulling your shoulder in the wrong direction. Then I'm gonna rotate your arm. When I do that, the pain's gonna go to an eleven for a second and then immediately drop to a two. Are you up for that?'

Peter said, 'No way.'

Evan kept massaging the knotted muscle at the back of Peter's shoulder. It was releasing ever so slightly. 'Why don't you tell me a story?'

'To distract me?'

'No,' Evan said. 'To distract *me*.'

'Okay. You know Girl Ryan?'

Evan took the boy's thin arm very gently. 'In Ms Croft-muffin's class?'

'*Bracegirdle*,' Peter said. 'Well, *last* month her dad went to Oswald.'

'Oswald?' Evan held Peter's forearm parallel to the floor, palm up, elbow in.

'You know,' Peter said. 'In Sweden.'

'Or Oslo,' Mia said. 'In Norway.'

'Whatever,' Peter said.

Evan stopped rubbing Peter's back and firmed his palm against the scapula.

'And you know how he always gets her cool travel gifts?' Peter said. 'So guess what he brought her back from Oswald?'

Evan tightened his grasp on Peter's forearm. 'Sherry-oak-cask-matured aquavit?'

'Moose socks!'

Evan rotated Peter's arm out as if opening it for a hug, keeping the elbow pinned to the boy's ribs. At the same time, he pushed the scapula in to catch the humerus, the bones meeting each other halfway, the shoulder reseating itself with a pleasing click.

Peter opened his mouth to scream but paused before any

sound could escape. Mia had covered her eyes, but she peeked between her fingers.

The silence stretched out a beat. Peter closed his mouth, lips tight over his braces.

Then he moved his arm gingerly. 'That feels *sooo* much better.'

Evan said to Mia, 'Will you please grab me a pillowcase?'

She nodded and headed up the hall.

Evan looked across at Peter. 'Were the socks actually *made* out of meese?'

Peter grinned. 'Mooses. And no. They had cartoons on them.'

Mia reappeared and flipped Evan the pillowcase. '*Moose*. Moose is the plural of moose. Like fish.'

'Except if you're talking about *species* of fish,' Peter said.

Mia said, 'Is that what Ms Dinglepants taught you?'

Peter sighed. 'You *guys*.'

'You should get it looked at by a doc,' Evan said, 'but it can wait till the morning.' He triangled the pillowcase and tied it in a loose sling. 'He can use this till then.'

'Okay. Thank God, Evan. Hang on . . . just . . . lemme get him to bed. Wait a sec for me?'

Evan said, 'Okay.'

With his good hand, Peter fist-bumped Evan, then blew it up, then squidded his fingers away, then turned them into a firework, and then Mia said, '*Peter*,' and he scampered ahead of her into his bedroom.

Evan waited on the couch, taking in the soft colors of the well-loved space. A broken Little League trophy on the mantel next to a picture of Peter in a wooden frame built of Popsicle sticks. A shoe box on the floor transformed into a robot head. A Post-it on the wall by the thermostat with a line from that Jordan Peterson book Mia was always quoting to Peter: '*Compare yourself to who you were yesterday, not to who someone else is today.*'

This childhood, this upbringing, this life so different from anything Evan had ever known.

And – in countless tiny, commonplace ways – so much better.

Mia reemerged, easing Peter's door closed. 'Sorry. Getting out of there at night is like backing out of a lion cage.' She ran a hand through her already mussed-up hair. 'That was amazing. Thank you.'

'No problem.' Evan stood. 'I have to go now.'

'Right now? Why?'

Still trying to kill the president.

Evan said, 'Work.'

'Okay. Sure you don't want, like, a Smirnoff Ice Pineapple or something?' She held a straight face for a few seconds but finally laughed at his expression. 'I'm kidding.'

'You're a very bad person.'

'Yes, I am.' She came over and hugged him. 'Thank you so much. Seriously. I'm good with cuts and blood and whatever, but dislocations gross me out.'

Her arms stayed wrapped tight around his lower back. He was holding her, pretending not to breathe the scent of her hair. Her cheek was pressed against his chest, her head snugged beneath his chin. He waited for her to let go, but she didn't, and he suddenly felt less in a rush than he was before.

'Ever notice how when they talk about dreams in movies they always make perfect sense?' she said, keeping her face against his chest. 'No one ever says, "I was ten years old at my childhood house, but it wasn't my childhood house, it was a school, and my whole fifth-grade class was there, but they weren't my classmates, they were all the criminals I've put away and they were gonna get me, but then I was an adult all of a sudden, and you came in and you were you but you were also my dear departed husband, and you took me by the hand and we walked outside, but outside was inside and we were in a bedroom, and then you kissed me and said everything was safe."'

Through his shirt Evan could feel the heat of her cheek.

He said, 'Did you have that dream?'

She pulled back and looked at him and then looked away, her mouth crooked with sheepish amusement. 'No,' she said.

He laughed.

But then they were serious again, her eyes so large beneath those long, dark lashes, and he kissed her. She tasted faintly like cinnamon toothpaste, and the smell of her, lemongrass mixed with lavender, came off her skin, and they were still kissing, but she was guiding them down the hall, an awkward walk-stumble that kept them together.

In her bedroom they finally broke apart, forehead to forehead, their breath intermingling, and then she lifted his shirt up and off.

'Wait a sec,' she said. 'Are these muscles real? Or spray-painted on?' She poked at his abs. 'I mean, *seriously*? If you think I'm gonna get naked after this –'

But then they were tangled in each other again, moving to the bed, and he was holding her face in his hands, her mouth so soft.

She leaned away, lips parted, breathing hard. 'Okay,' she said, 'fuck it,' and pulled off her shirt.

The soft mattress felt like an embrace. Throw pillows tumbled. She rolled him on top of her, unbuckling his belt. She kicked out of her jeans and shoved his the rest of the way off with her toes.

The smoothness of her bare belly against his. Her nails digging into his arms. Her teeth pressing into his shoulder.

Not aggressive.

But hungry.

Afterward he lay sunk in a swirl of duvet, spent, as she lay beside him, one leg slung over his hip, their skin meeting in a warm seal.

There was only the sound of their breathing, ragged at first and then slower, slower, yielding to a peaceful silence. She shifted off him, away, and bedded down on her stomach with one knee hitched up so her body formed a lowercase *h*.

She wasn't quite snoring, but she made a distinctive snuffle with each inhale that he found unreasonably charming.

He closed his eyes, enjoying the unexpected pleasure of this bed, her body beside his, this moment.

He couldn't remember ever wanting to not leave, but here he was getting more and more tired, listening to her sleep sounds, his blinks growing longer.

A faint humming noise jarred him back to alertness.

The RoamZone, set to vibrate.

He slipped from the bed and dug it from the pocket of his tangled jeans. Taking quiet steps, he moved to the bathroom so as not to wake Mia.

Caller ID showed a mobile number with a Los Angeles area code. A GPS dot pinned the location downtown near USC.

Evan answered as he always did. 'Do you need my help?'

A terrified voice said, 'Yes, please, sir. Yes, please.'

21. Heavy Weaponry

Naked in the bathroom, Judd Holt stared at his reflection. Rivulets from the shower streamed down his powerful body. From his calves to his biceps, his muscles were compact and pronounced, coiled springs. The wrinkles at the edges of his eyes had deepened into grooves that touched his temples, where the brown-copper hair turned the color of dust.

It had been a long time since Orphan A had truly looked at himself.

In prison mirrors were hard to come by – and for good reason. An instinct rose up in him – wrap a hand towel around his knuckles, smash the glass, search out a dagger-size shard.

Just to have it.

But there was no need for that. Not here.

He'd selected a hotel near Dupont Circle, closer to the action, and paid more for the room than he thought a mid-dling hotel should cost. Beneath the faucet an indentation in the porcelain held a petite lump of French vanilla soap, encased in fine paper and shaped like a scallop shell.

He unwrapped the lump, flung the wad of paper into the trash, then soaped his hands, forearms, and face, despite the fact that he'd just washed. It had been so long since he'd experienced a luxury scent of any kind, the sugary sweet-ness filling his nostrils like something from a remembered dream.

He toweled off and dressed quickly and then swiped a

wider circle of steam from the mirror. His beard was coming in aggressively, and he thought he'd let it keep coming, a Paul Bunyan show of strength.

The 1,779 days in prison had left his skin dry and chafed. Flakes of dandruff spotted the copper-wire tangle of his beard. With an old-fashioned black comb, he started grooming them out. They came, but the churning of the plastic teeth spawned more white flecks.

Orphan X invaded his thoughts once again. Not the man himself, whoever he was, since Holt had never laid eyes on him. But a shadowed face. A blurred darkness on a surveillance screen grab. The heel of a boot a split second before it vanished into an alley.

Holt scoured his beard harder and harder, the flakes multiplying like the goddamned broomsticks in that Mickey Mouse cartoon. He was thinking about what Orphan X had taken from him, how the fucker had dropped a fork in the road and forced Holt to veer left, wiping out an entire other life that might have been.

Instead Holt had remained what he was probably always meant to be. Orphan A, cleaning up messes for America.

His cheek was bleeding. He didn't notice until a blood drop struck the porcelain sink, ruby red and serrated at the edges like a sunburst.

He set down the comb and took a few deep breaths.

It was four in the morning, and he needed to sleep.

He exited the hotel bathroom. The bed had a bunch of those oddly shaped pillows, cylinders with tassels, ovals with velvet trim. A watercolor of a windsurfer hung above the headboard. On the nightstand a remote control as wide as a Ping-Pong paddle was studded with more buttons than he could count.

Holt stood in the hum of the regulated air from the vent and knew himself to be safe.

And yet everything in his body screamed otherwise.

He dressed quickly and then pulled on his socks, laced up his boots.

Then he lay atop the duvet, arms crossing his chest, a vampire in repose. He closed his eyes.

He imagined he was back in his cell, where his hours and thoughts were contained. This comforted him.

When he dozed off, he dreamed of a woman a lifetime ago. The scent of her on the bedsheets, her lyrical accent, that wavy dark hair. She was tough and beautiful and the only thing he'd ever known that had made life worth living.

He awakened two hours later, having moved not an inch.

On the desk, resting beside pamphlets touting Colonial Williamsburg and the Newseum, Wetzel's file contained the information on the federal prosecutor who had put Holt away.

He stared at the picture with enmity.

He certainly was not a fan. But still – a federal prosecutor.

His mistake last time was going with heavy weaponry. He couldn't risk being spotted with restricted guns, not during the warm-up round before the game went live.

He'd reserve heavy weaponry for when he really needed it, and he'd really need it soon enough. He knew that Wetzel and Bennett had processors sorting countless bits of data, scouring through the virtual universe. When X popped his head up, Holt would be waiting with a carbine, locked and loaded.

He memorized the specifics in the prosecutor's file and then lit it on fire, dropped it into the bathtub, and washed the clumped ashes down the drain.

When he drove away from the hotel, a moon floated brazenly in the slate-blue morning sky.

He parked at a Home Depot and walked inside, breezing past early-morning contractors smelling of beer breath and strong coffee.

He found what he was looking for in Aisle 10.

He laid it on the checkout counter.

The clerk glanced from him to it and back to him again. He'd been told more than once that his presence made sensible people feel uneasy.

She tittered, a burst of nervousness escaping. 'You sure that's all you need?'

He looked at her. Set down a twenty.

She rang him up, tapping the keys with her fingers splayed so as not to snap off her fake nails.

Her eyes jittered over him. She cleared her throat. 'Need a bag, sir?'

He picked up the clawhammer and walked out.

The two-story house rose from behind a wood-alternative picket fence. Michigan Park was located in Northeast DC, but this block, with its freestanding homes and grassy setbacks, could have been anywhere.

Holt stood at the end of the walk, hands stuffed in the pockets of a Carhartt coat. He was hesitating because this wasn't some high-value raghead or dickhead cartel hombre or off-the-rails Orphan, all of whom had it coming in one way or another. This was an attack on law and order itself, the kind of damage you sometimes had to do when you cut through critical structures to reach a deeper cancer.

The house itself looked warm and lived in, the kind of

ordinary place where ordinary folks lived out ordinary lives. Verdant green front lawn, three steps rising to a porch, Crayola-red bricks.

Languid suburban motion pervaded the street. A mom out for a morning jog, yoga pants adhered to her lower half, pushing before her a baby stroller that resembled a space pod. A few garage doors creaking up in unison. A low-end Mercedes easing out into the workday.

Holt unfastened the latch on the thigh-high fence, stepped through, and progressed to the porch. Behind the door he heard morning commotion.

A woman's voice. 'Did you feed Dylan before car pool?'

'Waffles. Frozen but multigrain!'

Holt rang the bell.

'Hang on.' A man threw open the door. Middle-aged, worn T-shirt from an old Stones tour, sandy blond beard, neatly trimmed. 'Hi, can I help –'

The feminine voice shouted from somewhere behind him. 'Honey! Have you seen my briefcase?'

'Sorry.' The man turned away from the door. 'On the chest in the playroom!'

'You're the best.' The woman blew into view, briefcase in hand, holding up earrings. 'These dangly ones okay? I have closing arguments today.'

The man said, 'I'd go with studs. More assured.'

'You're picking up car pool, right?' She turned, noticed Holt standing there mutely. 'Hi, sorry. Hi.'

Holt stared directly at her. 'You don't recognize me?'

She squinted, tilting her head as she slid a diamond stud into an earlobe. 'No. I'm sorry.'

Holt studied her a moment longer. Made a game-day decision.

'Must have the wrong house.' He seated his hands back into his pockets and turned to walk away.

He'd reached the edge of the porch when he heard her voice behind him. 'Wait! Four years ago – no, five. Possession of an illegal firearm, transporting across state lines.'

Holt paused, felt a weight bow his shoulders.

The sigh that left him made him feel every one of his fifty-two years.

Still facing away, he lifted the clawhammer from the deep inside pocket of his jacket.

Then he turned and moved swiftly for the open door.

22. The Small Gestures of Intimacy

Trevon Gaines's South Central apartment was small but so clean it met Evan's own diagnosable standards. Trevon sat on his bed scratching his biceps until his nails raised ashy streaks on the skin. He had on a pair of black-frame eyeglasses, thick lenses, one plastic temple secured at the hinge with a Band-Aid.

The bed was made up so tightly you could've bounced a sniper round on the comforter. Early-hours darkness still claimed the street, the quiet broken by the occasional car drifting past, music bumping from woofers. The building was close enough to USC to be relatively safe and far enough away to be interesting.

Evan stood in the shadow beside the bureau, away from the window, keeping a clear view of the bedroom door. He wore a Woolrich shirt held together with magnetic buttons that gave way readily in the event he made a quick grab for his weapon or someone made a quick grab for him. The shirt hid the Kydex high-guard holster riding his left hip, which held an ARES 1911 custom-forged from a solid block of aluminum, as untraceable as Evan himself. He'd fed the pistol a magazine filled with 230-grain Speer Gold Dot hollow points, a bonus round chambered in case a gunfight went nine deep in a hurry. Streamlined inner pockets of his tactical-discreet cargo pants hid extra mags and a folding Strider knife without showing so much as a bump. His Original S.W.A.T. boots were lighter than running shoes and looked perfectly ordinary with the pant legs pulled down.

The last words he'd spoken were, 'Tell me everything you remember.'

That had been forty-five minutes ago.

The story took longer than Evan had expected, longer than any story he'd ever been told. Trevon recounted every last detail. That Mama used Kentucky bluegrass for her back lawn because it reminded her of home. That Muscley One's truck was a Chevrolet Silverado kept very clean with a dangly tree air freshener that was blue which didn't make sense because trees aren't blue and they don't smell like new-car scent. That Trevon had taken 978 breaths between when they'd put the garbage bag back over his head and when they'd dumped him in an alley downtown.

Evan thought of the Seventh Commandment – *One mission at a time* – and felt frustration thrum to life in his gut. He had already embarked on the biggest mission of his life – perhaps the biggest solo mission in history – and was eager to get back to it. To proceed he had to get into the Secret Service databases through Naomi's phone. He'd booked his flight to Milan, to the one person with the hacking skills to possibly make it happen, and he was impatient to get airborne.

Mere hours ago he'd slipped out of the warmth of Mia's bed. He'd wanted to leave a note on one of her trademark Post-its but had struggled mightily with what to write. This was where his upbringing failed him; the small gestures of intimacy escaped him every time.

He'd settled on, '*Sorry. Work.*'

He'd made it quietly across the room before pausing for a three count, his hand on the doorknob. Then he'd reversed course, moving silently, and added, '*p.s.!*'

He noted his own rising restlessness now and created distance from it, observing it from afar. Before him was a young man in desperate need of help. Evan was getting useful information. And some not-so-useful information. But then again he couldn't yet know what would prove useful and what would not, so he cleared his mind and opened it wide. The First Commandment: *Assume nothing.*

As Trevon continued to describe what had been done to him, Evan forced himself to discard his anger. Anger was useless.

There were two tales unspooling, the one that Trevon was telling and the one that Evan was reconstructing in his head. When Trevon described the shipping container filled with $18 million of frozen fish from Suriname, Evan translated it to six hundred kilograms of cocaine smuggled inside large game fish that helped mask the scent from drug-sniffing dogs. The port of Paramaribo was a narcotics-transshipment point for cocaine of Peruvian origin, which meant Big Face was in deep to the cartel.

After another half hour, Trevon finally ran out of words. 'I was just following the rules.' He shook his head. 'I was just following the rules like you're supposed to.'

He was trembling, skinny arms crossed at his stomach.

Evan felt a surge of admiration for the young man, but that reaction, too, was emotional. It wouldn't get Evan from A to B, and right now that was all that mattered.

He leaned on the dustless bureau, his elbow touching the side of an old-fashioned TV with the bulk of an ice chest. 'Here's what's going to happen next.'

Trevon looked over at him, his already big eyes magnified through the thick lenses. On the neatly made bed behind him, there was a stuffed-animal frog, tucked in up to its chin.

'The cops will come,' Evan said. 'They'll tell you that your family has been killed.'

'What do I tell them?'

'That you're shocked and devastated. That you're scared you'll be targeted next. Act terrified. That shouldn't be hard.'

Trevon's teeth were chattering. 'No, sir.'

'They'll bring you to identify the bodies.'

Trevon covered his mouth and nodded.

'Your fingerprints are all over the house, but that's fine. You said you visit your mom a lot, right?'

He nodded again and murmured, 'Mama.'

'Don't tell the cops you went to the house last night.'

'But you're not supposed to lie to the cops. It's against the rules.'

'If you follow the rules,' Evan said, 'then Big Face will hurt you. And I don't want you to be hurt. So I need you to listen to me, okay? I need you to follow *my* rules.'

'Okay.'

'Your cheek's scuffed up a bit. If the cops ask where you got that, what are you gonna say?'

'I got it when Muscley One and Raw One threw me out of their truck.'

Evan gritted his teeth, searched again for patience, which was proving elusive. 'You can't mention them either, okay? Any of them. If you say anything about them, they'll find out, remember?'

'Okay.'

Evan looked away to hide his exasperation. On the bureau beside him was a notepad with neat handwriting that read:

Goals for the Day
1. Make more eye contact with folks.
2. Smile more when you see folks.

3. Ask a personal question when someone asks you one.
4. Don't overshare about stuff that bugs you.
5. Be yourself, 'cuz who else can you be!

Evan found that he'd been staring at the pad too long, and he looked away, reminded himself of the Fourth Commandment: *Never make it personal.*

He cleared his throat, a rare nonverbal tell. 'If the cops ask about the scrape on your cheek, tell them you got it moving a crate at the office.'

'Moving a crate at the office.'

'That's right. And you're gonna get up in the morning and go to work as if nothing's happened.'

Trevon's upper teeth pinched his lower lip, and Evan could see he was biting down very, very hard. Yet he nodded.

'Do not mention me,' Evan said. 'That's a rule. A very important rule. Understand? No matter what.'

'Mention who?'

'Me.'

'I was making a joke,' Trevon said.

'Oh.'

Evan did his best not to look at the list on the bureau, at the frog stuffed animal lovingly tucked in. He had to treat this mission like any other. Which meant treating Trevon like any other client.

'I have to figure out where to find the men who did this to you,' Evan said. 'You didn't overhear any names?'

'No, sir.'

'Can you tell me anything distinctive about the men?'

'Well, one had hair that was brown like chocolate brown and it was cut about two and a half inches –'

'I mean *really* distinctive. Piercings, tattoos, scars.'

'Muscley One had these tattoos on his inner forearms that were, like, each a half skull so when you put them together like this' – a quick demonstration – 'they'd make a whole skull. But I didn't get to see him do it.'

'That's good,' Evan said. 'That's helpful.'

'Thank you.'

'You don't know the location of the compound where they brought you?'

'No, sir. My head was covered and I lost count after we turned left, left, right –'

'Did you see the license plate of the truck?'

'It was a new truck with plates like from the dealer but they were dark so I couldn't read them. If it was new, I don't know why he added new-car smell 'cuz wouldn't it have that already and also he was worried I'd get puke on the new seats and so he made me wipe my mouth with a towel.'

'The towel you held on to,' Evan said. 'Like Blankie.'

'Yes, sir.'

'Do you still have the towel?'

Trevon stood up, but then his knees seemed to go weak, because he sat back down and leaned forward with his hands on his thighs, the mattress squeaking. Then he stood up again, and Evan followed him into the cramped front room of the apartment. Trevon went over to the yellow tile counter that passed for a kitchen, knelt, and pulled from the trash can what looked like a hand towel.

He handed it to Evan, the microfiber crusted with dried vomit, a ripe odor wafting off it.

Evan turned the white towel over, spotted the stitched decal on the other side: 24 HOUR FITNESS. He tore off the white tag, pocketed it, and handed the towel back to Trevon.

Trevon clutched it to his chest, his eyes starting to water. He squeezed them shut and muttered something to himself under his breath, repeating it in a loop, adjusting his eyeglasses again and again until the earpieces turned the skin above his ears raw.

'Trevon. *Trevon.*'

Trevon opened his eyes, sniffed hard. Then he leaned on the table as if he were dizzy.

'When's the last time you ate?'

Trevon thought for a moment. 'Yesterday at 12:05.'

'You're no good to us if you can't focus.'

'I'm sorry.'

Evan opened the refrigerator. It was filled with pineapple, cantaloupe, lemon chicken, apricot jam, squash soup, sweet potato, carrots, and oranges. On the counter were Cap'n Crunch's Orange Creampop Crunch, Cheerios, bananas, and a dozen boxes of mac and cheese.

Evan looked at him.

Trevon gave a faint cough, a nervous tic, then did it again. 'I only . . . I only eat food that's yellow or orange.'

'I understand,' Evan said. 'I only drink vodka.'

'Really?'

'And water.' Evan tossed him a banana. 'You need calories.'

Trevon peeled it, took a bite, then set it on the table. They were both still standing. 'I didn't ask not to be normal,' he said, with sudden anger.

'No,' Evan said.

'Even if I don't fit in, I'm still special. I still matter.'

Evan said, 'That's true.'

'I always mattered as much as anyone else to my family. Uncle Joe-Joe said blood's thicker than water. Now I don't have anyone to see me like that.'

Evan studied the angry twist of skin between Trevon's brows. 'It'll be hard.'

'You don't know!' Trevon shouted. 'You don't know how it feels to have someone try'n wipe you off the face of the whole entire planet like you were never even there!'

Evan thought of taping the surveillance photos to the wall of Apartment 705 in DC, all those other Orphans, their faces crossed out by Magic Marker, their lives redacted by the sitting president of the United States.

He didn't say anything, because there was nothing to say that would be useful.

Trevon raised a stiff hand and pressed his palm to the side of his head. This seemed to calm him. Finally he said, 'I wish Kiara was here.'

'Your sister. Can we reach her?'

'No,' Trevon said. 'Look.'

He went around the table to a tiny computer desk and came back with a glossy pamphlet. Evan scanned it. It detailed a three-month church mission designed to help provide potable water to Mayan Indians living in two hundred remote villages scattered through the jungles and mountains above the Río Dulce in Guatemala.

'There's no phones,' Trevon said. 'And she doesn't barely ever check e-mail. She doesn't even know what happened to Uncle Joe-Joe and Aisha and Mama . . .' He paused, drew a few breaths. 'Mama,' he repeated, and the grief in his voice was palpable enough to put a hitch in Evan's next breath.

'Your sister,' Evan said, getting them both back on track.

'There's no way to reach her.'

'That's good news, too,' Evan said. 'Because it means no one else can reach her either.'

Trevon chewed his lip and thought about that, and then his eyes changed. 'Right,' he said. 'Right.'

He took another bite of the banana and then set it down

again. 'I have to feed Cat-Cat,' he said, rushing to fill a plastic bowl with kibble. At the noise a slender tabby materialized from its hiding place behind the curtain. 'Mama bought me Cat-Cat. I'm responsible to him and he's responsible to me.'

'She sounds like she was a good mom.'

Trevon closed his eyes again, fiddled with his eyeglasses, and made the noises he'd made before below his breath. Some kind of mantra? At his feet Cat-Cat dined obliviously, crunching away.

'Trevon. What are you saying?'

He opened his eyes. 'We don't cry and we don't feel sorry for ourself.'

Evan took a moment to find words again. 'It's okay,' he said. 'You can cry.'

'No,' Trevon said. And then, more forcefully, '*No.*'

'All right.'

Trevon sank into the chair. That's all there was at the little breakfast table. One chair.

He looked up at Evan. 'Do *you* cry?'

'I didn't go through what you went through.'

'I'm *not* gonna cry.'

'Okay.' Evan took a step closer. 'I need to leave now, Trevon. I'm going to find the men who killed your family. And then I'm going to report back.'

'What if they come after me?'

'They're not going to hurt you. They need you alive and well to maximize your suffering.'

'Oh,' Trevon said. 'Oh, no.'

'The good news?' Evan said. 'From an operational perspective –' He caught himself. 'Right now there's no rush. For them nothing is pressing. Or urgent.'

'Pressing,' Trevon said. 'Or urgent.'

'That's right.'

'Okay.' His lips were wobbling. The half-eaten banana sat by his knuckles.

It seemed impossible that a banana could code for abject loneliness, but there it was.

Evan had to get out of here before he started anthropomorphizing the furniture. He started for the door.

'It's all my fault,' Trevon said to his back.

Evan stopped. Didn't turn around. *'No,'* he said.

'But they told me –'

Evan swung around. 'Everything that happened, every last thing, is on them. You did *nothing* wrong.'

Trevon's hands rested on the table, palms down. 'How do you know?'

'Because I wouldn't be here working for you if you had.'

'You work for *me*?'

'I do.'

Trevon swallowed, which seemed to take considerable effort. 'Can you stay for a little while?'

'No,' Evan said.

'Just till I fall asleep?'

'I don't do that. That's not what I'm for.'

'Okay.' Trevon shoved the heels of his hands into his eyes. 'I can . . . I can do it. I can put the TV on. It keeps me company.' He lowered his hands, and by dint of will his eyes were dry and his head held high. 'Mama said it's good to have a house full of voices and that's what she wishes for me someday.'

The chair legs screeched as Trevon pushed back from the table, and then he headed to the bedroom. A moment later Evan heard the TV click on, an exuberant weatherman discussing cold fronts fetishistically.

Evan bowed his head.

Cat-Cat sat at his feet and looked up at him.

Evan said, 'Be quiet.'

Cat-Cat looked at him some more.

'What do *you* know?' Evan said.

Cat-Cat flicked his tail and flounced back to his spot beneath the curtain, where he stared at Evan with recriminating eyes.

'Goddamn it,' Evan said.

He walked down the brief hall to the bedroom and found Trevon in bed wearing blue pajamas, having tucked himself in next to the stuffed frog. The lights were out, but his eyes were open, catching an ambient streetlamp glow through the window.

Evan sat across the room with his back to the wall, elbows resting on his knees. He thought about the painstakingly neat handwriting on the notepad: *'Be yourself 'cuz who else can you be!'* About the man across from him waking up every morning trying to do the best he could. And about the people who had obliterated everything he'd known.

The Fourth Commandment was out the window.

The Seventh Commandment was out the window.

Evan's hands had curled into fists. They were still loose, yes, but they were ready not to be.

Over on the bed, Trevon's blinks grew longer and longer. 'I followed the rules,' he mumbled, his voice slurred with exhaustion. 'You're supposed to be okay if you follow the rules.'

His head nodded to the side, and his breathing took on a rasping sound.

'Yeah, well,' Evan said to the dark room. 'Sometimes you have to break them.'

23. Backtracing an Outbreak

There were seventeen 24 Hour Fitnesses in the Greater Los Angeles Area. But here Evan was at the Magic Johnson Signature Club on the second floor of the Sherman Oaks Galleria. The gym was sandwiched between an upscale day spa and a wide staircase leading to a high-end movie theater.

Evan had arrived here by calling the gym towel manufacturer, which prided itself on producing hygienically clean textiles, a catchphrase with which he had been previously unfamiliar. Posing as an occupational-health safety inspector, Evan claimed he was backtracing an outbreak of *Staphylococcus aureus*, which seemed to be tied to laundry infection at a gym. If he provided a serial number from a specific towel, might the company be able to tell him to which location that particular batch of towels had shipped?

They might.

So now here he was in the open-air second level outside the gym entrance, wearing generic worker coveralls, replacing a wall outlet beside a shaggy ficus by the elevator. The impostor outlet he was installing, which was conveniently wired into the existing power source, contained a covert stationary video recorder. The tiny lens sat between the two plug receivers, flush with the plastic plate. Motion-activated, it recorded time-stamped footage to a microSD card hidden inside the unit.

Evan tweaked the button-size lens, angling it on the glass-doored entrance to the gym so it captured the people streaming in, seeking to break a pre-workday sweat.

The clientele, from what Evan could glean, consisted mostly of aspiring actors, dedicated muscleheads, and disciplined young moms in Lululemon eager to park their offspring at the on-site kids' club. The front desk featured an efficient check-in procedure – no card or key fob required. You just pressed your finger to a scanner on the counter and in you went.

Evan tightened the screws on the impostor outlet, pocketed his screwdriver, and moved the ficus another few inches to the right, its broad, glossy leaves whispering conspiratorially.

When he returned in a few days' time, he'd review the DVR footage until he spotted who he was looking for.

Muscley One.

A man with half-skull tattoos wrapping his forearms would be hard to miss.

Evan thumbed the elevator call button and rode the car down to the parking garage. He was running late for his flight, which he'd booked out of Las Vegas to obscure his trail. He'd stopped at a safe house earlier to switch out his Ford pickup with a backup vehicle. A fresh passport and supporting documents waited in the glove box.

As he pulled out of the shopping mall, he shot up Sepulveda and arced around onto the freeway, seating the pedal as low to the floor as he dared.

He had a plane to catch.

24. Worthy of Trust and Confidence

Naomi Templeton reached the building at H Street and 9th at 5:57 AM. There was no signage anywhere, no logos or plaques, nothing to indicate what the building in fact was. But if you looked closely, you might notice the sleek security cameras peeking out from the tan brick overhang near the front door. You might notice that there were no trash cans on the sidewalk outside, no USPS mailboxes or newspaper vending racks that might hide an IED.

She paused to consider the awesome task that had been lowered onto her shoulders at the start of the week. It was worth approaching this building and this day with an added measure of respect.

Entering the nine-story rise, she passed through the metal detector, taking a moment before the words written across the wall in silver letters: WORTHY OF TRUST AND CONFIDENCE.

She drifted through the central atrium in a kind of focused haze, ordering her mind for the briefing to come, the orders she'd give, the arms she'd have to twist. She moved beneath the catwalks, the beehive of glass-walled offices, so many agents bent to a common cause.

A succession of somber photographs in the hall commemorated those killed in the line of duty. This morning she didn't look at the clean-cut men and women with their stalwart eyes and proudly squared shoulders.

Instead she'd looked at the blank stretch of wall beyond

the last slain agent's portrait, the space allotted for future memorials.

If she didn't do her job, there would be more faces on this wall.

One of them might be her own.

Upstairs in the nerve center on the top floor, she presided over the Joint Operations Center. A string of agents was plugged into monitors, overseeing the movements of protectees as code names and coordinates blipped around in real time. The current location of POTUS was front and center on a large screen dominating the south wall, a clear and present illustration of what the Service's single top priority was.

A football team's worth of Protective Intelligence and Assessment agents rimmed the immense oval table, mostly men, mostly white. If it weren't for the shitty suits, it would've looked like a holiday lunch at a country club.

'. . . and I want full satellite monitoring on a continuous basis in a two-point-five-kilometer radius around the White House,' Naomi continued, her voice taking on a hoarse edge from all the talking. 'The same Unblinking Eye surveillance that McChrystal used in Iraq when they were hunting Zarqawi.'

'Uh, two point five klicks? Isn't that a touch arbitrary?' Agent Demme asked, snapping his gum.

'The longest sniper shot in history is two point forty-eight kilometers,' Naomi said. 'I'm not eager to have any records broken on my watch.'

'But our guy's not a dedicated sniper —'

'We don't know what he isn't,' she said. 'We don't know what he is. All we know is that one of our highest trained assets is hell-bent on getting Bennett in the crosshairs.'

She steepled her fingertips on the dossier sitting on the

polished surface before her. Ridiculously, the tab was redacted, the rectangle of ink blotting out the code name beneath: ORPHAN X.

This paper-thin file that Doug Wetzel had grudgingly released contained a minimum of information, either because that's all the agencies had or because that's all they were willing to give up. Evidently the Program was double-blind at every link of the chain, explicitly designed to maximize deniability up and down the command. With the various political messes President Bennett was mired in at the moment, it was clear that his office wasn't eager to lift the veil any further than was absolutely necessary.

Naomi didn't trust or like Wetzel. For her to do her job, she'd need more than the names of a few dead associates, a list of possible sightings, some vague details about suspected operations, and a shitty composite sketch generated from the memories of the DC cops who'd found themselves over-matched by matcha tea and a handful of salt. She vowed to catch the deputy chief of staff out of the White House on neutral ground and reach an in-person understanding on what she'd require to stop Orphan X.

But for now she needed to work with what she had. As Dad used to say, *You get to airtight one brick at a time.*

'If this guy has the training they say he does, he'll know to disguise himself from birds,' someone else chimed in.

'Right,' Naomi said. 'That's why we're covering all CCTV in Ward 2 – key alphabet streets, the Mall, monuments, everything. Priya's running that team' – a nod to the sole woman of color at the table – 'and Willemon's monitoring all flights, car rentals, train stations, tollbooths, bus stops, correct?'

Bob Willemon gave a wan smile. 'Down to every last tour bus.'

Naomi swiveled to the right flank of the table. 'Ted, I want facial recognition run on all posted data from all phones in the District – Instagram, Facebook, YouTube, Snapchat, the whole social-media landscape. You never know who we'll pick up passing through the background of a shot. Reach out to NSA – they're ahead of us on this with computational power.'

Demme's square jaw sawed sideways as he went at the gum, building up momentum and confidence. The promotion to SAC had come down to her or Demme, and she'd been better, pure and simple. Seeing her elevated further by presidential decree couldn't have been easy on his ego. In response he'd started growing out his sideburns and exceeding expectations on the job, one of which was working out nicely.

'So that's DC covered,' Demme said. 'What about the rest of the world?'

'I'm working up new advance-team procedures for transport and travel. I'd like your help with that, Demme. I saw your initiatives, and they're excellent.'

At this he let his palm rasp across his cheek, a flicker behind his eyes showing he felt conflicted about accepting the olive branch. She gave him her most serious stare, the one Dad used to reserve for broken curfews and prospective boyfriends.

Her stare said, *I mean what I say. I have no time for charity.*

'Happy to,' Demme said.

Naomi flipped open the woefully scant file. No name, no photographs, no fingerprints. 'I've also ordered sat footage on sites of importance to Orphan X.'

She scanned the partially redacted top page. There was a farmhouse in Arlington where Orphan X had supposedly spent some childhood years. The foster home he was taken from in Baltimore had been demolished last year. Perhaps he'd done some training at Fort Meade. There were a few more proper nouns, also unpromising.

She cleared her throat and added, 'Sites of *ostensible* importance. We don't have much, but you get to airtight one brick at a time. Orphan X's primary advantage is that he only has to get it right once. Our reliability is a precondition for his success. Which means we have to be unpredictable. So let's get to work on it. I'm putting the president's schedule in motion –'

'No shit.' Director Gonzalez leaned into the room, one hand gripping the doorframe, broad shoulders on tilt. 'I heard all about it from Wetzel, that weasel-faced fuck. All the schedule jostling's raising questions in the press. Rumors of internal problems with the cabinet, Bennett's not gonna want to see his approval ratings go any lower before midterms, blah-blah-blah. I told him you were trying to keep Bennett alive *for* the midterms, and that shut him up in a hurry. So keep at it, Templeton. Ruffle feathers, rattle cages, kick doors. The president's given you the power, and I have your back.'

The pouches under his eyes shifted. Sometimes they conveyed more emotion than his actual eyes. She dreaded the question before Gonzalez asked it.

'How's the old man holding up?'

Dad had mentored Gonzalez up through the ranks. Their relationship had evolved over the years, but their mutual affection had remained steady. For a good stretch after Dad retired and before Gonzalez ascended to the highest rank, they'd found a balance as peers, drinking and golfing together, swapping war stories.

And now Gonzalez had unwittingly undercut her authority with a single well-intentioned inquiry. There was an intimacy in the question he would not have presumed to pose at a round table were she a man.

'Doing great, thanks,' she said crisply.

He read her expression, those pouches bunching anew, registering regret. She caught up to herself, seeing through her anger that his motive was concern – concern and heartache – and felt a wash of regret herself.

Gonzalez knocked the door twice in closure and withdrew.

Naomi turned back to the dozen or so inquisitive faces, finding herself, for the first time in three hours, speechless. The mention of her father now, in this building, in this moment, had cut through her like a katana. Here she was projecting his strength while he languished in a facility, deteriorating by the minute, a puddle of flannel pajamas and English Leather. She locked down her face, felt her core tighten.

Demme broke the spell. Rocking forward in his chair, he found his feet, signaling the meeting's end. 'You heard the special agent in charge,' he said. 'Let's get to work.'

As the agents broke up, she rose to head to the Director's Crisis Center next door, where she was due to dry-run a few emergency-operation scenarios. When she looked up, Demme caught her eye across the long oval table.

She nodded her thanks and got on with her day.

25. Kick Like a Girl

Vera loved the silks, loved the feeling of climbing and twining, the combination of elegance and power required by *tissu*. She'd proven adept at aerial, graduating quickly to medium-stretch fabrics, the better to suspend herself gracefully above the gymnastic mats.

Her cover was equally graceful in its simplicity. She was a recently orphaned trust-funder, legally independent at eighteen years of age, here in the mountains of Switzerland to finish her schooling under the caring auspices of a fine English-speaking private academy.

In reality she was sixteen years old.

An Orphan Program runaway.

And a world-class hacker.

Like Evan, she had been pulled out of a foster home by the Mystery Man, a recruiter who had lingered outside the front yard and watched the kids play. She'd noted him there at the periphery with his wrinkled face and the Ray-Bans he wore all the time, even at night, as though they were nailed to his face. He seemed like something out of a fairy tale or a nightmare, a mystical figure come to carry kids away. When he'd chosen her, she'd been glad to get out, clutching at the opportunity as if it were a lifeline thrown to fish her out of stormy seas. He wore a loose gold watch and smoked cigarettes one after the other, conveying her into a new life on a magic-carpet stream of secondhand smoke.

It had not been the life she'd hoped for.

Here at the school, no one knew her name, her capabilities, her software superpowers. She toed the line and played the part. Her death had been ordered by no less than the president of the United States, and a thing like that tended to make a girl wary.

Evan had helped her and tucked her away here, hidden safely from the prying tentacles of the three-letter agencies. Joey Morales, the real her, was presumed dead, and she and Evan preferred to keep it that way.

But sometimes, even here, Joey still came out to play.

Across the gym a trio of rich Florentine boys practiced kickboxing on a heavy bag. They'd torn the sleeves off their workout T-shirts to show off their triceps, and they were talking too loudly, making sure everyone noticed.

Hanging upside down from the silks fifteen feet above the floor, Joey took a moment to assess their back kicks. Their form was for shit – poor body mechanics on the spin, sloppy counterbalancing, no foot-to-hip alignment on the heel strike – but they egged one another on. Lots of chest bumps and high fives.

Matteo, the ringleader, chinned at the girl on the other set of silks and muttered something to his compatriots, who grinned like jackals.

The other girl was Sara, Joey's lovely Dutch roommate.

At a secret-society party last month, Sara had drunk herself into oblivion, a stupid choice.

Still, a seventeen-year-old from a farming town in the northwest of Holland – or any girl from anywhere else – should be allowed to make stupid choices.

Suspended from the silks, Sara was practicing the midair splits, her eyes averted from the boys, her cheeks touched with color.

Joey braced herself, gathering the wraps around her legs, scaling higher yet and whipping herself upright twenty feet above the floor. She wound up in a foot lock, her back arched, gripping the bunched silks behind her, a Viking goddess commanding the prow of a ship. She felt a slight pull, the scar tissue in her thigh asserting itself, but that just made her feel more alive.

Below, inquisitive parents drifted through the gym, gazing up at the championship banners in the rafters with touristy wonderment. A presentation in the auditorium this evening would officially commence the year-end parents' weekend. Joey knew the drill: cheese plates and Viennese tortes, a PowerPoint augmented with endless blathering, the dads pretending not to be bored, the moms pretending not to radiate vicarious intensity. A gagworthy father-daughter dance capped the evening. It would be full of parental pride and familial warmth, all the shit a foster kid like her had learned to steer clear of.

She'd already set up her mission directives: feign menstrual cramps, hang out in her room, and stream *Veronica Mars* on her laptop.

After the last of the parents exited the gym, Matteo squared to Joey's roommate, still working hard on the silks. 'Nice spread, Sara. Heard you got in some extra practice last month.'

The trio laughed.

Beside Joey, Sara contracted in midair like a pill bug coiling in on itself, a visceral shame reaction.

Joey flipped her way down to the mat, unwinding from the silks in a controlled fall.

She had to get out of here or she was gonna kill somebody, and killing somebody would blow her cover for sure.

As she stepped off the blue rubber mat and walked past the crew of boys, Matteo leaned against the heavy bag and gave her a long-lashed gaze, flirty and handsome, sweat dripping from his dark brow. 'Wanna try?' he asked in lightly accented English. 'Let's see what those legs can do.'

Joey paused a few feet from the heavy bag, the muscles in her neck tightening.

She felt the eyes of the boys on her as if they were perusing something in a shop window. Her back was damp with perspiration. She could sense her heartbeat in the side of her neck.

She lifted the ball of her lead foot a few millimeters off the polished floorboards and pivoted it, locking into a side stance. She turned away, raised her knee up high, and threw herself into a spinning back kick, generating power through her base. She let her eyes lead the target.

Her foot hammered into the heavy bag, and Matteo flew back and slammed into the wall loudly enough to rattle the bleachers twenty feet away.

The wind left him in an explosive bark, and he fell to all fours, his mouth clutching for air, one hand pressed to his stomach.

'Sorry,' Joey said, continuing for the door. 'I kick like a girl.'

Joey pushed through the door into her dorm room, red-faced, her clavicles glistening with workout sweat. When she saw who was standing there, she came up short, her mouth slightly ajar. Her eyes welled.

Catching Joey speechless was something Evan relished.

It didn't last long.

'Fuck a *duck*,' she said.

He lifted a finger. 'Language.'

She swallowed hard, blinked harder, regaining her composure. On the floor beside her nightstand was an Original SWAT shoe box stuffed with letters. She stepped inside, sweeping it quickly out of sight beneath the bed.

Then she stared at him awkwardly. 'So are we supposed to hug or what?'

'I don't know,' Evan said.

The ninety-kilometer drive from Milan to Lugano had been gorgeous, snow flurrying with postcard perfection, the sun bronzing Lake Lugano with a dreamy haze. He'd forgotten how clean Swiss air tasted, ice and whiteness finished with a hint of pine.

He paused a moment to take her in. It had been six months since he'd seen her, and she looked healthy. Her skin tone was darker than tan; her last name indicated that she was part Hispanic, but she probably didn't know the full details of her ethnic background any more than he knew his.

She also looked a touch older, her features transforming into those of a young woman, the fullness of her face diminished ever so slightly. He was surprised at the glimmer of melancholy that brought forth in him. Did he expect her not to grow up? What an odd sentiment.

Before he could contemplate the matter, she said, 'Why are you here? I thought, you know, we weren't supposed to . . .'

'I need your help,' he said.

'Why doesn't *that* surprise me?'

'I hacked into the phone of a Secret Service agent.'

'Well, whoop-dee-do,' Joey said. 'I bet you can also program your DVR.'

She bit down a grin. He was glad to see her, too.

'Nice haircut,' he said.

She used to keep it shaved on the right side, but now she looked schoolgirl-proper.

'Hey. You're the one who put me here. The Third Commandment: *Master your surroundings.* Well, this is me mastering some shit. Plus, look.' She pulled up her tumbling black-brown locks to reveal the thinnest strip of shaved hair just above her ear. 'I'm still in here, bitches.'

He said, 'Language.'

She broke out that smile at last, the one that changed everything, like a light switch flicking on inside her.

She let her hair fall, and once again she was Vera, somber heiress to a middling trust fund. 'All right, all right. You need my help. With what?'

He presented the Boeing Black smartphone on his palm. 'I've mirrored the agent's phone,' he said. 'Using a Stingray.'

Joey stepped forward and pinched his cheek. 'Look at you, all grown up.'

'Joey.'

'Okay, okay.'

'I need to get into the Secret Service databases.'

She bit her lip. 'To kill the president.'

'Yes.'

'Who wanted to kill *me.*'

'Yes.'

Joey said, 'Okay.'

'The problem is, all Secret Service computers are air-gapped on a private secure network. No connection to the Internet or the outside world. Which means no way to get in.'

'Certainly not for a lesser brain like yours. You know how hard it is to keep an *entire network* hermetically sealed? Ask the DoD – they squirted epoxy into the USB ports of a hundred thousand PCs in the Pentagon to try'n block flash-drive exfiltration.' Joey plucked the phone from his hand. 'Leave it to the trained professional.'

They were standing close, and she was looking up at him and he down at her. She wound her hand into a fist around the phone, and then she leaned into him, hard, and it took a moment for him to catch up to the fact that she was hugging him.

He could feel the heat of her through his shirt, her hair soft and thick against his chin. He patted her shoulder, breathed in the scent of her – sweat and citrus – and realized with equal parts alarm and concern that she owned a small piece of him.

A brisk knock at the door startled them apart, and then the door opened and a portly man with ruddy cheeks and round eyeglasses entered. He wore a uniform with a nameplate that read CALVIN BLICKENSDERFER, SCHOOL PORTER.

'I'm sorry, Ms Vera. I was checking in to tell Ms Sara that the offensive graffiti on her locker has been removed.' He cleared this throat. 'And this is your . . . ?'

'Uncle,' Joey said at the precise instant that Evan said, 'Cousin.'

The porter gave a confused smile to fill the silence.

'My Uncle-Cousin,' Joey said. 'You know. It's weird, with my parents, the accident – some distant relatives have stepped up.'

'Oh,' the porter said, brightening, swinging his focus to Evan. 'You came to fill in for the father-daughter dance? How thoughtful!'

Evan felt the blood leave his face, saw the points of Joey's jaw flex as she clamped her teeth.

He said, 'Um . . .'

'The welcome reception for all parents kicks off in' – the porter consulted his polished silver watch, which no doubt kept exemplary Swiss time – 'twenty-three minutes. I'll make sure seats are held. You'd best hurry and get ready.'

'Yeah,' Joey said. 'Great.'

The porter gave another twinkly grin and withdrew, easing the door shut so it barely clicked in the frame.

Evan said, 'Fuck.'

Joey regarded him flatly. 'Language.'

26. Celebrating Individual Strengths

Evan and Joey sat in the rear of the dark auditorium as the PowerPoint continued, urged glacially onward by a matronly headmistress who seemed intent on reading every last bullet point.

'— our philosophy of fostering community while celebrating individual strengths.'

Evan leaned over. 'Is this really what school is like?'

Joey rolled her eyes over to him. 'She's gonna say "climate." Wait for it.'

A mother in flaking maroon lipstick and a mink stole turned around to hush them. Her kid shrugged apologetically at Joey.

Onstage the headmistress raised her remote control and another slide appeared: Diverse Kids Playing Frisbee in Quad.

'We seek to provide a climate that focuses on the individual student's interests, abilities, and educational goals.'

Joey muttered, '*Nailed* it.'

Evan had once sat a sniper post in a tree in Sierra Leone for fifteen hours without moving. He'd lain in wait beneath a bridge in Kirkuk, sipping from a CamelBak, eating protein bars, and pissing on the same spot on the wall for three days.

But this? This was actually going to kill him.

Not that the preceding twenty-three minutes and change had been any easier. On the way over, they'd run a gauntlet of teachers and administrators, each one stopping Evan to tell him what a wonderfully well-behaved student Vera was.

Now the headmistress was talking about mission statements and institutional values, pacing the stage like a charisma-challenged stand-up.

'How much longer?' Evan whispered, keeping his voice even lower so as not to draw the wrath of übermom in the row ahead.

Joey slid out of her seat and crooked a finger for him to follow. They moved in stealth mode out of the auditorium and into the corridor.

He hustled to keep up with her. He was still adjusting to seeing her wearing the school uniform – white polo, navy blue slacks, navy blue sweater, saddle shoes – rather than torn jeans and a loose flannel.

They turned the corner, running smack into an austere gentleman in a no-shit three-piece suit. He was lanky and tall enough to regard them down the length of his nose. 'Vera, what are you doing out here? The itinerary's very specific about –'

'I'm really sorry, Dean Anders.' Joey bent her knees slightly inward. 'It's just – I need to get to the bathroom. Girl problems, you know.'

The dean and Evan stiffened in uncomfortable tandem.

'Okay,' the dean said. 'And this is your – ?'

'Cousin-uncle,' Evan said, recovering and shaking the dean's bony hand. 'It's nice to meet you, sir. Vera was in some pain from, you know . . . cramps, so I thought I'd see her to the bathroom.'

'Very well,' the dean said. 'Hurry back.'

Evan wondered what kind of upbringing a person had to have to say 'very well.'

The dean coasted past them on an effluvium of aftershave. As the sound of his loafers clicked away, Joey's posture transformed and she grabbed Evan's arm. 'Move it.'

They cut up another corridor and paused before a locked door, Joey fishing a thin tension wrench and a hook pick from somewhere in her hair. She was through the dead bolt in seconds, and they were inside. She closed the door behind them and relocked it.

The windowless computer lab hummed with electricity from the monitors, a few dozen screen savers projecting patterns onto the walls. The room held the hot-metal scent of outlets working overtime.

'You're looking at my own personal robot army,' she said. 'After hours I reconfigured the network and code for all these stations to make it a compute cluster and harness all the computing power in the lab. Of course no one's figured it out yet 'cuz, you know, I'm me.'

She sat down at a station, slid a keyboard into her lap, and then her hands did that thing that made her look like a piano maestro playing Rachmaninoff in double time.

'I've been working on a chipset designed just for deep learning,' she said. 'I wrote a program that uses machine learning to, like, self-teach, self-improve, and ferret out data *I* don't even know is relevant. It's not rule-based – it's all analytics of Big Data now, ya know, scrutinizing massive sets of unstructured data to discover previously unknown connections. Like if someone searches for mouthwash effectiveness, it doesn't mean their next move is ordering Scope from Amazon, it means they make an OpenTable reservation for a date. Get it?'

'Not really.'

'Basically, I'm a warlock.'

'Copy that.'

Various windows proliferated on-screen – internal school documents, transcripts, confidential bank records, the search history and other documents pertaining to a male student named Matteo. Evan pointed to the raft of data about the handsome senior. 'What's that?'

'*That* is a fucking rapist. No – to call him a fucking rapist is too flattering. He's an aspiring necrophiliac molester of unconscious underage girls. But that takes too long to say. So: "fucking rapist." I'm gonna scorched-earth his ass. And destroy his family, too, while I'm at it. Seems his old man's tangled up in some insider trading, and let's just say CONSOB's gonna get an anonymous e-mail with attachments –'

'Joey.'

'Sorry. It's just . . . cyberworld's so much more interesting than meatworld.'

'Meatworld?'

Ignoring him, she plugged the Boeing Black smartphone into an ATX tower. 'Okay, what's your plan?'

'My plan?' Evan said. 'My plan is to ask you what to do.'

She grimaced at him. Then scanned the screen. Did some clicky things. Grimaced again. 'As I suspected, the Secret Service network isn't *totally* air-gapped.'

'How can you tell that?'

'Because your girl' – a squint at the screen – 'Agent Naomi Templeton, she logged in to her e-mail once through an encrypted program from a work computer.'

'So –'

'Don't talk.' Joey pinched the bridge of her nose, squeezed her eyes shut for a moment. 'Okay. Here's what we're gonna do. We're gonna infect the Secret Service's private secure network with a corrupt Windows update and let their secure update server pass it around their net. We make them infect themselves.'

'And you'll do that how?'

She tore off her sweater impatiently and hiked her sleeves over her deltoids. 'We're gonna get a sploit payload in through this broad's e-mail. We log in as her, put the bad payload in a PDF doc attachment, send it to herself, then modify it so it's, like, hidden inside the icon for a JPEG file. The next time she logs in on the secure network, my tiny little sploit execution engine uses that hidden code and actively modifies the private Windows update server with a series of corrupted patches. At the next update push – and they usually push at least biweekly on setups like this – it'll automatically install our modified patches to all the computers inside the private secure network. Once that goes down, my recon code'll probe around for a way through the outbound firewalls to find the Internet. It just takes one touch to the outside. Then we use, like, a hidden reverse SSH backdoor for you to get in at will and see whatever data you need. After that, all you have to do is sit on your ass, drink vodka, and watch the monitors. Got it?'

'I understood the sit-on-my-ass-and-drink-vodka part.'

'You should pay attention. This is some wicked shit. Crumbling-kingdoms kinda shit.'

Her hands moved in a blur, and more stuff happened on-screen. He watched with wonderment, feeling something akin to pride. For a time the only sound was the hammering of the keyboard.

Then Joey said, 'These rich kids suck. When can I come back to LA?'

She kept her eyes on the monitor, her fingers never slowing.

He hesitated.

'Not to live with you,' she added, still typing. 'I mean, that'd be a *nightmare*. But when?'

'If this mission goes well, it'll be safer for you. We can talk about it then.'

The scrolling code reflected in her striking emerald eyes. 'Is it gonna go well?'

He thought about it. 'I don't know. I've never tried anything like this.'

'Just don't die,' she said. 'I mean, that'd suck. Promise?'

He considered the odds, knew better than to answer. Instead he removed a burner satphone from his pocket and set it down on the mouse pad. 'If we need to be in touch about the code.'

Her eyes flicked over for a split second to take in the device. 'Wow. This is great. Did you get it from 1985? Lemme guess – the Beverly Hills Cop lent it to you?'

Evan sighed. 'You'd prefer we communicate through a draft file of an unsent e-mail?'

'Uh, *yeah.*'

'I'll get you my account and password.'

'Thanks, Kojak. And if we need to talk, I'll figure out an *actual* secure line.' She logged out and stood abruptly, the chair flying out from under her like something scared. 'Let's go.'

Again he hustled to keep up with her. In the corridor she used her lock-picking tools to reseat the dead bolt. Then she hurried up the hall, tugging down her sleeves and slinging her sweater back on an instant before a young teacher backed out of a classroom in front of them, cradling an armload of files against her chest.

'Vera!'

'Hi, Ms Bosch. We're just – This is my uncle-cousin. We're hurrying to make the end of the reception.'

The teacher brightened. 'Nice to meet you. Your cousin is a wonderfully –'

'Well-behaved student,' Evan said, pumping her hand. 'Yes, thank you.'

Minutes later Joey and Evan slipped back into their seats in the rear of the auditorium. The headmistress remained onstage facing the massive projection screen, arms crossed, wearing a beatific expression as she regarded a video showcasing the students' academic and athletic accomplishments.

Students jumped show horses, flung lacrosse balls, slide-tackled on lush pitches. A saccharine lily scent of perfume wafted off the woman with the mink stole. Evan was considering dozing off when the presentation suddenly fizzled out, the screen turned to static.

A blip of pure black.

A gritty sketch of the see-no-, hear-no-, speak-no-evil monkeys appeared briefly, a hacker's signature.

And then footage came up, low light, angled across a desk. A hijacked recording from a student's laptop webcam? A student – Matteo – sat facing the lens, staring at the invisible screen of his laptop intently.

A parent gasped.

It took a moment for Evan to assemble the imagery in his head: Matteo's contorted face, the grunts and groans emanating from his laptop, his hand pumping hard just below the sight line of the camera.

Suddenly there was pandemonium. People shouting, administrators rushing the stage, a swarm-of-bees hum of student voices. Someone tripped over a power cord, and the projection slid off kilter, mercifully before Matteo concluded. A mother – presumably Matteo's – was sobbing, and then the lights went out altogether. The sounds of a mini-stampede to the aisles filled the dark auditorium.

The headmistress's voice, sharper than before, cut through

the darkness. 'Please stay calm. We're going to ... um, perhaps ....Can I get ... can I get campus security up here? Going to cancel the scheduled ... the father-daughter dance until we can get a handle on just exactly ... So inappropriate ... We're very sorry. Security, please? ... Maybe just —'

Evan and Joey remained in their chairs, watching the swirling chaos before them, shadows in the darkness.

He looked across at her. 'Next semester?'

Joey smirked. 'Sure thing, Pops.'

She held out her fist, and he bumped it.

He was gone before the lights came back up.

27. The Good Guys

When Orphan A at last gave in and shaved his beard, the skin beneath was speckled with red nicks. He'd worked the comb too hard. He moisturized his face with coconut-hibiscus lotion from a sample tube by the sink.

What a weird fucking world.

He wandered out into the hotel room proper. On the bed lay a high-resolution photograph he'd taken of the federal prosecutor after he'd neutralized her. Proof of death.

He flipped over the photograph and stared up at the water-color windsurfer framed above the headboard. Braced with Hemingwayesque determination, the painted figure was breaking through the frothy cap of a wave, long hair slicked back across one cheek.

Holt wondered what emotion that was intended to evoke in guests staying at a midrange hotel near Dupont Circle. That there was a big, adventurous world out there ripe for the taking? That by traveling to DC you were embarking on one such adventure? Or maybe it wasn't anything like that at all. Maybe the colors and pattern had been focus-grouped and found to be soothing.

He stared a bit longer at the painting and wondered what emotion it evoked in him. All he felt was a sense of discon-nection, of being unplugged from the world of sentiments that everyone else seemingly drew power from.

At his feet were two Pelican cases, and inside those were various handguns, frag grenades, body armor, and a half dozen FN P90s, courtesy of the Secret Service's own White House armory. Designed in the eighties to penetrate Soviet titanium body armor, P90s took a 5.7 proprietary pistol cartridge, fifty rounds per mag. But that wasn't what made them special. What made them special was that each FN P90 stored its rounds horizontally alongside the barrel, which meant no mag sticking down out of the body. That made it half the size of most personal-defense weapons, a nice short *Star Wars*–looking motherfucker that gave so little kick that a reasonably strong woman could fire it one-handed.

It was totally ambidextrous, geared for unusual shooting positions, great for close quarters – in a car, a hallway, the cab of an elevator. The brass ejected straight down, which meant no hot casings flying around, pinging off your neck, landing in your shirt collar.

Considerations like this governed him. It seemed that living with them for so long had made hibiscus-coconut lotion and painted windsurfers less alluring.

Maybe that's what being an Orphan did, pressed the life force out of you until you were cold-blooded and slick-scaled, a creature bent to a single design.

A double rap came at the door. A pause. Another double rap.

Not room service.

He said, 'Unlocked.'

The door opened, and the Brothers Sound and Fury entered, stooping to duck beneath the frame. Pasty and hulking, they wore leather biker vests with the sleeves cut off, white-supremacist ink cluttering up their visible skin.

The Collins boys stood shoulder to shoulder, Wade tugging at his bushy Abe Lincoln chinstrap beard, Ricky's mouth bunched up so his face looked like a fist.

'Close the door,' Holt said.

'There's more of us,' Wade said. 'Cousins.'

He lifted his upper lip, part wolf, part rabbit, and sliced a whistle through his front teeth.

Five more men, slightly diminished versions of Sound and Fury, entered. Slightly diminished still put them at six-four, 230 each.

The last man in heeled the door shut, and then they crossed their arms in unison.

Orphan A took in the display. 'You can cut the choreography,' he said. 'This isn't synchronized swimming.'

Wade said, 'How 'bout you tell us exactly who the fuck you are and what you think we're gonna do for you?'

Holt appraised their outfits. 'We can't exactly make you inconspicuous, but I'll need you to dress like human fucking beings. Shave your beard, long sleeves to cover the arm tats, see about some cover-up for the Iron Crosses on the sides of your necks.'

Ricky sidled forward, Sound to Wade's Fury. 'I don't think you heard the man.'

Holt looked him dead in the eye. 'Lemme be clear. If you take one step closer, I'll crush your windpipe and turn your head a hundred and twenty degrees on your neck before you hit the ground. You and your brother are outta your cages because of me. The instant I'm unhappy, the secret-handshake men'll swarm your lives and put you back in your boxes to serve out the rest of your consecutive life sentences. So what do you say we cut the shit and get to work?'

The men locked eyes. Holt could smell the tang coming off Ricky, soured body chemistry and mental illness. He knew that he could make good on his promise, but the other Collins kin would extinguish him afterward. He wasn't sure which way the situation would go. He wasn't sure he particularly cared.

But then he thought of Orphan X and realized that he did.

What did it say that the only life-affirming glow that warmed his insides was the promise of revenge?

Ricky stepped back. 'What's the work?'

'Hunting,' Holt said.

This elicited grins from the cousins but nothing from the twin towers.

'We're going after someone who's going after the president,' Holt added.

'The president of what?' Wade said.

Holt gave him a dead stare until recognition dawned behind the grit and facial hair. 'I have access to SFI. Serious Fucking Intel. All the eyes inside all the devices.'

'How?'

'Don't worry about that.'

Ricky said, 'Why aren't the cops or whoever handling it?'

'Because it can't be handled the way cops handle it,' Holt said.

Wade scratched at his beard again. Evidently the Abe Lincoln look came at a cost to personal comfort. 'So we're supposed to kill this guy?'

Holt said, 'I didn't have you released from prison for your dinner-party etiquette.'

'What if we get busted?'

'You still don't get it.' Holt lifted a steel-tipped boot and laid open the top of the nearest Pelican case, revealing the gleaming ordnance beneath. 'We're the good guys now.'

28. A Touch to the Outside

Baseball cap pulled low, Evan sat in his rental car across from 6071 I Street, a pricey condo complex with a conveniently windowed lobby that showed off pods of leather couches, a few phallic cacti, and a wall of smoked mirror that would have been considered tacky a few years ago but now was retro cool. He wondered how Doug Wetzel afforded to live here on a deputy chief of staff's salary.

It was nearing 10:00 AM on Saturday, the DC streets clogged with tourists. A souvenir shop just past his parking meter received a steady influx of customers, clouding his car in a hurricane swirl of activity. He would have been jet-lagged had he bothered to notice, but he was busy sitting surveillance, waiting for Wetzel to show his bearded face.

Removing superglue from the backpack on the passenger seat, Evan applied another sheen to his fingertips, further obscuring his prints.

The familiar action tripped his memory, taking him back to 1997, riding a bus out of that gray Eastern European city to see a man about a copper-washed shell from a sniper round. He closed his eyes, pictured the little plastic bag, the Cyrillic lettering spelling out EYES ONLY. He'd reassembled that mission like a puzzle but was still missing a crucial piece that, to President Bennett, represented an existential threat.

Given that Wetzel was Bennett's go-to guy for dirty work, Evan wanted to search his condo in hopes he could find something to point at the puzzle piece that had landed him on the bull's-eye.

He blew on his fingers, waiting for the superglue to dry. In the backpack he had fingerprint adhesives as well, impressionable silicon composite films that were fifty microns thin, or half the width of a piece of hair. He'd acquired the DARPA-developed commodity at great expense and preferred to use the films sparingly. So, for now, superglue it was.

He pulled out his RoamZone and logged in to the.nwhr.man@gmail.com. He'd left a query for Joey inside the Drafts folder: '*Are we into Secret Service private secure network yet?*'

Her reply was where it should be, typed inside the same unsent message: '*no, mr patience.*'

Frowning, he thumbed: '*Keep me posted.*'

An instant later the draft updated: '*ya think?*'

Amused, he deleted the draft, killing it in its cradle. Another sense memory hit him – sitting on a ratty bed in a foreign hotel communicating with Jack inside a shared e-mail draft just like this. And now time had lurched forward and landed Evan in an iteration of his past, two lost souls communicating across the black expanse of the Atlantic.

His mind tugged to when Joey had caught him off guard with a hug and the epiphany that had followed – that she owned a small piece of him.

How had she gotten in?

Surely Jack was to blame. In cultivating not just Evan's lethality but his humanity, Jack had embedded a vulnerability in him as sure as every air-gapped system had a leak. What had Joey called it? *A touch to the outside.*

Evan's touch to the outside left him exposed, open to attack.

But it also left him open to the world and all the awesome, awful responsibility that came from living in it.

He thought about Mia and Peter, a single mother and a fatherless boy, and how if he were a better man with a better past, his missing pieces might fit with theirs.

Across the street the lobby of Wetzel's building remained empty. Through a break in foot traffic, Evan caught a glimpse of his own rental car cast back from the smoky mirror. In the space where he should be, the reflection showed nothing but the tinted glass of the driver's window.

He looked across at the souvenir shop with its red blaring sign: WE SELL ITEMS STRAIGHT FROM THE WHITE HOUSE GIFT SHOP!

Shouldering his backpack and its mission-essential valuables, he climbed out. Keeping an eye on the condo building, he perused the shop's offerings. He picked out a sleek half-moon plaque, custom-cast with a brass patina.

As he paid in cash, the shop owner asked, 'Want me to wrap it?'

Evan said, 'Yes.'

After the shop owner finished, Evan took the package, the size of a halved Frisbee, and shoved it into his backpack. When he looked up and across the street, he caught Wetzel emerging from the elevator into the lobby. He was dressed in a sharp suit, the tips of his mustache rising with speakeasy gusto.

Evan moved swiftly out from under the awning of the shop, keeping Wetzel in view. Evan expected him to cut through the back door into the parking garage, but instead Wetzel paused beside an industrial aluminum trash can near the tea-and-coffee counter.

Wetzel glanced around the lobby, making sure that no one was near. Then he put his hand on the trash can's metal swing lid, flipped it upside down, and checked beneath.

A dead drop.

Presumably he didn't find what he was looking for. Letting the lid fall back into place, he vanished through the rear door. Moments later he emerged from the parking gate behind the wheel of a Tesla S.

As Wetzel zoomed off, Evan decided not to search his place but to watch the dead drop instead.

He got back into his rented Nissan Altima, once again safe behind tinted glass.

Twenty minutes passed. Forty.

Near the hour mark, a man across the street caught Evan's attention. It wasn't his appearance but his sense of purpose, the way he cut through pedestrians, head lowered, his movements conveying latent power. Reddish brown hair cut short, receding but thick where it remained, clung to his skull like an ivy leaf laid over the crown. He was on the short side – maybe a whiff over five-eight – with a welterweight's build, wiry and dense at the same time.

Everything about him screamed *Orphan*.

Evan tracked him through the crowd but couldn't get a clear look at his face.

Still turned away, the man slowed at the entrance of Wetzel's building. Outside the lobby door, he tapped in a code, one arm raised, the sinewy forearm like knotted rope. Slipping inside, he tugged up his shirt and retrieved a buff clasp envelope tucked against the small of his back.

Through the window Evan watched the man beeline to the trash can. Barely slowing his pace, he flipped the swing lid, slapped the folder into place beneath, and continued up the brief hall toward the garage.

He banged through the rear door and was gone before the trash-can lid had stopped swaying.

Evan sat in the car for a few minutes. He remembered hearing whispers of Bennett's reliance on one of the Orphans – the *first* Orphan – back in his early DoD days. Evan had even uncovered a photo once, a decades-old surveillance shot taken in a bustling souk in Amman. It had captured a partial reflection of Orphan A's face in the side mirror of a parked car.

Evan hadn't caught a clear enough look at the features of the man now to compare. But the guy's age, somewhere in the mid-fifties, put him into consideration.

Evan waited a time longer, staring through the stream of pedestrians at that trash can and whatever had been hidden for Doug Wetzel beneath the lid.

Then he got out of the Altima.

Seating his backpack on his shoulders, he crossed the street and walked the same course as the likely Orphan had before him. He paused a few yards from the door and pretended to answer a cell-phone call.

A few moments later, an elderly woman with a rat-size dog trudged from the elevator to the front door. Evan caught it on the backswing and slipped into the cool lobby.

He moved swiftly to the trash can, flipped the lip upside down, and tore free the taped envelope beneath. He pinched the clasp, raised the flap, and slid out a high-res eight-by-ten photo of a woman who looked to have been battered to death with a blunt object.

Interesting.

It seemed the president's deputy chief of staff had been checking the dead drop for confirmation of an ordered kill.

Staring at the woman's sprawled form, the unhuman arrangement of the plates of her skull, Evan felt a bone-deep weariness overtake him. His life guaranteed that he saw ugliness in all its varied and gruesome forms. But that touch to the outside meant that he felt it, too.

Using the camera of his RoamZone, Evan sized up the frame and took a picture. Then he flipped the photograph over. On the back an address, a date, and a time had been rendered in meticulous block letters.

He took a picture of that, too, and then slid the photo home, reseated the clasp, and rotated the swing lid so he could seat the envelope back on its underside where he'd found it.

He sensed a shadow at the lobby entrance and glanced up, one hand grasping the envelope in plain view, the other holding the trash-can lid.

He found himself staring through the window at Agent Naomi Templeton, standing before her Cherokee on the sidewalk.

She was staring right back at him.

29. The Second-Oldest Profession

Naomi was frozen in place, as was Evan, the air between them like spun glass – one move and everything would shatter.

He noticed a sudden awareness tighten her focus.

He was, after all, standing in the lobby of the deputy chief of staff's building, his hand in the cookie jar of an evident dead drop.

Not a pose that screamed innocence.

He couldn't hear her through the thick window, but he watched her mouth the words, *Don't move!*

He stuffed the envelope into his front waistband, took a step back toward the door to the garage.

He barely had time to wonder how she'd react before her SIG Sauer cleared leather.

That was a lot of bullets to dodge.

He dove behind the nearest couch as the window blew inward, pebbled glass raining down on the tile. Sprawled on his back, the double pip of the shots still echoing in his head, he watched the rounds embed in the throwback cottage-cheese ceiling.

She'd fired not at him but up through the pane.

Which meant she was clearing the glass to take the quickest route from the sidewalk into the lobby.

He popped to his feet and sprinted for the rear door to the garage, backpack bobbing violently up and down on his shoulders.

Behind him she hurdled the window frame and landed with a grunt, her shoes crunching glass. 'Stop! Hands – *hands*!'

As he barreled into the garage, he heard her shouting for backup into her Boeing Black phone.

He skidded on an oil slick on the shiny floor, his boots giving him just enough traction to hold course. The obvious way out was the gated vehicle exit to the right, which led back onto I Street. But there was a service door to his left.

He spun in that direction, slammed through the service door into a back hall that reeked of cleaning solvent. Dodging mop buckets, he sprinted up its length and cut the corner hard away from the lobby. He battered through a side door into an alley.

Behind him a dead end.

Ahead I Street.

He ran forward onto the main street.

Twenty yards distant, Naomi stood on the sidewalk, facing away from him, aiming at the garage gate.

He took off in the other direction, knocking through the crowd.

Naomi's voice cut through the din. 'Stop!' And then, 'Suspect heading west on I Street!'

He pulled up a mental map of the surrounding blocks. As the Second Commandment mandated, he'd memorized every alley, doorway, and building. With alarm he noted that Secret Service headquarters was three and a half blocks away.

And that he was running toward it.

He hit the intersection with 7th to find a wall of cruisers bearing down from the convention center. At his appearance they amped into high gear, predators sighting prey. A multitude of sirens emitted overlapping screams. Light bars strobed the buildings, disco-balling windows all around.

Evan bolted south.

Whether by design or shitty luck, he was being herded to the doorstep of the Secret Service.

He moved between street and sidewalk, eluding cars, slicing through pedestrians. People were now gawking at him and at the vanguard of cruisers, a block back and closing.

So many units had been on standby.

For him.

He knocked over a guy handing out flyers, juked right just in time to avoid smashing into a baby stroller. The Smithsonian American Art Museum watched him fly past, its seen-it-all Greek Revival façade unimpressed, its colonnades like bared teeth.

About fifty yards behind him, Naomi blazed through the crowd, shouting for people to clear the way.

Most civilian vehicles had pulled over now, leaving the road open. Drawn by the commotion, onlookers spilled out of stores and restaurants, clotting the sidewalks, narrowing Evan's path to a high-wire sprint.

The screech of the sirens reached an earsplitting pitch. The cop cars would be on him in seconds.

He had to get to F Street, still gummed up with traffic. He barreled into a surge of tourists, the summer-fun smell of Coppertone and ice cream enveloping him. He bucked free of the press of bodies, emerging mere yards from the intersection.

Directly ahead of him, an officer stepped out of a Mexican joint, wiping his mouth with a cloth napkin, radio barking on his shoulder.

The officer sighted Evan, dropped his napkin, and drew his pistol.

Without breaking stride Evan threw his right arm free of the backpack strap, letting centrifugal force fling the heavy bag up the trajectory of his left arm. He caught the left strap as it flew by, whipped the backpack around like a softball pitcher winding up, and slammed the cop's pistol on the rise just as he fired into Evan's face.

The bullet trailed heat across the top of Evan's head, riffling his hair.

He slammed into the officer, shoulder to sternum, sending him airborne right back into the Mexican restaurant.

He let the backpack continue its rotation, threading the straps with one arm after another, and then he was wearing it again, still in a dead sprint.

The sirens were so loud it seemed they were inside his head.

Jackknifing past a parking meter, he cut up F Street. Behind him came a squeal of brakes and a crumple of fenders as the lead cars failed to make the turn. Already they were working their way free, tires spinning in reverse, horns blaring.

The sign for 8th Street flew by overhead. Casting a look back, he caught a flash of blond hair as Naomi tumbled around the corner, plunging into the crowd on the sidewalk. Office buildings and museums were emptying out all along the block, people hustling onto the sidewalks to find out what was going on.

He kept on, the next intersection coming up fast. Shooting a glance along 9th, he saw a half dozen G-rides screaming toward him, hot from Secret Service headquarters. From the south, two new Metro Police units accelerated at him.

He reversed course, plunging into the throng surging from storefronts.

Back at 7th, the cruisers had almost untangled themselves. He couldn't see Naomi for the moment.

He had three seconds, maybe five, before they picked him up again.

And nowhere to go.

Tightening his backpack straps, he wheeled around. The crowd pressed in on him, fear and excitement coming off bodies like an electric charge.

The mob ebbed and flowed around him. He fought against the prevailing tide, trying to get off the street. Stumbling up onto the curb, he came to a halt and stared at the marquee-style sign stretching before him.

INTERNATIONAL SPY MUSEUM.

He smiled.

The museum was still evacuating as Evan careened inside, sliding past reception and in through an exit door onto the museum's ground floor. He rooted in his backpack for the mirror phone that allowed him to listen in on Naomi's Black Boeing, thumbing it on as he darted forward.

Gray cobblestone was suddenly underfoot, and he looked up to find himself standing in Cold War Berlin. Sullen concrete barriers rose from the floor, routing him along like a rat in a maze. Agitprop flyers waved from kiosks. Graffiti brightened drab walls. A replica tunnel vanished into darkness, promising untold dangers.

He passed a *telefon* booth, gripped by a disorientation that brought him back half a lifetime to another gray street in another gray city when he was a nineteen-year-old Orphan laying the groundwork for an assassination.

Naomi's voice crackled through the phone into his ear, jarring him from his reverie: *lost sight of him.*

Copy that. We have PD units flooding the zone.

We need everything locked down between 9th and 7th. Empty every single building. Search ground floors first and heaviest – he won't want to go up and cut off his escape options.

That was exactly right.

So he'd do the opposite.

Swiftly he retraced his steps to the lobby, vectoring for the stairs next to the gift shop, where a headless bust displayed a shirt emblazoned with the words DENY EVERYTHING.

Naomi's voice again in his ear: *The Spy Museum. Let's see if he has a sense of humor. I'm going in.*

He cleared the doorframe into the stairwell an instant before he heard her strike the push plate of the lobby door.

Lunging all the way up to the vacated third floor, he charged out into the Covers & Legends room, the walls clad with ID cards and forged papers. A looping video explained that this was where visitors selected their new identity before partaking of the interactive exhibits ahead.

Searching for a hiding place, he moved through the circular floor plan, gadgets and artifacts blurring past him. Poisonous umbrellas and necktie cameras. Suitcase radios and a KGB lipstick gun. Surveillance stations and a grim interrogation room.

He was trapped inside a Disneyfied version of his life's work, the world's second-oldest profession repurposed as theme-park attraction.

In the background a recording played testimony from French Resistance saboteurs. When Naomi spoke through the mirror phone again, Evan had to hike the volume to hear her.

No one down on one or two. I'm going to three.

Copy that. I dispatched four units to sweep the ground floor behind you. Whistle if you get a hit, and I'll leapfrog 'em upstairs.

Evan sped up, searching frantically for a crevice he could slither into.

He heard Naomi's voice now in stereo, both over the line and at the third-floor entrance behind him. 'On the third floor, pressing forward. Status elsewhere?'

As the dispatch agent started rattling off other buildings that had been cleared, Naomi's exhalations fuzzed the line; she was jogging through the third floor, breathing hard, catching up to him.

Keeping the Boeing Black smartphone at his ear, Evan moved with light steps into the Ninja Suite. Ahead was the entrance to one of the interactive exhibits – an air-duct crawl.

He had a moment of unadulterated you-gotta-be-kidding-me.

The air duct's opening, a hatch cut into the wall, was cast in a red-light-district glow.

Evan stripped off his backpack, shoved it ahead of him, and pulled himself inside. He inchwormed along the elevated tunnel, pushing the backpack before him, his face drawing even with a vent. Pressing his fingers around the welded seams, he found an interior wire and tore it from its mooring, the illumination around the hatch dying just before Naomi came into the room.

She slowed her jog, pausing to catch her breath.

Hidden in the vent, Evan watched her scan the walls, her eyes passing over the shadowed opening to the air-duct crawl.

Was it dark enough that she'd miss it?

'Damn it,' she said into the phone.

The mirror phone, resting in the vent before Evan's face, gave a faint rattle as the words came through.

He watched her head crane, looking up in his direction.

With excruciating slowness, he reached forward and silenced the mirror phone.

'What?' Naomi said into her phone. And then, 'I was going over to talk to Wetzel. I saw a guy getting something from what looked like a dead drop in the lobby. I think . . .' She swiveled away, facing the precise spot where the air duct's opening lay barely hidden in shadow. 'I think it might've been Orphan X.'

She listened.

Evan watched, praying that her gaze wouldn't snag on the hatch in the wall.

'I have no fucking idea why Wetzel set up a dead drop,' she said. 'The only thing I know is there's no way he'll tell *me*.' A pause and then, 'No. No need. I already safed it. Let's expand the target zone down to D Street. Every building, every car, every alley.'

She turned away and walked out.

Long after her footsteps faded, Evan lay there in silence, holding his breath.

30. All Is Not What It Seems

The key card for Evan's room read NO NEED TO BREAK IN. The hotel phone system's internal number included 1972, a subtle nod to the infamous date. Less subtle was Nixon's voice, squawking over the urinals in the public bathrooms.

In the last few decades, it seemed, the Watergate Hotel had gotten itself a sense of humor.

Some years back the place had been bought by a new group, overhauled, and made trendy cool. Even the staff uniforms had a retro flourish; the receptionist had breathlessly informed Evan that they'd been 'envisioned' by the designer from *Mad Men*.

Welcome to the new world of metascandals and entertainment news.

On the ground floor, an undulating copper wall flowed into a whiskey bar with a few thousand backlit bottles precision-lined on floor-to-ceiling shelves, casting an amber glow across sleek red armchairs and young K Streeters seeking company.

Sitting at a corner table with his laptop, Evan studied the photograph of the woman's body he'd taken from the dead drop.

He'd waited for hours inside that faux air duct until the museum resumed operations and he'd been pushed out the other end by an onslaught of middle-schoolers on a field trip. Downstairs in the gift shop, he'd bought an oversize sweatshirt that read ALL IS NOT WHAT IT SEEMS, a facial-hair disguise kit, and a baseball cap stating I WAS NEVER HERE. In a bathroom stall, he applied a mustache and repositioned his backpack, wearing it in front under the roomy sweatshirt, where it bulged like a gut.

As he exited the museum, he'd thought, *Thanks for the memories.*

He'd gotten himself underground and onto the Metro as quickly as possible, acquiring a limp on his way. Police officers remained out in numbers, but he was just another overweight tourist shuffling by.

Once he was safely out of the city center, he'd made a stop to acquire a few items at Home Depot. The clerk had barely glanced at him as she'd rung him up, tapping the register slowly, careful not to snap her fake nails. After wondering if the consumers who'd come before him had endured the service with more patience, he'd taken his bag and waddled back to the train.

It had been a peaceful ride to Foggy Bottom.

A waiter drifted over now wearing a soul patch and a disaffected glower. Evan supposed that serving marked-up bourbon to lobbyists night in and night out might elicit a sour expression.

He placed the photograph facedown on the table. 'Do you have any vodka?'

'Whiskey,' the waiter said. 'It's a whiskey bar. That's why we're called, like, the Next Whisky Bar.'

'I want vodka.'

'Vodka's at the Top of the Gate bar,' the guy said. 'You know, on the roof?'

Evan stared at him.

Tougher men than Soul Patch had found that intimidating.

The guy blinked twice. 'What kind would you like sent down, sir?'

Evan told him.

As soon as the waiter backpedaled, Evan turned the photograph over again. He typed the address and date into Google, clicked on NEWS.

A federal prosecutor and her husband, bludgeoned to death in their own home. They'd left behind a third-grader named Zeke. No witnesses, no evidence, no motive.

Evan lifted the photograph, stared at it closely.

The woman's long lashes were parted, her left eye undamaged. A beautiful brown iris flecked with yellow. Eyes that had looked at her husband through a wedding veil, had gazed down lovingly on a newborn.

None of that was relevant now.

The pupil was.

Enlarged from the trauma, a black orb.

A black, *reflective* orb.

A face image recovered from a reflection in a victim's eye was thirty thousand times smaller than an actual face.

Evan plugged his RoamZone into the laptop and uploaded the high-resolution photo he'd taken of the high-resolution photo.

He zoomed and depixelated, thinking that maybe Joey would be impressed with him. But probably not.

A figure came into view, the photographer standing over the corpse. Face, upper torso, camera held out to take the picture.

Fortunately, the camera blocked only part of his jaw. Evan zeroed in on the face, let the software do its work.

The eyes achieved clarity first. Then the nose. At last the mouth achieved crispness, removing all doubt.

Orphan A.

The waiter returned, and Evan lowered the screen of his laptop.

'I brought the Spirytus, sir. How would you like it served?'

The Polish-made spirit claimed the title of the world's highest-proof vodka at 192 proof, or 96 percent alcohol content. The strongest booze on the US market, it had arrived here only after Eastern European communities from Brighton Beach to Sheepshead Bay had lobbied the New York State Liquor Authority.

By comparison, rubbing alcohol came in at 91 percent.

Evan said, 'I'll take the bottle.'

In honor of the hotel's notorious past, Evan elected to stay in Room 314.

Under the same false name, he'd booked a few other suites that could, in the event of a raid, serve the same purpose as President Bennett's dummy limousines.

The view was spectacular. The building's curving avant-garde architecture mirrored the flow of the Potomac, Evan's balcony looking across the slate-blue river at Theodore Roosevelt Island. To the south he could catch the edge of the JFK Center for the Performing Arts, a blocky rise set behind a respectable fringe of greenery.

But he wasn't focused on the view now.

He was focused on what he was mixing in the ice bucket. For an oxidizer he used pool chlorine in the form of powdered crystals. For fuel, superfine 600-mesh powdered aluminum – a common paint mixture that added surface shine.

Spirytus vodka was the last part of the explosive cocktail.

The high-proof liquor turned the concoction into a slurry,

keeping the compound stable, safer to handle, less suscep-
tible to static and percussion.

And it was good to drink.

He took another sip now, let it blaze its way down his food
pipe. Even on the rocks, it was an angry beverage, a longtime favorite of Siberian pilots, which was worrying for more
reasons than he cared to reflect on.

Once the slurry gooed up into formable shape, Evan
packed it into a foot-and-a-half length of tubular nylon, using
a wooden spoon to avoid any sparks.

He wound the nylon into a circle and left it on the table to
set. The alcohol would evaporate quickly as the compound
hardened, making it more sensitive. A simple electric blasting cap and a cell-phone initiator would take care of the
rest. When the time came, it would be like striking a match.

But sped up ten thousand times.

Evan crossed to the balcony and stared out at the water
sweeping by, a ceaseless current that stopped for nothing
and no one.

He thought about a third-grader named Zeke getting
pulled out of school by a social worker. What had the first
few days of being orphaned been like for him? Was he racked
with gut-searing grief? Or was he still lost in the concussive
aftermath of shock, his mind mercifully holding reality at
bay, letting it seep in a drop at a time? This would become
his story now: *When I was eight, my parents were murdered.*

Evan went back inside to his laptop and called up his
e-mail.

In the Drafts folder, he typed: *'Update?'*

A moment later the unsent e-mail refreshed: *'still nothing.
take a chill pill, mr patience.'*

Resting on the table to his right was the eight-by-ten of

the bludgeoned woman. A photograph left to confirm a murder likely ordered by Bennett and augmented by Wetzel. He thought about Wetzel driving out of his condo building, coasting away in a bubble of privilege.

He typed: *'What do you know about the Tesla S?'*

A moment later the draft e-mail updated with a single word: *'everything.'*

31. Strategic Planning Meeting

It was the neckties that got to him.

Small price to pay for proximity to the throne, but still, Doug Wetzel would have given his left nut to wear baggy jeans and a ratty Guster T-shirt from his college days.

Driving home from 1600 Penn, he loosened the knot at his throat and nudged the air-conditioning up another notch. This afternoon's strategic planning meeting had been unending, the president demanding that the army hold joint military exercises with India near the Chinese border as a response to Sino-Pakistan drills planned for next week. The Joint Chiefs were split and the debate at a low boil, but the president was decisive as always, issuing directives without breaking a sweat or elevating his voice.

When the president spoke, five hundred combined years of experience shut up, leaned in, and took orders.

Police cordons were still in effect, shutting down several blocks east of 14th, so Wetzel shot north up Connecticut and then cut off onto side streets to dodge traffic.

DC at night had a particular savage gleam, red taillights piercing through gloom, dingy alleys bookending martini-lounge hustle-bustle. And yet another realm hovered above in an angelic glow, the eye called to uplit white marble monuments, to rounded domes and thrusting peaks, to glowing penthouses floating above streets as dark as puddles. Everything that rose seemed to be mirrored in descent, the reflecting pool and the cool Potomac like portals to an underworld.

Wetzel had read somewhere that Hollywood directors liked to hose down streets to make the asphalt sparkle on film. Washington was like that naturally, a black-ice kind of town – lose focus and you'd slip and break your neck.

Earlier Naomi Templeton had briefed him on the day's events. She'd hinted around a dead drop at his building, but he didn't take the bait. He'd endured a stream of direct questions from her as well before shutting her down to get back to the business of governing.

He wasn't going home now, that much was certain, not after Orphan X had shown up in his lobby. He'd texted Orphan A from the disposable phone, requesting a meet in a dive bar in Tenleytown, a safe distance from the heated center of the city. After he powwowed with Orphan A, he'd return to the White House and sleep soundly in a guest room inside the fortress.

He passed an abandoned auto shop now, its windows boarded up. On the plywood someone had spray-painted I VOTED FOR BENNETT, AND ALL I GOT WAS THIS LOUSY DEMAGOGUE!

At a red light, Wetzel dialed the disposable phone for the third time in the past ten minutes. This time it rang.

A gruff voice answered, 'A.'

'Did you get my text? Where the fuck have you been?'

Orphan A said, 'Preparing.'

'We've had an incident,' Wetzel told him.

'I saw the news.'

'You think he followed you to my place? You think he's onto you?'

'"Onto me" doesn't happen. But I'm getting onto him. I called your hook at the DoD, had him run some scenarios for me. That correlative software shit you types are always on about.'

The light changed, and Wetzel accelerated off the line. 'Please elaborate.'

'You came to me because I think like him,' Orphan A said. 'So. If it was me, I'd set up safely outside the White House surveillance apparatus but close enough to be within striking distance. I'm thinking three to ten klicks out. Short-term condo rental or hotel, Metro and freeway access within a block. If a condo, it'll have an attached parking garage. If a hotel, he checked in with a rental car. I told your man to put the data in the genie lamp and tell me what comes out.'

'Fine. In the meantime, I need to see you.'

'Boy, aren't you paying attention? You're not safe to be in the world.'

Wetzel tried to swallow, but his throat gave only a dry click. He eyed the rearview, taking in the empty streets. Steam floated up from a sewer grate, wisps unfurling like tentacles. 'What's that supposed to mean?'

'If I was Orphan X, I wouldn't be watching the president. I'd be watching *you*.'

Sweat ran down the side of Wetzel's neck. He loosened his tie a bit more, unbuttoned his shirt's top button.

He wasn't sure what happened next, but he heard a screech of tires – his own – and his face smacked the top of the steering wheel. He pushed himself off, feeling a warm trickle ford his upper lip. He smelled iron and burned brake pads.

The phone had wound up somewhere on the dashboard. His briefcase had flown from the passenger seat and landed on the floor mat.

He gave the brake an exploratory tap, but it was still depressed.

Then his windshield wipers went on, scraping dryly across the glass.

He reached for the door, but it stayed locked.

At once the Tesla reversed, so fast that he had to brace against the steering wheel with his forearms, eliciting a baleful honk.

The Tesla spun around, smacking his head against the driver's-side window, the wheel spinning of its own accord. Driving itself, the car eased through a laid-open chain-link gate and coasted into the shadows in the far reaches of the dilapidated auto shop.

It stopped, shifting itself into park.

Dots clouding his vision, Wetzel white-knuckled the steering wheel, his hands quivering. He tried to shift gears, but the car wouldn't obey.

His thoughts roiled, a paranoid flurry. Someone had *hacked* his car?

The familiar hum made him start, a waft of night-cool breeze blowing across his face. His window had rolled down. He turned to look out and spotted a dark figure in the shadows no more than five feet away, sitting on the side steps that led to the old auto shop's office. The man was lit faintly by the glow of a laptop resting on the uneven wooden plank beside him. He removed his hands from the keys as if relinquishing a joystick.

The sweat seemed to freeze on Wetzel's face.

The figure rose.

Wetzel scrunched his eyes shut, a long-buried childish impulse. He heard the crunch of a footstep and then another.

He opened his eyes. The man was standing right there, the top of the window frame cutting him off above the chin.

A hand came at Wetzel's face, grabbed the lanyard around his neck, and tore the flash drive free. Next the disposable phone was plucked from the dashboard, the call presumably still active.

Wetzel watched the phone rise out of sight to the man's face.

The voice carried back to him. 'Orphan A,' it said. 'Wetzel first. Then everyone else who's helping you. Then you. Then *him.*'

Wetzel strangled a sob in his throat.

He heard the reply, tinny through the disposable phone. 'Not if I kill you first.'

The phone dropped to the ground. A heel crushed it into the asphalt.

The man leaned down, at last bringing his face into view.

'Hello, Doug,' Orphan X said. 'You and I need to have a talk.'

32. See Every Angle

Tonight's Class 3 threat was that Naomi's father was refusing to eat prunes.

Hank Templeton, legend of the Service and protector of presidents, was backed up from an array of meds and so far out of his right mind that he refused to cooperate with two nurses and the rounding physician. He shook his head back and forth like a child confronted with broccoli, grizzled lips clamped shut before the proffered prune.

Naomi had been called into her father's room, which smelled of urine and the too-strong detergent necessary for bedsheets in a facility like this. 'Dad, you have to –'

Hank knocked the prune out of her hand with his bone-lumpy knuckles. 'No, goddamn it. Where's Jason?'

'He's not here, Dad. It's just me.'

'Where's Robbie? Where are my sons? I need someone who can get something done around here.' His pronounced eyebrows bunched, his face set with familiar New England obstinacy.

A nurse unknown to Naomi leaned her father forward and started to untie his gown to change him. Naomi looked away. For her modesty or his? Clearly he didn't care. Fenway nuzzled into her side, wet nose in her palm.

Naomi took a step back, gathered her bangs in a fist, squeezed hard enough to feel the hair pull at the roots. She kept her eyes on the floor. 'Okay, Dad. Look, I brought Fenway. Do you want to see . . .'

Her voice went dry, and she lost the back half of the sentence.

Amanaki suddenly was at her side. 'I got it from here, honey. Why don't you take a moment?'

Not trusting her voice, Naomi nodded and relinquished the leash.

In the hall she called Jason and got voice mail. But she reached Robbie. In the background she could hear the sound of a family dinner in full swing.

'Hi, Nay-Nay,' he said.

'Robbie.' She pressed a knuckle to her lips. There was no crying in the Templeton family. 'I'm with Dad. I could really use your help.'

'Jesus, Naomi.' The full name now. 'I'm sending, what? Four grand a month? I have two kids in private school and –'

'Not money. Just someone else *here*. I'm dealing with . . . I have a thing at work and trying to manage that and Dad is a lot. Plus, you should see him. You should just see him.'

'Dad doesn't recognize anyone. He doesn't know who the hell we are anymore.'

'I don't need you to tell me that.'

'Maybe you do, okay? Because the way you frame it, to try and guilt me into dropping everything for *Dad*, it's bullshit. If you thought about it, you'd realize – you don't want me there for him. You want me there for you.'

She felt it then, a blowtorch flame of anger cutting through the grief. 'No, Robbie. It's so that when *you're* lying in a bed like . . . like a remnant of who you were, you can look back and not be embarrassed by how you acted when he needed you.'

'That's the thing. He doesn't need me. Never did. He never needed any of us.'

'Be a man,' she said. 'Not a child.'

She hung up and walked down the corridor, her head hot and thrumming. She sat on the plastic-cushioned chair, a shade of aqua not found outside waiting rooms, and tilted her face into her hands.

When had men gotten so small?

Her father, for all his flaws, had been forthright and loyal, shouldering responsibility and adhering to his own strict code. He'd always shown up, even when it was hard. *Especially* when it was hard.

It was difficult to square who he'd been with the boy-men her brothers were – let alone the dude-bros on the open market. Guys who were overmanicured and body-sprayed, who talked about little beyond microbrews and college basketball, who thought texting 'SUP? at booty-call hours constituted witty repartee. She replied the same every time: SERIOUSLY?

Her last date had been months ago, procured through one of the less-gropey dating apps. 'Wellesley,' he'd said over pork-belly sliders. 'Isn't that, like, a girls' college with no men?'

'No,' she'd said. 'It's, like, a women's college with no boys.'

She recalled the furrowing of his brow, more confusion than offense.

'Oh,' he'd said.

Like her, they'd been raised on YouTube and swipe-right screens. On every billboard and music video, there was the unattainable fantasy, curated personalities, skin smooth and shiny, glammed up and spray-tanned, and she knew it was all fake, a media creation or whatever, but it was still effective, still teasing some high-school not-belonging part of her. That was even more infuriating: to know it was a lie but to want to believe in it anyway.

To dive into that not-world and live there instead of inside a life of death and decay, of assassins probing for weaknesses and early-onset diseases that ravaged body and mind.

She wondered how it would have been to live back when there were real men like her father was, or like he *used to* be, real men who took care of themselves and took care of others and, yes – took care of the women in their lives, too.

What would it be like to have that comfort? To live in a real house with someone else instead of in a walk-up with a hand-me-down bed and an IKEA bookcase with lots of little-used consonants, named after a meatball.

A gravelly voice cut through her thoughts. 'Visiting your mother or your father?'

She lifted her head. An ancient gentleman, back domed like a turtle shell, had perched on the chair beside her. An oxygen tube fed his nose.

'My dad.'

'I'm sorry,' he said.

'Thank you. Me, too.' She took a breath. 'He's not . . . He can't tell what's going on anymore. Which I guess is ironic. He used to see every angle, everything coming down the pipeline. But he never could see what was right in front of him.'

Only in hindsight did she register her words as self-pitying.

The man gave a sage nod. 'It's funny how it goes.'

They weathered a momentary silence that was neither comfortable nor awkward. He fingered the oxygen tube, caught her watching his pruned fingers.

'When you're a kid,' he said, 'time lasts forever. You're immortal. When your grandparents die, it's not real. Not yet. Then your parents go, and . . . well, it's like there's no more insurance. You're next in line. You're that guy!' He laughed.

'The last one standing. The one everyone wants to make sure to see at Christmas, because you never know. You never know. I can see them grieving me even while I'm still here. And there's a comfort in that. A love. So maybe that's what you're giving your father by being here. Even if he doesn't know it in his brain, he knows it in his cells.'

Her throat was dry, and her eyes burned. She folded her hands, staring down at the ridgeline of her knuckles.

The man said, 'What?'

She cleared her throat. 'The mourning, it sucks, yeah, but no one tells you . . .'

He kept his gaze steady on her.

She forced out the words. 'No one tells you how hard it is not to get resentful.'

'Accept it,' he said. 'If you accept life, you accept all its rich, awful complexities. Because if you think about it, what's the alternative?'

She thought of pork-belly sliders and dude-bros thumbing their phones over dinner and the sweet bullshit promise of demo-targeted advertising.

She took the man's hand, skin draped over bone. 'Thank you.'

In her pocket her Boeing Black phone dinged with a text. Then another. A third and fourth on its heels.

And then it started ringing.

Alarm asserted itself in her chest as she stood and fished the phone from her pocket. 'Sir, will you please tell Amanaki to keep the dog for me?'

She didn't make out his reply.

She was already reading the screen, running for the door.

33. Big, Boomy Reds

Doug Wetzel stumbled up to the northwest gate of the White House, his face so ruddy and flushed it looked almost rubbery. As he reached the guardhouse, he thumbed the white button on the intercom and announced himself in a shaky voice.

The front gate rolled open.

He stepped into the embrace of the sally-port pen, credentials held aloft in a trembling hand.

Before he could approach the slot in the bulletproof glass, one of the Uniformed Division officers keyed to him, the voice made tinny by the speaker box. 'What's wrong? What's wrong?'

Wetzel broke, sobbing openly, saliva gumming at the corners of his mouth.

He tilted back his head, the well-trimmed beard lifting to show what had been secured around his neck.

A bomb collar made of tubular nylon.

'Hands! Hands! Don't move! Don't move!'

An emergency-response team materialized instantly out of the night fog.

As Wetzel spread his arms, his jacket pulled open and the duct tape ringed around his torso came visible, securing not explosive charges but manila files from his own briefcase.

A photograph pinned to his hated tie showed a federal prosecutor lying in a pool of her own blood in her foyer.

'Please God,' Wetzel said. 'Can anyone help me?'

President Bennett tipped back his big-bowled sommelier's glass and took a considered sip of Château Lafite Rothschild. He liked big, boomy reds – deep-throated burgundies and earthy bordeaux.

He enjoyed the moment of glorious aloneness in the West Sitting Hall, elaborate chandelier dimmed, the famous half-moon window an elegant portal to the night sky.

He had a full day tomorrow. Morning briefing, fifty-five minutes of world-leader calls, physician check-in regarding A-fib and blood draw, eye and vision examination if time permitted, bipartisan delegation for a foreign-policy meeting, tailor measurements for a new rack of suits, speechwriter meeting in the Oval, lunch with senior advisers, drop-by of counsel's office staff meeting, informal powwow with the secretary of state, a thrice-delayed photo with the NCAA Championship Wolverines, a Situation Room briefing, the daily wrap-up with the chief of staff, and then maybe – in the brief window between when Europe went to sleep and before the East woke up – a swim in Jerry Ford's pool.

The footsteps against the plush carpet were soft and soothing, but they portended bad news.

His assistant secretary moved toward him, lipsticked mouth trembling against her porcelain skin.

He set down his wineglass and stood.

The president assembled with a few staff members in the West Wing Situation Room, where he watched a live feed of the bunker where Doug Wetzel had been secured.

Wetzel stood alone, stark against the concrete walls, broad shoulders hunched. Though he'd run out of tears, he was keening hoarsely.

The emergency-response team had acted quickly to

contain the problem. Keeping a safe standoff distance from Wetzel, they'd steered him away from any public sight lines, marching him across the North Lawn. He'd kept twenty paces ahead of them, arms held wide, a prisoner walking to his execution. Following their shouted commands, he'd locked himself in a bomb-shelter room in the rear of the bunker, two blast layers removed from the world.

Over the high-def feed, Bennett could hear the ERT leader's voice through the door: *Take off your jacket!*

Wetzel squirmed out of the jacket, let it fall to the floor.

Arms wide! Raise your chin!

Wetzel complied, giving a good view of the files strapped to his body and the collar tight against his neck.

Bennett spoke into the starfish-shaped speakerphone unit. 'Doug. Calm down. Catch your breath.'

Wetzel was hyperventilating, chest seizing, head jittering. '. . . trying.'

'What does Orphan X want?'

Wetzel said something, the words blurred over a sob.

Bennett stood and neared the large screen, confronting Wetzel's life-size image. It was just like standing in the same room with him. 'What?' Bennett said. 'I can't understand you.'

Wetzel jerked in a few breaths. '. . . wants you . . . to see this.'

As the explosion came through the speakers, Bennett jolted back from the screen, banging his hip against the table's edge.

His palm had come up to cover his mouth.

On-screen, singed bits of paper fluttered in the air.

It was hard to look at the mess on the floor but harder *not* to look at it.

The secretary was neither screaming nor crying, but the

noises escaping her were an awful hybrid of both. To her credit, she'd kept her feet.

The other staffers were sunk into their chairs, pale, faces drawn. To a one, their blink rates had picked up – were it not for that, they would've looked like mannequins.

On the screen the bomb-shelter door swung inward, the team pouring in.

Bennett lowered his hand from his mouth. He noticed that he was still in a protective crouch and drew himself upright.

He gave a wave that was feebler than he would have liked, and someone cut the feed.

34. Mr Patience

Evan arrived back in his room at the Watergate, locked the door behind him, and threw the swing-bar guard. Setting down his backpack, he tilted his face to the ceiling and exhaled.

His neck had knotted up, and his hands smelled of chlorine and high-proof vodka.

Removing his laptop from the backpack, he logged in to his e-mail, opened his Drafts folder, and typed: *'Update?'*

He started to walk away, hesitated, then returned and signed the unsent note.

'– Mr Patience.'

That almost made him smile.

He passed through the wide door into the spa-like embrace of the marble bathroom, forgoing the freestanding bathtub for a punishingly hot shower. Setting both hands on the tile, he leaned into the powerful stream, letting the jets pound against his crown.

Wetzel had told Evan everything he knew, some of which Evan already knew himself. That Orphan A had been set on his trail. That A had recruited a death squad of down-and-dirty ringers headed up by two convicts, Ricky and Wade Collins. That once they killed Evan, they were going to track down and neutralize the remaining Orphans. That President Bennett was eliminating any trace of Evan's 1997 mission. When pressed – and Evan had pressed Wetzel in a fashion that would have produced results – Wetzel had no specifics about why the mission was so menacing to Bennett.

Whatever the secret was, Bennett couldn't even trust it to his own deputy chief of staff.

Evan turned off the shower, dressed, sat at the desk, and refreshed the screen.

Joey's reply was waiting: *'we're in.'*

A chill rippled across his back, his skin tightening. It wasn't a thrill so much as a predatory focus, the whiff of prey in the wind.

Beneath her two-word reply was a series of links.

He clicked.

All of a sudden, he was looking at the inner workings of the Secret Service, prized data and classified intel, private squabbles and dirty laundry.

It took him ten minutes to orient within the private network, another ten to start identifying areas of interest.

First he ran through the travel logs. President Bennett's schedule was in a state of upheaval; clearly there'd been a directive to move as many engagements and meetings around as close to scheduled dates as possible. The commitments were endless, more than Evan could review now, but he scanned them, searching for events that seemed difficult to reschedule.

Mid-September showed a promising fund-raiser in Los Angeles with the mayor and the senior state senator, mere miles from Evan's penthouse. But two months was a long time to wait, and there was no guarantee that the reception wouldn't be delayed or canceled.

Evan scrolled through other upcoming trips, assuming that catching the protection detail off their home turf would be easier. But the more he read, the more he realized that was not the case.

On domestic trips President Bennett was accompanied by more than three hundred civilian and military personnel, the ranks swelling to nearly a thousand for OCONUS forays. An advance team stacked with lead agents, transportation agents, countersurveillance agents, airport agents, event-site agents, Tech Security agents, intel agents, and a military comms team locked down every transition point and venue ahead of time. The Secret Service flew all equipment and vehicles, including Cadillac One, on C-130 cargo planes to ensure they wouldn't be tampered with. The gear was guarded around the clock, ready and waiting the moment Air Force One landed. At that point a working shift swung into effect as well, a whip directing a dozen agents and body men, backed by a counterassault team. Along the route safe houses were designated at regular intervals, spaced between hospitals and law-enforcement strongholds. At all times the president wore Level III flexible body armor made of synthetic fiber, fifteen hundred filaments per strand of yarn.

Evan had a backpack and a change of underwear.

If the president stayed in a hotel, the Secret Service booked the entire floor – and the floors above and below. Every room, every item in every room, and every square inch of carpet was swept and physically examined for surveillance devices, hidden explosives, and radioactivity. Multiple escape routes were charted. An elevator repairman remained on site to respond to irregularities. Every employee in the hotel received a thorough vetting and background check. Those with priors were given the day off; those without were ordered to wear color-coded pins. Food suppliers and delivery companies were checked in similar fashion. Secret Service agents stood posts in the kitchen, monitoring the chefs, sous-chefs, and waitstaff during all stages of food preparation. The agents waited until dishes were prepared and then selected plates at random for Bennett. Sporadically, the hotel kitchen was side-stepped entirely, a navy steward brought in to prepare the president's dishes.

Evan had a Baggie of leftover pool chlorine and a half bottle of high-proof vodka.

He dove deeper into the Secret Service databases, now focusing on White House security procedures. The water-purification system was tested semimonthly, Tech Security experts procuring a sample from every faucet and tap. The president had a weekly physical and bloodwork check, his robust medical file updated constantly. X-rays and MRIs could be provided on site, and peripheral health needs – optometry, pharmacy, and orthotics – were provided by specified outside contractors whose backgrounds, procedures, and operations had endured the full scrutiny of the Service. Food vendors, too, had been vetted within an inch of their lives, shipment records showing the president's dining proclivities. Receptions and state dinners were handled by one of three caterers, able to produce two thousand pounds of shrimp, five hundred bourbon-glazed Virginia hams, and a few hundred gallons of iced tea at a few hours' notice. Bennett's triweekly workout sessions with a trainer in the West Wing gym dotted his schedule, along with evening swims in the pool, but a glance at the past month showed frequent cancellations. Only cleared manufacturers could provide exercise equipment and pool chemicals; only approved janitors could service the facilities. All tailoring occurred inside the White House, with the textiles, thread, buttons, and zippers given rigorous scrutiny.

Evan had a laptop and a fake ID.

He rubbed his eyes, feeling uncharacteristically over-matched. He was a guy in a hotel room contending with all the protections that the Secret Service's $1.4 billion annual appropriation could buy Jonathan Bennett.

Evan gave himself three seconds to feel disheartened and then refocused on the databases, digging into the Service's response tactics and capabilities.

The best bet, it seemed, was targeting Bennett in DC but out of the White House. Which meant a motorcade assault. Evan read some of the operational procedures for the Uniformed Division countersnipers, who were issued .300 Win Mags and Stoner SR-25s. The training regs for Special Operations' counterassault team were even more rigorous, encompassing everything from close-quarters combat to ambush-defense tactics. CAT members operated in teams of six, a two-man element responding to the initial offensive while the others laid down heavy cover fire. They had a singular aim: suppress the attack long enough to give the president's limo time to get away. Clad in body armor and black BDUs, they wielded SIG P229s and full-auto SR-16s and carried flashbangs and smoke grenades.

When the time came, Evan vowed, it wouldn't be enough.

Determining that time, unfortunately, was the biggest problem of all. It was everything. Without a definitive advance-notice When and Where, he'd never even get to the starting gate.

A knot of frustration asserted itself at the base of his throat, and he closed his eyes, breathing it away. There were promises to keep and files to read before he slept, but he had to recharge or his effectiveness would dim.

He was about to shut down the laptop when his eye snagged on a red-tagged folder at the bottom of the highest-classification directory.

It was labeled x.

He hovered the mouse over it a moment, took a breath, and then opened it.

What he saw inside made him lean forward to bring his face closer to the screen.

Photos of his former foster home in East Baltimore. Various hangars at Fort Meade. Jack's farmhouse, the paint peeling, shingles worn through in patches. Naomi Templeton had ordered continuous sat footage on key locations in case Evan popped his head up. The file also contained a few fragments of operations past. A high-value target gone missing in Mogadishu in 1999. A questionable passport at the Al Karamah border crossing in 2005. A bloody fight on the Las Vegas Strip in 2015.

It was barely anything, but he was amazed they had assembled even that.

After another moment reviewing these fragments of his past, he powered down the laptop.

Removing everything from his backpack, he spread the few items out on the carpet and then repacked meticulously. His laptop slid into a padded pouch just beneath Peter's gift. He stowed Wetzel's flash drive in the back pocket. Though the intel files it held on the other Orphans were heavily redacted, they could still provide enough for Orphan A and his goons to pick up the scent. It was a sober reminder for Evan of the stakes should he fail.

Which meant failure was not an option.

He finished zipping up his belongings in the backpack. Traveling light meant he could depart on an instant's notice without leaving a trace.

He set the backpack on the foot of the mattress and lay on top of the goose-down comforter, fully clothed, boots tightly laced. Resting his left hand on his stomach, his right on his chest, he let his mind range over the incalculable number of safeguards and contingencies the Secret Service had erected around President Bennett.

Endless impediments, endless complications.

An idea nibbled at the back of his brain, expanding until he saw, sketched in his mind's eye, the rough outline of a plan. An insane, Hail Mary pass of a plan.

It was a start.

He mused on the impossibility of what lay before him until he fell asleep.

Sitting in the passenger seat bathed in darkness, Orphan A felt the sweat bead along his widow's peak.

Excitement.

That's what life had become for him now. All it held. A jungle cat's momentary thrill when the right kind of movement flickered across its visual field.

In the other seats, he could sense Wade and Ricky Collins and their cousins displacing a large quantity of air. The van was turned off, its lights killed, the interior laden with the smell of gun oil and hardware.

'Weapons check,' Holt said.

Various clinks and metallic clanks answered him.

Ricky's blocklike fists encircled the steering wheel. He wore a fully loaded grenade-carrier vest, camo design, over Kevlar body armor. The pockets covering the front of the vest were unsnapped, flaps raised for ready access to the safety-pin rings. He looked ready for an assault on the Ho Chi Minh Trail.

Ricky's brother and the five cousins had likewise gone militia chic, bedecking themselves in army-surplus offerings with fetishistic delight.

It was overboard, all right, but Holt was fine with that. They'd require overboard if they hoped to get X. Part of the Collinses' job was to loom large anyway. Ultimately they were decoys to draw X's attention so Holt could get the kill shot.

The hotel parking structure was dimly lit and sparsely attended, the van cloaked in shadow. Zeroing in on the Watergate had taken a hefty amount of computing power. The DoD had put Holt's hypotheticals through their magic machine, and it had spit out a reservation.

Though only one man had checked in, there were three rooms registered under the same name.

On the part of X, this was smart business. In case he had surveillance in place, Holt and his crew would have to hit all three rooms simultaneously. Divide to conquer.

The only benefit to splitting up was that it would make them less conspicuous. They wore trench coats that fastened at the belt to cover up the gear, but still, if the sight of two Collinses drew attention, seven would elicit widespread panic. They'd break into three teams and infiltrate the hotel through different entrances. Holt would float in a central location, at the ready to respond once the firefight broke out.

Twenty minutes earlier they'd driven unnoticed into the structure and taken the only spot available on the ground floor, in the southwest corner. Unfortunately, that pinned them in, the parking-attendant booth positioned between the van and both exits.

From the shadows they watched the attendant, a heavyset Hispanic man with bulges at the back of his neck. If the guy didn't exit the booth soon to take a bathroom break, Holt planned to call in a phony alert.

'Let's go,' Ricky hissed through his teeth, the words riding a tobacco-scented stream.

'Sure thing,' Holt said. 'We'll just clank out of the van and file past him, all eight of us in full battle rattle.'

'We got trench coats.'

'Have you *seen* you motherfuckers? Police response to this location averages seven minutes. Believe me, we're gonna need all seven. That countdown can't start till we engage X.'

'I don't need seven minutes to cap some bitch,' Wade said from the middle bench seat.

Holt lifted his eyes to the rearview, catching Wade's reflection in the green glow of an exit sign. His cheeks looked raw from shaving, a few nicks at the jawline.

'This isn't a fistfight behind a biker bar,' Holt said. 'If you know that, you might have a chance.'

'A chance at what?'

'Surviving.'

The parking attendant rose from his stool, stretched, and exited the booth.

'Finally,' Ricky said.

The man looked around and then pulled a pack of American Spirits from his sagging pants and started walking.

Directly toward the van.

'Shit,' Wade said. 'He's coming over here to sneak a smoke.'

'What do we do?' Ricky racked his SIG. 'Put him down?'

'It'll be loud,' Wade said. 'But worth it.'

'One in the chest, one in the head,' a cousin piped in. '*Pap-pap*. People'll think it's a car backfiring.'

Holt watched the attendant draw near. The guy had a brick-size radio clipped to his belt. One click of a button and they'd be looking at a whole new set of variables. Holt swept his gaze around the concrete structure, gauged the acoustics of a fired shot.

The attendant stopped a few yards from the van.

By unspoken accord Holt and the Collins crew stayed frozen in their seats.

The attendant tilted his head to light up, and in the flare of light, his name tag came visible: ERNESTO. He sucked in a lungful, leaned back, and dispensed a plume of smoke overhead.

In the rear row of the van, another Collins boy tightened his grip on his FN P90. He spoke quietly, a whisper through clenched teeth. 'I say we kick this shit off here, go full Benghazi. Take care of business hard and then run and gun straight for the three rooms.'

In his peripheral vision, Holt noted Ricky's hand on the door handle.

Ricky said, 'We go on my three.'

Moving his hand slowly, Holt opened the glove box. Inside rested the clawhammer.

'*One* . . .'

Ernesto's pivot felt inevitable, his gaze drawn to the pent-up energy emanating through the windshield. He looked at the van loaded with men and weaponry, his forehead furled with curiosity, not yet processing what his eyes were telling him.

'. . . *two* . . .'

Holt climbed out of the van and strode toward the man, spinning the hammer a half turn in his hand. Ernesto managed to say, 'Hey. Um . . . ?' before Holt clipped him beneath the chin on the rise.

When the deadweight hit the concrete floor, it sounded like a dropped sandbag.

Holt turned back to the van. 'Coming?'

35. Shadow and Shape and Nothing More

The door to 314 smashed inward, the latch assembly splintering the frame, the swing bar tearing the fastened bolt free.

Evan was airborne before he was fully awake, a lifetime of muscle memory moving him from horizontal to vertical. His consciousness caught up to his body an instant before his boots struck the floor, and he had a split second to contemplate why no one was charging the room when a small blur of movement from the doorway caught his focus.

A bouncing ball, thudding on the carpet once, twice, spinning to a stop in the dead center of the room.

Not a bouncing ball.

A frag grenade.

Evan bounded once, twice, clearing the threshold of the bathroom and diving for the bathtub.

He struck the cast-iron side hard, bucketing into the bottom as the floor heaved, accompanied by a rush of sound and heat. A metal-on-metal clang rocked the tub, the side studding in, black denting through the enameled white surface at the impact points.

Dust powdered the air, cut through with a torrent of sparks from a shattered ceiling light above. A buzz-saw whine filled Evan's head, his ears vibrating with a concussive roar.

He flipped over in the tub, shards from the blown-out light crunching beneath his elbows and shoulder blades.

Over the wavering white-noise rush, he heard a voice. 'The fuck is he? Is he here?'

'I thought I saw him.'

'Safe the bathroom, Carl. I'll go balcony.'

Footsteps thudded the floor, muted taps Evan registered as if he were underwater.

A gunshot shattered the shower enclosure, the pane giving way in strobe-light bursts thrown from the sparking wires.

A form cut through the pixelated air, pistol swinging down at the bathtub.

Evan reared up.

He caught Carl's gun hand at the wrist and hooked his other thumb so it rode the knuckle of Carl's trigger finger. Evan fired down twice, once through the meat of the thigh, once through the top of the foot.

Carl sagged forward, clutching Evan in a limp hug, howling in his ear. Over Carl's shoulder Evan spotted a massive figure pivoting back in from the balcony, phone raised to his mouth – Ricky Collins.

Evan hooked an arm around Carl, holding him upright, a two-hundred-plus-pound shield. Blood spurted from Carl's thigh, painting the wall beside them. Inches from Evan's cheek, the bellowing continued.

Evan couldn't hear Ricky, but he read his lips against the nighttime lights spilling in from outside – *Here, he's here!*

Ricky hoisted an FN P90, but there was no shooting Evan without shooting the slab of meat between them.

Evan released Carl, his hands blurring. In the instant before gravity caught up, Evan seized Carl's meaty forearm, firmed his clamp on the pistol, and drove the man's arm back through the resistance point of the elbow, hyperextending it ninety degrees.

Carl's scream reached operatic heights.

The barrel was now aimed directly behind Carl, his arm bent precisely the wrong way. Evan stayed behind the gun-turret safety of Carl's mass, chin resting on the ledge of the man's shoulder, their cheeks slapped together, faces pointing in opposite ways.

Evan jerked his thumb backward against Carl's trigger finger twice, firing the upside-down gun across the room at Ricky. The first shot missed, but the second clipped his shoulder, sending him in a half spin to the floor.

Carl fell away, the pistol spinning loose and clattering off into the darkness by the toilet. He reached weakly with both hands to clamp the arterial gush.

Evan stepped out of the bathtub, kicking Carl's right hand off the wound and grinding it into the shard-layered floor. Bones popped.

He'd be unable to stop the bleeding now.

Ricky rolled onto all fours as Evan darted through the ragged doorway into the main room. Ricky rose, yanking the FN P90 across his barrel chest, catching Evan in its wobbling sights.

The submachine gun purred, unleashing lead at a rate of 850 rounds per minute. Evan dove at Ricky, rolling over a shoulder, sensing the air vibrate around him, the wall disintegrating at his back.

He came up beneath the gun, driving it up, the barrel smacking Ricky's jaw before the weapon was knocked free.

But now he was in the grasp of the big man.

Ricky bear-hugged him, tilting back so Evan's boots lifted off the carpet. Without a base, Evan dangled ineffectively in the vise grip, his chest mashed to Ricky's vest, which looked to be laden with grenades, an explosive overlay to the Kevlar vest beneath.

Ricky drove his face forward, head-butting Evan.

Evan dipped his face, letting his forehead take the brunt, a clack of bone on bone. He crumpled, free-falling, and didn't realize he'd been laid flat until his head smacked against his backpack, blown onto the floor by the explosion.

Ricky readied to deliver a kick to Evan's face, and Evan scissored his legs, spinning around the pivot of his hip, hooking Ricky's planted ankle.

The leg sweep worked, knocked Ricky flat on his back beside Evan. Ricky hammered the bar of his forearm at Evan's face, Evan catching it just before it smashed the bridge of his nose.

Ricky followed with a kidney punch, the men grappling on the wreckage of the floor, planks poking up into them. The bullet wound at Ricky's shoulder didn't slow him at all.

The big man quickly got the upper hand, rolling on top of Evan. One sweaty palm shoved into Evan's jaw, twisting his head back so hard it felt as though it might pop off.

The excruciating upside-down perspective gave Evan a whirligig view across the room, the front door hanging crookedly from one remaining hinge.

A smaller man filled the frame, compact muscle and hunched build, silhouetted by light from the hall.

Orphan A.

The pressure on Evan's jaw intensified. Evan sensed Ricky draw back a fist. If he landed a direct punch, it was over.

Evan bucked, Ricky's palm slipping off his face.

For a suspended moment, Evan had both arms free. He grabbed blindly at Ricky's grenade-loaded vest, fingers spread, gathering safety-pin rings in both hands.

He caught a few and ripped them free.

Stunned, Ricky looked down at his vest, now studded with live grenades.

Evan flipped free, a grappling reversal. He knocked Ricky over, slapping him facedown into the crater of the floor. Then he rolled atop the big man and crouched with one knee planted between the impossibly broad shoulder blades.

He looked up at the doorway.

Orphan A's hands moved and produced a pistol, a picture-perfect shooting stance. He was backlit, shadow and shape and nothing more.

Evan's backpack rested an arm's length away. He grabbed it by a strap, hauled it into his gut, and curled over it.

The grenades detonated, the effect propagating as one after another caught.

Evan pressed himself into Ricky's back, shielded by two layers of the man's oversize Kevlar vest. Shrapnel flew up all around him, a cone of destruction, Evan in the eye of a man-made hurricane.

And then he was falling, the already damaged floor giving way entirely.

His stomach lurched as he tumbled into the void.

He rode what remained of Ricky down and hit the floor below with a wet thud.

A woman had backed herself against the headboard, clutching a sheet to her breasts as her panicked paramour stood at the nightstand, phone cord coiled around his bare ass.

Evan stood up, one leg buckling before he righted himself.

'Excuse me,' he said, and bolted for the sliding-glass door.

Raking aside the curtains, he threw the lock and shoved the door open. He glanced back at the blast hole in the ceiling in time to see Orphan A step into view.

Two muzzle flares lit Orphan A's face, rounds embedding in the floor at Evan's feet. The man holding the telephone screamed.

Evan stumbled across the threshold onto the balcony of 214, straddled the stone ledge, and looked around. The neighboring balcony was out of reach. If he jumped down, he'd risk shattering a leg or blowing out a knee on the service driveway running below. He glanced up the driveway's length, spotting a laundry truck as it rumbled away from a loading dock.

Already he could hear sirens on the breeze, not far away.

As Orphan A appeared on the balcony above, Evan let himself fall out of sight, gripping a stone post, his legs dangling.

A round grazed the ledge above, showering stone chips across his head.

Evan held, held, gauging the sound of the truck engine as it neared.

The box truck coasted underfoot, and Evan swung away from the balcony, falling five feet and landing lightly atop the cargo area.

He stood up, the breeze riffling his hair, and looked back. Before the truck banked around the building's curve, Orphan A came into view on the balcony above. He stared across the widening distance at Evan.

Evan stared back.

The laundry truck turned onto the main road, wiping Orphan A from sight.

36. What We're Not Dealing With

Chaos.

It was nearly impossible to focus amid the raised voices and overlapping arguments in the Oval. Bennett sat on the couch, leaning forward with his fingertips pressed together, taking in the crossfire. It was almost three in the morning, the air thick with stale breath and body heat.

His vice president was talking at him – or, more precisely, talking at the top of his head. Victoria Donahue-Carr had a grating voice to begin with, but it reached new heights of stridency now. '– been in a seventy-two-hour knife fight with the Committee on Oversight and Government Reform –'

Without moving he tuned his focus behind him to a heated debate taking place between his chief of staff and three senior advisers. '– have to get out ahead of the story on Wetzel to deflect –'

'– only going to add to questions about what the hell is –'

'– analysis on why Doug was targeted?'

Donahue-Carr's voice bored back in on the action. '– and believe me when I say, Jonathan, that I can't hold off that congressional subpoena another minute. This is no longer a question. Something has to give.'

'Quiet!'

The room silenced.

It was the first time Bennett had raised his voice since taking office.

'Everyone out,' he said quietly. 'Eva, bring in Naomi Templeton.'

Eva Wong snapped off a nod. The longtime special assistant to the president, Eva had hastily been promoted to fill Wetzel's shoes. Bennett couldn't trust her as much as he trusted Wetzel, but then again trust was illusory, a lie that weak men drew false comfort from. Relationships were about holding influence, the right cards, the reins.

Wetzel's murder had been a shot across the bow from X. It had the added benefit of cutting off Bennett from his most trusted man, isolating him further.

As the room emptied out, Naomi Templeton entered, blading her body as she moved against the current. The door sucked closed, and Bennett finally moved, pulling himself upright, knuckling his glasses back into place.

'The files strapped to Wetzel,' Templeton said, 'were lost in the explosion. We're down to ash. What were they?'

'You're not going to offer any niceties about Doug's passing?' Bennett asked.

Templeton sat on the facing couch from which Donahue-Carr had assailed him moments before. 'I'd prefer not to waste time,' she said.

Bennett nodded. 'I have no idea what files were strapped to him.'

'The few scraps that we recovered had redaction markings.'

He stared at her. She hadn't asked a question, so he didn't offer a response.

'I'm assuming that they have something to do with you,' she continued. 'Or else why send them onto White House grounds strapped to your deputy chief of staff?'

Bennett said, 'It appears clear that a would-be assassin

was hoping to smuggle in the bomb on Doug to get it within range of me.'

'We both know this wasn't an assassination attempt,' she said.

Bennett skewered her with eye contact. 'It appears clear that a would-be assassin was hoping to smuggle in the bomb on Doug to get it within range of me,' he told her again.

Her slender throat pulsed. She pursed her lips. Hesitated. Said, 'I understand.'

He softened his face, if barely. 'I'm glad we're clear.'

'How about the photograph pinned to Wetzel's tie?' she asked. 'The murdered prosecutor? My guys pulled a screen grab from the footage.'

'I assume Orphan X killed her and wanted us to know.'

'Why?' she asked.

'I gleaned from the briefing that she's had a long and storied career. Maybe she went after him or one of his interests in the past.'

He didn't like how Templeton was looking at him. 'You're implying,' he said, 'that Orphan X has some kind of information on me.'

'Or that he *believes* he does,' she said. 'We're clearly dealing with a highly paranoid suspect.'

He noted that she'd adjusted her tone to strike a careful note. They were talking beneath the words. His preferred kind of conversation.

'If he did have any information,' Bennett said, 'it would be classified at the highest level. Beyond your security clearance. Or anyone else's. The content needn't concern you.'

A hint of perspiration sparkled at her hairline. 'In this . . . scenario, why wouldn't he just release what he has to the press?'

'That's no longer good enough for him,' Bennett said. 'Theoretically. And, theoretically, he'd be uncomfortable leaving the matter in the hands of others. He'd have a healthy and justified respect for my ability to protect myself in the political arena.'

'So what's he telling you, then? With all this, the files?' Quickly, she added, 'Theoretically.'

'That he's gonna keep digging until he finds what he's looking for. And that he'll let the world know. After.'

She said, 'After he's killed you?'

Bennett moved his head up, down.

'To obliterate your reputation. Your legacy.'

'Yes,' Bennett said.

She exhaled. It seemed she'd been holding her breath.

'So,' he said. 'Do you understand what we're dealing with? And what we're *not* dealing with?'

'I do.'

'Thank you, Agent Templeton.'

He waited for her to exit.

The questions surrounding Wetzel's death could be deflected, yes, but Bennett was already taking incoming fire from enough fronts that his presidency was nearing a crisis point.

Crisis management, he'd learned, generally balanced on getting others to focus on a *different* crisis, one of his choosing. Bait and switch, sleight of hand, a gentle tap to send the news cycle into a different spin.

Phones were omnipresent at 1600 Pennsylvania Avenue, always within arm's reach. He leaned for the nearest table and dialed the assistant secretary.

Two minutes and thirty seconds later, Eva Wong appeared, pad and pen in hand, her razor-straight bangs cut high on her forehead. 'Mr President.'

'Tell the congressional committee that I will be happy to appear next week – *voluntarily*. There is no need for a subpoena, and there is not to *be* a subpoena or I will stonewall them for the next three and a half years. When's the press briefing announcing Doug's death?'

She fumbled through her stack to check. 'We have it at ten AM.'

'Hold another in the late afternoon regarding my cooperation with the committee. We need voters to know how obliging and transparent I am. That I'm eager to help them get to the bottom of this and to set the record straight. That there's no smoking gun here.'

She was scribbling notes furiously. 'Mr President, given the timing, a hearing could be –'

'Eva, I have the vice chair and five of nine committee members in my pocket. It's a dog and pony.'

He watched her attempt to digest this.

'But the vice president said –'

'What Victoria doesn't understand is that I've *also* been busy these past seventy-two hours.'

He stood to convey that Wong was dismissed. Still jotting notes, she took a few backward steps toward the door. 'Sorry,' she said. 'Just trying to keep up.'

'Don't worry,' he said, bestowing upon her a rare smile. 'You'll figure out how this works soon enough.'

37. My Business

Crouching outside the 24 Hour Fitness at the Sherman Oaks Galleria, Evan unscrewed the impostor outlet he'd installed three days prior. Though he'd flown a circuitous route home, he'd driven here straight from the airport in the inconspicuous Ford Taurus he used as one of his many backup vehicles.

He popped off the outlet's cover plate to access the microSD slot. After withdrawing the card, he sat on a metal bench by the elevator and accessed the footage on his laptop. He played it on 5x fast-forward, slowing down to look at particularly hulking men, of which there were quite a few. He focused on patrons only as they exited the gym, since that provided the best view of their forearms.

He was looking for those half-skull tattoos that Trevon had described.

It took him three-quarters of an hour to get a hit. A man pushed out through the gym's glass front doors wearing a deep-collar tank top torn down the sides to show off bulging lats. The shoulder straps were thin, stretched up over his traps, giving the shirt an oddly feminine vibe, like a bikini top designed to expose maximum flesh.

As the man lowered his arms and headed for the elevator, walking directly toward the hidden lens, the half-skull tattoos came clear.

Evan rewound until he spotted the man on his way *into* the gym and then checked the time stamp of his arrival: 3:57 PM.

On a hunch he zipped the footage forward to 3:50 the next afternoon. Sure enough, at 3:59 the same man appeared.

You don't build muscle like that without committing to a routine.

Evan pulled out his RoamZone and called Trevon Gaines. He answered right away. 'Hello?'

'Trevon. It's me. How are you doing?'

'I'm okay, thank you. How are you?'

Goal for the Day #3: *Ask a personal question when someone asks you one.*

'No,' Evan said. 'I actually mean how are you doing?'

'Oh. I'm awful. They made me take bereavement leave from work, but I don't like . . . um, I don't like when I can't go to work. And now I'm just sitting here at home trying not to think certain thoughts in my head. And I didn't get to fill out my shift reports and they're just sitting there at work all not-filled-out and we always do our job and do it well, but they won't let me come back for two whole weeks.'

'Did the cops talk to you?'

'Yeah. I did like you said. I didn't even have to act.'

'Okay. I'm going to text you a picture of a man.' Evan took a screen shot of the man and sent it. Over the line he heard the ding of the arriving text. 'I want you to tell me if he's Muscley One.'

'I don't . . . I don't want to look.'

'Trevon. I need you to look.'

'I'm too scared.'

Evan took a breath, held it. 'We don't cry and we don't feel sorry for ourself.'

He could hear Trevon breathing across the receiver. Then some rustling came over the line. 'That's –' His voice cracked. 'That's him.'

His terror was undeniable. What did it feel like to behold the face of a man who'd slaughtered every single person you cared about?

'Thank you, Trevon.'

'What are you gonna do to him?'

'You don't want to know that.'

Trevon said, 'Okay.'

Evan cut the connection.

It was a bit past two o'clock now, which gave him some time before Muscley One appeared.

At an athletics shop downstairs, Evan bought some workout gear. He went out to his car and changed.

In the privacy of the driver's seat, he took stock of his injuries. His cheek stung beneath his left eye, where he'd picked out a half dozen splinters that had embedded themselves there when he'd blasted through the floor of the Watergate room. The superficial cuts on his elbows had mostly healed, but one laceration hurt every time he bent his arm. He made a mental note to dig in it more later in case he'd missed a sliver of glass. After the firefight, he'd detoured on his way out of DC, executing a break-in at a key location. He was getting his pieces into position on the chessboard, one painstaking move at a time.

Refocusing, he fished in his backpack and came out with a metal case the size of a deck of playing cards. Inside were two dozen ovals of silicon composite film, each vacuum-sealed inside a glass tab that resembled a microscope slide.

The fingerprint adhesives.

He removed one.

He caught himself rubbing his eyes and realized how exhausted he was. Setting his internal alarm, he napped deeply for an hour and fifteen minutes and awoke refreshed.

Leaving the ARES 1911 behind in the glove box, he rode the escalators back up and picked the lock of a service door on the gym's lower level. Coming up the stairs, he pretended to stretch on the mats behind the check-in desk, giving him a clear view of the elevators through the glass front doors.

3:50.

Customers trickled in at intervals, pressing their index fingers to the print reader on the front counter. When the sensor blinked green, they passed inside.

After an eight-minute wait, the elevator doors parted, revealing Muscley One.

Evan walked briskly to the check-in desk. 'Hey, man,' he said to the sales associate. 'Someone just puked in the Jacuzzi in the locker room. It's a mess, and it looks like a fight might break out.'

'Shit.' The guy snatched up the phone, his voice issuing over the PA system. 'All personnel to the locker room.'

He hung up and hustled to the back.

Alone at the check-in counter, Evan pulled the glass slide from where he'd tucked it into his waistband. He cracked the seal, carefully removed the transparent fifty-micron film, and laid it across the fingerprint reader. Once exposed to air, the adhesive acted like candle wax; it had a thirty-second window to receive an impression before it hardened.

He sensed a big form looming behind him.

'C'mon, dude. Move it. You're taking all day.'

'Sorry,' Evan said, and stepped aside.

He pretended to tie his shoelaces while Muscley One pressed his finger to the sensor. The laser read his print through the transparent film, the green light clearing him to enter.

As Muscley One ambled away, Evan peeled the print from the reader, reversing it onto his own finger pad, where it

245

clung and hardened. He circled the counter quickly so that he was standing before the computer monitor.

Over the tops of the exercise machines, Evan sensed movement – the sales associate emerging from the rear hall, returning to his post.

Swinging the reader around, Evan pressed his appareled fingertip to the glass window. The green light came on again, the member identity popping up on the screen.

Bo Clague.

Beneath the photo, an address in Panorama City.

Bo Clague entered his house, stripping off his weight-lifting belt and hanging it on the coat hook by the front door. Shaking out his arms, he stepped through the foyer into the kitchen.

Evan sat at the breakfast table.

Bo halted, surprise flaring his wide-set eyes and then giving way to anger.

Evan said, 'Sit down.'

'Don't you fucking tell me what to do in my own house. You'd better have a gun. You'd better *pray* you have a gun.'

Bo's upper body was swollen from the workout, protruding muscle tapering in a V. Like most muscleheads, he favored vanity over fitness. Contrasted with the bulk of his torso, his slender legs looked like they belonged on another body.

That would prove useful.

Evan nudged a two-pound jug of whey protein aside with his knuckles. 'Do you know why people hit the floor when they're in pain?'

Bo's body stayed tense, but his head cocked. 'Motherfucker, *what?*'

'The vasovagal response. Strong emotional or physical

246

distress activates the vagus nerve, which in turn widens blood vessels. That reduces blood flow to the heart, which slows down the heart rate and impedes circulation to the head. Which in turn causes light-headedness and – that's right – fainting. You're probably wondering what evolutionary purpose is served by our bodies' having such an odd response.'

Bo blinked at him.

It did not look like that was what he was wondering at all.

'When you hit the floor, you're horizontal,' Evan said. 'So that increases blood flow to the brain again. Which in turn restores consciousness. Permit me to demonstrate.'

He stood and lobbed the jug of protein powder at Bo's face. When Bo reflexively caught it, Evan skip-stepped forward, chambering his right knee high to the side like a piston, and hammered his heel down and forward through Bo's woefully overloaded knee. The *dum tek* oblique kick blew the joint straight back, Bo's body crumbling.

The oversize torso slapped the linoleum, Bo momentarily unconscious.

Evan walked back to the table, pulled out the nearest chair, and took his seat again.

A few seconds later, Bo blinked back to life. He looked down at his ruined leg and gagged a little. Above the damage, his big hands encircled the thigh as if to choke it. His mouth was open, and he didn't seem capable of closing it.

Evan nodded at the chair he'd pulled out. 'Sit down.'

Bo dragged himself across the linoleum and pulled himself up onto the chair. He'd gone red, veins standing out in his forehead and throat. 'Who are you?'

'I'm a representative.'

'Okay.' Bo spread his hands on the surface of the table,

grabbing maximum surface area as if he were concerned about slipping off. 'Okay, my employer and I can work with that. We know there have been some irregularities. It can be worked out. Which supplier do you represent?'

'Trevon Gaines.'

Evan watched the flush drain slowly from Bo's face, leaving his lips with a bluish tinge.

'I want your employer's name. And I want the name of the other man, too. The one who helped you kill Trevon Gaines's family.'

'I can't . . .' Bo clung to the life raft of the table. 'You don't understand. You don't know what he'll do to me.'

'Will it be worse than what I'll do to you?'

'*Yes.*'

They sat a moment, two friends at a breakfast table.

'I understand you're scared,' Evan said. 'Let me fast-forward to one hour from now. Your other knee will be shattered. Both elbows. Your wrists. Every finger. Your jaw, broken so badly you'll be gagging on your own blood. Which will make it that much harder for you to choke out the names that you're going to give me anyway.' He leaned forward. 'I will get my answers. And you will die. The only question is, how do you want to spend the next hour?'

Bo bent his head down, nostrils flaring as he drew breath. 'Why do I have to die?'

'How many people did you kill at Trevon's mother's house?'

He closed his eyes. 'That was different.'

'Not to me.'

'That was business.'

'And this is my business.'

'Please, God.' Reality was dawning now. Bo palmed his

forehead, which had gone shiny with sweat. 'There's gotta be another way. Money. Something. I can set it right.'

'Seventeen dead. You ruined Trevon Gaines's life. You *terrorized* that young man.'

'It was my orders.'

Evan thought about Trevon's notepad with his goals for the day. The stuffed frog tucked in up to its chin. *It's all my fault.*

He stood. 'I'm done talking now.'

Bo bolted back in his chair, held up his hand. '*Okay*. Okay.'

He told Evan what he needed to know.

Afterward Evan walked over to the gas stove, flopped down the door, and turned it on high. He found a matchbook in one of the drawers, bent a matchstick around the front flap, and thumb-flicked it against the striker.

'Wait. Jesus Christ . . . you can't just – Motherfucker, *wait!*'

On his way to the door, Evan left the matchbook on the end of the counter, the stick burning down toward the rest of the pack, a makeshift fuse. Already the smell of gas laced the air.

Bo fell out of the chair and struck the floor with a yelp. Gritting his teeth, he started pulling himself arm over arm across the kitchen toward the matchbook.

Evan adjusted the pistol in his hip holster and walked out.

He crossed the street, got into his Taurus, and pulled away from the curb.

He'd gone half a block when he heard the boom.

38. As Long a Long Shot
As Ever There Was

Evan was in desperate need of vodka. Aside from the hour-and-fifteen-minute nap he'd grabbed in his car, he hadn't stopped moving in four days. Driving the speed limit south on the 405, he headed for a long-term-parking lot near LAX, where he'd changed out his truck for the Taurus. He never returned to Castle Heights after a leg of a mission without at least one vehicle switch.

He pictured the slender bottle of Tigre Blanc in his freezer, the smooth French wheat vodka a world apart from the Spirytus he'd utilized in DC to scorch his esophagus and to liberate Doug Wetzel's head from his body.

It was still early in the day, but given his travels Evan hadn't yet caught up to Pacific Standard Time. Half of his internal clock was set to East Coast time, while the other half readied itself for bed in Europe.

The soporific thrum of his tires across the asphalt was making his head nod. He was just reaching to blast the air-conditioning into his face when his RoamZone gave its distinctive ring.

The car's hands-free audio system pulled the incoming call through the dashboard, and Evan found himself confronting a mobile number he didn't recognize on the screen.

The Seventh Commandment decreed that he take only one mission at a time. His last client had already chosen Trevon Gaines, which meant that no one else should be calling the Nowhere Man's encrypted line.

He clicked to answer, hesitated, then said, 'Do you need my help?'

'No ...' The familiar feminine voice shattered through his grogginess like a mainlined hit of epinephrine. 'But you need mine.'

Over the past few years, Orphan V and Evan had tried to kill each other on numerous occasions. As elusive and deadly as Evan, Candy McClure had an array of specialties, among them making the bodies of her targets disappear. While defending himself, Evan had kicked her onto her own bottles of concentrated hydrofluoric acid, her back and shoulders taking the brunt of the damage.

She'd not forgotten that.

The past half year had brought Evan a number of revelations, among them an awareness that Candy's allegiances might have shifted away from the Program. The files on the flash drive he'd lifted from Doug Wetzel seemed to bear that out; she was now among the targets on the president's wish list.

Before making contact with Evan, she'd come to Los Angeles, a decent guess since a number of their run-ins had been in this city. She'd given a meet location and hung up before he could argue.

He parked a full ten blocks away and approached the destination cautiously, taking side streets and cutting through people eddied around gourmet-food trucks.

From the safety of a crowded sidewalk, he stared across Wilshire Boulevard at the entrance to the Los Angeles County Museum of Art. Restored streetlamps from the 1920s and '30s formed a large-scale assemblage in the front. The two-hundred-plus cast-iron lamps had been painted a flat gray and placed neatly on a tight grid. At dusk they imbued the air with a Hollywood glow, part dream, part drunken fantasy.

Patrons threaded among them now, a few unoriginal souls striking Gene Kelly poses for iPhone shots. Evan scanned the rooftops, the parked vehicles, the faces in the crowd. When he looked back at the forest of streetlamps, Candy was standing among them, perfectly motionless.

At first glance she was tough to identify, having changed her hair color and appearance yet again. She was masterful at drawing attention to her body – which was worth drawing attention to – and changing her carriage and posture. Today she wore a long-sleeved bodysuit top stretched tightly down into a pair of dark blue jeans. Half circles of skin showed at her hips where the leg holes pulled high above her thick leather belt. Black cowboy boots, dark glasses, glossy pink lipstick. Her hair, dyed a vibrant rose gold, hung down her back in a knotted rope, swaying like a horse's tail.

Everyone noticed her, yes. But she directed the eye in such a way that not one male or female observer would be able to recall her facial features with any detail.

Before revealing himself, Evan watched her, looking for any tell that she had backup in the area. It was impossible to read her eyes behind the dark shades, and her training was such that she was unlikely to supply any nonverbal cues.

He gave a final look around and stepped out from the cover of the crowd.

She picked him up as he was entering the crosswalk and turned away, casting a glance over her shoulder that in another context would have been seductive. He followed her inside, sidestepping museum visitors to keep her in view. She carved west from the entrance, and he came up behind her, close enough to hear the taps of her boots against the concrete.

They passed through the Sunday throng, children bicker-ing, parents grabbing sippy cups from beneath strollers, a foursome of flirty college kids huddling over a museum-campus map, giddy from the proximity. Evan kept part of his focus on Candy, the rest on the periphery. Orphans oper-ated in the shadows, navigating their way through the underbelly of the world everyone else lived in. But much of their work was also out in the wide open, their footprints invisible to everyone but conspiracy theorists and fellow intelligencers.

Ahead in the LACMA courtyard, a thick multitude of durable tubes fell from a raised steel grid, forming a pene-trable sculpture. A few kids spun inside the exhibit, arms spread, the yellow-lime hoses draping their arms and shoulders.

Candy stepped into the embrace of the piece, the tubes rustling and then shaping around her form like dense jungle vines. Evan followed her in, parting the way with bladed hands.

The hoses stretched up a full story, giving them heft, and they tugged at his face and chest as they billowed about him. The effect was whimsical and disorienting, like twining one-self in giant spaghetti.

Reading the car-wash oscillation of the tubes, he could discern Candy's shape ahead. They cat-and-moused their way through, and when Evan broke free of the curtain's edge, she was several paces ahead of him, veering for the Broad Contemporary Art building.

She passed a Japanese tour guide waving a telescopic flag, a janitor mopping up spilled coffee, a sign on a distinguished gold stand reading RAIN ROOM CLOSED FOR SCHEDULED MAINTENANCE.

As she brushed up against the janitor, Evan heard her drawl, ' 'Scuse me, sir.' When Evan passed the spilled coffee, the janitor was still staring after her in a daze.

Evan kept on her as she cut inside the lobby of the Broad. Spinning the janitor's keys around her index finger, she sidestepped the groups massing for the main exhibit and disappeared up the brief corridor leading to the Rain Room.

As Evan came around the corner, she was gone, but the key remained inserted into the lock, the laden ring beneath it still swaying. A placard on the door read IMMER-SIVE ENVIRONMENT.

He stepped forward, turned the key, and entered, already sliding his hand beneath his shirt to unholster his pistol.

Inside, it was raining, a perpetual downpour unleashed by what must have been a network of pump-fed ceiling tiles. The room was dark, lit only by a few pinprick spotlights. Rainfall echoed off the hard interior surfaces, cacophonous and hypnotic.

ARES raised, Evan edged forward, scanning the space. Before him a square of rain paused, clearing the way for him to step forward onto the metal-grate floor. He paused, enchanted, and then accepted the invitation to progress. As he did, the next tile ceased its output overhead, opening up a path. He had no time to contemplate the invisible sensors as he edged farther in, the storm parting for him.

Across the room, through overlapping sheets of falling water, he spotted her.

Her curvy form was backlit like something from an album cover, the pencil-thin streaks of water around her catching the sparse illumination irregularly, flickers of white. He couldn't see her face, and judging from the light spilling over his shoulder, she couldn't see his.

She shifted, and her gun hand came visible, raised like his, sighted on his face.

She stepped and paused to match his pace, the two of them spiraling to the center until they stood in a patch of broken downpour, the muzzles of their pistols paralleled.

They had circled each other for so many months that it seemed bizarre to be standing face-to-face at last. Over the years he had built her into something of his own making, and he knew that he represented something mythical to her, too, something bigger than what he was.

'I figured this was a nice spot,' she said. 'Romantic.'

The reverberation, he realized, had the benefit of drowning out any potential audio surveillance.

One side of her face intercepted the light, a crescent of smooth cheek, and he thought about the ravaged flesh of her back, burned beyond recognition.

'I like the cowgirl getup,' he said.

'Oh, this old thang?' She smiled. Her mouth was wider than most. 'I'm tired of waiting for you to come after me. And I'm not gonna spend the rest of my life looking over my shoulder. So we either have this conversation now or we kill each other.'

'What conversation?'

'What do you say we lower our pistols? If I was gonna shoot you, I would've done it the second you walked in the room. Like I said, I'm here to help you.'

'Hard to take you at your word,' he said. 'Given how many times you've tried to kill me in the past.'

'I know you stashed the girl in a boarding school in Lugano.'

All at once he was aware of the moisture in the air, the way his shirt clung to his body. It took everything he had to keep his expression impassive. 'Is that a threat?'

'God no,' she said. 'It's an offering. I'm the only one who knows she's alive, remember? I figured out *months* ago where you parked her. The secret's safe with me.'

He stared at her a beat longer. Then he eased back the hammer and lowered his pistol. For a moment he stared down the black bore of her gun. He saw her thinking about it.

A stray drop traced the edge of her temple. 'It's not like I've forgiven you or anything.'

He said, 'Not aware I asked.'

Finally she lowered her pistol as well. 'You're going after Bennett,' she said.

He gave a little nod.

Again with the smile. 'Revenge,' she said. 'It's a loser's game. You're better than that.'

'It's not just revenge,' he said.

'It's what's right.' Her tone held mockery.

'Yes. And to prevent what's still to come.'

'The list of targets,' she said. 'How many Orphans are left?'

He bit his lip. Around their umbrellaed dome, rain fell unremittingly, hammering the floor, making the metal tremble beneath his boots.

'How many?' she asked again.

'Nineteen. As soon as Bennett finishes with me, he moves on to them.'

'They're spies. Not innocents. You don't know them any more than you know the average guy on the street. You're a professional – or at least you were. When did you grow a conscience?'

Her tone was driven, and he found himself wondering whether she was arguing with him or with herself.

'I don't know,' he said. 'Somewhere along the way, it happened.'

'So you're gonna stop killing by killing.'

'Yes.'

'Doesn't that strike you as hypocritical?'

'Yes.'

'So why do it?'

He considered her question, the rain crashing down around them. 'It's the only thing I know how to do.'

She stared at him. He watched her chest rise and fall, the puff of condensation brought by each breath.

'Why do you want to help me?' he said.

'Because I'm one of those nineteen names,' she said.

Evan studied her closely, knew her to be lying. She cared about more than that, but her shifting morality didn't interest him.

'Once you take out Bennett,' she said, 'it's over. He's the head of the snake.'

He said, 'And?'

'You need another operator at your skill level.' She blinked innocently. 'Or better. And we all know there's only one of me out there. And afterward . . . who knows?' She licked a raindrop off her lips. 'Maybe you and I could move in together and have ninja babies.'

'House with a white picket fence.'

'Join a wine-of-the-month club. Buy a fucking Volvo.'

Evan holstered his ARES. 'No wine-of-the-month club, no Volvo. And no working together. I operate solo.'

'Never believe a man's first reaction,' she said. 'It's one of two rules I live by.'

'What's the other?'

'Nothing good ever comes of dating guys named Travis.'

He smirked, looked away.

She took a step closer, set a hand on his cheek. 'Oh,

sweetie,' she said. 'You're still in denial about what you're up against.' She turned his face until he was looking into her eyes. 'You'll never be able to pull this off by yourself.'

She lowered her hand and stepped back, the rain parting behind her and then resuming between their faces.

'You have the number I called you from,' she said. 'I'll be waiting for you to come to your senses.' She hesitated. 'Even with both of us, it's as long a long shot as ever there was.'

She eased away again, the rain thickening between them. One more step and the darkness enveloped her.

He stood listening to the pounding rain and his own beating heart.

39. A Method to the Madness

Furrows of rain clouds turned the sky into a field of gray. Evan stood between the Taurus and his Ford pickup on the top level of the long-term-parking complex, his head still humming from his encounter with Candy McClure. Her offer seemed to be legit, but there was a reason that the first of the Commandments proclaimed: *Assume nothing.*

Given her exceptional dangerousness, he couldn't trust his usual procedures to cover his tracks.

He had the rooftop to himself. Most travelers didn't want to leave their vehicles up here, exposed to the elements, especially when there were so many spots available on lower levels. And now was the midday lull between morning departures and afternoon arrivals.

He stripped naked, threw his clothes and boots into the back of the Taurus, and then dressed in an identical outfit, which he'd stored in the trunk. He transferred his backpack and everything else from the Taurus into the rectangular truck vaults installed over the bed of his F-150 pickup.

Then he took a hose and a gas can from the truck and suck-started a stream of gasoline from the Taurus's tank. When he had enough, he doused the car's seats and his clothes and lit them on fire.

He left the Taurus burning on the rooftop, sending a plume of black smoke up to join the charcoal sky.

He arrived back at Castle Heights without further incident and hustled across the lobby to catch the elevator as the doors closed. Too late, he picked up the scent of old-lady perfume, but his momentum carried him across the threshold next to the stubby and venomous Ida Rosenbaum of 6G.

She glowered up at him, her eyes pronounced behind her glasses.

He nodded at her. 'Ma'am.'

'Again with the ma'am.'

They rose a few floors in awkward silence, Evan gripping his backpack before him. He hoped his hands didn't smell too strongly of gasoline. Her nose twitched once and then again.

Before she could ask anything, he quickly diverted her. 'It's nice out today.'

Her painted eyebrows rose. 'Know what my Herb used to say, may he rest in peace?'

'No, ma'am.'

'That talking about the weather is dull enough. But to talk about the weather in Los Angeles? You have to be *pathologically* dull.'

'Copy that, ma'am.'

Mercifully, the elevator doors parted on the sixth floor and Mrs Rosenbaum shuffled out with an absence of alacrity that signaled either a hip condition or deep-seated passive-aggressiveness.

Evan exited on Mia's floor and removed the present he'd picked up for Peter in DC, still wrapped in brown paper from the gift shop.

As he neared the door of 12B, it occurred to him that he had nothing for Mia. Given that his last visit had wound up in her bed, was this poor form? He hesitated, finger extended to the doorbell, arguing with himself. It wasn't like he was empty-handed. But was a gift for Peter enough? Or did that make it more insulting that he had nothing for Mia? What did ordinary people do? A bouquet of roses? Chocolates? Both options seemed crass and vaguely humiliating, as if he took his cues from TV commercials.

He could elude half of DC's police force, but this is where he fell down: negotiating the nuances of everyday relationships. Nothing in his background or training had provided any guidance on how an actual second date went and whether he was supposed to show up with a heart-shaped box of fucking truffles.

He rang the bell. Waited.

No answer.

He was surprised at how much relief he felt. This would give him time to fall back, rethink his position, and strategize.

He removed a notepad from the backpack and jotted on the top sheet, *'Stopped by to say hi. Sorry I missed you. – Evan.'*

Direct, efficient, to the point. He had to play to his strengths.

He slotted the note in the crack above the doorknob and started walking back to the elevator. Then he stopped and dropped the backpack, frustrated.

Returning, he unfolded the note and wrote *'P.S. It was nice seeing you.'*

He scowled at the bland addition. That sounded nothing like him. He crumpled up the sheet, re-created the first note, and left before he could rethink his position again.

Upstairs, he put away his gear and then settled into a cross-legged pose on the Turkish area rug in the great room. He veiled his eyes, holding them not entirely open or closed, letting the room turn into a blur. He sensed the weight of his body, the complaints of his sore muscles. And he listened to the sound of his breath through his nose, the hiss of air from a distant vent, the hum of the Sub-Zero way across in the kitchen. His body felt warm, sweat beading on his forehead, the old scar in his stomach pulsing with a faint heat. The aim was to feel his body as if for the first time. To enter this moment as if only this moment existed.

He was alert and relaxed. They weren't opposites, not exactly. They were two opposing forces that held him steady in the center, the wave line of the yin-yang. A perfect balance, one foot in either domain, the eyes of the tadpoles.

He breathed and breathed some more.

An image sailed into the haze of his meditation. The naked Ukrainian girl, no more than fifteen years old, standing in the office doorway of an abandoned textile factory. Her haunted eyes, the skin around them black with toxins. The filthy mattress on the floor behind her. A metal cup and plate.

All those years ago, Evan had killed the Estonian gun dealer and left her with a cigar box stuffed with currency.

Could he have done more?

His eyes were open now, fully open. Rising, he headed to the nearest workout station.

It seemed he'd lost his stomach for meditation.

In the Vault, Evan had President Bennett's schedule projected onto three walls. He pored over convoy routes, upcoming events, and travel logs. Then he analyzed the schedule changes to see if there was a method to the madness, but there was none that he could discern.

Sighing, he cocked back in his chair. From her bowl of glass pebbles, Vera II looked at him, clearly unimpressed.

'I'll figure it out,' he told her.

She stared at him some more, smugly photosynthesizing.

'Okay,' he said. 'You want to see some headway?'

He minimized all the projected windows from the Secret Service private network, cracked his knuckles, and switched tracks, refocusing on the Nowhere Man mission. He'd gotten two names out of the musclehead.

Terrance DeGraw, aka Raw One, was the other man who'd helped exterminate Trevon Gaines's extended family. An address and a rap sheet filled with priors was quickly forthcoming.

DeGraw would get a visit soon.

But right now Evan was focused on the kingpin.

Russell Gadds.

Evan called up Gadds's booking photo and slid it onto the opposite wall so the giant face stared back at him.

Trevon Gaines had nicknamed the man well.

Gadds had a thick, doughy nose, extra meat around the flanges, his cheeks textured with pronounced pores. A thick tousle of shiny black curls hung over his forehead. His lips were too pink and too moist, almost beaklike. They might have looked sensuous on another face. He was striking and ugly, and yet there was a virile handsomeness to him. He made a forceful impression, as forceful men often did.

Building a picture, Evan went deep-diving through NCIC, CLETS, and a half dozen other state and federal databases. Gadds had served a few short stints in federal penitentiaries, mostly for pled-down drug charges. He'd been brought up on assault numerous times, often against women, and ordered to attend court-mandated anger-management courses. Hearsay linked him to several murders, and he'd been twice investigated for trafficking. The DEA had an active but stalled-out continuing criminal-enterprise case; the lead agent had assembled a list of eighteen known associates, whom he'd characterized as impressive in their depravity and blind devotion.

Gadds had seemingly learned his lesson from the CCE case, his personal and business addresses vanishing off the radar a few years back. Everything now was off-the-books or buried in shell corps, his bills sent to mail-forwarding services or PO boxes.

Evan knew that drill well enough.

He dug around in old criminal records until he produced a cell number.

He dialed.

It rang once, twice, three times. Just as Evan was about to cut the line, a man answered. 'Who's this?'

The voice was deep, sonorous, but also nasal, the septum blown out from cocaine.

Evan said, 'Russell Gadds?'

'Who's calling my private line?'

Evan had the man's attention. That was good. The more distracted Gadds was, the less likely he'd bat Trevon around like a toy mouse.

Evan stared at the photograph of the big face still floating before him. 'I hear you're weakened. I hear you've lost your supplier. I want you to know: I'm coming for your business. I'm coming for you.'

The line crackled for a moment, and then Gadds laughed, a few booming notes that sounded wet and angry. 'Who are you?'

'I'm the guy who's gonna kill you.'

Another laugh, this one wheezing and a touch strained. 'Who are you?'

Evan hung up.

He rose, clipped his holstered ARES to his hip, and exited the Vault.

40. Making Good Choices

Russell Gadds kept his office dark because it reminded him of offices in movies, the ones with parchment-colored globes hiding decanters of scotch and walnut bookshelves with brass fittings. So when he'd bedded the operation down in this sprawling cinder-block building, he'd turned the central room into the study of his fantasies. He'd even selected the blotter online, a chocolate leather beauty with two swiveling fourteen-karat-gold-plated pen holders.

Before him, the bullet-resistant one-way mirror gave him oversight of his men in the blastproof front room. Behind him, halls wound back to various operation centers.

He was, he realized, still gripping his phone, though the dead line was bleating in his ear. As usual, Hurtada was standing just behind his shoulder, breathing heavily, the fat fuck taking his right-hand-man designation literally.

Gadds struggled to maintain his composure. It had been years since anyone had dared to threaten him directly. And now some anonymous bastard had dialed his private line – his private line! – and told him he was *weakened*.

The course had taught him to become aware of physical cues, to note what was happening when he was still between a One and a Seven. Seven was his personal Rubicon. Once he crossed Seven, he was no longer rational.

Right now he was redlining the barrier. Setting down the phone, he closed his eyes and paid attention to his body. Pulse rate elevated. Heat in his stomach. Fingernails indenting his palms.

'You okay, chief?'

'Is the room ready?' Gadds said. 'I need the room ready.'

He noted the volume of his voice – high – and the pitch – higher. Two more cues to let him know he was on the verge of losing control.

He was supposed to search for other emotions swirling around inside him, the primary sentiments that his rage was covering for, but he wasn't having much luck. His hands were balled up now, the knuckles bulging and bloodless.

Hurtada took a step back and held open the door on the left. 'Sure it is.'

Gadds shoved back from the chair, sensing the heat welling up from his stomach now as he tried to shut out the memory of that smug-fuck caller – *I hear you're weakened* – and peg his anger on that scale of One to Ten.

Seven now, and rising.

He charged down the hall.

The Rage Room's door was padded and soundproofed, and it autolocked behind him. Inside were an array of items selected for their fragility. An antique lamp on a slender side table. A sixteen-piece china set arranged on a hutch. A variety of vases. A freestanding bookcase hosting a menagerie of glass figurines.

It was as though he'd stepped onto the showcase floor of a Beverly Hills furniture store.

A catcher's mask dangled from a peg on the wall. He donned it.

The steel baseball bat was end-weighted, heat-treated, and double-walled – illegal for most men's leagues.

He hefted it and confronted an old-fashioned stereo stack, the record player on top begging for the first blow.

He felt his anger cross the Rubicon, and he yielded to it.

For a time he raged.

It might have been fifteen minutes. It might have been thirty.

When he came to a halt, panting and winded, his hands cramped and sore, the Rage Room was decimated. It was much more satisfying to take his anger out on some*one* rather than some*thing*, but this was what his course leader had called Making Good Choices.

He tilted the bat against the wall beside a golf club and returned the catcher's mask to its peg on the wall. He felt clearheaded now, ready to make some business decisions.

When he emerged, Hurtada was waiting in the hall, a gym towel folded over one chubby forearm as if he were a waiter from the Roaring Twenties. He wore the same nervous expression he always had when greeting Gadds outside the Rage Room.

'The way things are going,' Gadds said, 'you'd best restock the room.' He snapped the towel off Hurtada's arm and mopped his face. 'This can't stand. None of it. Charter a jet. I have to go down to South America. I'll kiss a few rings, negotiate a goddamned dangerous new line of credit, and get the distribution flow unfucked.'

'On it,' Hurtada said.

Gadds was already moving up the hall, Hurtada wobbling along at his side. 'Chief? Chief? I got an update for you.' Hurtada produced a fax. 'On the other matter.'

Gadds snatched the paper and looked down at it.

Then he smiled.

This was good. A more pleasing target for his rage.

Some*one* always beat some*thing*.

'Let the retard know,' he said.

*

Trevon was sitting on the couch alone with himself and the Scaredy Bugs, and alone with them wasn't a good place to be. He flattened his hand and pressed his palm to the side of his head, pushing hard, his head tilted. He didn't know why it felt good, but it did, like he was holding all the pressure in, like he was holding himself when there was no one else there to do it for him. Mama told him it looked weird and he should be careful about doing it in front of other people.

Mama.

He was making noises now out of his mouth and hearing them like it wasn't him, and he didn't know what else to do since they wouldn't let him work and there was no more family and he couldn't talk to the cops or anyone else or Big Face would get him. He wanted to call his friend, the Nowhere Man, but Mama told him that friendships had to be reciprocal and you can't just keep calling folks, you have to wait for them to call you back even if sometimes they never did.

He felt something touch his legs and he jerked back, but it was just Cat-Cat twining between his ankles. Cat-Cat looked up at him and meowed twice, which meant he was hungry.

Trevon didn't feel like he could move, let alone stand up, but he had to, 'cuz he was responsible to Cat-Cat and Cat-Cat was responsible to him. That was what the rules were, and the rules kept him calm and kept Cat-Cat fed.

He was shaking some kibble into Cat-Cat's bowl when the doorbell rang.

The doorbell rang again, and he realized that he'd frozen there over Cat-Cat's bowl. 'Who is it?'

'Delivery.'

Trevon set down the bag, walked over, and peeped through the peephole. It was a FedEx guy.

'Okay,' Trevon said.

'Can you open up, please, sir?'

'How come?'

'I need you to sign.'

'Can I see your badge?'

'I don't . . .' The guy scratched his nose. 'I don't have a badge.'

Trevon pressed his head some more.

'Sir? I don't have all day.'

Trevon undid the chain real slow-like and opened the door. The guy stared at him a sec. Then thrust an electronic pad at him.

Trevon signed. His fingers were shaking. He couldn't remember the last time he ate.

The guy took a small box from beneath his arm and handed it to Trevon. 'Have a nice day.'

'Thank you, sir. You have a nice day, too.'

Trevon shut the door and locked it and rehooked the security chain.

He got a pair of scissors and walked to the table, holding the closed blades in his fist like he was taught. Then he sat down and opened the box.

Inside was a small black clock.

But it didn't tell the time.

It said 10 DAYS, 23 HOURS, 09 MINUTES, 11 SECONDS.

It was counting down.

But for what?

The only thing Trevon knew of that counted down was –

He dove away from the table, gathered Cat-Cat up in his arms, and huddled against the kitchen cabinets. He stayed like that for a time, Cat-Cat meowing to get back to his food.

After a while he let Cat-Cat go.

He tried to relax.

A bomb didn't make sense.

Like the Nowhere Man said, Big Face needed Trevon alive and well to maximize his suffering.

He crawled back over to the kitchen table, then drew his eyes up so he could see the clock: 10 DAYS, 23 HOURS, 07 MINUTES, 54 SECONDS.

He watched till it counted down to 10 DAYS, 23 HOURS, 05 MINUTES, 30 SECONDS.

What could it be?

When it reached 2 MINUTES, he got a horrible feeling in his gut.

He stood up and went to his computer. He logged in.

The horrible feeling got worse when he saw he had an e-mail from Kiara.

Hey, Tre!

The program's wrapping up a little early due to some funding issues, so I'm flying back a week from Thursday. I e-mailed Mama already but wanted to let you know. I probably won't be able to get to a computer again to check e-mail but I hope you can go with her to pick me up at the airport. Miss you!

xo – K

His heart was pounding loud enough that he could hear it in his ears.

He double-clicked on the attached itinerary.

She was on a Spirit Airlines flight that landed at LAX June 29 at 12:35 PM.

Today was June 18.

He squeezed his eyes shut, saw the numbers in his head,

the days and minutes and seconds. He opened his eyes and looked over at the clock on the kitchen table.

They matched.

His jaw started watering like he was gonna throw up. Before he could, his cell phone rang. He fumbled it out. 'H-hullo? Who is it, please?'

'Trevon.'

It was Big Face.

'Yes, sir?'

'They say a decapitated head can still see for three seconds, but I've always wondered. My thinking is that you'd pass out from the shock without so much as a blink of recognition. But when your sister gets home? We're gonna find out.'

'Hello? Sir? Please don't. Please let's not find out.'

But Big Face had already hung up.

Trevon's mouth watered even worse than before. He barely got the trash can out from under the desk in time.

41. Customer Service

Terrance DeGraw lived in Chatsworth off a winding canyon road on an isolated patch of land that might've once passed for a ranch. Yellow weeds covered the earth, and one of the walls of the stable had rotted away, revealing the empty stalls. The house was falling apart, windows shattered, screen door rusting on its hinges.

Evan parked and crossed through the front gate, dead leaves crunching underfoot. He didn't get halfway up the front walk before the door opened and two men came out.

Evan identified Terrance immediately from Trevon's description. Raw One certainly earned his sobriquet. Skin stretched taut across high, hard cheekbones. Lips pulled thin in a permanent scowl. He wore a T-shirt with the sleeves torn off, showing bony shoulders, and when the breeze picked up the hem, his ribs came visible, ridging the pale white skin.

The man at his side was more filled out, hefty and jittery, with an Amish fringe of beard hanging off his jawline. He held what looked like a Colt .45, the barrel pointed at the ground beside him.

'Can we help you?' Terrance said.

Evan said, 'I hope so.'

They met halfway up the walk, the closed gate hanging crookedly behind Evan, the house looming beyond in all its *Texas Chainsaw* glory.

Evan jerked a chin at the front door. 'You the only two here?'

'Why would you ask a thing like that?' Terrance said.

'Trying to figure out how many of you I have to kill today.'

Terrance coughed out a note of disbelief. 'You hear that, Darren? He wants to know how many of us he has to kill today.'

Darren lifted the Colt and aimed it at Evan's chest, his wrist loose, the pistol lolling lazily to one side. 'Just us two.'

Evan's ARES remained in his Kydex high-guard hip holster. There'd be no need for it.

'Mind telling us who you are, friend?' Terrance said.

'I'm the guy who killed Bo Clague.'

'Bo's not dead.'

'When's the last time you talked to him?'

Terrance licked his cracked lips but didn't say anything.

'Wanna give him a try?' Evan said. 'I can lend you my phone.'

Darren bunched his mouth a few times, as if he were working tobacco.

Terrance squinted at Evan. 'You the one who called the chief earlier? We got word to be on alert.'

'Is that why Darren's here? Buddy system?' Evan shook his head. 'It won't help.'

Darren took a step forward, jabbing the .45 at Evan. 'We should just do him here.'

Terrance held up a hand. 'You heard the chief. He wants to talk to him.' He smiled. 'The chief likes to take his time with folks. Give 'em his full attention.'

Darren said, 'Doesn't mean I won't pistol-whip your ass into submission first.' The muzzle swung slightly right. 'Or put a round through your shoulder.'

'Darren,' Evan said. 'There are two of you and one of me. You have your pistol drawn, aimed at my critical mass from three feet away. We're on secluded land far enough from the nearest neighbors that no one'll hear a gunshot, and even if they do, they won't think much of it. You've got the drop on me in every conceivable way. But I want you to look at me. Look into my eyes. And ask yourself: Do I look scared?'

'Yeah, actually. You *do* look –'

Evan's hands blurred. He caught the barrel of the Colt in the thumb webbing of his right hand, shoving the pistol upward as his left hand chopped Darren's elbow, forcing the arm to bend. The Colt .45 snapped vertical just as Darren tugged the trigger, the round blowing off his face.

Darren swayed on his feet, the pistol tumbling free, the front of his head little more than a bubbling sheet of red. He collapsed to his knees, clawing at himself, and then his weight tugged him forward and deposited him flat on his chest. He twitched on the weeds pushing through the cracked concrete of the walkway and then was still.

A moment of perfect silence followed, Terrance staring down at his friend, chin wobbling, mouth ajar as if trying to produce sound.

Evan stood calmly, as he had an instant before. The breeze was pleasant, scented of sage and rosemary.

Terrance gave a cry and lunged for the fallen Colt. Evan heel-hammered him, breaking the wrist.

Terrance rolled on the ground, gripping his hand, choking down howls.

Evan said, 'Get up.'

Terrance obeyed and stood stooped, the Hunchback of Chatsworth. 'The *fuck*, man. Who do you work for?'

'Trevon Gaines.'

'Oh, no. C'mon, man. That was just . . . that was just orders. What do you want?'

'I want to issue a complaint about Russell Gadds's business practices. You're customer service. I want to see the CEO. Right now.'

Terrance blinked the sweat off his eyelashes. 'But he's gone. Had to fly down to Lima and Paramaribo, straighten some shit out. I swear, man. I *swear*. But he's back next week. Sunday night.'

'I'll be waiting,' Evan said. 'Tell me where.'

'Where what?' Terrance stared at the Colt on the ground by his feet, just out of reach.

'The place you took Trevon. The operation center.'

Terrance cradled his arm. 'You'll never get in there. Place is a fucking fortress. Especially after this clusterfuck with the . . . with the missing shipment. Competitors are smelling blood. Gadds has the office on high alert. It's crawling with men. All of them tougher than you are.'

Evan shifted toward Terrance, and Terrance cowered, hugging his broken wrist.

Evan said, 'I'll take my chances.'

'Okay, man. Okay.'

'Where?'

Terrance gave him an address in the wholesale district downtown.

Evan crouched and picked up the Colt .45.

'C'mon, man. Please. I got . . . I got people.'

The gunshot lifted a murder of crows from the ancient oak tree by the porch.

Evan dropped the .45 next to the bodies and walked back to his pickup.

The canyon was a rare out-of-service spot for his Roam-Zone, so he waited to drive out of the canyon before turning it back on.

It showed twenty-three missed calls.

'I'm sorry I called you so much,' Trevon said.

Evan sat across from him at the small kitchen table, the clock between them counting down to Kiara's arrival. Darkness turned the windows opaque, the night sounds of East LA filtering through, a man bellowing drunkenly, someone laying on the horn with gusto, Mexipop blaring from a radio.

Trevon continued to jerk in shallow breaths so rapidly that he seemed at risk of hyperventilating. A Band-Aid still secured his glasses at one temple.

Evan said, 'That's okay.'

'She gets home on the twenty-ninth.'

'Then we'll have to solve the problem before then.'

'Can you?'

Evan said, 'Yes.'

'Promise?'

'Yes.'

Russell Gadds would get back from his trip to Paramaribo and Lima in one week, which gave Evan a four-day window to eliminate him and his operation before Kiara hit US soil.

Cat-Cat rubbed up against Evan's calf, and he leaned over to scratch him. The cat hissed, clawed his knuckles, and then scuttled away.

Charming.

Trevon didn't seem to take note. 'I have no Mama no more. No relatives. I'm a orphan now. All by myself.'

Evan stared at him.

'If they kill Kiara,' Trevon said, 'I'll be all alone in the world.'

'I won't let that happen to you.'

Trevon's chest shuddered with each inhalation. Evan

rested a hand on his shoulder for a few minutes until his breathing slowed. 'Will you stay just till I fall asleep?' Trevon finally said.

'Sure.'

Evan followed him to the bedroom, and Trevon climbed heavily into bed. He adjusted the stuffed frog beside him and lay in the darkness. 'Will you turn the TV on, please, sir? It's good to have a house full of voices.'

Evan clicked on the television and sat in the same spot on the floor, his back to the wall. It was quiet for a long time, just the Channel Five sports anchor running down scores and Mexipop pumping from up the block.

Trevon said sleepily, 'We don't cry and we don't feel sorry for ourself.'

Evan wasn't sure if Trevon was talking to himself or to Evan, so he said nothing. A few moments later, Trevon's breathing grew regular and took on that familiar rasp.

As Evan rose to sneak out, a breaking-news update cut in on the television. '— confirmed that President Bennett *will* appear before the Committee on Oversight and Government Reform this Friday to respond to long-standing questions about improper relationships with defense contractors before he assumed office, one of a host of scandals that have plagued Bennett since he's taken office. The press secretary stressed that this is a voluntary appearance, that Bennett is devoted to full transparency, and that he is eager to set the record straight.'

Evan paused in the doorway before easing out of the room. He had the sense that another stopwatch had begun, another clock counting down the days and minutes. But he felt excitement also, a quickening of the blood.

At last he had a time and place. A When and Where.

Now he just had to nail down the How.

42. Cut Both Ways

The wholesale district, known on official zoning maps as Central City North, was an unlovely throw of warehouses, refrigerated-storage facilities, and factories slapped down between the LA River, Alameda Street, and the Union Pacific Railroad Line. It was even more depressing at night. To the north sparkled the not-quite-famous downtown skyline, a jagged rise of domino tiles. The glow of the city backdropped rows of palm trees that shot skyward like frozen fireworks, all tails and bursts.

Evan had set up on the roof of a commercial bakery, posting up next to a vent that smelled of yeast. Various pipes exhaled cumulus clouds of condensation, shrouding him from view.

The elevation gave him a good vantage over the high fence next door lined with privacy filler strips and topped with concertina wire.

Terrance DeGraw was right. A fucking fortress. The cinder-block building was virtually windowless. A control pad and a security-controlled metal door defended what seemed to be the sole point of entry; the other doors had been boarded up with metal plates. Anyone who entered was trapped inside.

Of course, that could cut both ways.

The front entrance opened now, a fat man emerging, and as the door swung shut, Evan glimpsed the front room. It had been reinforced as Trevon had described, a DIY sally port with blastproof walls. A cadre of armed men became visible for a moment. Evan doubted they were the only guards posted up inside.

The fat man boasted a handgun on either hip like a Turner Classics cowboy. He joined four others already patrolling the area like junkyard dogs. News of their colleagues' untimely demises must have reached them by now, as they were clearly on highest alert, covering all sides of the building. Carrying AK-47s, they circled the various shipping containers littering the yard, moving in and out of cover.

If Evan picked off one or two with a sniper rifle, the others would fall back to reinforced positions.

If he made a full-frontal assault through the gate, he could take out several, but there'd be no getting through that reinforced-steel security door to the others waiting inside.

He wanted them all.

He wanted to eradicate Russell Gadds's operation like Gadds had eradicated Trevon's family.

Gadds didn't return until June 25. That afforded Evan some much-needed time to devote his attention to Bennett.

Given Bennett's Friday appointment on the Hill, Evan had to get home and start assessing the variables and charting the plan of attack. When he thought of the airtight security measures in place, he felt a creeping concern that Candy McClure might be right, that the job was impossible.

And after the promise he'd made to Trevon, he couldn't get killed in DC. That wouldn't just be inconvenient. It would be inconsiderate.

He stared down once more at the heavily armed guards and the daunting barriers of razor wire, cinder block, and steel. Between Russell Gadds and Jonathan Bennett, Evan faced two herculean challenges.

In his next life, he vowed, he'd be a Starbucks barista.

He drew back from the edge of the roof and vanished into the billows of rising exhaust.

43. Wolves in Wolves' Clothing

The morning gave way to afternoon, not that Evan could tell inside the Vault. His eyes ached, and his hands cramped from pounding the keyboard for hours. He'd risen at 5:00 AM for a workout and then gone straight through the looking glass of his shower wall to the Secret Service databases, burying himself in route assessments, security updates, and GPS imaging of the blocks between the White House and the Hill.

Choosing the exact method was even more challenging than he'd anticipated. The plan, such as it was, had to be impeccably executed. He whittled away at the options until he saw maps and calculations floating ghostlike behind his lids when he closed his eyes.

It was barely, barely possible.

But not as a solo operation.

As he neared the eight-hour mark at his desk, he rose and stretched his stiff back.

Vera II eyed him from her glass bowl.

'I'm not bad at asking for help,' he told her. 'I just prefer not to.'

She sagely withheld further counsel.

He paced in front of his desk, the projected classified data scrolling over his body, shadow and light, shadow and light.

Now that he'd had more time to scour the Secret Service databases, he'd seen that they did not contain a single detail pertaining to the 1997 mission. Whatever mystery President Bennett was guarding against, he'd kept it even from the agency sworn to protect him. Evan was beginning to think that the secret had been redacted so thoroughly that it now existed only in Bennett's mind. If so, Evan would never get the answers he sought.

Sitting heavily in his chair, he brought up the Drafts folder of his Gmail account. *'You there?'*

A moment later: *'i'm in calculus. so yeah. this shit is boring. + easy.'*

'Glad you're getting the most out of your education.'

An eye-rolling emoji bleeped onto the screen.

He grimaced, fingers poised above the keyboard. Then he typed: *'I can't find anything about 1997 in the Service databases.'*

'97? like the mission Dear Leader wants you dead 4?'

'That's right. I've checked call logs, visitor records, official movements, off-site meetings. Maybe I'm not looking in the right places. Anything you can scare up with your algorithms or whatever, let me know.'

'algorithms. yer cute.'

'Need me to open up a portal to get you on my system?'

The light rippled within the Vault, and he realized that Joey had replied inside his own computer, projecting her answer onto the wall before him.

'dummy,' it read, *'i'm already in.'*

Vera II smirked at him.

He typed, 'Oh.'

'i'll look into it after class. any luck picking your spot?'

'Yes. Can you do some route analysis? I need specs on wind factor, visibility, height above target, distance, ease of access, stability, etc.'

'not remote. haveta be onsite for that. happy to fly to d.c. it'd get me outta this final.'

'Not safe. I'll figure it out.'

He deleted the rough draft, erasing their correspondence.

He stood up and paced around some more, doing his best

not to think about the bottle of Tigre Blanc waiting for him in the freezer. A few fingers of ice-cold vodka might take the edge off the upcoming phone call he had to make.

He plucked his RoamZone off the desk, glowering at Vera II. 'All right, all right.'

He dialed.

As it rang, he continued walking in tight circles.

Candy McClure's voice came like a purr across the line. 'I thought you'd never call. Here I am, all dolled up and nowhere to go.'

'I need you in DC.'

'I'm already here.'

'Why?'

'I saw the press briefing, too. Bennett just announced precisely when he's gonna be on the mark. I knew you'd jump at it. You'd better hope Bennett's not playing you.'

'I thought about that. But I don't think he'll pull out of a congressional testimony. He'd lose more political capital than he can afford right now.'

'What do you need?'

'Secret Service protocols designate three primary high-alert routes from the White House to Capitol Hill, ranging from 1.9 to 2.3 miles. They're all circuitous, so we can't count on the straight shot up Pennsylvania Ave. Right now that stretch of blocks is under heavier surveillance than anywhere on the planet. I can't risk being seen in the area again, not until the day of. I've identified three potential perches. Can you go to them and get me a comprehensive set of data for each hide?' He told her the measurements he required. 'I need it down to the inch.'

'I was thinking to the millimeter,' she said. 'But if you want me to work sloppy, I can back off my game.'

'I'm down to ninety hours, and I still have to procure the weapon. I need this ASAP.'

'I'm out the door,' she said. 'But, X? One more thing to consider.'

'What's that?'

'If I can predict you, they can, too.'

Orphan A sat on the edge of the bed in his hotel room, hands folded. The four surviving Collins cousins had departed earlier that morning, but Wade remained hunkered down on the Pelican case, hefting various weapons. He refused to leave. He wanted to be right here at command central, manning the fort so he'd know the instant his shot at revenge came through the line.

His face was red from crying, blood vessels blown out around his nose and eyes. He was the only person Holt had ever seen whose sobbing conveyed not grief but rage.

There was no more Sound. Only Fury.

The authorities had identified what remained of his cousin's and brother's bodies and leaked a story about a drug heist gone bad. The speed and deftness of the cover-up was particularly impressive – amazing what got done behind the scenes when the commander-in-chief was tugging the marionette strings. People who said the government was inefficient didn't know the right parts of the government. The media was having a field day with the incident, calling it Watergate-gate.

Wade and his cousins failed to find it amusing.

Holt's disposable phone vibrated.

Wade's hands stopped moving at last, the pistol at rest between his massive palms.

Holt looked at the text, the sender ID nothing more than a redacted space. FRIDAY. BE READY.

Holt rose and handed Wade the phone as he passed him. Resting by the front door was a black duffel bag that had arrived earlier this morning. It was zippered shut and secured with zip-ties.

Wade read the message and rose from his perch.

It seemed, for a time, that he kept rising.

'I'll round up the boys,' he said. 'You get us within range of him. That's all you need to do. Just get us within range.' He wiped at his nose. 'Can you do that?'

Holt crouched over the duffel, flicked out a folding knife, and severed the zip-tie. He tugged the duffel open and dumped its contents by Wade's feet.

Scattered on the floor were emergency-response-team jackets, Secret Service badges, department-issued combat-utility uniforms.

Holt grinned. 'Wolves in wolves' clothing.'

44. Shock-and-Awe Charm

When Mia opened the door, she noted what Evan was holding and her face froze with surprise.

It wasn't the expression Evan had been hoping for.

He stood there dumbly, Peter's wrapped present tucked under an arm, a bulky gift for Mia front and center. He offloaded it to her, and she struggled a bit under its weight.

'It's – wow, cool – a . . . um, first-aid kit.'

'It's actually a Black Hawk medical pack, designed to SEAL-team medic specs. I packed it with essentials – syringes, field dressing, alcohol pads. I guess the morphine vials are a little much.'

She hefted the immense olive-drab pack onto an accent table, displacing a mound of LEGOs. 'Maybe so.'

'There's a sternum clasp and cinch straps for the sides to help maintain load integrity during stress maneuvers. Not that, you know . . . But I figured after Peter's injury . . .' He read her eyes and stopped. 'I'm not very good at this, am I?'

'No. But you're *so* bad that it actually makes you good.'

'Pity factor?'

'No,' she said. 'More like shock-and-awe charm.'

'I'll take it.' He followed her inside, the condo filled with the scent of fresh-baked pie. The TV was on in the background, a commercial featuring a silver-haired couple toasting with umbrella drinks while a rugged voice ran down a list of horrifying side effects. 'I'm sorry I've been gone. Traveling for work.'

She started clearing dirty plates off the kitchen table. 'No worries. Been busy here, too.'

'I brought something for Peter, too. Is he –'

'Evan Smoak! Check it out!' Peter shot out of his room. He rotated his right arm in the socket, showing off the healed shoulder even as he streaked toward Evan. Then he saw the wrapped package and froze: Flying Hug Interruptus. 'What is it? What is it?'

Evan handed it to him, and Peter sat on the carpet to unwrap it. The half-moon plaque came clear. 'It's . . . um . . . ?'

'A plaque,' Evan said. 'From the White House gift shop.'

'Like, the *actual* White House?'

'The very one.'

Peter went to lift the plaque, but it came apart, a clean break splitting the brass patina. 'Oh, shoot. It's broken.' He looked up at Evan, his charcoal eyes wide. 'What happened?'

I cracked it over the head of an MPD officer.

Or it shattered from the overpressure of a frag grenade in my hotel room.

Or it fractured when I crashed through the floor on top of an assassin and used it to break my fall.

Evan cleared his throat. 'Must've been mishandled by airline baggage.'

Mia came around from the kitchen and crouched behind Evan. 'Let's have a look.'

'Don't worry,' Evan said. 'I know exactly who can fix this. I'll bring it back soon, good as new.'

Across the room the news had taken over from the Cialis commercial. '– *new information about the death of the deputy chief of staff, who we've now learned heroically intercepted a bomb intended for the president, taking the brunt of the blast* –'

Out of the corner of his eye, Evan noticed Mia's head rotate to the TV. She did a double take. In the reflection of the screen, he saw her look down at the White House plaque. Then she shook off the notion, rolling her eyes at herself.

Evan folded the broken gift back in the paper and rose quickly to help with the dishes.

Later he sat on the couch next to Mia, spooning fresh rhubarb pie into his mouth as she sipped coffee. Peter had gone to bed after demanding two stories, a glass of water, a closet check, a search under his bed, and a trip to the bathroom. Evan had taken care of all but the latter.

'So,' Mia said. 'Whaddaya say we break in that Navy SEAL medic kit and get crazy? I can make a string bikini out of adhesive tape. You could oil down your chest with triple-antibiotic ointment.'

He had to fight off a smile. 'It was either that or a catheter kit. So be grateful.'

She reached across and brushed his temple with her knuckles. 'I am,' she said. 'Grateful.'

'Plus, it's not a Navy SEAL medic kit. It's designed to SEAL-team *specs*.'

She was laughing at him now.

'Here's where I should stop talking?'

She said, 'Here's where you should stop talking.'

She leaned to kiss him when her cell phone rang. She answered. 'Mia Hall.'

As she listened, her expression altered, the warmth and softness draining out of it. 'Don't you dare try to intimidate me. I will bring the full weight of the law down on your head, and I will *crush* you.'

She looked at the phone, the screen showing that the call had been severed. She hurled it aside onto the cushions. 'I won't let that piece of shit scare me,' she said. 'I won't.'

But her voice was shaking.

'Who is it?' Evan asked.

'Remember that case I closed?'

Seven felony counts. Oscar Esposito. Case number PA338724. Four-year-old girl who knew her name only as 'Idiot.'

'Remind me,' Evan said.

'Domestic abuse.'

'That's right.'

'He was out of custody throughout the court process, so the judge allowed a surrender date later than the date of sentencing so he could, you know, get his affairs in order. Like he's an international mogul instead of a strung-out reprobate renting a by-the-day room at the Voyager Motor Inn in Huntington Park. So he's out there free till the end of the month. I objected, of course, flight risk, blah-blah, but she said if he was gonna run, he would've done so before the conviction happened. I pulled every lever, but ultimately I'm limited in what I can do.' She scowled, bunching the faint freckles on the bridge of her nose. 'So of course he's been blowing up his soon-to-be-ex wife's phone, trying to figure out which domestic-abuse shelter she's staying at. If she caves, I think he'll kill her and the little girl.'

Evan set down his plate on the coffee table. 'Restraining order?'

'Three hundred feet. But until he violates it, he's out there. Free to make anonymous threatening calls. To her *and* me.'

'What's he threatening you with?'

Mia waved him off. 'The usual. He's gonna rape me. Kidnap me and keep me in a cellar. That when he's done, I'll beg to be put out of my misery.'

Her eyes belied the hard-bitten tone.

Evan realized he'd come forward on the couch, his legs

tensed. She took note of the shift in his posture. 'Whoa, whoa, whoa,' she said. 'I'm telling you this in confidence. Nothing better happen. Not like the other time. Okay?'

He pushed his thoughts away.

He had a president to assassinate and a criminal enterprise to take down. His plate was full enough.

'Okay,' he said.

'This is none of your business.'

'I understand.'

He stood to go, but she took hold of his hand.

'That doesn't mean leave,' she said.

He lay in the softness of Mia's bed, her skin glowing milk-white in the spill of light through the window. The sweat had dried on his chest, his body a lovely confusion of heat and coolness.

She rested on her side, her eyes closed, and he could barely make out the birthmark at her temple beneath the tumble of her hair. Three stretch marks rode the hump of her hip, a Japanese fan, the skin looking so feather-soft he had to lean to press his lips to it.

She gave a pleased murmur he felt in his spine, and then she shifted onto her belly.

Somewhere in the dark room, his phone hummed.

He got out of bed silently, located the RoamZone in his heap of cast-off clothes, and stepped into the bathroom, easing the door shut behind him.

He answered, 'V?'

'I have the field specs on all three locations,' Candy said. 'Texting them now.'

His phone buzzed and buzzed some more, the data coming through. Measurements, dimensions, elevations.

She said, 'Tell me I'm the best.'

'You're the best.'

'No shit,' Candy said. 'Let me know when you're ready to come out and play.'

She hung up.

As he studied the data on the three perches, one came clear as the most suitable.

A soft tapping issued through the door. He opened it to find Mia standing there, wearing his T-shirt, the hem falling to mid-thigh. Her eyes were at half-mast.

'Is it a woman?' she asked.

Evan hesitated. 'Yes,' he said.

'Are you sleeping with her?'

'No.'

'Okay,' she said, kissed him, and trudged back to bed.

The afterimpression of her lips lingered on his. In his hand the RoamZone's screen displayed the coordinates he required to end the life of the president of the United States.

He wondered if he could ever bring these two lives of his into alignment without destroying one or the other.

For a long time, he stood on the cold tiles of the bathroom, phone in hand, staring across the threshold at Mia's nestled form on the bed.

Then he dressed quietly and slipped out.

45. The Entitlement of the Mighty

Martin's Tavern had hosted every president since Give 'Em Hell Harry, a slice of DC lore that the Martin clan didn't hesitate to advertise at every turn.

President Bennett sat at 'The Proposal Booth,' where JFK had allegedly popped the question to Jackie. Commemorated by a brass plaque screwed into the wall, the apocryphal event had recently been corroborated by an aging eyewitness, a former ambassador named Marion Smoak, who recalled watching the young senator from Massachusetts consummate the political alliance that would serve as the cornerstone of Camelot.

The Georgetown eatery, nearly a hundred years old, made every effort to look its age – dimly lit wooden booths, antique fox-hunt engravings in warped frames, charmingly hideous stained-glass lamps hanging over a bar worn from decades of forearms and workday stress.

In the cramped space between booths, tables were arranged cheek to jowl. If you weren't the president, you'd have to watch your elbows.

At Agent Templeton's request, the Service had cleared out the restaurant. Through the window Bennett could see agents at intervals all up the sidewalk, hands crossed over their groins, the trademark posture. At least a third of the plainclothes 'civilians' in eyeshot, at closer look, sported surveillance kits, earpieces snugged into place, pockets bulging with radio transmitters.

Until recently Bennett had felt like the king of all he surveyed.

Since Orphan X had announced himself, the world had remained just as vast, but it seemed the space from which Bennett could view it was shrinking.

Naomi Templeton sat across from him, that blunt-cut blond hair framing an obstinate face. '– hoping you will reconsider and cancel, Mr President. It's like sending a Google Maps route to Orphan X.'

Bennett dragged the tines of his fork through the gravy-covered slab of turkey. He could taste the giblets in the sauce, rich and meaty. He looked across at Johnson's favorite table.

And then at Nixon's.

'My appearance before Congress is a gesture of grace, Templeton. Backing away from it would be disastrous. I am not going to let an assassin dictate the operations of the highest office in the nation.'

'Mr President –'

He set down his fork firmly, the slender handle plinking on the rim of his plate. 'I'm the leader of the free world. At your disposal you have the most advanced and resource-rich security apparatus history has ever known. If you can't get me seventeen blocks safely, we both deserve to die.'

She opened her mouth. Closed it. 'Yes, sir.'

He nodded. 'Continue.'

She returned her focus to the leather-bound folder before her. 'It'll be the formal motorcade package, forty vehicles, and extra SUVs to accommodate a second CAT team. I want our backup to have backup. We'll cordon off the blocks along the route and send an intel car in the lead, running real-time facial recognition on everyone behind the barriers. Let's see.' She tapped her pen against her chin, her eyes scanning down the page. 'Motorcycle units blocking side streets, post standers at every intersection, three Park Police helos in the air the whole way.'

'And the ground game?'

'We're locking down all the buildings along the primary route as well as the two contingency routes – that means each doorway, entrance, and exit secured. By the time the motorcade pulls out of 1600 Penn, not a single window between you and the Capitol will be open. My men are already acquiring master keys to every condo building, every office, every hotel room. We'll secure utility rooms, roof access points, circuit boards – anything that could throw a wrench. FSD – sorry, Forensic Services Division – has worked up interactive 3-D digital models of every structure along the trajectory, complete with floor-by-floor blueprints. This afternoon I'm personally leading the briefing to walk everyone through the route one square foot at a time. Thursday morning we're getting EOD on loan from the army to spot-weld manhole covers shut, remove mailboxes, all that jazz. They'll run dogs through alleys and garages, make sure we pass the sniff test. Building-extraction scenarios are complex when we're dealing with the Capitol Building, but we've worked up several . . .'

As she continued, Bennett took a measured sip of the 1865 Château Lafite that Billy kept stored in the back for him. The grapes had been harvested the year the Confederacy surrendered, and they'd aged through both world wars and a host of others, through the polio epidemic and the Great Depression, the airplane and the A-bomb, space travel and supercomputers, only to spend themselves in a moment's pleasure upon his palate.

The world flowered in order to be picked by the daring. It was a privilege, yes. And the entitlement of the mighty.

'. . . full-body scanners at the door,' Templeton was saying. 'Airspace will be cleared, of course, but we'll also shut down drone flights, model aircraft, everything. Capitol police will have two mobile command centers in the vicinity, feeding directly into the White House Communications Agency switchboard . . .'

Most presidents didn't require this level of detail.

Most presidents didn't cut their teeth in the DoD.

Most presidents hadn't been hunted by Orphan X.

It would have been easier in a dozen different ways to receive the brief from Templeton in the Oval, but he'd insisted on the excursion to Georgetown over her strenuous objections. He needed to make a point. The bottle on the table had waited more than 150 years for him to consume it – three times the span of his own life. Time waited on him, acquiesced to his desires, bowed before him.

Not vice versa.

He leaned back, taking in the storied walls of the tavern. The entryway featured another Victorian flourish, beveled leaded-glass windows announcing the restaurant. He stared at the tavern's name sandblasted into the black flashed glass, thinking of everything that had come before him and everything that would come after.

For the first time, he truly entertained the notion that Orphan X could succeed. Victoria Donahue-Carr would assume the Resolute desk. The media would rejoice. The sun would rise on another day.

And he would be nothing more than another brass placard screwed into another table here in Martin's Tavern, like Nixon but remembered less fondly.

He found himself staring out the window, considering the passing cars, the facing windows, the pedestrians across the street.

Everything a threat.

The heat of the gravy wafted up to him, heavy with the

scent of organ meat. For the first time he could remember, he'd lost focus.

Abruptly, he directed his attention back at Templeton. 'How many agents are here?'

He'd cut her off, a rare show of impulsivity.

She was taken aback, her head slightly withdrawn. 'Seventy-five. We have G-rides circling the area as well. Are you concerned?'

He said, 'No.'

He could sense her eyes on his face, studying him.

'Was it really worth it?' she said. 'To eat here?'

'Yes.' He pushed his plate aside. 'To show I'm not afraid.'

He reacted instantly at the bang – a startling percussion from deep in the restaurant. The agents by the entryway swung around, their SIGs clearing leather. Templeton was already halfway over the table, one hand grabbing his arm, forcing him down.

He'd ducked beneath the windowsill, flattening against the weathered wood of the booth. Crimson dripped down past his face, and for a moment he thought it was his own blood, that he was staring at what had an instant before rushed through his veins and arteries.

The smell of bordeaux reached his nostrils.

And then the sound worked its way from the stem of his brain to the white matter, allowing him to process it as a metallic clang from the kitchen.

A dropped pan.

He pulled himself upright as the last of the Lafite dribbled from the knocked-over bottle, pattering onto his thighs.

He righted the bottle, thumping it down on the table again.

He said, 'I'm ready to head back.'

46. Comprehensively Impossible

Unimpressed, Tommy Stojack stared down at the cracked half-moon plaque from the White House gift shop. 'Does it explode?'

Evan stared at him across the armorer's workbench, littered with firing pins and stray rounds. 'No.'

At the edge of the counter, coffee gurgled in a cauldron of a pot, strong enough to be considered weaponized. A welder's mask rode the top of Tommy's head like a shoved-back Halloween mask. He worked a wedge of tobacco dip from one side of his gumline to the other, his biker mustache rippling from the effort. A Camel Wide spiked out from between his fingers. When he held it to his lips, the cherry crackled and lurched a good half inch, dangerously close to the tip of his battered nose.

Tommy waved the butt at the plaque, scattering ash across its face. 'It's constructed out of an undetectable contact poison?'

'No.'

'It's hiding a shiv and a Beretta Nano?'

'No.'

'Then that raises the inevitable question. Which is this: What the motherfuck? I mean, a decorative tchotchke? It's to . . . what? Prettify your fucking powder room? Hang it above the decorative antique butter churn in the corner? Or, no – wait – use it as a backdrop to spruce up your Hummel collection?'

'Tommy . . . It's just . . . it's for a friend.' Evan held up his hands. 'It's got a brass patina, and I figured you'd know how to solder it.'

'Oh, yeah. This ain't below my pay grade or nothing. You want I should cut you a spare set of house keys while I'm at it?'

Tommy specialized in procurement and R&D for specified government-sanctioned black groups. He was the finest armorer Evan had ever met, able to machine up a ghost pistol or produce a next-gen sniper scope at a moment's notice. They knew little about each other's background or current extracurriculars, but Evan had learned enough to know that he could trust Tommy absolutely and that their moral bearings were aligned.

To acquire specialty gear, Evan visited Tommy's shop on the outskirts of Las Vegas. The exterior looked like just another auto shop, but inside, it was a dungeon, its oil-spotted floor buried under mills and lathes, RPGs and munitions crates, cutting torches and test-firing tubes. If few people knew of the lair hidden by the banal exterior, fewer yet were afforded the respect of having the surveillance cameras unplugged before they arrived. But Tommy honored Evan's request that they meet only under full-black protocols.

On the drive to Vegas, Evan had kept the mirror Boeing Black resting on the passenger seat in speaker mode. Again he'd activated the mike on Naomi Templeton's phone, allowing him to listen in on her lunchtime conversation with the president. By the time he'd arrived at Tommy's shop, he – like the president – had received her full security brief.

Right now Evan breathed in the scent of gun oil and steroidal coffee and tried to refocus his friend. 'Like I said, I'm happy to –'

Tommy snapped down the welder's mask and fired up a

butane microtorch. Sparks flew up against the dark rectangle banding his eyes. He made slow but meticulous progress, smoothing out the lines until the plaque had been restored to its previous glory.

The mask snapped back up. 'Now can we please get to some real fucking work? Or do you need me to sew knee patches onto your corduroys?'

Evan said, 'I need you to design and field-test a weapon for me. By Thursday.'

'What is it?'

Evan told him.

Tommy's bird's-nest eyebrows hoisted up to touch the forehead band of the welder's mask. He whistled. 'That's a whole other Oprah,' he said. 'You sure you don't want something more straightforward? Mosey on up to the bad guys and spit out copious amounts of brass and lead?'

'Straightforward's not an option.'

Evan removed a folded sheet from his pocket that contained the calculations of his chosen perch and slid it across the workbench. Tommy scowled down at the paper before donning a pair of rectangular reading glasses better suited to a librarian. He read everything over again.

'Look,' he said. 'I know I'm your RKI, but I gotta say –'

'RKI?'

'Reasonably Knowledgeable Individual.' Tommy smiled his gap-toothed grin. 'But this?' He shook the paper. 'By Thursday? Is asking a lot.'

'I also need it to meet me in DC,' Evan said. 'I can't travel with it.'

'Oh, well. Of fucking course. You sure you don't prefer Dubai? I could airlift it in, set it down on top of the Burj Khalifa.'

'Some supporting weaponry also. Explosives. Oh, and I need less lethal options. Make sure the wrong people don't get hurt. There's a list of specialized gear on the back of the page –'

Tommy held up both hands, closed his eyes against the apparent strain of it all. 'Can you pretend you're not comprehensively impossible? Just for, like, a minute? Lie to me? Whisper sweet nothings? Tell me my ass don't look fat in these cargo pants?'

'I'm prepared to pay heavy.'

'Well, that's fortunate, 'cuz it's gonna cost you heavy. I mean, fixed location, single shot, no adjustments. It'll have to be more perfect than perfect.' His basset-hound eyes peered down at the data through the ridiculously tiny eyeglass lenses. He looked like Santa Claus if Santa Claus were a qualified marksman. 'This survey of site better be dead-on.'

'It is.'

'I gotta duplicate the elevation *precisely*. It's not like I can wander out into the desert and find a dune at the same height. Nah, I'll have to rent a scaffolding platform lift and drive it out to a remote location so I can range-test a whole goddamned bunch.'

'Whatever you need to do.'

Eyes on the paper, Tommy flicked a hand at the coffeepot. 'Pour me a cup of shut-the-fuck-up, would ya?'

Evan found Tommy's sticky mug beside the salvaged ship's porthole he used as an ashtray and coaxed a stream of sludge from the pot.

He handed it off to Tommy, who was already muttering to himself under his breath: '. . . looking at two hundred sixty-six meters to impact area, which means time of flight has to be . . .'

He shifted the cigarette to the side of his mouth, sipped

coffee across a lip still pouched with Skoal Wintergreen. His hand patted his shirt until it came up with a well-chewed pencil, and he started jotting equations down next to the numbers Evan had supplied – overpressure calculations, projectile angle and velocity, speed of the moving target. His forefinger had been blown off at the knuckle, one of countless injuries, but he gripped the pencil between the stub and his thumb.

He was a hard man to slow down once he got going.

'Tommy?' Evan said.

Tommy did not look up. 'I only got three days. Why are you still here talking at me?'

Evan stood another moment watching Tommy work and then withdrew. He threaded through the shadowy shop to the door, escorted out by just the echo of his own footsteps.

47. Roused Beast

Driving home, Evan watched the sun bury itself in the horizon. Its dying glow washed the hills in gold, the sepia-toned filter of another era. The sky, too, was hyper-real, the kind of soft lavender reserved for children's sketches of sunsets. Soon enough darkness prevailed, headlights and freeway overheads spot-bleaching the endless black strip of the 10.

As Evan neared downtown, the vehicles proliferated like prairie mammals. In short order the freeway grew constipated even by LA traffic standards, so he looped south on the 710 and cut west across Slauson Avenue. Given the streetlights, it would probably take him just as long to get home, but there was a pleasure in keeping the Ford pickup on the move, a sense of hard-won progress.

Huntington Park was three square miles of densely packed Hispanic working-class folks living mostly above the poverty line. It felt dreary and vibrant at the same time, nightclubs and health centers, shops and run-down apartments. When Mexico beat Croatia in the World Cup a few years back, the whole neighborhood had taken to the streets, prompting LAPD to dispatch mounted officers in riot gear to ensure that the celebration didn't tip into lawlessness.

Evan almost didn't notice the sign as he drove past.

In hindsight he wished he hadn't.

Waiting for the light to change, he read the reversed words in the reflection off his windshield, a neon-pink glare: NNI ROTOM REGAYOV.

Then he turned and stared at the seedy motel.

Mia's words came back to him: *Like he's an international mogul instead of a strung-out reprobate renting a by-the-day room at the Voyager Motor Inn in Huntington Park.*

'Goddamn it,' Evan said.

The light changed. The car behind him honked, the window cranking down, an upturned hand helping convey a stream of profane Spanish in his direction.

He coasted through the light and then pulled to the curb. His eyes gazed back at him from the rearview, issuing a clear warning.

This was stupid.

Mia had told him not to get involved.

It was none of his business.

It wasn't like he didn't have enough to worry about.

But he thought about the taste of the sun-kissed skin at her shoulder. Her bottom lip between his teeth. The light freckles across her nose, visible only at close quarters. Then he remembered how her expression had changed when she'd answered the phone. *I won't let that piece of shit scare me.* What had the man told her? That he was going to rape her. Kidnap her and keep her in a cellar. That when he was done, she'd beg to be put out of her misery.

Mia was right. It wasn't Evan's business. He wasn't going to get involved.

Already he was out of the truck, walking up the sidewalk, head lowered.

The door of the lobby clanged against a mounted bell, the cheery ring adding a discordant note to the decidedly uncheery interior. Stuffing protruded from a gut-slashed love seat. The floorboards had rotted away in an amoeba by the front desk, releasing the sweet smell of mold. An obese receptionist rested her head on a propped fist, her jowls dimpled into concentric folds above her knuckles. She was watching *The Silence of the Lambs* on a television no bigger than a toaster. Hannibal Lecter bragged about eating the census taker's liver with some fava beans and a nice Chianti, then rabbit-sucked his teeth with epicurean relish.

As Evan approached, the woman slid her eyes over to him but didn't otherwise move.

'Is Oscar Esposito staying here?' Evan asked.

'Why?'

'He's a friend.'

'Then I don't much want to help you.'

'Why?'

'Because he's a *culo*.'

Evan supposed that a man whose four-year-old daughter answered to 'Idiot' generally didn't make a winning impression on women.

He said, 'Then I'm an enemy.'

At this she moved, shifting her considerable weight on her chair. 'What do you want to do to him?'

'Just have a talk.'

'A talk.'

'Yes.'

'That might not be the worst thing.' She fanned her fingers, considered. 'Too bad, though. You just missed him. He flew out of here.'

'Drunk?'

'No. Like, with a purpose, you know?'

A ripple of heat moved across Evan's shoulders. 'Do you know where he was heading?'

The woman shrugged. 'Course not.'

'Does he have a car?'

'Not that I know of. *Cara de mierda* takes the bus.'

Mounted on the wall behind her, a plywood board housed columns of hooks, some of which held room keys.

Evan said, 'You can't tell me what room he's staying in, right?'

'That's right.'

Evan stared at her.

She stared back.

And then she stretched, a great expansive gesture, her sweater swooping beneath her capacious arms like a set of wings. She finished with a finger landing on an empty gold hook, her pretty dark eyes peering pointedly at Evan from beneath elaborate fake lashes.

The keys on either side dangled from cheap plastic key chains labeled with blue Magic Marker – 13 and 15.

Evan said, 'If you'll excuse me, I need to use the restroom.'

She gave a Vanna White flip of her hand. 'Right down that hall, sir.'

He hustled up the corridor. Room 14 was conveniently unlocked, saving the half minute it would have taken him to pick the crappy dead bolt.

Given the prison-small space, it took Evan all of fifteen seconds to rifle through Oscar Esposito's few belongings. He paused, scanning the room, his gaze coming to rest on a beige telephone propped on an old-fashioned radiator.

He picked up the handset, hit REDIAL.

A woman answered, her voice hoarse. 'Look, O, I give up, okay? I give up. I told you where we at. Just come get us. I'll come home with you. Just don't hurt Aurora no more.' Her sobs came over the line. 'I give up. I give up.'

Reseating the handset, Evan eyed the number on the

cracked caller-display screen. On his RoamZone he accessed a classified reverse telephone directory and thumbed in the number.

NEW HAVEN WOMEN AND CHILDREN TRANSITIONAL HOUSING.

An address 2.4 miles away.

That was a short bus ride.

Oscar Esposito was on tilt, all lean muscle and bone flying up the sidewalk, face thrust forward, leading the charge with his scowl. He wore black 501s tugged low enough to reveal a good six inches of Tommy Hilfiger boxer briefs and the grip of a nickel-plated .22. His leather jacket fluttered behind him as he cut between two parking meters and charged for the front door of the shelter.

Nearing the steps, he reached behind him and tugged the gun free.

That was when his momentum stopped.

It was puzzling at first, his foot raised before him, frozen above the sidewalk, ready to set down. The tightening pressure around his chest. His arms pinned at his sides.

He squinted down at the band of paracord lassoed around his torso.

It tightened some more.

And then he was whisked off his feet, flying backward into the alley next to the shelter.

He hit the ground hard, the wind knocked out of him, his gun skittering off. His mouth gaped, but nothing came out. And no air came in.

The alley walls were feathered with torn-off corners of flyers. A breeze rushed across his sweat-washed face, making the triangles of paper flap on their tabs of tape like the wings of injured butterflies. Through the gap between rooftops, a few stars shone through a bleary sky.

And then they were blotted out by a man-shaped form.

A boot lowered to Oscar's chest, compressing his ribs, and at last his lungs released with a shudder. He gasped and then gasped again.

The voice came down at him as if from the heavens.

'Listen to me closely. When you regain consciousness, the cops will find you hog-tied on the doorstep of the shelter, in violation of your restraining order. Resting beside your cheek will be that gun, which I assume is unlicensed. It will be unloaded, not that you'll be able to reach for it.'

The wind picked up even more, the torn bits of flyers fluttering with wounded fury, transforming the alley into something living, the hide of a roused beast.

'After you've served your time, if you try to hurt your wife or daughter again or *ever* contact the woman who prosecuted you, I will come back for you. Blink twice if you understand me.'

Oscar could hear his own breath screeching in and out of his lungs, but it didn't sound like it was coming from him; it sounded like a growl issued from the chest of the alley.

He blinked twice.

All at once Oscar was flipped over onto his stomach, the rope coiled around his wrists and ankles, creaking with tension. The paracord zippered into a knot, cranking his shoulders and hips back in their sockets. His spinal cord bent in a painful reverse arc, strung like a bow.

The voice was lower now, calm and sharp, a dagger in his ear. 'If I have to come back for you, I will make you hurt. Understand?'

Oscar blinked again.

This time everything stayed dark.

48. Dirty Work

Beltway insiders referred to the Washington Hilton as the 'Hinckley Hilton,' a macabre nod to the failed songwriter who, in a *Taxi Driver*–inspired act of obsessive love for Jodie Foster, put a bullet into the lung of Ronald Reagan at the hotel's T Street exit.

The room Candy had rented, perhaps by design, was high on the northwest corner, looking down at that fateful stretch of sidewalk, which shimmered now in the moonlight, wet with night dew. Evan paused by the cold pane, gazing below, taking it in.

Tomorrow was going to be a very big day.

As neither the Secret Service nor Orphan A's band of misfits were on alert for a single woman, Candy had procured the room.

This morning Evan had collected the shipments Tommy had arranged for him. As promised, Tommy had left them in the trunk of a beater car in a salvage yard on the city outskirts. Evan had simply climbed in and driven off.

Between Evan and Candy now on the floor were all three of Tommy's weatherproof Hardigg Storm Cases, lids raised to show off the gear nestled into the foam lining.

In the bluish flicker of the TV, Evan knelt to remove the two-foot weapon, taking a moment to admire Tommy's superb craftsmanship before tucking it inside the skateboard backpack he'd purchased this afternoon. Earlier today he'd dragged the backpack behind the car for a few blocks; the more well-loved something was, the less it stood out.

Adhered to the rear of the pack by buckle carry straps was a road-worn Santa Cruz Slasher board that Evan had bought used at a skate shop. It nicely hid the bulk beneath.

CNN flickered in the background, clean-cut pundits running pregame commentary on the president's congressional appearance. Their discussion of the security measures had taken on a fetishistic air, the familiar phrases trotted out with breathless delight. *Taking every precaution. No stone unturned. Intense scrutiny of the event zone.*

As they delved into often-incorrect specifics, Evan wondered how much of it was ignorance and how much disinformation. After all, Bennett was a master of counter-intelligence.

Through the lens of a new laser range finder, Candy watched with amusement as Evan tested the heft of the backpack. He finally glanced up at her. She looked ridiculous, the tag from the golf-pro shop dangling down over her nose.

She tossed the range finder onto the bed. Then she peeled off her shirt.

For a moment she stood brazenly, hands on her hips, physical assets on full display. From the front none of her mottled flesh was visible.

'This routine?' he said. 'You don't have to do it. I know it's your training talking.'

'Like you didn't have the same training. Fun, wasn't it?'

He was silent.

'Oh,' she said. 'Right. You want it to be *special.*'

He had a hard time holding his focus on her face.

The pope would have, too.

'One condition,' Candy said. 'I have to be on top.'

He cleared his throat. 'Because of your scars?'

She smirked, bit her lip. '*No.*'

She kicked off one shoe and then the other.

'This doesn't interest me,' he said. 'We have a job to do.'

She shifted her weight, crossing her arms self-consciously. 'Don't be so literal.' Slowly she turned, bringing the ruined flesh of her back into view. 'I just need some help . . . dressing this before the mission. I can't always reach, and . . .' She gave him her profile over a shoulder, her face downturned. 'I'm ashamed.'

He walked over to her. 'I have gauze in my pack.' He rested a hand gently on her shoulder, just beneath her chin. 'We're all scarred one way or another.'

She took his hand in hers and turned to look up at him, her eyes huge and fragile, her fingers clutching his. She put a hand on his cheek and started to pull his face to hers.

Then she laughed and pushed him away. 'You liked that?' Her eyes shone with predaceous pleasure. 'Le Wounded Bird routine? God, men are *so easy*. If one lever doesn't work, just move to the next and give a little tug.'

She walked past him, bumping his hip with hers, making him stumble to keep his balance. 'Remember, some of us have more work to do tonight. I have to change. That doesn't mean I want to fuck you. But when I saw you pretending not to look at me, the picture of strained virtue . . . well, I couldn't resist.'

As she wriggled out of her pants, his RoamZone rang. He noted the caller ID, forwarded on from his rarely used home line. Grimacing, he moved back to the window before answering.

Mia got right to it. 'What the *hell*, Evan?'

He said, 'Sorry?'

'You should be. Wanna tell me what went down with Oscar Esposito?'

He paused a beat. 'Who?'

'You know exactly who. Oscar Esposito, case number PA338724. You said it to me when you were bragging about your forensic noticing skills.'

He thought, *Fuck*.

He shot a glance at Candy, lowering his voice even more. 'I can't get into this right now.'

Over the silence he could hear Mia breathing.

'Don't worry about it,' she said. 'No need.'

And she hung up.

Evan pursed his lips, stared at the phone as if it could tell him something he wanted to hear.

'Marital problems?' Candy said from across the room.

He turned to find her dressed in dark jeans and a black sweatshirt, the better to disguise her upcoming night maneuvers. Even so she looked working-class competent, her rose-gold hair twisted up in a bun beneath a stylish army cap, her makeup wiped off, her boots replaced with sensible sneakers. A Hardigg case rested at either side of her. They could have held concert equipment, tools, computer hardware.

'Nothing like that,' Evan said.

'Good. That shit doesn't work with us. You should know better.'

He said, 'I do.'

He thought he sensed a flicker of longing move across her face, but he wasn't sure if he'd imagined it, casting his own doubts across the shadowed room so she could wear them instead of him.

They stood in perfect stillness, mirror images facing off over a stretch of patterned carpet.

'You did good work,' he said. 'The survey of site. With what's coming tomorrow . . .' The words did not come easily. 'I'm glad you got my six.'

'That's what I'm good for.' She bent at the knees and with some effort lifted the Storm Cases. 'The dirty work.'

49. Kill Zone

Evan lay flat on his back, staring up at the unbroken DC sky. To his right, a barred metal overhang shaded the extended open terrace cupping the southern edge of the Newseum's top floor. Six stories below that, eight lanes of Pennsylvania Avenue swept by, stretching less than a mile to Capitol Hill. Flanking the traffic, leafy crowns of trees swayed in a faint wind, green wads of cotton. This precise thoroughfare was the site of countless processions, parades, and – especially under Bennett's administration – protests.

To Evan's left, the backpack rested on the rooftop. Five hours earlier he'd skated up the sidewalk to the museum, slinging the Santa Cruz Slasher board through the backpack's carry straps before entering so it would shield the bulky cargo. Disguised in a youthful hoodie and mirrored surfer shades, Evan sported a pair of high-top Vans to complete the look.

He remained still, only tilting his head slightly now and then to check the sight lines. Next door the Canadian embassy rose, the red maple leaf fluttering at high mast. Under the Vienna Convention, its premises were immune from requisition by the host country, which meant the Secret Service couldn't station countersnipers on its roof. This offered Evan a key swath of invisibility.

Across the way in the opposite direction, the Federal Trade Commission Building forged into view like the prow of a steamship, its rounded face fanged with limestone colonnades. Peeking over its shoulder, the Washington Monument's arrow tip caught the midday glare.

The motorcade's route was not the straight line between the White House and Capitol Hill that lay before Evan. The twisting course they'd mapped out, designed to thwart malignant planning, lay well beyond his range. The two contingency routes carried the motorcade even farther afield from his location.

That was what Candy was for.

To herd the prey.

He rolled his head toward Pennsylvania Ave. A plastic grocery bag snared on a telephone line above the wide street wobbled in the faint breeze.

From far in the distance, the sound of chopping rotors reached him.

Candy's voice came through his earpiece. 'It's go time.'

Staying flat on the roof, Evan reached beside him, unzipped the backpack, and removed the weapon.

President Bennett ducked into the first of the three limousines, the helicopters low enough to blow his hair out of place. His body man, a Secret Service agent, and Eva Wong were waiting in the rear compartment. He settled into the leather, noting the sparkle of sweat at Wong's temple.

'Nervous?' he asked.

She shook her head too rapidly, a cunicular tic.

He laid a presidential hand on her knee. 'It'll be fine.'

The agent's body was tense; his jacket flapped open to grant him quicker access to his SIG P229.

As the three matching limos eased out of the protective shield of trees to join the convoy, Bennett took a moment to smooth down his hair. He found himself breathing a bit more deeply than usual.

All at once the driver tapped the brakes, causing them to lurch in their seats.

Wong cried out, and the agent drew his weapon.

Bennett found himself gripping his seat belt. He gave a laugh that sounded a touch strained even to his own ears and let go. The dummy vehicles behind had halted as well.

A rap came on the agent's window, followed by a fall of blond hair as Agent Templeton leaned over.

Since the windows didn't open, the agent cracked the door to talk to her.

'Come on,' she said to the agent, gesturing for him to climb out. 'I'm taking the ride myself.'

The agent hesitated.

Naomi said, 'Get out.'

He obeyed.

She took his place, sitting heavily, the plush leather seat giving out a sigh of air.

Bennett said, 'You sure you want to join me here on the bull's-eye?'

She kept her seat belt unbuckled, her eyes pegged to the window. 'Like you said: If I can't get you seventeen blocks safely, we both deserve to die.'

She rapped the divider, and they pulled out and away from the White House.

Courier bag slung over one shoulder, Candy McClure sliced through the pedestrians behind the blockades, unnoticed by the motorcade cops guarding the intersections. She held an iPhone live-streaming from a camera she'd hidden in Lafayette Square on the right foot of the statue of the French general himself. The tiny lens was angled on the northeast gate of the White House, through which Evan's intel had indicated that the presidential motorcade would exit.

And indeed that's where the three limousines appeared now, sandwiched in the middle of a host of G-rides, the footage crisp and seamless. The limos halted at the gate, waiting to insert themselves into the stream of the bigger convoy.

Holding the phone tightly, she watched the tires as Evan had instructed.

The back vehicles ground their wheels against the gravel before accelerating, but the lead limo turned them gradually as it eased forward.

The target had been identified.

Threading closer to the sawhorses, she smiled. Misreading her, one of the motorcade cops tipped his head to her, a tough-guy flirt. She let her smile widen.

Drifting past the curved marquee of the Shakespeare Theatre Company, she took a position on the corner that gave her a clear view up E Street. Swiping the live feed off her iPhone, she called up her telephone favorites.

In place of names, the entries were simply numbered *1* through *10*.

A hush of excitement rippled through the crowd, and she looked up as the presidential motorcade swung into view, a cavalry charge of G-rides and SUVs. She waited as the river of dark steel snaked through the turn, the presidential limos finally appearing. Each flew miniature flags on either side of the hood, Old Glory and the Presidential Standard. Three helos tracked the limos overhead, spread like hawks.

The front SUV of the motorcade had reached her corner now, whipping past the sawhorses, Cadillac One still a quarter mile back. Candy wet her lips, her focus narrowing to the vehicles blurring across the 9th Street intersection a full block away.

Her finger hovered over the first telephone number.

She waited.

Pairs of vehicles shot through the target intersection, as fast as shuffled cards – SUVs, G-rides, another set of SUVs.

She didn't move, didn't breathe.

And then Cadillac One's grand grille appeared, the limo hurtling forward. The rear tires had just cleared the cross-walk when she thumbed the first telephone number.

The manhole cover in the intersection exploded, blasting twenty feet into the sky, severing Cadillac One from the vehicles behind it.

There was an instantaneous eruption of activity.

Four sets of G-rides screeched to the sides, forming a chevron, Cadillac One and its protective SUVs accelerating through them. The dummy limos split north and south, all three limos peeling apart, putting distance between them-selves, their respective choppers shadowing them overhead. The motorcade cops scrambled, parting the crowd, shoving sawhorses aside to open up escape routes.

Candy focused only on Cadillac One.

As it raced toward her, readying to bank into a turn around her corner, she thumbed phone number 3, blowing the man-hole cover right behind her, forcing what remained of the convoy to veer back on course and continue along E Street. The Park Police helicopter tilted abruptly to dodge the flying disk, which missed the left skid by no more than a foot.

For good measure she tapped 4 and 5 next, blowing man-hole covers to the north of the upcoming intersections so Cadillac One wouldn't deviate from its course. She sprinted along the sidewalk, keeping it in sight.

Rather than drop low into the building corridor again, the helo swooped to a greater height, providing better overwatch.

Sirens blared. Some of the agents lunged out of their vehicles, weapons drawn, shouting into radios – *AOP! We have an AOP! Attack on Protectee in progress! Repeat: in progress.*

Candy fixed her attention only on the presidential limo. As it neared 6th Street, a quick dial of phone number *8* blasted another cast-iron saucer skyward, steering the limo south. The EOD's protective measure of spot-welding the manhole covers only added to the explosive force from the charges Candy had placed beneath them last night.

Courier bag bouncing on her hip, she ran after the convoy as it swept out of sight ahead. Onlookers screamed, stampeding up the sidewalks, providing her some cover. But she was running against the current, with purpose, which made her conspicuous. Sure enough the flirtatious motorcycle cop picked her up, his helmet swiveling in her direction.

He revved the bike and accelerated at her hard, steering between G-rides and up onto the sidewalk. She got off calls to *9* and *10*, initiating the Indiana Avenue charges on either side of 6th, funneling the convoy ahead so it would pass behind the Newseum. She couldn't see the explosions – she hadn't reached the corner yet – but she heard the eruptions even over the commotion of the crowd.

As Orphan X's forward observer, she had to get to the intersection to establish visual on Cadillac One and call the shot. If she couldn't, all their meticulously laid groundwork would be wasted.

The motorcycle cop closed in, a chirp of his brakes shifting his weight forward on the bike. As he drew alongside her, she flipped the phone into his front wheel.

It hit the spokes with a buzz-saw whine, disintegrating into a thousand glittering pieces. The hitch was enough to rip the cop up over the handlebars, an airborne somersault that landed him in a five-foot skid up the sidewalk, his bul-letproof vest giving off a fingernails-on-chalkboard screech.

Her contribution to the accident went unnoticed, leaving her free to whip between fleeing onlookers and bolt around the turn in time to catch sight of Cadillac One speeding away. Edging out to the brink of the curb, she thrust her hand into the courier bag, gripped the speed gun, and aimed its nose out through the mesh opening at the trunk of the quickly receding limo.

Red numbers glowed up at her: 53 MPH.

That put the target vehicle smack in the middle of the highest range Orphan X had calculated on the speed chart.

Which meant the visual for the green-light call would be when the limo passed the *second* old-fashioned streetlamp on the east side of the street.

All she had to do was wait.

She activated her earpiece. 'They're in the chute. Wait for my signal.'

X answered, 'Copy that.'

Three SUVs careened around the corner, causing her to jerk back from the curb so they wouldn't take off her knee-caps. They accelerated to catch up to Cadillac One and assume a rear guard.

Unfortunately, they also cut off her vantage of the target.

She had no choice now but to step out into the cleared center of the street, putting her in the wide, suspicious open.

Cloaked in official emergency-response-team garb, Service creds dangling in full view from lanyards, Orphan A and the Collins brood had been able to move freely, strolling in front of the sawhorses, their FN P90s at low ready. Overzealous agents had checked their credentials twice, but the documents were – if fake – authentic government-issue.

Irate over Ricky's death, Wade was running on a high simmer, breathing so hard his nostrils quivered. Holt didn't know if he'd kicked something extra into his bloodstream – a shot of epinephrine, a hit of PCP, the blood of a Spanish bull.

Holt had positioned his team in the dense network of streets north of Pennsylvania Avenue because that was the corridor he would have chosen were *he* plotting the assassination. They'd started in a wolf pack, then spread out gradually, Holt going solo but splitting the remaining Collinses into teams of two. He directed them over the radio, maintaining close contact.

When he'd heard the explosions, he was in position near the Grand Army of the Republic Memorial, a triangular granite shaft with bronze reliefs depicting Union soldiers holding stately poses. Ideally located at the intersection of 7th, Indiana, and Pennsylvania, the circular plaza gave him clear sight lines through a good swath of Penn Quarter.

His first reaction was to not react. He'd hopped up onto a bus bench, widening his focus, reading the river. Looking two blocks north, he'd caught the convoy as it blasted along E Street. Moments later two more charges detonated up Indiana Avenue.

Now he understood.

X was guiding Bennett into a kill zone.

Holt looked overhead now, using the helicopter to chart the location of the lead limo beneath it. It was vectoring south hard toward Pennsylvania Avenue.

At last he moved, sprinting a half block south and spilling onto the wide thoroughfare a block from where Cadillac One would intercept it. He looked wildly up the street, searching for something, anything, that could pass for a sniper's wind indicator.

There it was.

A plastic grocery bag stuck artfully on a telephone line over the dead center of the street by the Newseum, high enough to catch the sight line of a roof shooter. The bag fluttered in a low breeze.

Already he was sprinting for the nearest building, activating the radio. 'He's set up for a shot somewhere near Sixth and Pennsylvania. Get here *now.*'

Slinging his submachine gun, he plowed into the Federal Trade Commission Building, flashing his badge at the security guard – *'Emergency! Emergency!'* – and smashing through the door into the stairwell. Pounding up three at a time, he headed for the roof, shouting, 'Do you copy?'

At last Wade's voice came back. 'I got eyes on a woman standing in the middle of the intersection at E and Sixth. I think she's spotting for him.' The connection crackled and then came clear once more. 'Me and my boy gonna take the bitch now.'

50. A Sleek Instrument of Destruction

Candy had to straddle the center line of 6th Street to hold the presidential limo in view, and even then it was a challenge with the SUVs weaving side to side behind it. She ran south down the middle of the street, courier bag smacking against her lower back.

Cadillac One crossed D Street, hurtling away from her.

There were still enough panicked pedestrians dashing across the road to cover Candy for the moment, but the area was dotted with agents, so it was only a matter of time before –

She sensed him from the corner of her eye, a hulking figure wrapped in an ERT combat-utility uniform, stepping out from between two parked police motorcycles.

His energy drew her focus immediately, something off about him – not just size but a ferality behind the eyes. He was sweating heavily, a trickle running down the side of his throat leaving a bluish stain.

No – not a stain.

A makeup-covered tattoo.

That happened to be a swastika.

His shadow stepped out from behind him, and she realized it wasn't his shadow but a slightly less enormous version of him.

Wade Collins and one of his cousins. Bob or Jimmy. Either way it wasn't going to go well for him.

In her ear came X's voice. *'Standing by.'*

She looked ahead at the vanishing rear of the presidential limo and then back over at the men confronting her.

A still moment, as fragile as a spiderweb, all of them connected by silk threads and trembles in the air.

And then Wade charged, his cousin at his heels. Stray tourists were still darting between them, so Wade dropped his FN P90, letting it dangle from the sling, and opted for the SIG in his hip holster.

Instead of running away, she ran *at* him.

She had to intercept him before his arm got to horizontal. She barely did.

Seizing his rising wrist with her left hand, she planted a foot on his thigh and literally ran up his body, seating her other boot in his gut before flipping backward and locking up his arm between both of her legs. Her weight ripped him forward off his feet, and they pitched together to the asphalt. Even as they fell, she reached to his side with her free hand, grabbing the swaying submachine gun, and squeezed off a burst under his armpit.

Impact with the street was brutal, Wade's weight crushing her into her courier bag.

But she held the arm bar, keeping his limb clamped between her legs, the elbow flexed outward, a breaking hold.

Behind them Bob or Jimmy held his feet a moment, staring down at them. Then crimson spots bloomed through his ERT uniform like shirt buttons, a neat line up his torso.

He toppled.

Screams split the air, leading to another mini-stampede, nearby agents and cops strobing in and out of view in the seething crowd. A few alerted to the gunfire and started forging toward them.

Keeping pressure on Wade's arm, Candy twisted hard over her shoulder and stared down 6th Street.

Between the bodies in motion, the motorcade cops, and

the weaving SUVs, Cadillac One flashed into view a quarter mile away. It crossed the first streetlamp on the eastern side, and then she lost it.

When it reappeared, it had barreled across C Street.

She strained to snap Wade's arm, but it was too goddamned thick, a log of muscle. Wade bellowed and bucked, the force lifting her off the ground and pounding her shoulder blades into the street again. Her vision blurred.

It clarified just in time to see Cadillac One occlude the second streetlamp.

She released Wade, flipping free and scissor-kicking him as hard as she could in the side of the head. As she spun up onto her feet, she initiated the earpiece to get out the command.

The weapon Evan had set up on the rooftop beside him was indirect fire, which meant he'd have to shoot it blind.

Tommy had machined the mortar out of a solid chunk, the same drawn-over-mandrel manufacturing process he used for Evan's ARES pistols. The mortar was two feet long with a baseplate and a bipod – two legs that folded down off a stainless-steel, heavy-wall, high-pressure tube.

A sleek instrument of destruction with no welded seams. It had no instrumentation, just a simple drop-and-shoot like the improvised mortars perfected by the IRA.

All calculations had to be made beforehand.

Tommy had range-tested the weapon, calibrating it for a precise distance and altitude from the target.

Candy had lased the measurements to the millimeter.

Evan had worked up a speed chart, figuring out how much he needed to offset the interception point ahead of the traveling vehicle – a sniper's trapping technique. Cadillac One was a full eighteen feet long, which gave him a lot of slop.

He'd doped the breeze with the average rate for this time of day in this location, so as long as the shopping bag on the telephone pole didn't move to horizontal, indicating a full-value wind, he'd be good to go.

The custom mortar shell was already locked and loaded. Given Evan's requirements, Tommy had opted to supply a high-explosive squash-head projectile. The tech was generally defunct, having enjoyed wide use in the Second World War and Korea. Before armor penetrators were developed, soldiers had to rely on armor *defeaters.*

Squash heads featured two key components: a hollow ballistic windscreen of a nose cone, and the C4 load, stored in a bag behind it.

On impact the aerodynamic front collapsed and stuck to the armor, sending the C4 crashing forward inside the shell to make contact with the surface and detonate.

Tommy had weighed the C4 to a tenth of a grain. For the effect Evan required, the explosion could be neither a speck too powerful nor a speck too weak.

Since the charge wasn't dependent on kinetic energy to penetrate the target, Evan could fire it nice and low over the breadth of the Newseum, keeping it out of the wind. Like lobbing a water balloon – he just had to deliver it and let physics do the rest.

His RoamZone vibrated. If Candy had switched comms from the earpiece to the RoamZone, something must have gone wrong.

He snapped the phone to his face. 'What happened?'

'The Scaredy Bugs are back.'

Evan could see the helicopter now, blazing through the airway over 6th Street.

He gritted his teeth. 'It's not the best time.'

Trevon said, 'I saw . . . um, um, I saw the countdown clock had moved, okay? It jumped ahead seventy-two hours and I didn't know why, but then I got another e-mail from Kiara and it said she was coming home three days earlier 'cuz she ran outta money and now that's only three days till she's here and Big Face can get her.'

Within seconds Evan would be spotted by the helicopter pilot. Below him on the balcony, he could hear the museum patrons milling about, confused by the mayhem outside.

He could not afford three fewer days.

He could not afford to be carrying out missions of this magnitude simultaneously on both coasts.

He could not afford to be talking to Trevon right now.

Rising up onto one knee next to the mortar, he pinched the phone between cheek and shoulder and looked back to check the subtle wind indicator one last time. The trash bag showed a moderate wind factor.

On the other end of the phone, Trevon was crying.

'I promised you I would handle it,' Evan said. 'And I will. But I have to go now.'

A movement all the way across Pennsylvania Avenue caught his eye.

A man sprinting to the edge of the rooftop of the Federal Trade Commission Building, an FN P90 pinned under one elbow.

Orphan A.

Even through his alarm, Evan felt a stab of admiration. How many hypotheticals had A considered to track Evan to this location at this moment?

Evan let the phone slip from his shoulder, thumbing open a cargo pocket to catch it as it fell.

Orphan A neared the edge of the rooftop across from Evan.

The helicopter was louder now, the sound of its approach thundering off the walls of the surrounding buildings.

Candy's voice crackled over the earpiece, cutting through Evan's thoughts. 'Shot out!'

Orphan A drew to a halt at the brink of the roof.

Evan gave him a little nod in greeting and then fired the mortar.

It left the tube with a pop.

The shell floated up over the building, past the windscreen of the helicopter, and plummeted from view. Evan saw the pilot's eyes rise to meet his.

He swung back in the other direction in time to see Orphan A hoist his submachine gun to aim at him.

Rolling onto the metal overhang, Evan gripped the edge with one hand and snatched the backpack with the other. He swung down onto the balcony among the patrons and vanished into the museum's sixth floor.

The squash-head round sailed down at the speeding limousine, striking directly above the back right seat of the rear compartment.

Cadillac One's passengers had a split second to register the thud of the charge sticking onto the roof.

Wong screamed.

The body man covered his head, his cry muffled through his arms.

Naomi jerked her eyes and the muzzle of her pistol upward.

Bennett's head rotated, too, dread pulling down on his face, gathering his skin at the jowls.

The charge detonated.

51. Breaking News

Candy blazed through the crowd, running at a full sprint. A block and a half and then she could lose herself underground.

Wade had recovered from the kick to the jaw, hustling in pursuit, but she wasn't worried about him. He was linebacker-huge without the speed.

The agents and motorcade cops were more worrisome. They'd already started to communicate through the confusion of the crowd, radios squawking as they coordinated how to close in.

She tucked in high on the sidewalk next to the buildings so she wouldn't have to cover her right flank. As a motorcade cop wheeled out of a parking lot in front of her, she darted into a throng of tourists milling like fish trapped in a tank.

She stumbled out of the press of bodies onto the opposite curb and hurdled a low hedge, her shoulder brushing a rectangular post announcing the Judiciary Square Metro Station.

Hemming in the square were multiple courthouses and the US Attorney's Office. One block south loomed the Metropolitan Police Headquarters. She was running against expectations, sprinting into the heart of DC, into the heart of authority itself.

She shot a glance over her shoulder. Three agents pursued her on foot and two motorcycle cops – wait, three.

Ahead, the exposed escalators burrowed into the earth, slanting to the Metro station below.

Without slowing she jumped onto the metal slope between

the up and down escalators and rocketed into the hot breath of the underground. As she slid past, the rising courtgoers blinked into the light of day, confused.

Riding down on her ass, she dug in her courier bag and yanked out a fat industrial razor, a 380-watt beast designed for shearing sheep. She hit the Metro platform, dumped the bag into a trash can, and shouldered into the spill of an emptying train. Ducking her head, she raked the razor through her hair.

Five wide swoops left her long rose-gold locks on the concrete floor. All that remained were blond roots bristling in a buzz cut. Next she ran the razor up her shirtfront, peeling it away and dumping it onto the tracks. She wore a bright pink jog bra.

Her gestures were largely lost in the herd, though a little boy holding his mom's hand looked up at Candy with wide eyes. She winked at him as she fastened a magnetic septum bar into place between her nostrils.

A new train screeched up to the platform.

As the agents and cops tumbled down off the escalator, she popped in headphones and bopped her head, watching them in the reflection of the subway windows.

The doors parted.

She got in and turned around, keeping herself in full view at the window. A half dozen officers filed past, checking the cars frantically, their gazes sweeping right over her.

The doors closed, and she pulled away from the station.

Despite the disruption outside, the Newseum was still filled with patrons. Evan made it through *Today's Front Pages* and *Reporting Vietnam* to the stairs, but shouts carrying up the stairwell forced him out into *Breaking News* on the fifth floor.

He jabbed his finger at the DOWN button of the elevator,

waiting for it to arrive. The wrong set of doors dinged open, and he cursed himself for not asking Candy to prep both cars. With agonizing slowness the car clanked shut and departed.

He clicked the DOWN button again.

Shouted commands reached him, ever louder.

He waited for the other elevator to arrive. He didn't punch the button more than once. He didn't bounce impatiently on his boots. He didn't crowd the doors.

It took all of his training to stand there and wait.

Without the mortar and squash head, the backpack felt light on his shoulders. He prayed the shell had hit home.

Behind him he heard the stairwell door bang open.

At last the doors spread to welcome him. He stepped inside the enormous hydraulic elevator and turned to the others waiting to board. Over their shoulders a stream of agents poured into sight.

Evan held up his hands, blocking the patrons. 'You don't want to be in here. Trust me.'

The rubber bumpers closed on a dozen startled faces.

The huge transparent car, wall-to-wall glass, had a capacity of seventy passengers.

He'd need all the room.

Dumping his skateboard backpack on the floor, he hopped up onto the handrails and tilted the third ceiling panel on the right. A load-out duffel bag slid into his hands.

He ripped out what looked like a stubby mutant rifle. The Lake Erie gas gun, named in honor of the location of the lab that engineered it, was a single-shot break-open with a tube barrel. Tommy had sawed off the butt stock behind the action, the whole thing no more than a foot and a half.

Two ballistic-nylon pouches were prepped and waiting,

filled with less lethal thirty-seven-millimeter rubber bullets, the same baton rounds the Brits had used during the Troubles in Northern Ireland. The pouches clipped onto his belt, their dilated elastic tops ensuring that he wouldn't lose any spare rounds as long as he didn't go upside down.

As the elevator dropped, the cavernous atrium of the museum yawned before him, a 3-D maze of mezzanines, floating staircases, and dangling displays.

Agents and cops scurried on the steps and across various levels, an Escheresque confusion of activity.

He tucked to the right side, partially hidden behind a massive piston nearly two feet in diameter. He'd not been noticed. For now.

Holding the gas gun low by his leg, he passed the fourth floor.

The third floor was coming up. None of the officers or agents had taken note of him descending here in near-plain view.

Then, without any warning, the neighboring car swooped up, its passengers suddenly right beside him through two glass walls and a few feet of open air.

Its passengers happened to be four Secret Service agents, their SIGs at the ready.

As they rose and he dropped, two sides of a pulley, the agents clocked the rifle at his side.

He threw himself flat in a sprawl a split second before their rounds shattered the transparent walls of his elevator, spraying him with pebbled safety glass.

An instant of onslaught and then they'd swept up out of range.

When he rose, the scene before him in the atrium had frozen, as though the plug had been pulled on an elaborate windup toy. From various levels and staircases, at least a dozen cops and agents stared at him, scrolling slowly by as he continued to descend.

The volley of nine-millimeter rounds had converted the car into a platform elevator. This was good because there would be no refraction on his outgoing shots.

It was bad for everything else.

He picked out a cop on the balcony just below, raised the gas gun, and fired a rubber bullet across the open divide. It struck the cop in the thigh, spinning him in a 180 and knocking him to the floor. It would leave a nasty bruise, but nothing more.

Evan stepped back from the brink and waited for incoming.

Bullets and sparks blew out the rest of the glass clinging to the maw of the frames. Evan waited for a break in the action and then eased forward and popped off another sabot round at an agent standing on the concourse level two floors below. Reloading, Evan knocked down another agent on the ground floor just before the guy could squeeze off a shot.

Clearing a path.

A hefty cop made heftier by a Kevlar vest bulled through the front door into the lobby, well out of rubber-bullet range.

Pulling back from the edge once more, Evan slung the gas gun down, thumbing the barrel release with his left hand so he could maintain a firing grip while his other hand dug in the ballistic pouch. The weapon broke open as his fingers closed on the cool metal he was looking for – a D-cell battery in the bottom of the pouch.

The battery's weight gave him greater range.

Sweeping the spent cartridge out, he slotted the battery into place and snapped the barrel up with a jerk. He was drawing fire now from above and below, though the moving car made pinning him down tricky, the sight lines constantly shifting. If he stayed back from the lip, most of the shots hit the car's ceiling and floor in front of him.

He hoped not to catch a ricochet.

Laboring downward, the elevator was just above the concourse level now. The displays dangling in the atrium provided sporadic cover as Evan stepped forward and sighted on the hefty cop's sternum.

'Sorry,' he said, and fired.

As he jerked back, he heard the ping of the D cell against the armor plate of the vest, the cop giving a bark that echoed up the six-story rise of the atrium.

Gunfire answered furiously, cops and agents raining lead down from the open staircases and balconies. Sprawled on his stomach, squinting against the sparks, Evan fumbled in another round. Then he jerked the skateboard free of the straps on the rear of the backpack.

He gauged the elevator's descent, the ground floor coming up fast. From outside the building, muffled voices reached him, agents shouting to fall back and set a perimeter.

Hugging the gas gun, Evan rolled through the open mouth of the elevator, falling five feet onto the concourse, the skateboard bouncing after him. He hit the slick floor beneath a rippling banner that shielded him from the sight lines above.

He looked at the skateboard, his brain taking a microsecond to dismiss the idea of riding it as idiotic. Then he was sprinting unevenly toward the door past the cops he'd felled. Rounds bit the floor behind him.

Using the hanging displays as cover, he ran for the entrance. As he neared, the door boomed inward, the frame filled with a big man in an ERT jacket, squaring to raise an FN P90.

The world went to slow motion except for Evan's brain, which made the tactical assessment in real time.

Even if he struck the man with a rubber round, the guy would be able to get off a blast from the submachine gun. Evan's only chance would be to kill the man, and he was unwilling to kill a Secret Service agent.

His momentum carried him forward, bringing him closer to the muzzle.

He thought of the promise he'd made Trevon to protect him and his sister.

The promise he'd have to break.

52. Decades-Long Fuse

As Evan bore down on the ERT agent, the man's submachine gun reached horizontal.

Evan focused on the eyes of the man he was about to let kill him.

Recognized them.

The set of the features, the stubble, the pronounced ridges of the nose.

Evan had seen this face before when he'd pulled files after Doug Wetzel had alerted him to Ricky and Wade Collins.

A cousin.

The pounding of Evan's footsteps and the whine of ricochets at his heels revved back from slow motion into normal time. He snapped the gas gun up and shot a rubber bullet through the impostor's eye.

The big man spun violently, one hand tailing up. He fell, his boot pinning the door open. Evan hurdled him, stumbling onto the sidewalk.

Outside, MPD was scrambling to set a perimeter. Evan flew into the mix. If they shot at him, they'd kill one another with crossfire. The primary risk to Evan would come from the countersnipers on the opposing rooftops.

Dodging a crisscross of stunned officers, Evan flung the gas gun aside and grabbed his RoamZone from his pocket. He heard the first whine of a sniper bullet pass his ear. Another round chipped the sidewalk in front of him, spraying grit across his shins.

A deep engine rumble added its voice to the commotion, matched with a vibration of dread inside his own chest. Across the huge street, an SUV screeched to a halt, doors blowing open, CAT members flying out wielding SR-16s. Between them and the countersnipers, Evan had to keep his time on the street to a dead minimum.

He thumbed the first saved number, and a manhole cover blew in the center of Pennsylvania Avenue.

The diversion would buy him two seconds, maybe three, before the countersnipers would reset and pepper his torso.

Across eight cleared traffic lanes, the CAT members reeled back from the manhole explosion, weapons flung skyward. Before they could regroup, Evan sprinted into the middle of the street, directly toward them.

A quarter block away, he saw Orphan A burst out of the Federal Trade Commission Building and wheel to a stop, gaping up the street.

They locked eyes – a split-second connection – as Evan slid across the final three feet of asphalt and dropped through the hole into the sewer.

As he fell, he managed to claw onto the top rung, his body racked punishingly against the steel bars beneath. In the circle of daylight above, bullets rent the air. He fell down onto the ledge below, where another load-out bag awaited him.

The hot reek and dank concrete reminded him of another sewer in another country, the mission that had set this decades-long fuse burning.

He stripped in seconds, kicking his clothes off into the stream of muck to kill any trace DNA.

Naked save for his boxer briefs, he ripped open the bag.

Inside, a hazmat diving suit.

He squirmed into the specialized dry suit, the double-layer

vulcanized rubber bunching infuriatingly at his ankles and waist. Yelled commands came from above; the agents would have to approach the open manhole tactically, which would buy him a few more precious seconds.

He raked the zipper up over his chest and then across his back, the second skin clinging to his flesh, sealing at every joint, a perfect insulation. He tugged on the positive-pressure helmet, the special intake valve wheezing into effect, preventing hostile contaminants from entering his lungs.

He noted a shadow above and looked up through the hole in the street to Orphan A. The glare on his face was homicidal.

Another memory flash jolted Evan back beneath the street of that gray foreign city. How young he'd been, patriotic blood flowing through his veins. He'd still thought he could remain above it, pristine and righteous.

He'd thought he could stay clean.

Orphan A reared back, whipping the submachine gun around to aim down into the sewer.

Still looking up at him, Evan stepped off the ledge and vanished into the black murk.

53. Antianxiety

Cadillac One screeched back through the White House gates, a shell of its former self. Windows shattered, rear tires shredded, the Presidential Standard flag snapped off the hood.

Conveyed between the half dozen battered SUVs representing the remaining convoy, it sped to a secure area, slamming down a ramp to a blastproofed emergency bunker, its undercarriage throwing up sparks.

It skidded to a halt.

Hosts of agents, emergency medical personnel, and the White House physician waited with held breath.

The limo was still.

Steam rose from the hood. Foam bulged from a punctured tire. Radio chatter filled the bunker, overlapping waves of commands from the crisis center at Secret Service HQ.

And then the rear door creaked open, releasing a spill of bullet-resistant glass, revealing Naomi lying across Bennett's inert form. She'd piled on top of him as the charge initiated.

She peeled herself off him now.

Bennett coughed, the sound driving everyone into motion.

'Mr President, we need to get you —'

'— cut off his shirt and let's find a —'

'Goddamn it, everyone off me.' Bennett's face poked up, his glasses shattered, crooked on his face. They fell free, trampled underfoot as he shoved himself clear of the limo and the throng of personnel. 'I'm *fine*.'

Behind him Eva Wong and the body man exited, hands pressed to their heads. They were steered immediately to rolling gurneys.

Bennett's chest heaved. His watch face was cracked. The skin beneath his right eye twitched. He rubbed his face, coughed some more, holding out a hand to keep the others at bay.

Naomi raked her fingers through her hair, freeing bits of glass. 'You need to let the physician check you, Mr President.'

'I need to find out what the hell just happened.'

'It looks like a mortar round of some sort –'

'You allowed a *mortar round* to drop on my goddamned limousine?' His voice, ordinarily so calm, shook with rage. 'You're lucky I'm still alive.'

A flush crept up Naomi's throat, invading her cheeks. 'Yes, I am, Mr President. But right now you need medical attention. You need to let the physician –'

Again paramedics attempted to move in but Bennett swung an arm to hold them off, a drunk wielding a broken bottle. 'What kind of charge did he use?' he said, dangerously close to shouting. 'What did Orphan X use?'

Naomi stepped forward, allowing cover for the paramedics to position the gurney closer. 'Forensic Services will be here any –'

'A bigger charge would've gotten it done,' Bennett said. An uncharacteristic wildness touched his eyes – desperation or maybe even fear. 'It would've killed me for sure. Why didn't he use a bigger charge?'

'Maybe he wasn't trying to kill you,' she said. 'Maybe he was trying to ring your bell.'

Bennett straightened up, clutching his lower back. 'It'll take a lot more than that.'

Everyone stiffened at once, staring at him.

'What?' he said. *'What?'*

He felt warmth trickle from his ear, reached up. His finger pad came away glossy with his own blood.

Naomi said, 'The physician, Mr President.'

Bennett rubbed the blood between his thumb and forefinger, watched it spread across the pads. He felt his mouth settle into a scowl, though he hadn't told it to.

He sat on the gurney.

Naomi perched at the edge of an overstuffed chair in the West Sitting Hall, the red leather cool through her pants. Bennett reclined on the chesterfield sofa across from her, tie missing, collar still spotted with blood.

The room was soothing with its peach walls and antique wooden tables, its ferns and bowls of carnations. The framed double doors that opened onto the hall and staircase were closed, squaring the room. A number of staffers and medical personnel orbited the space or conferred in hushed tones in the far-flung seating areas. Eva Wong sat alone over by the fireplace, at the ready for a snap of the president's fingers. After being diagnosed with minor tinnitus and released from care, she'd scurried right back to the president's side.

This was an all-hands-on-deck moment.

Though there remained more questions than answers, Naomi had downloaded Bennett on the preliminary report from the Forensic Division, and given his reaction, she couldn't blame the others in the room for maintaining a healthy standoff distance.

'A squash head?' Bennett said. 'Why's he using outdated weapons tech?'

'The hypothesis we're working with is that he wanted to shatter the ballistic windows to clear the way.'

'For what?'

'A shot at you. But the protective convoy did its job, got you away safely.'

An aide entered with a silver tray holding a fresh shirt and a replacement pair of eyeglasses. Bennett tore off his tie and changed his shirt in full view of everyone. Propriety had been washed aside by the exigencies of the situation.

'A job well done, is that what you're telling me?' He polished the lenses carefully before donning the new glasses. 'Convenient how that hypothesis lets the Service off the hook.'

'If you'll forgive me for saying so, Mr President, I'm not feeling particularly off the hook at the moment.'

'Okay,' Bennett said. 'So he wanted to break the glass to get at me. The rear compartment of Cadillac One is a closed container, which means he had to pull off a balancing act between concussing it enough to shatter the windows – which he'd know is impossible, by the way – and producing too much overpressure, which would kill everyone inside. Hence the question: Why not just do the latter and kill everyone inside?'

'I have a feeling . . .'

'What?'

'I have a feeling that he didn't want to kill the rest of us.'

Bennett's eyes crinkled at the edges with amusement. 'You think Orphan X cares about collateral damage?'

'He was cornered by cops in that café two weeks ago –'

'I recall.'

'Well,' she said, 'a man who throws matcha tea and salt when confronted with armed police officers doesn't sound like someone who doesn't care about collateral damage. A man who uses rubber bullets to effect his escape doesn't sound like someone who doesn't care about killing innocents.'

'According to Director Gonzalez, Orphan X killed two Secret Service agents today.'

'About that . . .' Naomi shot a glance at the iconic lunette window, realized her breath was held. She took the plunge. 'We've discovered that the two emergency-response-team members who were killed were actually impostor agents.'

Bennett stared at her with incredulity. 'You allowed outsiders to penetrate the Secret Service? Along my motorcade route?'

Though chagrined to the bone, she found herself wondering whether Bennett was feigning his reaction. 'Agent Demme remembers clearing them during the advance sweep.' She nodded to Demme, who was waiting nervously across the room, doing his best to pretend he hadn't heard his name spoken. 'He double-checked their creds, said they checked out in the databases. But now any record of them is gone.'

'You're telling me you've got moles in your agency, Templeton?'

'I'm worried we have moles outside the Service, people with clearance high enough to alter top-secret databases. Someone authorized inside State, NSA, DoD.'

Bennett's gaze was steady, but in her peripheral vision Naomi saw Wong's face swivel to him. Naomi had no idea what that was about, but she felt paranoia squirm to life in her belly, the sense that there were vast mechanisms at work beneath the surface so well cloaked that she'd never comprehend them.

She focused on the job at hand, which was itself big enough to drown in. 'It seems these impostors were targeting Orphan X, and he targeted them – and *only* them – right back.'

'No,' Bennett said. 'No, no, no. Nothing with X is a direct line. Not the men he killed, not his reason for shattering the limousine. It's all part of a more complex strategy. We're missing something. What are we missing?' He ran his thumb back and forth across his fingertips repetitively.

Bennett's shift in affect was upsetting. Naomi was accustomed to seeing him completely in control, never a tremor in his voice or a sheen of sweat across his brow. Now he looked disheveled in his rumpled clothes.

'Perhaps you're right,' she said, hoping a conciliatory tone might take his agitation down a notch. 'Perhaps he miscalculated the charge.'

'The man penetrated an impenetrable security zone, sent a mortar round a half block in moderate wind conditions toward a target moving fifty-five miles per hour and hit the nail on the head.' Bennett clenched his hands together. 'That doesn't sound like someone who *miscalculates*.'

'No,' she said.

'So we need to figure out what the hell he's up to. You're not thinking hard enough.'

Before Naomi could respond, the physician approached, orange bottle in hand. 'Mr President, after the strain of the day, I think it's imperative that you take a low dose of Buspar —'

Bennett said, 'I don't need an antianxiety. I never take that crap, Frank. You know this. Don't want to get in the habit.'

The physician kept his voice calm and steady. 'It's not every day that you're nearly assassinated.'

Bennett tensed, his stare locked on the bottle. 'Where was this prescription filled?'

'The usual pharmacy.'

Bennett knocked the bottle out of the physician's hands,

sending it tumbling across the carpet. The doctor drew upright, taken aback.

'Nothing is usual anymore,' Bennett said. 'Have those pills been tested?'

The physician said, 'I assure you –'

Bennett's glare found Naomi. 'Have them tested. This is a perfect ploy, see? The attack gets my heart rate up, after which my doc will likely recommend I take a med. Pills can be contaminated. That's how he thinks. Every single thing is strategic.' He got up, snatched the bottle off the carpet, and held it before Naomi's face. 'I would have thought that after what you just witnessed, you might understand what we're up against.'

She gestured Demme over and handed him the bottle. 'Can you get Tech Security in here, please?'

'What other logical actions can be predicted in the wake of an explosion like that?' Bennett said, loud enough now to address the entire room. 'I give a speech. So. Where's my speech?'

A wiry man in the far corner held up a notepad and a sheaf of papers. 'Not quite there yet, Mr President.'

Bennett pointed. 'Those papers. The notepad. Take them to the lab. They need to be checked.' He rubbed his wrist. 'Where's my watch?'

Across the room the assistant secretary was on her feet. 'Already en route to Geneva to be fixed, Mr President.'

'No, *no*. I want it fixed here in the US. Orphan X could intercept it, apply contact poison to the band.' Abruptly, he removed his new pair of wire-frame eyeglasses and regarded them. His other hand worked the top of his shirt, unbuttoning it. 'And these. Did someone check these for toxins?'

Naomi said, 'Every item that goes on your body is acquired

from a security-cleared vendor and is double-checked before it enters the White House.'

'Were they checked *again* for toxins and poisons? After the attack but before they were brought to me on a silver tray?'

Demme cleared his throat. 'They were, Mr President, right before they were brought in.'

Reluctantly, Bennett slid his glasses back on and released his shirt, which gapped open at the throat.

Demme continued nervously, 'After an AOP, we take nothing for granted. Every conceivable measure is –'

'How about my other clothes? The bedsheets? He could sneak a contaminant into the detergent.'

'I have two agents down at laundry operations right now, Mr President,' Naomi said. 'One from Protective Intelligence and Assessment, the other from the Technical Security Division. We understand the level of this threat, and we are tightening operations to an unprecedented level. We'll even be adding more panic buttons through the residential areas of the White House. They'll be disguised as Presidential Seals embedded in surfaces and on the walls –'

The double doors opened, and a team of agents entered with cameras. They began systematically photographing the room.

'Who are they?' Bennett said.

'I'm having our advance-team techs sweep all the rooms in the White House,' Naomi said. 'They'll photograph everything so we can make sure nothing has been touched or moved. This is the baseline series.'

'Do you *personally* recognize these men?'

'I do.'

'I want those cameras taken apart,' Bennett said. 'Orphan X, he would have predicted this measure in the wake of the limo attack. He could have planted a charge *inside* the cameras. You need to start thinking like him.'

The agents stopped taking pictures and stood awkwardly, the offending cameras in hand. Demme started over to them.

'Not while I'm here,' Bennett said. 'Templeton, come with me.'

He exited the sitting room swiftly.

Naomi hurried to keep pace, flipping through her notebook. 'Mr President, until we can get our arms around this situation, we have to make some adjustments. No more rope lines or jogging, no unmagged crowds, wider buffer zones –'

She looked up from her notebook, realizing only now that they'd arrived in the master bedroom. That broad plain of brown carpet, the rounded north side, the oddly delicate letter desk. Bennett had opened his closet door, an inset panel that had been papered like the rest of the wall. He had a necktie in hand, which he regarded with evident suspicion. The muscles of his back flexed like scales, a physical tell of his mounting frustration.

She said, 'For right now I'd like to cancel *all* public appearances, meals eaten out –'

He whipped around, jabbing his finger in her direction. 'I'm the most powerful person on this planet. I won't be trapped in my own goddamned house, no matter how big it is.'

She heard her father's voice reminding her that ultimately a Secret Service agent was a babysitter, and she kept her mouth shut. Even so, she could feel her face burning.

Bennett looked down at the tie in his hand. He dropped it on the floor. His shoulders sank, and then he walked heavily across the room and sat on his bed.

All the heat had gone out of him.

He snickered, a single note muffled in his throat. 'After a time you forget the privilege of this place,' he said, his voice hoarse. 'Everywhere you look.' He gestured at an ornate gold clock resting on the nightstand. 'What do you think of that?'

She stared at the scrolled acanthus leaves and cherubs floating around the white face. She pocketed her notebook. 'I think it's hideous.'

This seemed to amuse him. 'It's a French mid-nineteenth-century Louis XVI ormolu,' he said. 'It cost a hundred seventy-five thousand dollars.'

'That doesn't make it pretty.'

'No. I suppose not.'

'It looks like something my gamma would've had on the mantel next to a velvet Jesus painting.'

He was silent for a time.

Then he said, 'I know why I do this job. At least I used to. Why do you do yours?'

She pictured her dad again, a husk of what he used to be. She thought of his countless stories, his undying pride in the Service, his sureness of his place in the world.

She said, 'I can change history.'

'How do you mean?'

She shrugged. 'If Robert Kennedy doesn't get shot in '68, Nixon doesn't become president.'

'And if I don't get killed by Orphan X? Then what?'

She studied the carpet, perhaps for too long. When she finally looked up, his gaze was waiting, as steady as she'd ever seen it.

She said, 'I suppose that's up to you, Mr President.'

54. Too Damaged

In the shower's stream, Evan soaped himself from head to toe and then did it again. On the third go, he finally felt he'd gotten the sewer muck off himself, but he went a fourth round anyway. Technically none of the waste had touched his flesh, but he felt it, a phantom contamination in his nostrils, his lungs.

Myriad aches had taken up residence in his muscles, but he refused to acknowledge them directly. There would be time enough to be sore when the mission was over.

After toweling off, he leaned against the counter of the sink and checked the Drafts folder of his Gmail account.

The message, twelve hours old, was only two sentences. And yet they seemed to carry the weight of the world.

'can't find anything in secure SS databases re: 1997 mission. sorry. x, j.'

His frustration brimmed, spilling over and assailing him with impressions. A man slumped over a table, chair shoved back, face in his bowl of soup. A fastidious Estonian arms dealer bleeding out beside a loom in an abandoned textile factory. A naked girl, skin tented across her bones, curled on a mattress beside a metal folding chair holding a heroin kit. The foreign minister falling back, his eyes bulging in a final instant of awareness, a hole the size of a 7.62×54mmR round replacing his left cheek. His wife's stretched-wide mouth, her scream buried beneath the swelling uproar of the crowd. The generals surrounding them in the open sedan, stolid and loyal. Or not.

And the bits and pieces sent into motion by that single squeeze of a trigger. A copper-washed steel cartridge holding an invisible fingerprint, left on a sewer ledge. The untold grief and rage left in the wake of the murdered. The power vacuum after the foreign minister and his hawkish views on nuclear development had been dispatched. What fault lines and tectonic shifts had Bennett's order set into motion? What hurricane had been unleashed by the flapping of a butterfly's wing? How the hell had a nineteen-year-old's first mission evolved into a storm sufficient to threaten the president of the United States?

Evan stared at his reflection, a ghostly form in the fogged glass. For the first time in years, he felt a stab of self-pity, wishing that the Mystery Man had never showed up to peruse the offerings of the Pride House Group Home in East Baltimore. The foster home had proven a rich recruiting ground for the Program. The boys used to jostle at the window, hoping for a glimpse of the man lingering by the chain-link surrounding the cracked basketball courts across the street. They were unsure who he was or where he'd come from, but they sensed he was there for them. There were rumors of boys pulled off the street, boys who had gone on to fresh lives. There were rumors of sex-slave operations and stolen-organ rings, too, but those weren't strong enough to quell their curiosity.

They all had so little to lose.

If the Mystery Man hadn't chosen Evan – or, more precisely, if Evan hadn't gotten himself chosen – he would never have had Jack. He wouldn't have become an Orphan. He wouldn't have been sent halfway around the world at the age of nineteen to a country he didn't know to assassinate the foreign minister of a government he cared nothing about.

He probably would have died of a drug overdose or in a prison cell. But maybe, just maybe, he might have seen himself clear to a normal life. A life where he wasn't hunted by the most powerful man on the planet.

A life where he might have met a single-mother district attorney and her nine-year-old son and figured out how to be with them.

He saw himself punching the mirror, spiderwebbing it into a thousand fragments as impossible to put together as his own past. He imagined the blood dripping from his knuckles, the wounds that would slow him, imperfections he could not afford.

He finished dressing and emerged into the hotel room.

Candy faced away, wearing jeans, readying a shirt to pull over her head. The TV was muted, but the news – with its apoplectic hosts, blaring chyrons, and manic breaking-news scroll – seemed to be screaming anyway.

She turned quickly to hide the burned flesh of her back, but he'd seen it already. It looked scraped up, probably from the fight with Wade, the ruined skin cracked and weeping.

The front of her was unmarred. She held the shirt low by her stomach, her breasts exposed.

Her shorn hair accented the shape of her head – beautiful, regal – and the absence of her locks made her curves more pronounced. She looked like a different person and more like herself all at once, as if she'd been laid bare, distilled to her essence.

She locked down a wince of pain, said, 'I'll be fine.'

He said, 'Okay.'

She looked over at the news, annoyed. She turned off the screen and threw the remote onto the couch with more force than seemed necessary. Then she stood a moment, breathing, T-shirt still bunched in her hands as if she couldn't bring herself to pull it on.

'A cool washcloth helps sometimes,' she said.

She did not meet his eyes.

He said, 'Okay.'

He returned to the bathroom. When he emerged with the washcloth in hand, she was lying on her stomach on the bed, shirt mopped around one fist.

He stood a moment, regarding the damage that he had wrought. Then he went over, sat next to her, and dabbed gently at the whorled, angry flesh.

She did not flinch.

After a time she said, 'The person who called you the other night. Was it a woman?'

Evan said, 'I have some gauze in my backpack.'

'Doesn't help. It just sticks, and then it's worse when I have to peel it off.'

He folded the washcloth, applied the cool compress to a gouge on her right shoulder.

'What if we're too damaged?' she said. 'For anything . . . real? Ever think about that?'

He folded the washcloth once more and kept at it.

'All the time,' he said.

He finished blotting her lower back, and then she spun off the bed and pulled on her T-shirt. It was odd to see her move so gingerly. Already the wounds started to spot through the fabric.

She looked over her shoulder, noticing.

'I have a jacket,' she said.

He gathered his stuff and she gathered hers.

They met at the door.

'We did exactly what we needed to,' he said. 'I got it from here.'

Her lips softened in a smile that seemed more sad than not. 'I'm gonna miss trying to kill you, X.'

They stepped out into the hall and walked away in opposite directions.

Neither looked back.

55. A Social Call

Naomi awoke from a deep slumber fully dressed, flopped facedown into her fluffy duvet like a ditzy lead in a rom-com. The air blanketed her, middle-of-the-night heavy. And yet something felt different, an aspect of the space around her.

She pushed herself up, wiped drool from the corner of her mouth.

Her bedroom door was open.

She never slept with the door open, couldn't relax with that black rectangle of exposed space staring back at her from across the room.

Like it was staring at her now.

She scrambled across the mattress, dove for her night-stand drawer, came up with her service weapon.

Rolling off the bed, she hit her knees on the far side, aiming at the doorway.

Not a sound aside from her own labored breathing.

Over on his round corduroy cushion, Fenway lifted his head sleepily, offered a curled-tongue yawn, and went back to sleep.

Useless dog.

Maybe it was nothing. Maybe a draft had sucked the door open. Maybe having a mortar round dropped on her head had made her jumpy.

Naomi clenched the checkered grip of the P229. It was a

highly effective weapon but even so, it felt less than comforting right now.

She waited a full minute, listening, but heard nothing from within the apartment.

Rising with her pistol locked before her, she circled the bed, inching for the door.

Slowly, slowly – and then she sprang into the hall, sighting up its length.

The front door to her apartment was standing open.

It took an extra half second for her to register this simple fact, an undeniable breach of her space. She had to wrestle the image from the realm of nightmares and seat it in the present reality.

An intruder.

Had come into her apartment.

While she slept.

She waited another full minute for her breathing to slow, and then she moved for the front door, letting her shoulder whisper along the wall.

Her Boeing Black phone charged on the table in the entry, emitting a bluish glow. Keeping her muzzle aimed at the door, she snatched up the phone and thumbed a 911 text to HQ.

In the silence of the hall, the whoosh of the sent text sounded like a tidal wave. She cringed, letting the noise recede before stepping into the outside corridor.

No one in the open.

No one by the elevator.

But at the far side of the hall, the window to the fire escape had been unlocked, the pane bumping in the midnight breeze.

Click-click. Click-click.

Swallowing hard, she made her way painstakingly to the window.

Click-click. Click-click.

She reached for the pane, stilled it with her hand.

Nothing on the landing.

Nothing beyond.

She stepped through into the night chill.

Fog rolled over the courtyard below, wisps trailing above the cobblestone with Victorian menace. Flakes of rust poked her bare hand as she gripped the steep rail of the fire escape.

She descended.

She couldn't see the fountain in the center of the fog-filled courtyard, but she heard its gurgling, like an old man choking.

'Backup's on the way,' she said, pleased with how strong her voice came out. 'You picked the wrong apartment to break in to.'

A wind cut through the courtyard, lifting a curtain of fog, and she saw a form standing there indistinct in the darkness.

Orphan X?

She said, *'Put your hands up.'*

He did not.

'Put your fucking hands up.'

'Atlas carries the world on his shoulders,' he said. 'And I used to think about how miserable he must be. You know how the Greeks love suffering. But then I realized – he's not suffering. He's fortunate to shoulder a responsibility of that magnitude. It's enough weight to make him useful, to give him self-respect. If he put down his load, he'd be meaningless.'

A streamer of fog drifted by, occluding Orphan X for a moment. Her gun hand was trembling. 'You have a pretty high view of yourself.'

'Not me,' he said. 'You.'

Her throat felt suddenly dry. She forced a swallow. 'Why didn't you kill the president with the explosion?'

'Because you were in the vehicle,' he said. 'You, the body man, the new deputy chief of staff, the driver.'

'You were willing to kill others,' she said. 'If you'd been cornered in that museum –'

'Then I would've taken what was coming to me. Whether that meant an arrest or a bullet.' The mist swirled, and he was there and gone, there and gone. 'If your men took me alive, I'd have to be condemned, sentenced, put away, or put to death. It would be necessary. I accept that.' For a second, only the band of his eyes was visible. 'It's just not enough to stop me.'

'So that's it,' she said. 'You think you're the good guy.'

'There are no good guys. There are no bad guys. There's only what needs to be done.'

She firmed her grip on the pistol, her arms starting to ache. 'Why does *this* need to be done? Why do you want Bennett dead?'

'You see what's wrong,' he said. 'Open your eyes wider.'

She thought about the two dead impostor agents whom Demme had just linked to the ostensible drug murders at the Watergate. There'd been no record of either man in the databases, though Demme had sworn up and down he'd seen them there. Who had the power to create and delete an authentic Secret Service agent's profile while leaving no fingerprints?

'Something happened in 1997,' Orphan X said. 'Something he's been trying to cover up since he took office. Something he would handle personally. Look harder.'

She remembered the surveillance photographs Orphan X

had left with the sniper rifle in Apartment 705, all those neutralized Orphans, their faces crossed out with Magic Marker.
The files strapped to Doug Wetzel's chest. In the wake of the
explosion, they'd recovered nothing but ash and singed
scraps with redaction markings. She felt that same paranoid
uptick in her blood, the sense that she was listening in on a
conversation between Orphan X and the president of the
United States, only they were speaking in a tongue unknown
to her.

'It's not my job to investigate the president,' she said. 'It's
my job to stop you from harming him. I know you've got a
conspiracy theory you believe in deeply. I know you believe
he's committed some terrible wrong. But if you're as honor-
able as you claim, what about due process?'

'Bennett's Teflon. Nothing sticks.'

His hand dove to his pocket, and she fired.

The dry click reached her ears and – *fuck* – through a rush
of adrenaline – *misfire* – she pulled the trigger again, and it
cycled double-action once more and clicked uselessly, the
slide not actuating – *no bullets, how are there no bullets?* – and she
saw his hand jerk clear of his pocket.

He threw a scattering of bullets at her. The brass bounced
over her boots and rolled on the concrete, snagging in cracks.

It took a moment for the dime to drop.

He'd been in her bedroom, in her nightstand, in her
pistol.

The tap of metal on the ground stopped, the bullets set-
tling. Sweat filmed her back, her neck.

'Are –' Her throat clutched. 'Are you gonna kill me?'

'No,' he said. 'This is a social call.'

She stared in disbelief, the gauzy air sheeting between them.
At last came the sweet, sweet sound of sirens approaching,

music on the night breeze. She was still rooted in place, her head numb, her legs made of concrete.

'Besides,' he said, 'if I killed you, who would feed Fenway?'

She crouched, thumbed a few rounds into the mag with shaking hands, seated it with a smack of her hand.

When she jerked her head, he was gone.

56. Are We Ready?

Evan was burying the rental sedan in the darkness of an alley across from the target location when his RoamZone rang.

Immediately after leaving Naomi Templeton's building, he'd saved a new message in the Drafts folder of the.nwhr.man@gmail.com.

'Request phone contact. Total privacy. Secure line.'

In the intervening hours while he waited for the sun to rise over Switzerland, he'd run a series of fast-strike break-ins focused on White House-approved vendors.

Remaining in his tucked-away vehicle, he answered.

Her voice came through, a burst of exuberance. 'Holy *shit-monkeys*! Did you see the news?'

He tilted his head back, took a deep breath, and summoned patience. The moonroof showed only the impenetrable black sheet of the sky.

'I was there,' he said. 'I don't need to see the news. Is this line secure?'

'More secure than yours,' Joey said. 'But mission wasn't accomplished. He wasn't neutralized.'

'I noticed,' Evan said. 'Listen. Our friend, the agent? I just put her into motion.'

A brief pause while Joey regrouped. 'Pertaining to what?'

'Pertaining to 1997. That should open up new avenues for you, new intel. I need you to use her phone to monitor her trail. GPS, parallel queries she might make in the databases, what new intel she pulls in. She'll be on the trail, but I want you to hound-dog out ahead of her.'

'Given the tsunami you just put into motion after the motorcade attack, does this really matter anymore? Whatever went down in '97? I mean, at this point –'

'Yes,' he said.

'Why?'

'I need to know.'

He'd allowed a rare uptick in his tone, a sharpness that surprised even him. While he'd been advancing the operation, the mystery of his first mission had been working on him like a thorn, burrowing deeper, growing inflamed.

To no avail, he'd scoured an ocean of intel. His only hope for an answer now lay with what Naomi Templeton, in her capacity as a special agent in charge, might uncover from the inside.

A deadness claimed the connection, highlighting every one of the four thousand miles between him and Joey.

'Okay,' she said.

Evan moved to hang up, but Joey said, 'I did notice something important while I was poking around. The surveillance feed of past locations they flagged for you? The site where your foster home used to be and stuff? The code's been hijacked.'

'Which means?'

'The imagery analysis is being siphoned off before the Secret Service sees it. Guess where it's going?'

Evan recalled those whispers about Bennett's early years in the Department of Defense, how he'd relied on the first Orphan to help steer his operational directives.

He said, 'DoD.'

'That's right,' Joey said. 'It's set up to autoforward through the DoD to an unknown source. The Service gets it on a three-hour lag.'

Evan said, 'A lot can happen in three hours.'

'Yes it can,' she said. 'Look, about the other thing with Agent Templeton. I can't promise that whatever new intel she brings will give me enough to get you what you're looking for. But I'll try.'

'You take point on the past,' he said. 'I'll keep her busy in the present.'

He hung up, got out, and headed into the commercial kitchen across the street.

The security guard hefted his pants, the belt orbiting his pronounced waist like a line drawn around an egg. He wore a mustache that he thought enhanced his masculinity but in reality made him resemble a third Mario brother.

As he ambled around the corner of the blocky brick building, he clicked on his Maglite and dutifully checked the surveillance camera hidden under the overhang of the gutter.

The thick black power cord was severed.

Leaning back on his heels, he stared up at the cross section of tube for a moment, the dot of copper conductor glinting inside its rubber insulation.

His radio was at his lips. 'This is Bill, location five. Intrusion. We have an intrusion.'

Bill hustled around to the rear entrance, wheezing now from fear and lack of gym time. The door rested slightly open, a black seam showing at the frame. The alarm hadn't gone off, which was shocking. Given whom the catering company serviced, it was not an easy system to disarm.

The bright yellow backup security patrol car was there

within seconds, his two colleagues easing the doors shut quietly so as not to alert any intruders who might be inside.

They circled up, Glocks drawn, nervous.

Bill gestured silently with two fingers, directing their movements like military guys did in movies.

Jayla wrinkled her forehead at him. 'Why you waving your pudgy fingers all at us?'

'Just listen, okay,' he whispered, resisting the urge to put his hands on his knees to catch his breath. 'You go in the side entrance. I'll go in the front. Luis, take the other side. We'll corner whoever's in there.'

'And leave the rear entrance open?' Luis said.

'Well, there are three of us,' Bill said. 'And four doors.'

'So why don't we take the sides and the rear?'

'I say we take the rear door, this side, and the front,' Jayla said.

'This isn't a democracy,' Bill said.

'Why not?'

'Because . . . well, I called it in,' Bill said. 'We're going side, side, front.'

Jayla rolled her eyes elaborately.

Bill said, 'Let's move.'

Jayla and Luis exchanged a look of forbearance before they left the huddle.

Bill fumbled the master keys out of his pocket and entered the commercial kitchen from the front. The frigid air hit him, cooling the sweat at the back of his neck. He passed a row of refrigerated units humming like slumbering beasts, his reflection wobbly in the stainless-steel panels. Fat padlocks dangled from several of the units – the ones with contents designated for 1600 Pennsylvania Avenue.

He kept his finger outside the trigger guard alongside the

barrel, because he didn't want to shoot some kid who'd broken in on a lark.

Not that a kid could slice through a surveillance system installed by the Secret Service.

Bill cleared the corridor and emerged onto the main floor. Beyond several floating cooktops arrayed like craps tables, a wide half-moon dais floated several steps above the floor, elevating one cooking display higher than the others for instructional purposes. Behind a butcher-block island adorned with carrots, mixers, blenders, bags of flour and sugar, a plate of sushi, and a vibrant green bunch of parsley, a man sat on a barstool.

Backlit by a single lamp dangling from an exposed beam in the ceiling, he remained so still that Bill considered – hoped – that he was a mannequin propped in place on the showroomlike stage.

Movement wavered in Bill's peripheral vision, Jayla and Luis edging into view from either side.

'Don't move,' Bill said.

The man said, 'I'm not moving.'

Bill blinked sweat from his eyes. 'Right,' he said. 'Stay not moving.'

From his left he heard Jayla exhale with dismay.

'Listen carefully,' the man said. 'I'm going to tell you what's gonna happen next.'

He remained on that barstool, hands resting casually on the butcher block before him. Behind him to one side, the wind sucked at the rear door, clicking the latch assembly against the strike plate. The sound was unnerving, a doomed animal scratching at a cage door.

'You're gonna let me walk out of here,' the man said.

Jayla stepped forward, weapon raised. 'You're staring at three guns,' she said. 'And you got empty hands.'

'The thing is, you're all perspiring already. Your eyes wider than normal. Nostrils flaring because you're breathing hard. Which means you've already shifted into emergency mode. Which means a whole lot is going on inside you that you're not even aware of. Your cortisol levels are up, your right and left cortices have activated, and your limbic system's disinhibited. That's what's making you sweat, making you tremble. It's eroding your fine-motor precision, even your perception.'

'Don't matter,' Jayla said, her suddenly high voice ringing off the walls and the lofty ceiling. 'We have numbers.'

'But you've drawn too close together,' the man said helpfully. 'Which puts you all into range.' His hands stayed where they were, but his eyes ticked to the stovetop to his side. 'This pot is filled with boiling water,' he said. 'To which I've added oil, which makes it cling to the flesh and burn. The first thing I'll do is knock it right off the burner, spraying you all. Then I'm gonna come over the top of this island with that pan.' His eyes indicated said pan, within reach of his left hand. 'I have elevation, which means good momentum on the drop. While you two are clawing at your faces, I'll hit you' – and now the eyes skewered Bill – 'on the wrist of your gun hand. The pan's cast iron, so that'll do the job. Then I'll turn my focus to you two.' The eyes found Jayla. 'Leg sweep and you're on the floor, wind knocked out of you.' Luis. 'Back kick to your ribs, cracking the seventh and sixth. Maybe the fifth.' His jaw shifted. 'I haven't made up my mind on that yet.'

The man folded his hands on the table, as calm and resigned as a banker denying a loan. He regarded the three of them, frozen where they stood. 'So,' he said. 'What's it gonna be?'

Jayla seemed to be speechless. The tip of Luis's gun lowered a few inches.

Bill tried to speak, but his mouth had gummed up. He cleared his throat, an undignified harrumph, and said, 'I'm sorry, sir. But I have a duty, and if I don't honor that duty, then I won't be able to look my fiancée in the eye when I go home tonight.' His voice shook a bit.

He did not add his next thought: *If I'm lucky enough to make it home tonight.*

'Okay, then,' the man said. He spread his hands calmly so they hovered a few inches above the butcher block. 'Are we ready?'

Bill said, 'Let's just –'

A pan flew upward, the deafening clang of its impact with the lamp accompanied by total darkness. Something hit Bill in the face, and he screamed, pawing at the hot liquid. Only his responsible trigger-finger placement kept him from firing blindly.

Luis grunted, and Jayla's boots shuffled against the floor, and then Bill sucked something into his lungs and coughed so hard he thought he might hyperventilate.

He managed to click his Maglite on, the beam stabbing the darkness. Particles textured the air, everything turned to Ground Zero grit, and there was no man behind the island, no man among them, no man behind him.

Bill kept whirling around, the beam painting the darkness with yellow swipes. Two more beams joined his, Jayla and Luis getting in on the act, and then Bill spit twice to clear his mouth and realized that what had hit him in the face wasn't boiling water and oil but flour from the burst sack resting on the island.

All three of the flashlights zeroed in on the rear door,

which now stood wide open, a rush of night wind parting the flour-filled air like the Red Sea.

The three guards stood shoulder to shoulder, still breathing audibly.

Jayla's voice came in a hoarse croak. 'The fuck,' she said, 'was *that* about?'

57. Negative Space

'He wouldn't get caught,' Bennett said. 'Not by a second-rate security patrol. No – he *wanted* to get caught. That commercial kitchen is merely the place he chose to be seen. We're not reading the chessboard right. We need to figure out what we *aren't* looking at. The chemicals in the swimming pool? My newly tailored suits? The water supply to my shower?'

Continuing to pace, he pulled off his jacket and flipped it onto the desk, tugging at his tie. His face looked flushed, a vein bulging in his forehead. Naomi stood perfectly still between the couches, letting him revolve around her like an electron.

For the first time, it seemed he was having trouble focusing. She'd had to cover the basics with him several times.

That a security patrol had intercepted Orphan X in the commercial kitchen of the White House's primary caterer.

That he'd left behind two pieces of fugu sushi, the white slabs of puffer fish rich with deadly tetrodotoxin.

That KAZ Sushi Bistro in Foggy Bottom had reported a burglary earlier in the night, several of the rare fish stolen before they could be expertly prepared by the chef.

That each fish contained enough toxin to kill thirty men.

That a pinhead drop of tetrodotoxin, ten thousand times more lethal than cyanide, was sufficient to paralyze the diaphragm and the intercostal muscles and halt breathing.

That there was no antidote.

That break-ins had been reported in three other kitchens

and two food plants last night and early this morning, all of them on the approved-vendor list.

That the Service was unsure if more intrusions had been executed but remained as of yet undetected.

Though Bennett had refused to eat anything since the news emerged early this morning, he looked poisoned now, with his red face, agitated gestures, and patch of flesh twitching beneath his eye. He was under tremendous stress and holding up relatively well, but even so she found the unraveling of his famously perfect composure to be sobering.

Not that she felt any better. After filing a report on Orphan X's social call last night, she'd gone straight into HQ. Though she hadn't repeated X's claims of a presidential cover-up pertaining to a 1997 incident, her curiosity had been piqued. The impostor ERT agents, the tampered-with database entries, and Bennett's increasingly erratic behavior had raised enough red flags to motivate her to undertake some reckless digging.

Orphan X had clearly stated that the matter was sufficiently explosive that Bennett would have handled it – or at least part of it – personally. Which would require off-the-books contact with an intermediary. But the president's official movements were well known and well documented. If he beckoned someone to the White House, the name would show up in the visitor logs. Phone calls, even highly classified ones, were memorialized by date, time, and participants.

What Naomi needed to uncover were the president's *unofficial* movements. Since taking office Bennett could go nowhere without Secret Service protection. From her father she knew precisely how this kind of covert outing would work. In order to identify the negative space, she had to shade in the terrain around it.

Which meant: Don't follow the president. Follow the agents.

So, against her better judgment, in the first glow of dawn she had started digging around to find what she could about off-duty outings by the Presidential Protective Detail. From digital deep storage, she'd excavated time sheets, work logs, travel movements, and hotel and restaurant receipts and set her software running on it.

Before she could get up a head of steam, she'd been called away on the kitchen intrusion, and the day had cascaded sloppily downhill from there.

Bennett broke in on her thoughts. 'How the hell does he know which vendors we're using?'

'We're still trying to –'

'You said you didn't find any more traces of poison at the other locations?'

'That's correct. Except for the two pieces of sushi he left out at –'

'Is it possible he could be using poisons that don't show up on initial tests but appear later?'

'I've been assured that's impossible.'

Bennett's shirt had darkened beneath the arms. His glare held no sign of the warmth from the momentary rapport they'd shared yesterday over the ugly clock. 'When it comes to X, nothing is impossible.'

'We're switching food suppliers, of course –'

'That's what he's anticipating.'

'It doesn't matter. We need to get new long-term procedures in place. As one solution we're thinking about having agents buy food off supermarket shelves at random –'

'There *is* no random. There are algorithms for that. Deep-learning data-mining software that can identify which supermarkets your men are most likely to choose, which ones are located along oft-driven routes of particular agents, which foods I commonly eat.'

'You think he'd risk randomly poisoning civilians?'

'You have *no idea* what he'd do to get me.'

Bennett circled behind his desk again, and as she turned to keep him in sight, her gaze snagged on a pill bottle on the blotter. The label showed it to be Buspar, the antianxiety med his physician had prescribed after the near miss in the limo. Before Bennett would consent to taking it, Agent Demme had overseen the testing of the pills, a five-hour affair that involved three different labs and a team of PhDs.

Bennett saw that she saw the pill bottle, and something in his gaze hardened until it felt palpable, designed to impale her. He swept the bottle out of sight into a drawer.

'He showed us a hand. Not *his* hand. *A* hand. We cannot react accordingly.' He closed his eyes and pressed his palm to his forehead, as if warding off a migraine. 'All this talk about tetrodotoxin's making me nauseous.'

She checked her watch. 'Agent Demme is due any minute with food that's cleared our short-term emergency protocols.'

'What are those protocols?'

'Until we can determine precisely what Orphan X is up to, we're shutting down all domestic food supply. We'll feed you only from shipments that arrive via direct routes from dealers in Europe. The minute I got the call, I had our logistics team place orders in Oslo, Vienna, Paris, and Provence –'

'We have to assume he knows *all* our approved vendors, even international.'

'I had our team switch to unspecified vendors with zero notice when they ordered. The first shipment arrived an hour ago and has been tested comprehensively upon arrival. It's a new system, special chemicals developed by a professor from Johns Hopkins.'

Bennett finally stopped moving. He closed his eyes and blew out a breath. 'Okay,' he said. 'I suppose I have to eat something. Now, where are you with my protective-detail request?'

'We're looking at a ten-percent manpower increase.'

Her private phone vibrated in her pocket and she inched it out, subtly tilting the screen to read the incoming text from Sunrise Villa: PROBLEM WITH YOUR FATHER. PLEASE CALL IMMEDIATELY.

A familiar sense of dread coalesced in her stomach.

'Ten percent isn't sufficient,' Bennett was saying. 'When I step outside again, I want an *army* of agents surrounding me.'

'We've already borrowed agents from field offices, which is leaving us thin –'

'How about the UN?'

She hesitated. 'We have the General Assembly in Manhattan next week. That's a hundred and thirty heads of state, most of them with spouses. It's contingent upon us to provide a full detail. That means CAT and countersnipers –'

'Knock them down to a dot detail. A leader and two agents.'

'Mr President, that's just window dressing. We can't –'

'I'm the president. That means I can. Which means *we* can.'

She closed her mouth, forced herself to nod.

'If you get any friction,' Bennett said, 'have Director Gonzalez call me.'

She wondered at a man who would hang out UN reps with minimal protection to bolster his own already fortified defenses.

The panel door swung inward, and the assistant secretary appeared. 'The vice president is on the phone.'

'Not now.' Bennett glanced at Naomi. 'The only good part of this attack is that I can use it to get the vice president and Congress off my ass.'

Naomi had already seen him turn away requests from the secretary of the treasury and the ambassador to China. From what she'd gleaned, India's prime minister was waiting in the Rose Garden.

In her pocket another text announced itself, no doubt the escalating crisis at Sunrise Villa.

'Very well, sir,' the assistant secretary said. 'Also, Agent Demme is here.'

Demme appeared bearing a tray uneasily, a man unaccustomed to serving. He stood awkwardly until Bennett nodded at the round table in the corner, and then he set down the service with a clunk.

The White House china held endives with what looked like walnuts and blue cheese, a side of pâté with crostini, and two slices of boeuf en croûte. A glass of red wine rested to the side, a thin daytime pour.

Demme gave a deferential nod and withdrew, leaving Naomi and Bennett alone with the savory scent of his lunch.

'Someone eats it before I eat it,' Bennett said. 'Every single item.'

It took a moment for her to grasp his meaning.

'You don't trust me,' she said. 'The Service, the lab, the protocols.'

'This is your job,' he said. 'To take a bullet. Eating pâté is simply a more pleasant version of that.'

She stared at him.

He crossed to the tray, used the edge of a fork to pinch a bite of each item onto a side plate.

Then he stared at her. 'Eat it.'

His eyes shone behind the lenses, but whether from anger or excitement she couldn't tell. The fact that it was a question at all, she realized, indicated that she understood him differently now.

She picked up the fork, took a bite of each item, wadding them all together in her mouth and forcing them down with one big swallow.

Bennett pointed to the wineglass, and she paused, humiliated, before taking a sip.

He studied her for a minute or two, though she wasn't sure what he expected. Vomiting? Collapse? Hemorrhaging from the eyes?

The food sat heavily in her stomach.

After another full minute passed, he snapped out his napkin, sat, and began to dine. 'There is no measure of paranoia too great when you're dealing with Orphan X.' He paused, head downtilted, offering her a gaze through his glasses. 'You still don't understand who you're dealing with, do you?'

She set her jaw, said, 'I'm beginning to get the picture.'

58. What's Not There

With its open-spandrel, concrete-and-steel design, the Key Bridge is the oldest surviving bridge to cross the Potomac. Evan had driven from Georgetown to the Arlington side, where he'd pulled off and parked, letting the six lanes of traffic stream by.

Somewhere miles and miles ahead as the crow flew, twin stone pillars marked a sloping dirt road that cut through an oak forest, leading to the apron of cleared land upon which Jack's two-story farmhouse sat.

That was the home Evan had grown up in from the age of twelve. An old-fashioned porch and shuttered windows. Plush brown corduroy couches in the living room, pots hanging from a brass rack in the kitchen. A fireplace in the study casting an orange glow on the bookshelves, on the framed photograph of Jack's dear departed wife, on the faces of Jack and nineteen-year-old Evan as they massaged his first operational alias into place, wrapping it around him like a second skin.

Now he sat and stared at taillights and office buildings cloaked in a haze of car exhaust.

This was the closest he'd come to home since that bleak gray morning in 1997 when Jack had driven him to Dulles International and dropped him at Departures.

Though he was expecting the call, he didn't fully register the RoamZone until the second ring. He answered sluggishly, 'Yeah?'

'What's wrong?' Joey said.

He cleared his throat, lowered his eyes from the horizon. 'Nothing. What do you have?'

'As usual, you're asking the wrong question.'

'Just spit it out, Joey.'

'You've been looking at what's there. You need to look at what's *not* there. Agent Templeton understood that better than you. And I understand it better than her.'

'Which means?'

'Early this morning Templeton pulled in all the information on Secret Service schedules – the Presidential Protective Detail in particular. But she's looking to see when they worked off-hours, say, or logged an unusual outing that didn't line up with the official schedule. But the thing is, she's underestimating our target. He's DoD-trained, deep, deep black protocols. Which means if he did take an extracurricular outing, he would ensure that his PPD agents didn't log any time at all. So. Among the cadre of inner agents, I looked at workday absences. Sure enough, a pair of his men had missing half days that correlated. They took the same two mornings off, once in October of last year, once last month. Those mornings also happen to align precisely with gaps in the target's official schedule.'

Evan could sense his pulse quicken ever so slightly. 'So he ducked out without the detail. Just two agents and a sedan.'

'Looks that way,' Joey said. 'Next, I hacked into the iCals of the agents' wives. No family vacay, no medical appointments listed, no kids' soccer games. Both had an entry that their husbands were gone for the day. Too much of a coincidence.'

'So they snuck the target out.'

'More like he snuck them out,' Joey said. 'The agents just had to play chauffeur. No knowledge of what they were participating in, no official record – technically they weren't even working those mornings.'

'How can we figure out where they went?'

'Each Service vehicle has GPS,' Joey said. 'Both days, same location. A house in Bethesda.' She rattled off the address, then paused. 'You'll never guess who it belongs to.'

She told him.

After a moment she said, 'You still there?'

'I am.'

'I saw a picture,' she said. 'It's him.'

He waited for his inner disturbance to still. It wasn't turmoil he felt, not precisely, more like a vibration of his cells. A trip wire that stretched back nearly three decades had been plucked like a guitar string, and the bone-deep resonance refused to recede.

He'd follow it, the trip wire, no matter the course, no matter the cost.

It would lead to the answers he sought.

Hanging up, he pulled out into traffic and pointed the car for Bethesda.

59. Sharp Edges

When Naomi at last arrived at Sunrise Villa, she rushed up the corridor to see two burly orderlies pinning down her father to administer a shot. He was bellowing unintelligibly, bucking with all the force left in his failing body.

Judging by the state of the room, he still had a considerable amount of strength left. The lunch tray had been knocked over, a comet of green Jell-O painting the wall above the TV. A bedpan lay upside down on the floor. In the corner Amanaki applied a Band-Aid to the finger of an angry male nurse.

Naomi stood in the doorway and let the orderlies do their job. The Versed finally took effect, and her father ceased thrashing, though he looked far from subdued.

She eased into the room. 'I'm sorry about this.'

Amanaki said, 'Nothing you need to apologize for. He's just been more . . . agitated than usual.'

The male nurse said, 'He bit my finger.'

'However bad it is for you,' Amanaki said, 'it's worse for him.'

Gripping his hand, the nurse exited.

Naomi turned to face her father. 'You can't keep doing this.'

She felt Amanaki's hand, cool on her arm. 'He's confused, honey,' she said. 'He doesn't know what he's doing.' She said to the orderlies, 'He'll be fine now. Thank you, gentlemen. Let's give them some time.'

They departed, leaving Naomi alone with her dad.

His eyes looked sunken; dark hollows in a skull. In his face she could see the waiting grave.

'Where are my boys?' he said, his hoarse voice laced with accusation.

'They're not . . . They can't make it, Dad.'

'They'd talk to these people, get me taken care of.'

'You *are* being taken care of.'

He glared around the room, his pale arms twitching on the sheets. He looked so goddamned frail in that hospital gown, like a plucked bird.

'Is that what you call this?' he said. 'Jason and Robbie, they would never stand for it.'

She felt a rise in temperature, a flush creeping up her neck. 'This is a nice place. The staff does a lot for you, Dad. *I* do a lot for you.'

'My boys would never let me be treated like this.'

Something in her chest broke, spilling heat through her insides. 'God*damn it*, Dad! Jason can't be bothered to see you, okay?' Her face was wet now, the room blurring. 'And Robbie, Robbie doesn't give a shit about anyone but himself. They mail their checks so they don't have to bother with you.'

She wiped angrily at her eyes.

Her father lay there, stunned. His lips, framed with gray stubble, wobbled disconcertingly.

Remorse crushed in on her, chased with guilt so intense she felt it as a swirling void in the pit of her gut.

For a moment she thought she might die.

She tried to breathe, but the black hole in her stomach snatched the oxygen away like a cry in the wind. It took a few seconds for her to force her gaze up to her dad again.

'I'm sorry you feel so alone,' she said, and now she was

crying, really crying. 'I tried. I tried my hardest. And it still didn't matter.'

Standing there dumbly by the foot of the bed, she cried for a while. When she was done, her father was staring at her, the same expression frozen on his face.

'You know the best part of being an adult?' he said. 'It teaches you to forgive yourself.'

She snatched a tissue from a box angrily. 'Well, that's great, Dad. I'm glad you can forgive yourself.'

But she was shocked to see his grizzled cheeks glittering.

'No,' he said. 'Not like that. Because I had to. Because I couldn't get it right. Not with my boys. And not . . . not with my daughter.'

She stared at him, spellbound. This language, the language of emotion, of regret, was not how her father talked.

'I was in the Secret Service,' he told her. 'I always had to control everything. Every variable. Every outcome. That was my job. But a baby girl?' He shook his head, overcome. 'When they were little, their mother carpeted every surface. No sharp edges. She carpeted over the hearth, wrapped the pillars in the living room, everything. I remember that. I remember . . .'

He trailed off, losing the thread. Balanced on the razor's edge, Naomi waited to see if he'd find it again or if fate and illness would deny her this one last story as well.

'The problem is . . .' He cleared his throat. 'The problem is, the world's full of sharp edges. It was fine for the boys, but when my baby girl came along, I tore all that padding out. Her mom and I, we had a good row about that. And I told her, I told her the world would let the boys figure it out later. But a girl? *My* girl?' His face hardened, wiry brows lowering over a suddenly adamant stare. 'I wanted her to learn. I needed her to learn. So she'd never get caught off guard. So she'd never get surprised.' His mouth trembled. He bit down on his grief, firmed his jaw. 'So she'd never get hurt.'

She blinked, freeing fresh tears. 'That's not possible, Dad. Everyone gets hurt.'

'I know.' His Adam's apple jerked in the wattle of his neck. 'But when you have a daughter, you don't care about what's possible.'

His head lifted weakly from the pillow. For an instant he seemed to recognize her, but then his eyes lost focus. He sank back onto the pillow, his voice growing weaker as the benzo worked its way through his bloodstream, blurring the words together. 'I had to be hard on her . . . harder than on the boys, harder than on anyone. And if I didn't figure out how to try to forgive myself for that, I woulda . . . woulda been taken to pieces long ago. Even worse than this.'

The monitors bleeped and hummed. His blinks grew longer.

She sat on the bed next to him and then leaned to put her head on his chest. She listened to the breath rattling through him, so fragile, so resolute.

With great effort he lifted a hand trailing tubes and stroked her hair.

60. Death Itself

The two-story Colonial home was disappointingly banal, faded brick and shingled roof, a wide grassy lot with mower stripes, the periphery dotted with what realtors like to call mature trees.

Evan wasn't sure what he'd been expecting, but it certainly wasn't this.

He headed for the front walk, noting the signs of life. Mailbox flag raised. Bulging trash bag at the side of the house. Beat-up Honda Accord in the driveway – probably a cleaning lady or the pool guy.

The doors were ornate, dated wood and glass, brass hardware. Evan knew he should approach more cautiously than he was, but a weariness at the center of him made him uncharacteristically rash. He was tired of the foreign minister and the trim Estonian and the strung-out girl and the round man with the loose-fitting clothes. He was tired of the Russell Gaddses and the Jonathan Bennetts, men of immense means and power who took their pounds of flesh from those who could not defend themselves. He was tired of his own past, of his training and missions, of the lives he'd ended by lead or blade or garrote, and the silent, baleful chorus of the dead who rode his shoulders, good angels and bad.

He rang the doorbell, blading his body, ready to fight or flee depending on what answered his call.

The door creaked open.

A stout Hispanic woman wearing teal scrubs. 'Jes?'

'Is he home?'

'Jes, of course.'

She gestured down an unlit hall to her right. Near the end a door lay open, freeing a triangle of light from a room. Just outside, a wheelchair waited. In its seat rested a medical-waste bucket, the kind used to dispose of needles. Evan focused on two shapes in the shadows beyond that looked like antitank missiles stood on end.

Oxygen tanks.

And then he understood.

'I'm his nephew,' Evan said. 'Haven't seen him in years. I heard from my mom, and . . . well, I flew in from Tallahassee to surprise him and, you know, pay my last respects.'

She nodded solemnly. 'I have some errands to run. You can be with him for one hour until I get back?'

'That will be fine.'

'Any problems, my phone number is on the clipboard.'

She walked past him, leaving the door ajar.

Evan entered, eased the door shut behind him, and stood breathing the scented air. The interior was 1990's idea of modern, marble floors and prints in gleaming black frames. A spray of calla lilies rose from a vase in the foyer, no doubt sent by some well-wisher and arranged by the home-care nurse he'd just met.

How odd to find flowers here. Or vases. Or well-wishers.

A textured bamboo wallpaper darkened the hall, the house growing cooler as Evan moved back toward the lit room.

From the doorway he saw only a pair of feet bumped up beneath a woven blanket.

He eased inside.

The Mystery Man lay in a double-railed hospital bed that took up a good measure of the room. His hair had grown thin and wispy, receded to a severe widow's peak. An oxygen tube ran beneath his nose, and a wide-bore needle was sunk to the hilt into the back of one thick-veined hand. His clavicles were pronounced, as was the bump of the ulna at his wrist, the gold watch dangling loosely around the bone.

An imposing wooden desk remained at one end of the converted study, flanked by file cabinets, but the rest of the space had been transformed into a makeshift hospice suite. Glass-fronted mini-refrigerators stored bags of saline and various vials. There were IV poles and washcloths, cups holding ice chips, backup sheets crisply folded and stuffed onto bookshelves.

It had been twenty-seven years since Evan had laid eyes on the man.

He had a name, of course, which Joey had unearthed, but the name didn't match the memory Evan had been living with for all this time.

When Evan was twelve, the Mystery Man had appeared like the boogeyman, running his fingers along the chain-link across the street from the Pride House Group Home, his ever-present cigarette exhaling a thin banner of smoke. From a scared distance, the boys had jockeyed for the right to be taken, to be exploited, to get the fuck out of East Baltimore. None of them could have known that he was a recruiter for the Program. Evan had gotten over the grueling hurdles, one after another, and his prize had been Jack Johns and a two-story farmhouse in the woods outside Arlington. It had been a dormer bedroom, three meals a day, and a sniper rifle. It had been a mission following his nineteenth birthday, the first of countless.

After Evan had gone rogue, the Mystery Man had served the Program's purposes for many more years, even as it grew increasingly twisted and brutal. He had played a role in corrupting countless foster kids. And in hurting Joey.

Evan had been waiting a long time to kill him.

The Mystery Man's breathing was irregular, rapid deep inhalations interspersed with shallow panting.

Evan walked over and stood at the foot of the bed.

The Ray-Bans rested on the nightstand. The Mystery Man stared up at Evan. His lazy left eye wandered to the opposite wall, but the other was alert, its intensity undulled.

'I've been hoping you'd come,' he said, his voice a dry rasp. He seemed short of breath, as if he couldn't quite get enough oxygen to relax the muscles of his face. 'I never wanted you, you know,' he said.

Evan said, 'I know.'

'But you proved me wrong. You were the best. You were always the best.'

Evan said, 'There is an advantage to being underestimated.'

'I suppose so.'

Evan circled to the nightstand and opened the drawer. There lay the gleaming handgun he knew all too well, its image having been branded onto his twelve-year-old brain. In the intervening years, he'd been able to retrospectively identify the weapon, a snub-nosed Smith & Wesson .357. He lifted it from its place beside a box of tissues.

The Mystery Man looked up at him, helpless to intervene. His etched skin was crepe-paper thin, mottled with bluish patches, shiny with sweat. A gurgle accompanied his exhalation, rising in volume until Evan was worried that he'd die here and now before giving up any answers.

But he coughed a few times, partially clearing his throat.

'They call it the death rattle,' he said. 'Fluid buildup in the lungs.'

'The cigarettes?' Evan asked.

'Yeah. But it was worth it. My one true love.' He smiled weakly. 'Now it's metastasized in my brain. You're lucky you got here in time to kill me. A week or two later, you'd've missed your chance.'

'I'm here for something else, too.'

'I figured as much.' His finger rose a half inch, pointed at the television bracketed to the wall. 'I watch the news. It's about all I do anymore.'

'Bennett came to see you twice. Last October and last month. What about?'

'About 1997.'

Evan hadn't expected him to arrive so directly on the point, but maybe dying made a man less circuitous. Evan's relief was quickly undercut by gnawing dread for what was to come. 'My first mission.'

'Yes. I was involved. As was Orphan A. Bennett needed to know that we were airtight, every last loose end severed.' His chest rattled up and down, the good eye fixing on Evan pointedly. 'Of course, one remains.'

'I killed a lot of people,' Evan said. 'Unsanctioned kills, cutout jobs, no US footprint. Each mission is a live grenade, top-level classified. What makes '97 so threatening?'

'I've spent most of the days of my life with information in my head that I can't unknow. I don't have anything to care about anymore. Not my life, not protecting the past, certainly not Jonathan Bennett. But I can protect you, especially after I cost you so much.' He gazed up at Evan, and Evan could smell his breath, sour and sickly, the smell of death itself. 'You know what you did. But you don't want to know what you *really* did.'

'Tell me.'

The Mystery Man lay there, his lips pouched.

Evan hefted the revolver in his palm. 'I know you're in pain. But there can always be more pain.'

'You're the best there is, X, but you got nothing on cancer.'

The Mystery Man breathed for a time, and Evan let him.

'Okay,' he finally said. 'I'll tell you a story. Once upon a time, there was an undersecretary of defense. He was an ambitious soul with designs on the throne. But he was also greedy. Not for money but for power. He understood that the more of the former he accrued for the right people, the more of the latter he'd inherit.'

'Who are "the right people"?' Evan asked.

'Think, boy. I've been watching the news. Have you?'

Evan turned his head to the television screen, though it was dark. 'The congressional subpoena,' he said. 'A multibillion-dollar investigation into Bennett's relationships with defense contractors.'

'Relationships that date back to his early days at the DoD.'

'I understand,' Evan said. 'But so what? We both know that's how the game's played. Influence, money, and war have always gone hand in hand. So the administration's moves a few decades ago benefited the military-industrial complex and vice versa. That kind of quid pro quo can always be covered up and spun, buried beneath half-truths and fake news. Any moves Bennett made would have been conducted behind a haze of full deniability. Illegal and immoral, sure. But why does it constitute a clear and present danger now?'

'What if we're not talking about illegal and immoral?' the Mystery Man said. 'But about treason?'

'Treason?' Evan eased back a step and slid the gun into his waistband. 'How do you get to treason? The powers that be wanted a hawkish foreign minister dispatched —'

'The foreign minister you assassinated was *publicly* hawkish, yes. Beating the drums about nukes. Lots of carefully cultivated sound bites to the media. That's how he rose to power. But in private? He was willing to accede to our demands.'

'He was under US influence?'

'Yes. And he also happened to be very close to Milošević. In fact, he was plotting his execution. With our help, no less.'

'But the president decided to change course?'

'No. The undersecretary of defense did.'

Evan's skin tightened against the cool of the room. 'You're telling me that as undersecretary of defense, Jonathan Bennett ordered a political assassination in violation of the wishes and policy directives of the sitting US president?'

'I am telling you precisely that.'

'And no one found out?'

The Mystery Man's hand pulsed around a wandlike control, releasing another hit of morphine. He sighed, relief mixed with pleasure. 'That's the point of black programs,' he said. 'No one can see them.'

Evan pictured the minister's wife in her billowing aubergine dress, her mouth stretched wide, a scream of primal grief. He forced down a swallow. 'Bennett would take that risk just to line the pockets of his defense-contractor cronies so they'd . . . what? Put him in the Oval Office one day? How much financial gain can be had from the murder of one foreign minister?'

The Mystery Man's cracked lips stretched in a smile. 'All the gain in the world,' he said. 'Thanks to you, Slobodan Milošević was not killed. We lost our opportunity – and our window. Weeks after you dispatched the foreign minister, Milošević expanded his title from president of Serbia to president of Yugoslavia. And we know where *that* led. You see, Bennett and his backers didn't want an ally in the foreign minister. They required an enemy in Milošević.'

'Why?'

'Had the Butcher of Belgrade been killed in 1997, that would have precluded the need for the bombings in Serbia a year and a half later.'

'They can't have known that,' Evan said. 'No one could have predicted that.'

'Not *that* specifically. But if you were a warmonger with chips to bet in 1997? You would've put every last one on a madman despot in the Balkans.' A smile moved the cracked lips. 'Do you recall that bombing campaign?'

Evan wiped his mouth. 'NATO ran thousands of air strikes. Almost every single town was targeted. Combat aircraft fired four hundred twenty thousand missiles and dropped almost forty thousand cluster bombs. They used graphite bombs to take down the power system.'

He paused to regain his composure. When it came to ordnance and war campaigns, Jack had drilled into him an aptitude for specifics. His head swam with them now: 25,000 housing units damaged or destroyed, 500 kilometers of roads, 600 kilometers of railways, 14 airports, 19 hospitals, 20 health centers, 44 bridges, 87 schools.

He found his voice again. 'More than four thousand dead, thirteen thousand injured, half of them civilians, children. A billion dollars of damage to the infrastructure.'

'Ah,' the Mystery Man said. 'But it *made* much more than that.'

Evan's face slackened with disgust.

'Not just the bombs and the planes, the armored vehicles and the artillery,' the Mystery Man continued. 'But you have to understand, you can't *buy* a testing ground like that. Our defense firms finally got to flex their muscles, haul all that gear out of R&D and see what it could do. Ordnance and explosives testing in a real theater at zero cost. And that was just the start. You remember what was politically noteworthy about the bombing campaign, don't you?'

The answer spun just out of reach, like a flicked coin. And then it settled, and Evan saw the face of it. 'It was the first time NATO ever used military force without the approval of the UN Security Council.'

'Correct. Which allowed the Pentagon, on the heels of that attack, to seize a thousand acres of land in Kosovo. They built a colossal US military base there, one of the biggest in the world.'

'Camp Bondsteel.'

'We're talking seven thousand troops, fifty-two helipads, twenty-some Black Hawks, a few dozen tanks. The contracts that were awarded *then*?' The Mystery Man gave a weak whistle. 'More commas than a Russian novel. And the thing is? We don't even *need* it. We never did. It's not an air base. It's not connected to the sea. It doesn't hold a strategic position. Truth is, we should've mothballed it years ago. And yet we've been paying to supply it for nearly two decades.'

The recycled air with its whiff of rubbing alcohol and iodine was making Evan feel sick.

'So let's return to your question,' the Mystery Man said. 'How much financial gain *can* be had from the murder of one foreign minister?' He tried to lift his head again, but it just rustled dryly against the pillowcase. 'A kingdom's worth.'

Evan took an unsteady step back and sat on the sill of the box window.

The Mystery Man read his face. 'You were a nineteen-year-old kid.'

'I pulled the trigger.'

The relentless hiss of the oxygen kept on, a backdrop for Evan's mounting dismay. A single bullet had opened the floodgates. A war crime. Treason. A nation destroyed, four thousand dead, and a new chapter in American imperialism. The weight of it threatened to crush him.

Remorse spread through him, heated and seething. He tried to get his arms around it, wrestle it down, reshape it into something sharp and unforgiving, something he could weaponize.

The Mystery Man adjusted the tube beneath his nose. 'You ensured that this was all pinned on an anonymous Chechen shooter. If you were to say now that you were behind the scope, it would point to America. And if it points to us, it'll point to Bennett. Now you understand why he has to have you killed.' He shook his head, the tufts of hair sparse and thin. 'The wolves are massing at the White House gates. You can bet he hears them howling every night when he goes to sleep.' He closed his eyes, the lids translucent and veined. 'I hear them myself sometimes.'

Evan stood again. The light from the window streamed over his shoulders, his shadow falling across the Mystery Man. Evan waited for him to open his eyes again.

Then he asked, 'Why are *you* still alive? Why did Bennett let you live?'

'Is that what you call this? Living?' The Mystery Man grinned flatly. 'Because clearly I don't represent a threat. At least for many more days. Plus, I had an insurance policy.'

He lifted a hand and pointed past the desk, a shawl of loose skin draped around the bone of his forearm. 'Left file cabinet. Bottom drawer.'

Evan circled the desk, crouched, and slid the drawer open.

It held a number of hanging files. He thumbed through them. Redacted operation reports, redacted intelligence briefings, redacted after-action reviews.

Evan looked from the blacked-out papers across the room to the Mystery Man. 'These are useless.'

The answer came as a wheeze. '*Behind* the drawer.'

Evan pulled the drawer out all the way and then wiggled it free of its tracks. Lying flat on the floor, he peered into the empty slot.

A hatch had been cut into the metal rear of the cabinet.

Aligned with a jagged mouth of drywall.

Inside the wall rested a single manila file.

Mashing his cheek to the cabinet, Evan strained to reach it. With his fingertips he managed to slide it out.

The file held yellowed logistics reports from 1997, brittle with age, the corners flaking. A transcript from a call to the round man. A report on the acquisition of the 7.62 × 54mmR round with its damning fingerprint. Surveillance photos of the foreign minister, an assembled schedule of his movements.

Evan lost himself in the file so thoroughly that he'd forgotten that the Mystery Man was in the room until he heard the strained voice from behind him. 'You can go public now.'

Evan turned to face him. 'Not my style. I prefer to take care of things myself.'

'Be careful. Orphan A is a very dangerous man. And he's had his sights on you for a long time.'

Evan started for the bed. 'Once I neutralize Bennett, Orphan A will be irrelevant.'

'No. Killing you, it's personal for him.'

Evan halted. 'Why?'

'I honestly don't know.'

'Well,' Evan said. 'I'm going to find out.'

'When?'

'Now.'

Evan pulled the .357 from his waistband.

The Mystery Man's voice was weak, but his stare was not. 'You'll never pull it off. Bennett. It's impossible.'

Evan said, 'He's already dead.'

He thumbed the lever to open the well-greased wheel and spun it, watching the six brass heads roll. With a snap of his wrist, he reseated the cylinder.

It would do.

The Mystery Man settled back on the bed. Then he nodded. 'I suppose we should get to the next part now.' He let his eyes draw shut for the last time, that death rattle sounding in his chest.

A few seconds passed and then a few more, but still the rattle persisted, reminding him that he continued to draw breath.

When at last he opened his eyes, the room was empty.

61. A Knot Tightening

A flyer flapping beneath the knocker on the front door announced that the house was in probate.

Even worse, it was in disrepair.

Rusting gutters heaped with leaves. Wood panels warped up off the nails. One of the address numbers had fallen from its perch, leaving a 7 of fresh paint floating on the weather-bleached post. A bundle of heavy-duty rattraps, no doubt left on the porch swing by the probate realtor, answered the question of what had chewed through the underbelly of the porch. Most of the screens had fallen from the panes.

Evan stood beneath the cover of the oak trees, staring across the weed-addled front yard, holding his emotions in check.

Jack had ministered to this house scrupulously, showing it the kind of rigor that for him expressed love. He'd once spent an entire morning polishing the door hinges with white toothpaste and an old gun cloth. When he was done, each plate threw off a reflection as clear as a mirror.

How you do anything is how you do everything.

Evan remembered waking up that first morning of his new life, how the dormer bedroom seemed to float above the forest, above Earth itself. A comfortable bed with clean sheets. Shelves holding books ordered by height. The surface of the desk polished to a high shine. A bouquet of unsharpened pencils rising from a mug, the bloom of possibility itself.

It had been the first place he could ever call his own.

A blue jay hopped from branch to branch overhead, plumed head nodding as it emitted a balloon-losing-air squeal. The dusky scent of the woods filled Evan's nostrils. He knew the smell of this place in his bones.

He gazed at the front window until he pictured Jack standing there gazing out, baseball-catcher build and bulldog head, his bunched crow's-feet lending his eyes that perennial hint of amusement. Jack, who always knew the answers before Evan did. Jack, who'd cracked open the world and served it to Evan on a platter. Jack, the closest thing to family he'd ever known.

Jack beckoned impatiently with a hand. *Waiting for a red carpet, X? C'mon, let's get 'er done.*

Evan stepped out of the tree line onto the apron of cleared land.

Keeping his face pointed at the ground, he walked to the center of the front yard and paused in the wide open, exposed to the heavens.

There were eyes up there.

The four men approached from the points of the compass rose, a knot tightening around the two-story farmhouse.

Wade Collins.

Two cousins.

One Orphan.

Communicating through Secret Service–issue earpieces, they paused in their respective spots at the forest's edge.

North, south, west, east.

Holt gave the order, and they closed in.

Evan perched on a wooden stool he'd found on its side in the kitchen, its edges smoothed and oiled by the touch of countless hands. Jack had once sat watch on this very stool in this very spot at the rear of the entryway facing the front door, his back to the dark cavern of the kitchen.

Evan remembered his quiet focus across the seventy-two-hour span, the way the shotgun lay across his knees, how he'd drunk from a thermos and otherwise never moved. His vigilance had allowed seventeen-year-old Evan to more or less go about his normal existence, training in the garage, studying in his bedroom, eating over the kitchen sink. The threat had passed, but the image of Jack's sentinel form on the stool, unbudging and proficient, had stayed with Evan.

It said, *This is how we protect what is dear to us.*

Soon enough, given Naomi's order to keep the farmhouse under constant satellite surveillance, Evan would have a chance to follow Jack's lead.

Night had descended on the patch of Virginia forest. Aside from a pale starlight glow at the windows, the house was full dark. Most of the furniture had been carted off already, leaving the floors bare and unacceptably dusty. Evan felt as though he were inhabiting the shell of his former life.

He knew the sounds of this house. Every last creaking board, every squeak of a doorknob.

He sensed the men's approach before he heard them. A vibration of the floor. A scent in the air. A pressure against his skin.

He heard the melody of a slender rake tickling lock cylinders at the back door. Beneath the kitchen window, a boot tread compressed a dead leaf. In the living room, the pane issued a complaint as it pressed against the frame. Straight ahead, the doorknob turned silently.

They were attacking from the cardinal points, requiring him to cover 360 degrees. But it also disadvantaged them, since they'd have to mind their crossfire. Evan guessed that Orphan A would hold back, use the Collins boys for cannon fodder, and strike once Evan's attention was compromised.

One thing was certain: When it went down, it was going to go down fast.

Evan lifted the .357 from its resting place on his thigh.

And he closed his eyes.

Listening as if he were a newborn, as if he were hearing every sound for the first time.

The back door was breached first, creaking inward. There came a loud snap and then a muffled cry of pain as the heavy-duty rattrap taped over the light switch deployed.

Evan wheeled off the stool, striking a modified Weaver stance, sighting across the kitchen island. With the rush of bracing air, an earthy forest smell gusted in at him. Beside the partially open door, a dark form was silhouetted against the slice of night blackness, one elongated hand flapping in agony, his chest presented conveniently wide, spread like a shooting-target.

Evan put a round through his thorax and chased it with a head shot.

The man fell away and landed with a peaceful puff on the fallen leaves outside.

Behind him Evan heard the front door yawn open, and he threw himself to the side, rolling over his shoulder and coming up in a high-kneel shooting position.

The man – the last Collins cousin – came in with the FN P90 already barking, chewing up the stool that Evan had occupied a half second before. Evan shot him through the hollow of the throat.

Oil welled from the hole, and the man went to his knees, shuddering the planks of the foyer, his mouth agape.

Evan put the next shot between his teeth, knocking him back across the threshold onto the porch.

Evan's position by the front door ensured that friendly-fire concerns would prevent the two remaining men from lighting up the entryway.

Already he heard the whine of the compressed floorboard in the living room, the spot where the corner of the Navajo throw rug used to lie. He started to pivot when he sensed a wall of movement flying in from the side, Wade Collins gripping the compact submachine gun in both hands, punching the butt end at Evan.

Evan wouldn't have time to bring the barrel around, so he ducked the blow, clenched the steel frame of the Smith & Wesson, and brought knuckles and steel to bear in an upper cut. He connected squarely, the jaw giving off a pleasing crack.

He was alarmed at how little the big man swayed from the impact.

Wade was gargantuan, sheathed in muscle, his torso the girth of a refrigerator. If Evan allowed him to get his bearings, he'd be destroyed.

Before Wade could recover, Evan dug his feet into the floor to firm his base and threw a horizontal elbow into the broken bone, knocking Wade's jaw right off the hinge.

This drew a reaction.

Bellowing through his shattered face, Wade grabbed Evan, toppling onto him and smashing him into the floor. The FN P90 clattered away. Wade's earpiece popped free, bouncing on its clear coil. Evan's gun hand was pinned beneath Wade's mass, his finger wrenched clear of the trigger guard.

Ramming the bar of his forearm across Evan's throat, Wade pressured down with all his weight, then clutched at his hip holster and came up with a SIG P229. With his free hand, Evan caught Wade's wrist, forcing the pistol to the side. It fired into the floorboard a half foot from Evan's head.

Evan's ears screamed, a barbed hum shearing through the center of his skull. He caught a twisted, upside-down view of the doorway to the kitchen just as Orphan A pivoted around the corner, submachine gun raised.

Evan's gun hand was trapped beneath Wade's leg, the revolver out of reach.

Wade's forearm crushed into Evan's windpipe, cinching off air.

The P229 wobbled in Wade's massive grip as he forced it through Evan's resistance back toward his face.

Evan couldn't hold him off much longer; the meat of Wade's biceps was the size of a softball. He stared up into the broken maw of Wade's mouth, a few teeth loosed from the gums.

Behind him he sensed Orphan A clear the threshold into the entryway.

Evan slowed everything down.

He sensed the trickle of sweat making a snail-like crawl down his temple.

Watched the drop of blood fall from Wade's lip and splash against his forehead.

Noted the descent of Orphan A's lead boot to the floor.

Evan took the predicament apart and put it together again to his own liking.

The moves went faster than the beats of a drumroll.

He released Wade's gun hand, the abrupt lack of resistance causing the SIG to swing straight across Evan's face to the other side before Wade could react and pull the trigger.

The bullet bucked the floor two inches from the left side

of Evan's head, pain stunning his eardrum. Wade's weight shifted, his gun hand flailing and then thumping to the floor as he righted his balance.

Evan lunged for the dropped submachine gun on the floor and squeezed off a burst at Orphan A. The FN P90 was designed for the smallest kick possible, allowing Evan to get off a good number of rounds even one-handed, even stretched out flat on his back, even firing upside down.

The rounds flew wild, peppering the ceiling, but they were sufficient to make Orphan A dive back into the kitchen, pinball off the island, and scramble for cover.

The shells ejected out of the bottom of the inverted FN P90, spouting up into the air, the hot brass pinging off Wade's ruined face.

Wade knocked the submachine gun from Evan's grip, and Evan rolled with his lunge, the two men tussling on the floor. Evan's revolver slid off by the stairs, both men gripping Wade's pistol, which wavered beneath their faces, the barrel rising parallel to their noses.

The slide was actuated from the last shot, the hammer back in single-action mode. Once the gun was aimed, the trigger would require only 4.4 pounds of pressure.

Given Wade's size, the arm-wrestling match could end only one way. Before Wade could force the muzzle to Evan's head, Evan relaxed pressure, jerking an elbow into the wreckage of Wade's jaw. As Wade recoiled in pain, Evan flipped them once more so he was on top.

He couldn't overpower Wade to turn the gun, so he reared back and then jammed his full weight down on the SIG, pressing its side into Wade's cheek.

Wade's eyes flared as Evan tugged the trigger.

As the pistol fired off blindly into the kitchen, the slide

snapped back an inch and three-quarters, its sharp lower edge gouging through Wade's cheek.

Instinctively, Wade released the pistol, flinching away, and Evan rotated the gun around and shot him through the side of the head.

He looked up to see Orphan A staring back from the kitchen, his eyes poked up over the top of the island, submachine gun aimed.

Evan dove off Wade, rolling for the stairs, gathering his Smith & Wesson along the way.

Rounds chased him to the second floor, chewing up the balustrade and rails. He dove across the landing, tumbling gracelessly down the length of the hall and smashing through the door of his old dormer bedroom.

He had a single instant to take in his cramped childhood room – the single bed now missing the mattress, the desk yanked out from the wall, the rows of empty bookshelves looking down like toothless mouths.

He heard Orphan A slot a fresh fifty-round mag into his weapon downstairs. Rising, he looked wildly around. There was nowhere to go.

He had a wheel gun with two bullets, and he was up against a fellow Orphan brandishing a submachine gun that would bring nearly a thousand rounds a minute.

The familiar nighttime view looked back at him from the window, unmarred by any screen.

He eased the pane up and stepped outside, the heels of his boots finding the half-inch ledge of flashing securing the first-floor gutter. Gripping the peeling shutter with one hand, he eased the window closed and flattened to the side of the house just as Orphan A's shadow darkened the hall.

One heel slipped off the tiny ledge, and Evan strained to

force it back. Tightening his grip on the shutter with his right hand, he aimed the Smith & Wesson at the window with his left.

A bank of clouds obscured the moon, disseminating its glow across the oak-tree canopy, a blanket of silver.

He tried not to breathe too hard.

He tried not to breathe at all.

A burst of rounds nearly startled him off the side of the house. They shattered out the window, erupting through the wall just above his head.

He ducked hard, the shutter wobbling away from the wall, swinging him out onto one heel again. The shutter started to give.

Even over the high warble of the ringing in his ears, he heard chunks of the wall hitting the floor inside.

He tried to edge himself back onto the ledge but saw now that the top shutter hinge was pulling free of the wall, the screw protruding enough to show off a finger's width of threading.

As Evan stared helplessly at the loosening hinge, Orphan A's boots creaked into the bedroom.

62. Final Look Back

Rotated out away from the second-floor wall, a leg swinging in the open air, Evan fought to keep one heel dug into the flashing. His fingers cramped around the top of the shutter. The hinge plate strained against the screw, forcing it out another quarter twist. If Evan fell, he'd either break a leg or wind up an open target on the ground below.

He rammed the gun through his belt, yanked his knife from a cargo pocket, and snapped it open. With his full weight fighting against him, he seated the tip of the knife in the flathead slot of the screw, cranking it a half turn to the right. He adjusted his grip on the knife handle and cranked it again, the screw tightening back into the wall.

Just enough for the hinge to hold.

A darkness fell across the sill.

Evan dropped the folding knife.

Yanked the pistol from his belt.

As the shutter swung him wide once more, he fired through the window.

He heard the smack of lead hitting meat.

The submachine gun knocking against the floor.

The hinge ripped the screw loose, the shutter tearing away from the wall. Evan grabbed for the window, his hands landing on the lower frame, the teeth of the remaining shards slicing through his flesh.

But he didn't let go.

He hauled himself up over the sill, jagged glass scraping his stomach, and tumbled into his old bedroom.

No sign of Orphan A.

A pool of blood glimmered on the floor by Evan's face. The FN P90 rested over by the desk, still rocking. Near the doorway Orphan A's pistol lay discarded.

Evan stood.

He walked out into the hall.

The drops of blood made Orphan A easy to track. A streak pointed into Jack's room, the second on the left past the stairs.

Evan followed. Before he could reach the doorway, he heard the thump of Orphan A's shoulders hitting the wall right beside him.

He heard the man slide to a sitting position.

Evan put his own shoulders to the wall and lowered himself to sit back-to-back with him.

Two Orphans, separated by a single wall.

Evan said, 'How you doing?'

'Not so hot,' Orphan A said. 'Thanks for asking.'

A dull ache throbbed in Evan's eardrums, the volume turned down on the world, his head stuffed with gauze. He checked his palms. Broken glass glinted in the bloody slits. 'Critical?' he asked.

'Gut shot, so yeah. Looks that way.'

Four and a half inches away, Orphan A's head tilted back to thump his side of the wall.

Evan said, 'I was told you had a score to settle with me. Beyond Bennett, I mean.'

'You could say that.' Orphan A's breaths took on a wheeze. 'It was that woman you killed.'

It took a moment for the words to sink in.

'The heroin addict?' he asked. 'The one I left in the abandoned textile factory?'

'What? No. No.'

Evan waited for Orphan A to catch his breath.

Finally A spoke again. 'I was developing her as an asset, but it developed into more than that. Like it does, I guess. I don't know. Never happened to me before. Never since.' A few more ragged breaths. 'A Chechen girl. Man, she was a princess-warrior all right. Jet-black hair down to the middle of her back. Hazel eyes that *glowed*. I was supposed to gather DNA from her. You know, strands of hair. Cells from her toothbrush.' Orphan A paused. 'A copper-washed steel shell of a sniper round with her fingerprint on it.'

Evan would have thought that the last strain of punishing revelations had hardened him against further injury, but there it was, a new blade twisting between his ribs.

Orphan A continued. 'She was pregnant, turns out. I didn't know till later. The Russians caught up to her soon enough, put her in a forced-labor camp in Krasnoyarsk.' He coughed a few times. 'Chechen women don't do so well there. Pregnant Chechen women do even worse. They kept locking her in the ice insulator – a cold-punishment cell the size of a roomy coffin. She was tough. She made it through the first fifteen-day sentence. And the second.' His labored breaths filled the pause. 'It was the fifth that got her.'

Evan cradled the revolver in his hands.

Down to one round.

'I'm sorry,' he said.

'I never knew I was supplying the shell that would get her killed,' Orphan A said. 'Guess I never wanted to know. It's my fault, really. For thinking I could have more in this life.'

Another wet cough. 'At the end of the day, isn't it always our fault?'

Evan placed the snub nose of the revolver against the dry wall to his side.

'Yeah,' he said. 'It is.'

He fired.

He heard Orphan A's body absorb the shot and then slump over onto the floor.

He sat for a while breathing the scent of his old house.

It was all so goddamned sad if he thought about it.

He imagined Jack emerging from his bedroom door, brow twisted in disdain. *You done bellyaching yet? That's good, because you got work to do. On your feet, son. On your feet.*

Evan shoved himself up.

Limping out, he dialed the RoamZone, his fingers leaving bloody smears on the screen.

When Trevon picked up, he sounded exhausted, wrung out. 'Hello?'

'It's me. How you hanging in?'

'I'm fine, thank you. How are you?'

Ask a personal question when someone asks you one.

Evan smiled. 'I'm hanging in, too, Trevon.'

'Kiara gets home in one day, eleven hours, four minutes, and nineteen seconds,' Trevon said. 'Now it's one day, eleven hours, four minutes, and *fourteen* seconds.'

Evan stepped out onto the porch and cast a final look back at the house where his second life had begun.

For better or worse, this was who he was now.

This was what he did.

'Well then,' he said. 'I'd better hurry.'

63. Why Fuck Around?

Evan didn't have time for a better plan.

The DC mission had cramped him on one end, Kiara's pending flight on the other.

Big Face had flown back today from Suriname, probably landing about the same time Evan had landed himself. But Russell Gadds would have taken a direct flight on a private jet, whereas Evan had flown a switchback route in economy, arriving at Orange County's John Wayne Airport with an ache in his lower back reminding him of parachute landings that were bad and fist-to-fist clashes that were worse.

After going to a safe house to clean up the cuts on his hands, grab some load-out gear, and switch vehicles to an old Ram pickup, Evan had driven straight to the wholesale district.

From the roof of the neighboring bakery, he'd intercepted enough radio comms with a parabolic mike to know that Gadds was on premises along with his sixteen remaining associates, that they were braced and ready for an attack, and that the cinder-block building was virtually unassailable.

Though Evan was vastly outnumbered, all the targets were gathered in one location, and with Kiara due to touch down around noon tomorrow, he couldn't risk letting any of them leave that building alive.

Not if he was to keep his promise to Trevon.

Evan pressed his palms on the thighs of his cargo pants once more to blot the blood from his cuts. Then he gripped the steering wheel with one hand and with the other lifted his ARES 1911. The contour of the grip, the high-profile straight-eight sights, the matte-black finish that gave off neither glint nor gleam – it felt like home.

He'd loaded it with 230-grain Speer Gold Dot hollow points, because why fuck around?

The industrial neighborhood was deserted for the night, the surrounding streets and buildings empty. The back edge of twilight leached from the sky, stars visible overhead even through the downtown smog.

He would have preferred more time for operational planning.

But sometimes you had to go with a full-frontal assault.

A cooling breeze blew through the pickup's rolled-down windows, riffling Evan's hair. Idling across the street from the compound, he watched the flicker of movement between the fence-filler strips that obscured any clear view through the chain-link.

Gadds's men were on high alert, walking overlapping patrols around the building.

Evan waited for two of them to cross by the front gate.

Then he seated the accelerator against the floor.

The Ram shot forward, 240 horses and 420 pound-feet of torque powering more than two tons of Detroit Steel through the perimeter fence.

The gate smashed down, crushing both men.

As a bonus the impact yanked down the neighboring sections of fence, the concertina wire snaring another man beneath it.

Screeching to a halt, Evan fired through the open passenger window, putting the trapped man down as he tried to untangle his bloody torso to lift his Kalashnikov.

Before the men guarding the entrance could react, Evan

shot out the windshield and drilled them each with a round, painting the metal door behind him with their blood.

Kicking open the driver's door, he jumped out and sprinted for the row of shipping containers on the west side of the yard.

More of Gadds's men sped around the corners of the building, responding to the threat. Their rap sheets had been helpfully listed on the DEA chart, Evan pairing an identity with each shot he fired.

Richard Brewer, a dime in Lompoc for second-degree murder – center mass.

Hector DeJean, good-behaviored out for kidnapping and assault with a deadly weapon – bridge of the nose.

Esau Corona, convicted and released serial rapist – left clavicle entry, dinner-plate-size chunk of shoulder blade blown out the other side.

Eight men down.

Eight left.

Return fire came from the others, AKs coughing out rounds, strafing the shipping containers. They held the weapons improperly, arms winged out, unleashing long spray-and-pray bursts with ample muzzle rise. They were clearly not expert assaulters, but at these numbers they didn't have to be. The assault was war-zone relentless, the illicit full-auto weapons clearly an added perk of Gadds's import operation.

Evan knifed between two of the massive metal boxes, ducking as ricochets flew overhead, ping-ponging between the containers.

He ran through the tight space, corrugated metal sandpapering both shoulders, and popped out the rear as two more men shot into sight at the end of the row.

Evan was off balance, firing into the blaze of Kalashnikovs.

Again the men gripped the AKs inexpertly, all wrists and elbows, the lack of resistance causing one gun to short-cycle and the other to unload high.

David Stade, assault with a deadly weapon – left eye, right eye.

Jay Gordon, human trafficking – scalp.

As Gordon went down, he swung the AK, forcing Evan to dive back between the containers to avoid the incoming volley.

Six men left on the premises.

And Russell Gadds.

The ARES was empty, the slide locked to the rear. The aggressive front-frame checkering and specialized Simonich gunner grips had opened up the cuts on Evan's hands again, blood snaking down his forearms. Slamming his back to the metal rise and bracing his boots against the opposite wall, Evan slid down, hitting the slide release and dropping the mag.

As he slapped the fresh mag home, wincing as the base bit into his palm, he could hear shouting as the others circled the shipping containers, hemming him in. His vantage was limited, none of the men daring to venture across the mouth of the aisle on either side.

He went to chamber a round, but his fingers, greased with blood, slipped on the slide. Before he could try again, the men unleashed. The percussive roar came at him from all directions, threatening to swallow him up.

He flattened to the ground, burying his face in the dirt, enduring nearly ten seconds of sustained fire.

Ten seconds could be a very long time.

He heard the men approaching now and did his best to force his cramped hands around the ARES, but it fell from his grasp. He worked his phone from his pocket, leaving the fabric darkly smeared, and thumbed it on.

But he had no one to call.

He was all alone with what remained of his plan.

Stuck in the cramped space, he stared up the narrow alley, the ambient city lights guttering, blocked by the shadows of men moving in.

He turned and looked in the other direction, noting the same.

He thought of Trevon in his humble East LA apartment with Cat-Cat and a breakfast table with one chair. Kiara, who was at this moment obliviously airborne, winging her way to Los Angeles. Jonathan Bennett, who was regrouping in the White House, no doubt planning future assaults that would spell disaster for the other Orphans who had fought so hard to move on and get by.

Evan looked down at his fallen pistol, the opened lacerations on his palms.

He clenched his fists against the pain. Dark spots appeared in the dirt below.

He'd never take six men wielding AKs. Not like this.

'Wait!' he called out. 'Just – *wait!* I'm done! I'm coming out!'

A rough voice answered him, 'Throw your gun first! Now!'

Evan picked up his ARES and hurled it clear of the containers.

The voice was closer now. 'Walk out. Hands laced behind your neck.'

Evan complied, his palms sticky against his skin. As he shuffled between the containers, he heard men pile into the makeshift alley behind him, blocking off any escape route.

He stepped from between the shipping containers into a semicircle of four men. They were fanned out around him at a fifteen-foot standoff, automatic weapons raised. The remaining pair of men pushed free of the alley behind Evan and completed the ring.

Even if he still had his weapon, there'd be nothing he could do.

They could end him right here, but Evan knew that Russell Gadds was a talker and a sadist. He'd want to look into Evan's eyes. He'd want him to know what was coming. Gadds's henchman, Terrance DeGraw, had told him as much: *The chief likes to take his time with folks. Give 'em his full attention.*

The bitter tinge of body odor, fear, and fury hung in the air, the scent of a posse ready to do its worst. Evan stood very still, not wanting to give them an excuse.

The speaker – Danny Hurtada, murder two – gestured with the tip of his AK, the flab of his arms rolling with the motion. 'Search him.'

One of the others stepped forward and clocked Evan in the face. He crumpled, briefly blacking out, but the impact with the ground jarred him back to consciousness.

Hands frisked him, seizing his phone from his pocket.

A steel-toed kick cracked a rib, and then the others closed in on him.

'Hang on,' Hurtada said. 'Chief is gonna want to see this motherfucker.'

Menacing faces glared down at him, silhouettes against the night sky.

For a moment Evan thought they might beat him to death despite Hurtada's orders.

But then he was hoisted to his feet.

Scott Marcus – manslaughter – pocketed the RoamZone and spit on Evan's boots.

Fernando Cortés – murder one, fugitive – frisked Evan roughly and then prodded him toward the building with the muzzle of his AK. Evan's legs felt heavy, his head still clouded from the blow.

At the entry Hurtada input a code into the control pad, and the metal door buzzed open. It looked thick enough to withstand a battering ram. Flecks of blood were still making their way down the façade, a snail's-pace crawl that felt hallucinatory.

Evan was propelled into the front room with enough force to make him stumble. Steel plating covered the walls entirely, save for a huge rectangle of one-way glass that Evan guessed was composed of Lexan.

The room was twenty-two by eighteen feet, precisely as Trevon had described.

Hurtada and Cortés slotted their automatics into a gun rack lining one wall. Hurtada sported two handguns, one on each hip. He drew them both, handing one off to Cortés.

Aiming at Evan from either side, they steered him across the room and stood him before the glass.

He stared at his reflection. Dark beads dripped from his fingertips. His left eye throbbed, a bulge coming up under the brow, crowding the upper lid.

He'd looked better.

An electronic click announced itself over hidden speakers, and Russell Gadds's voice came over the loudspeakers. 'How many of my men did you kill?'

'So far?' Evan said. 'Ten.'

'Doesn't look like you'll be doing any more damage now.'

When Evan blinked, he felt the bite of crusted blood. He looked down at his slashed-up palms. 'No. I guess not. I guess I'm finished.'

The voice came back on and said, 'Did you frisk him?'

Cortés nodded at Evan's ARES and the RoamZone, resting on the battle-scarred table behind them. 'Head to toe, chief.'

'Bring him in.'

Hurtada and Cortés pushed Evan toward another reinforced door, which clicked open, and then he was through into an office.

This, too, was just as Trevon had described it. A fancy desk with a leather blotter, complete with gold-plated swivel pen holders. Tables with digital scales and packing materials. Doors leading back down dim corridors, the building octopusing out across the property.

Hurtada and Cortés flanked Evan, guns raised. They were taking no chances. Behind him Evan heard the door shut with a weighty clank that spelled finality.

Russell Gadds was parked at the desk, a pair of cowboy boots resting up on the edge of the desk, looking like a soap-opera bad guy. His bloodshot eyes bulged, pronounced beneath a tumble of shiny dark curls.

He regarded Evan and seemed unimpressed with what he saw. 'You're the one who's cost me so much?'

Evan said, 'Yes.'

'Who hired you?'

'Trevon Gaines.'

Gadds's boots thunked to the floor as he rocked forward in the chair, his eyes bulging a bit more, one hand slapping the blotter. And then his lips parted, his teeth bared. He made a sound like a laugh.

He covered his mouth, sealing in the sound, and blinked a few times rapidly. Then he took a measured breath. Another. With each one he sank back further into his chair.

Finally he said, 'Do you have *any idea* what I'm gonna do to that retard when I'm done with you?'

Evan said, 'No.'

Through the bullet-resistant glass, Evan could hear the other men huddled around the table, joking and laughing.

Gadds made a noise like a whinny, which he muffled beneath closed lips. 'Know what they taught me in the classes?'

Evan had no idea what he was talking about.

'They taught me that anger is a secondary emotion. That it usually covers fear, sadness, guilt. I thought this was helpful at first. I spent so much time trying to excavate the feelings that lay beneath, to see if that would help me control myself better.' Gadds's meaty features had turned ruddy. He looked more than slightly unhinged. 'But do you know what I discovered?'

Evan said, 'No.'

'For me? Anger just covers *more anger.*'

'They say knowing others is wisdom, knowing yourself is enlightenment.'

'Who says that?'

'People who quote Lao-tzu.'

Gadds swept his shiny locks back off his forehead. 'Who the hell *are* you?'

Evan said, 'The Nowhere Man.'

Gadds had no immediate reaction, but from the corner of his eye Evan sensed Hurtada's face loosen slightly.

'The Nowhere Man?' Gadds said. 'That some sort of secret identity?'

'Something like that.'

'I heard of him, chief,' Hurtada said. Sweat glistened in his buzz cut. The wrist of his gun hand was slightly slack, the muzzle dipping. 'People call him, and he helps them, like some kinda vengeance service. I thought he was . . . you know, like a urban legend.'

'Well,' Gadds said, 'looks like he bleeds the same as

everyone else.' He stood up, pressed his knuckles into the chocolate leather of his blotter. 'So what is it exactly that you do, Nowhere Man?'

'Why don't you call my number and find out?'

With some effort Gadds converted his scowl into a smile. He dragged the phone closer on his desk and punched the speaker button. The dull whine of the dial tone filled the office. He stared at Evan expectantly.

Evan said, 'It's 1-855-2-NOWHERE.'

'I get it,' Gadds said. 'That's cute.'

He snatched one of the pens from the gold-plated swivel and began punching in the numbers. The men stood expectantly. Evan watched closely.

'And also?' Evan said.

Gadds finished dialing, looked up.

Evan said, 'Thanks for gathering all your men in one place for me.'

Gadds's head jerked down at the phone speaker as the call went through.

In the blastproofed front room, Evan's RoamZone did not ring.

Instead it forwarded the call.

To the tiny circuit-wired detonator inside the fresh magazine he'd inserted into his ARES 1911.

That magazine wasn't packed with bullets.

It was packed with C4.

The boom was impressive.

The aluminum forging of the ARES provided plenty of shrapnel. The plates on the walls turned the room into a steel box, amplifying the overpressure waves that Evan had calculated from the precise dimensions of the space supplied by Trevon.

The four men were dead instantly, cut through by flying chunks of aluminum, their organs collapsed from blast pressure.

A weighty throw of flung spatter thrummed the bullet-resistant window in its frame.

Of the men inside the office, only Evan was expecting the explosion.

He skipped back from between the two men guarding him, grabbing the wrist of Hurtada's gun hand as he fired, aiming the shot past his own chest into Cortés's.

He twisted the fat man around, seized the remaining pen conveniently presented by the gold-plated swivel on the blotter, and jabbed it twice into the side of Hurtada's neck.

The carotid spurt shot straight up, tapping the ceiling. It attained less height with the next heartbeat.

Evan dropped the pen and turned around. One of the doors leading back from the office still trembled on its hinges.

Russell Gadds was gone.

Panting audibly, Gadds ran through the warren of corridors, passing storage bays, packing rooms, surgical tables dusted with baking soda, an assemblage of recycled lab equipment, heaps of gas masks.

He couldn't rate his anger on a scale of one to ten, but it was safe to say his terror was at an eleven.

Rounding a corner, he tripped over a shipping box filled with jugs of paint stripper. As they rattled on the concrete floor, he stared behind him up the long, unlit corridor, waiting for the Nowhere Man to appear.

Nothing.

Shoving himself to his feet, Gadds doubled back, cut through an open galley kitchen, and stumbled into a parallel hall.

Way up its length, he could see another of the doors to his office laid open.

Hurtada sprawled on the floor, one hand covering his throat, the other at his side. He was long gone, but darkness still oozed between his fingers, slowed to a trickle.

Sensing a change in the air, Gadds spun around frantically, but there was no one behind him.

With a moan he lunged up the hall to the Rage Room with its padded, soundproofed door, as secure as a vault.

He lurched in, slamming the door shut behind him and shoving it until he heard the autolock engage. The room had been replenished at his command, a new stock of delicate furniture and valuables there for the smashing.

For a few seconds, he stood at the door, his sweaty forehead pressed to the padding, trying to get his breathing under control. He told himself to pay attention to his body cues.

Pulse rate galloping. Fire in his belly. Pins and needles pricking his scalp.

The same tricks that worked to control anger should work to control fear. He grabbed for one technique after the other, but nothing worked to slow the torrent.

He backed away from the door, brushing against an accent table and toppling a Tiffany-style lamp. At the crash he whirled around.

A figure stepped out from behind the china hutch.

He wore a catcher's mask.

He held a baseball bat, end-weighted, heat-treated, and double-walled.

Blood dripped from his hands, dotting the floor at his feet as he approached.

'I take it back,' he said. 'Maybe I'm not finished just yet.'

64. Let It All Out

Trevon Gaines sat at his little breakfast table, an open can of corn centered on a place mat, a spoon handle sticking out of the top.

Evan said, 'Can't you eat?'

Trevon said, 'No, sir.'

'But it's yellow.'

'All my food is yellow. And orange.' Trevon was at last wearing new eyeglasses, having dispensed with the ones he'd taped at the hinge. He knuckled the new pair up the bridge of his nose.

It took him a few seconds to lift his stare from the can, and Evan was reminded once again of his goals for the day: *1. Make more eye contact with folks.*

Trevon looked at Evan for as long as he seemed able to manage and then looked away again. 'So that's my only job now? To repay you? I find someone else in trouble like me, and then I tell them to call you?'

'That's it.'

'But that doesn't repay *you*. It just pays someone else.'

'Well,' Evan said. 'It helps me keep repaying what I owe.'

'I don't get it.'

'That's okay,' Evan said. 'I don't always get it either.'

Cat-Cat emerged from his spot beneath the curtain, struck a bellicose pose, and hissed at Evan.

Evan said, 'Why does your cat hate me?'

'Cat-Cat doesn't hate you. He's just moody.' Trevon blinked

a few times and then scratched at his elbow a little too hard, his fingernails raising flakes of dry skin. 'I wish I coulda saved them.'

His breath hitched in his chest, and he closed his eyes, pressed the side of his head with his palm, and started murmuring to himself.

Evan couldn't make out the words, but he knew what Trevon was saying.

We don't cry and we don't feel sorry for ourself. We don't cry and we don't feel sorry for ourself. We don't cry and we don't feel sorry for ourself.

'Trevon? *Trevon?*'

At last he opened his eyes.

'I'm proud to know you,' Evan said.

'Thank you.' Trevon's eyes darted away uncomfortably. 'Thank you for everything.'

'Maybe,' Evan said, 'it's okay to cry now.'

'*No*, that's not what Mama . . .' Again Trevon trailed off, squeezing his eyes shut. But he pulled himself together, bobbing his head. 'I hafta take the bus to meet Kiara. She called me from her connection in Houston, and I told her. I told her everything – 'cept about you. She was . . . I never heard her cry like that. I never heard *anyone* cry like that. And it's just me she's coming home to now, and I'm worried . . .'

'What?'

'I'm worried I'm gonna disappoint her. 'Cuz . . . 'Cuz . . . I know I'm special, but I don't know how to act normal.' His voice had dropped to a hoarse whisper. 'And that can be frustrating for people. I don't want to be frustrating for her, 'cuz I'm all she has left. And what if . . .'

Evan waited, gave him the space to fight the thought to the surface.

'What if I'm not enough?' Trevon pushed the can of corn

away. 'What should I do?' His eyes implored Evan. 'I don't know what to do.'

Evan thought of Trevon's neatly made bed, his stuffed frog, the scrawled list of goals for the day.

'Just be yourself,' Evan said. 'Because who else can you be?'

Trevon stared at him, his eyes wide.

And he smiled.

It took three different buses to get to LAX and traffic was bad, but Trevon didn't mind so much 'cuz he could look at the different cars on the freeway and see all the people making different faces and guess what they were feeling.

It was a good game to teach him about how to read social cues, and the social cue from the woman driving the white Range Rover next to them said she didn't like her husband in the passenger seat very much.

He couldn't wait to see Kiara 'cuz she was the oldest and the sweetest and his favorite and she always understood him better than anyone. But then he felt bad 'cuz here she was flying in from helping tribes in Guatemala and the first thing he'd done was make her cry over the phone.

The bus hissed up the ramp to Arrivals, and then it got all lurchy-like, people honking and cutting each other off and one guy flipping the bird, which wasn't a hard social cue to read, not at all.

They finally stopped by Terminal 4: International Arrivals, which was also named Tom Bradley, which was dumb 'cuz if you were gonna name a airport terminal after a football quarterback you'd think you'd bother to spell his name right.

Trevon hesitated after they stopped, and the bus driver stared at him and said, 'Didn't you say this was your stop?'

and Trevon said, 'Yeah,' but still couldn't get his legs to move. The bus driver said, 'It's your dollar seventy-five, pal,' and started to close the doors but Trevon stood up and said, 'Okay. I'm ready to go,' and the bus driver said, 'I'll alert the *LA Times*,' and let him out.

Trevon walked over to Baggage and waited by the elevators, and people kept coming down and down like there was a people-making factory on the floor above, and he was getting tired of waiting and the Scaredy Bugs were starting to dance around in his tummy and then he realized they weren't the Scaredy Bugs, not anymore, but the Muddy Waters.

And then, before he could clear his head, there Kiara was riding the escalator down, holding a hand over her mouth and waving at him. And then she was running over to him, crying and saying, 'Tre, honey, honey —' and he said, 'Welcome home. I'm sorry it's only me and not . . . and not Mama . . .'

Mama.

MamaMamaMamaLeoUncleJoe-JoeAuntieTishaGran'mamaAisha—

And his face was bent to her shoulder and he was holding her and she was holding him, patting his back and saying, 'That's it, Tre. That's okay. I'm here. I'm here now. We still got each other. You just let it all out now. You just let it all out.'

65. The Flip Side of Intimacy

'What happened to your eye?' Peter was sitting froggy style in his living room, legs bent back behind him.

Evan leaned forward on the couch, elbows on his knees. 'I walked into a door.'

'Ouch.'

'Yeah,' Evan said. 'But you should see the door.'

Peter laughed.

Mia did not.

She was sitting way down at the end of the couch, a safe distance from Evan to avoid any communicable diseases. Any further and she'd fall off.

Evan said, 'I stopped by because I had your gift fixed, so I wanted to –'

Mia said, 'Peter, why don't you give us a minute?'

Peter's charcoal eyes lingered on the bag at Evan's feet. 'But it's never a minute. It's always, like, a hour, and I've been waiting forever to get my gift back.'

Mia said, 'Five minutes.'

'Which is it? *A* minute or *five* minutes?'

'Peter.'

'*Fine.*'

He scampered off to his room.

Evan looked down at the union of his hands floating between his knees. He kept them clasped to hide the damage to his palms.

Mia said, 'How about your hands?'

He should have known that nothing would escape her district-attorney eye.

He said, 'Fell down the stairs.'

'If we don't have trust, Evan, we don't have anything.'

'I'm trustworthy,' he said. 'I just have limits on disclosure.'

She made a noise in her throat that showed what she thought of that.

He tried not to recall the two nights he'd spent with her. Her mouth pressed to his shoulder, their bodies entwined. After she'd rested her head on his chest, her ear had left an imprint on his skin, the sine wave of the yin-yang. Everything an inside joke, as if they were building a language of their own.

And now this arctic freeze, the two of them riding ice floes drifting slowly apart. Was this the flip side of intimacy? You get closer and closer until you can no longer discern each other?

'My case was neatly tied up,' she said. 'Literally. Oscar Esposito hog-tied on the front steps of the domestic shelter.' Her gaze was unremitting. 'Happy day.'

He nodded.

'How did you – Wait, don't answer that. I can't . . . I shouldn't know.' She scrunched her eyes as if warding off a headache. 'Look, there's no way that we can . . . I mean . . . You and I, with what we do – or don't do – we keep trying, but we can't be together when this interplay of law and . . . and *not* . . .' She shook her head. 'I can't talk to you intimately and have it domino into something out there.'

'Allegedly,' he said.

'Allegedly.'

'If I *had* done it,' Evan said, 'would that be bad?'

'Yes.'

'If someone hadn't stopped him in that moment, then his wife and daughter would have been harmed. If not killed.'

'That's right. That's the awful, awful cost of living with laws.'

He considered. 'Can you say that you regret the outcome? Would you rather he –'

'*No.* Of course not. But that's the part no one talks about, right? The old TV scenario. Would you torture a terrorist to get the location of a nuclear device that would kill millions of people?'

Evan said, '*Yes.*'

'Me, too. But that's where most people stop. They don't think beyond it. But you *have to* think beyond it. Because that's not the whole answer, is it?'

'No,' he said. 'It's not.'

'Afterward, in order to protect society, in order to protect the Constitution, in order to preserve order and uphold the law –'

'I'd have to answer for what I did. I'd have to be accountable.'

Her eyes welled. 'Right,' she said.

'That's the cost that has to be paid,' Evan said. 'The sacrifice that has to be made.'

Mia pulled her legs beneath her and leaned back, dimpling the cushion. Her lush, messy curls were taken up in a loose ponytail, showing off the slope of her neck. A stray crayon mark stained the fabric, a periwinkle flare. A candle on the kitchen counter threw off autumnal scents. On the cooktop a pot simmered, dinner in the making.

Evan thought about how much he would miss this place. He had nowhere else like it in his life. He never had. He figured he never would.

Mia said, 'I have to go into a courthouse next week repre-senting the largest district attorney's office in the United States, with the full power of the state of California behind me. I have to prosecute Oscar Esposito on new charges des-pite the fact that I know –'

Evan cut her off sharply. 'You don't know anything,' he said. 'Do you?'

She didn't answer.

'You don't know anything about what happened to Oscar Esposito,' he said. 'And you don't know anything about me.'

It was the only way to protect her.

She bit her lower lip, her face warring between sadness and anger. 'No. I guess I don't.'

Peter came out of his bedroom. 'It's been like *nine hours.*'

Evan said, 'Sorry, bud,' and lifted the bag.

Peter scampered over and claimed it. He tore at the wrap-ping, revealing the half-moon plaque. 'Wow. So cool. Is she a goddess?'

'Sort of.'

Tommy had done an impeccable job with the soldering, nothing more than a hairline crack visible through the cast-ing of Lady Justice.

'The sword she holds represents justice and reason,' Evan said. 'And it shows she's prepared to carry out her verdict. The scales symbolize fairness. As she weighs the merits of each case, she has to be objective. She can't show the slightest prejudice.'

'I thought she was blindfolded,' Peter said.

'Not originally.' Evan looked across at Mia. 'She sees what she has to do. And she does it anyway.'

Mia blinked a few times.

Peter held up the plaque, regarding it with awe. 'I can't wait to show this to Ms Bracegirdle.'

Evan rose and ruffled his hair. 'Good-bye, Peter.'

'Good-bye, Evan Smoak.'

Evan sat at his usual table, eyeing the glowing glass shelves above the bar as if hoping that a bottle of superior vodka might materialize on them.

To his side was the booth with the older woman who was, as always, dining alone. She wore a navy-blue pantsuit, dressed up with a string of freshwater pearls, and her silver hair was styled with care and pride. She sipped her solitary glass of white wine. Her cell phone rested beside her bread plate, her reflection captured in the obsidian glass of her phone, the screen that never lit up.

He pictured Mia and Peter in the soft glow of 12B. They'd be eating dinner now, Peter misbehaving just the right amount, Mia laughing that openmouthed laugh. She'd have lit more candles, and the plates on the table would be mismatched.

Evan sipped his Pellegrino.

A new waiter circled, too handsome to have come to LA to serve branzino. 'Are we ready?' he asked.

Evan pointed over at the parking meters. 'That vet still around? The one who used to camp out there on the sidewalk?'

'Nah. Management had him removed. People don't like to look at that, you know, when they're eating.' He readied pen and pad. 'Have you had a chance to read the menu?'

'No,' Evan said. 'But that's okay. I think I'm done here.'

The waiter wrinkled his nose and slid the padded check presenter onto the table.

As Evan set down a twenty and rose to leave, he noticed a family filing in. A bald gentleman in an expensive sweater, two grown daughters, three grandchildren. They clustered around the older woman, her face lighting up as they slid into the booth around her.

Evan caught a snatch of conversation from the man. 'Sorry to cut in on your quiet time, my love, but these monsters stopped by to surprise us, and . . .'

The rest lost beneath the din of children's laughter.

Evan looked down at his glass of sparkling water, the two-top table set for one, and wondered who, all these months, he'd really been sad for.

66. A Long Time Coming

The Map Room earned its name during the Second World War when FDR agonized over the war's progress within these four walls, charting his army's headway across the continent and a scattering of blood-drenched Pacific islands. A half century later, Bill Clinton provided closed-circuit testimony to Ken Starr from this same space, the only time a sitting president gave evidence under oath while being investigated.

The waitstaff moved silently in the background, clearing out dishes from the tea that Bennett had just completed with his press secretary and the chief of staff.

The room's stuffed-back armchairs and Chippendale-style case goods brought an Old World luster to the White House, a sense of gravity.

Which Naomi tried to summon now, here, before the president.

She'd quietly recounted for him her investigations and what they had yielded. That the Service's satellite feed of the Arlington farmhouse had been hijacked by the DoD and forwarded on to the Orphan whose body had been recovered at the scene. That the same Orphan appeared to have been in contact with the late Doug Wetzel. That the other three bodies had been tentatively linked to the missing impostor profiles in the databases as well as to the bloodbath at the Watergate. That the more strings she pulled, the more she seemed to find.

Bennett snapped his fingers, and the room cleared instantly.

He dug in his pocket, palmed another pill into his mouth, swallowed it dry. Leaning against the rear side of a couch, he crossed his arms but couldn't manage to keep still, instead scratching at the nape of his neck. 'So that's what you've been doing? Investigating me instead of the man trying to kill me?'

'The latter led to the former,' she said. 'Which is why . . .' She took a moment to steady her voice. 'Which is why I can no longer in good faith be responsible for your protection. I can't have an instant's hesitation about stepping between you and a bullet. Or ordering my agents to do the same.'

Bennett's face glimmered with sweat. He bit at his lower lip, rolled it between his teeth. 'But you do. Why is that?'

'I'm no longer certain that protecting you is in the best interest of the United States.'

Even from this distance, she could feel the heat coming off him. Waves of barely suppressed rage.

His jaw clenched. 'Your name will be scraped off your office door before you reach your car.'

She hoped he couldn't read how shaken she was. Drawing an uneven breath, she started out.

She'd just reached the door when he said, 'You need to be careful, Templeton. The world's got a lot of sharp edges.'

She read the threat beneath the surface, and for an instant it scared her to the core.

Then she thought of her father's chest rising and falling beneath the hospital gown.

She paused, looked back.

She said, 'I'm not afraid of sharp edges.'

A snack waited for him back in the Oval, the silver tray bearing a Double Gloucester cheese and an aged Gouda, flown in this morning. He ate quickly, washing them down with a

1985 Richebourg Grand Cru from Côte de Nuits, which cost slightly less than a Volkswagen.

He circled to the Resolute desk, plucking up the phone to get Director Gonzalez on the line.

That's when it happened.

A weakness in his legs pulling him down into the chair. His temperature spiked, a film of sweat covering his flesh, making his shirt and pants cling to him. His heartbeat ramped up to a drumroll that seemed to vibrate under his skin.

An awareness dawned, as certain as the walls around him. In the marrow of his bones, he knew that he was about to die.

Through his confusion and terror, he managed a single clear thought: how unjust that he was going to expire here in the safest room in the world.

He fumbled his hand up to the telephone, the black one on the left that allowed him direct access to an outside line.

With a shuddering hand, he managed to dial the familiar number.

Evan removed the bottle of Tigre Blanc from the freezer drawer, the French wheat vodka swirling inside. He loaded a cocktail shaker with ice cubes and poured in two fingers.

His RoamZone rang.

As he saw the 202 area code, he knew.

When he answered, he could hear Bennett gasping on the other end of the line.

Bennett forced out the word: *'How?'*

Evan set down the shaker. 'Your eyeglasses,' he said. 'I swapped out the nose pads and temple tips.'

The president's schedule had shown him to be due for a prescription update. Before the limo strike, Evan broke into the designated optometrist's office. Bennett's glasses and supplies were stored separately under lock and key.

Not a superb lock and key.

Evan said, 'The new ones were coated with a high-dose antidepressant medication administered through the skin.'

Emsam, a common med, wouldn't show up on any poison or toxin scans – at least not on any panel used by the Technical Security Division. It was intended to be administered only once a day. But Bennett had been getting around-the-clock transdermal delivery of a monoamine oxidase inhibitor.

'It elicits a host of nasty interactions,' Evan said. 'Headaches, agitation, nausea, tremors, rapid heart rate, heavy sweating. Which any reasonable doctor would misattribute to stress and treat with – of course – an antianxiety med. Which doubles down on the effects.'

Over the line Bennett's breaths turned into screeches as he raked in air, trying to breathe.

'But to *weaponize* it,' Evan continued, 'it has to be combined with specific foods. Organ meats, hard cheese, fava beans, red wine, or any other tyramine-heavy cuisine.'

That included the majority of Bennett's favorite dishes, which he asked to have imported internationally. By throwing a scare into the Service about domestic food supply, Evan had ensured that they leaned more heavily on foreign vendors.

Everything had relied on Bennett's being the person he was. Paranoid, manipulative, strategic, solipsistic. There'd been holes in the plan, yes. But Bennett had filled them.

Evan watched frost creep around the base of the cocktail shaker. 'The combination of MAOIs and tyramine potentiate a hypertensive crisis, which leads to a heart attack,' he said. 'That's what you're experiencing now.'

Bennett tried to say something, but all that came out was a throaty rush of air.

Evan heard the thump of a body striking the plush Oval Office rug.

He hung up.

Picking up the shaker, he rattled it until his hands stuck to the stainless steel, the chill pleasing against his still-healing palms. Then he wrapped a dish towel around it and shook it some more.

Retrieving a martini glass from the freezer, he poured the frosty vodka and garnished it with a leaf of basil from the vertical garden.

Jonathan Bennett had had the full force of the United States government behind him, the military-industrial complex, and all the alphabet-soup agencies.

Evan had Vera II and a living wall.

Bennett had boundless resources and boundless manpower.

Evan had a sixteen-year-old foster girl and a nine-fingered armorer.

Bennett had a willingness to do anything to get what he wanted.

Evan had a willingness to do what needed to be done.

And now, at the ragged end of the long road, Bennett lay sprawled on the Oval Office rug and Evan stood here, far from the corridors of power, cloaked in anonymity, protected by his very unimportance.

He had a chilled glass of high-end vodka and a piece of quiet in his clean, well-lit place. Perhaps that was all he needed.

Perhaps it was all he deserved.

He strolled before the floor-to-ceiling Lexan windows that constituted the penthouse's east wall. The discreet armor sunshades shielded him from sight and sniper bullets while still letting in the view through the finely woven metal links.

He looked out across Wilshire Boulevard to the glimmering rise of downtown. All those twinkling lights, so many lives in progress behind windshields and windows, people doing the best they could with their private trials and tribulations, their everyday triumphs and tragedies.

He saw his own window as if from afar, one anonymous dot among millions.

He was a part of the living hive of the city and apart from it, too. Like everyone else, he found comfort where he could. Like many others, he tried to give some comfort as well.

He took a sip of the Tigre Blanc. It had been distilled five times, getting it down to its essence. Clean nose, a touch of fruit, maybe a hint of pepper on the finish.

He closed his eyes and enjoyed the drink.

It had been a long time coming.

67. A Damning Light

The funeral was an all-out affair. The flag-draped coffin making its solemn descent into the earth. State troopers firing a three-gun salute. Speeches about a life dedicated to public service. And then the bagpipes, which never failed to make Naomi mist up.

Robbie and Jason managed to show up for once, to say good-bye to their father.

The former president was due to go into the ground next week, but given the recent torrent of revelations, White House officials were still figuring out how to deal with the pomp and ceremony of the state funeral.

Two days ago the Newseum had been breached, a full display showing up in the *Today's Front Pages* installation on the sixth floor. It contained logistics reports from a three-decades-old mission that cast a damning light across Jonathan Bennett and his entire scandal-riddled legacy. The display was effective if unartful, an impeccably neat tiling of pinned documents behind glass.

Naomi had a guess who'd curated the illicit display.

When she'd woken up this morning, the light streaming beneath her shade had caught something on the lip of the nightstand drawer where she stored her service weapon. A gummy dime-size disk, slightly oblong, that on further inspection proved to be an adhesive made of silicon composite. When she'd held it up to the light, she'd seen a print pressed into its surface.

And a *second* print on the other side.

Which meant that one was fake – but one had to be real. After all, he'd been wearing it.

Orphan X, she was sure, had no prints on record. If she brought the adhesive in to the Forensic Services Division after the funeral, she could add one key piece of evidence to the exceedingly thin file that had been provided to her what felt like a lifetime ago.

As Robbie and Jason tipped shovelfuls of dirt into the open grave, she lifted the fingerprint adhesive from her pocket and stared at it there, perched on her thumb.

Director Gonzalez approached, and she lowered her hand to her side. 'Ready to get back at it tomorrow?' he asked.

'Yeah,' she said. 'I am.'

He hugged her before taking the shovel from Robbie and stepping around the waiting backhoe to the grave.

Naomi stood with her brothers watching another throw of dirt fall and then another, covering their father, the legend of the Service.

Robbie pursed his lips. 'He was tough.'

Yeah, Naomi thought. *And so am I.*

As her brothers drifted away with the other mourners, she stayed a moment, just her and the open wound of the rectangle marring the green grass. Maybe there would be peace now. For her father, for herself, for Orphan X, even for President Bennett.

Stepping forward, she flicked the fingerprint adhesive into the grave, and then the backhoe did its work, layering over the coffin, her father, the past.

Acknowledgments

Orphan X would like to convey his gratitude to his Special Operations Group:

– Keith Kahla, Andrew Martin, Sally Richardson, Don Weisberg, Jennifer Enderlin, Alice Pfeifer, Hector DeJean, Paul Hochman, Kelley Ragland, and Martin Quinn at Minotaur Books

– Rowland White and his team at Michael Joseph/Penguin Group UK

– Lisa Erbach Vance and Aaron Priest of the Aaron Priest Agency

– Caspian Dennis of the Abner Stein Agency

– Trevor Astbury, Rob Kenneally, Peter Micelli, and Michelle Weiner of Creative Artists Agency

– Marc H. Glick of Glick & Weintraub and Stephen F. Breimer of Bloom Hergott Diemer et al.

– Geoff Baehr, Philip Eisner, Dr Melissa Hurwitz, Jay Karnes, Dana Kaye, Dr Bret Nelson, Billy Stojack (R.I.P.), and Kurata Tadashi

– Simba and Cairo, the lion hunters

– And my favorite trio, Delinah, Rose, and Natalie